PRAISE FOR THE SAPPHIRE TALISMAN

"An enticing and compelling follow up to [...] plot twists and defined characters helped m[...]

— Liem, [...] s

"The Sapphire Talisman forever left me on the tips of my toes with all the twist and turns it managed to pack in between the characters and their relationships. It's definitely one of the best sequels I've read in a long time. . ."

— *Lauren, Lauren's Crammed Bookshelf*

"A well written and unique series that will appeal to all kinds of readers. Whenever I thought I might know what was going to happen, Brenda threw a curve ball and completely took me by surprise."

Kelsey, The Book Scout

"By the time I got to the end of the book I was biting my fingernails and hoping for the best."

— *Katie, Katie's Book Blog*

"A roller coaster ride from the beginning to the end."

— *Yara, Once Upon a Twilight*

"I am still reeling from just recently finishing the last page."

— *Jessica, A Fanatics Book Blog*

"An outstanding, and worthy, successor to The Emerald Talisman . . . engaging and deliciously vampiric read."

—*Corrine, Lost For Words*

"A stellar follow up to The Emerald Talisman! Once again I found myself turning pages late into the night because I had to know what happened next!

—*Jennifer, Extreme Reader Book Reviews*

Other books by Brenda Pandos

The Talisman Series:
The Emerald Talisman: Book One
The Onyx Talisman: Book Three
Blood Wars: Book Four
Out for Blood: Phil's Story

Mer Tales:
Everblue
Evergreen
Everlost

Lost in Time:
Glitch
Switch

THE
Sapphire
TALISMAN
THE TALISMAN SERIES - BOOK TWO

BRENDA PANDOS

OBSIDIAN MOUNTAIN PUBLISHING

Pandos, Brenda, 1972 –
The Sapphire Talisman: A novel/by Brenda Pandos

Cover design and layout by the author herself.
www.designbybrenda.com
Cover image © Iuliia - Fotolia.com

Published by Obsidian Mountain Publishing
www.obsidianmtpublishing.com
P.O. Box 601901
Sacramento, CA 95860

Summary: Julia and Nicholas try to begin a somewhat normal life together. Bound by secrecy from a shape shifter determined to see Julia's world-saving prediction come to fruition, Julia isn't allowed to tell Nicholas the leader survived, ransacking her happiness with guilt. When Alora returns, bent on revenge, everything changes.

Printed in the United States of America
ISBN: 978-0-982-90332-2
LCCN - 2010916966

1 2 3 4 5 6 7 8 9

To Lucy – My Wonder Woman

Do not be overcome with evil,

But overcome evil with good.

Romans 12:21

Chapter One

I sat in the waiting room together with my older brother Luke, my dad, and Erin, my uncle's sister, in upholstered chairs with wooden arms, my internal experience vastly different from anyone else's. Our scenery consisted of four white walls adorned with pastel flower paintings and a TV hung in the corner, playing a late night talk show. My eyes kept drifting to the large red "NO SMOKING" and "NO CELL PHONE USE" signs, reading them over and over, wishing I didn't have the ability to read other people's emotions, especially in a maternity ward. When another wave of pain would arrive, I'd close my eyes and place my hands under my legs to grip the edge of the chair where no one could see, desperately trying to ignore the stifling agony. Relief only came when invisible explosions of incredible elation burst forth, sweetly followed by Brahms lullaby tinkling throughout the corridors.

With each passing episode though, I hoped the last one would be for us. Suddenly, my uncle John appeared in the hallway, dressed in a blue smock and booties, overflowing with love.

"It's a girl!" he exclaimed.

We all jumped to our feet simultaneously. The wait was finally over.

"A girl," Dad said in jubilation while putting his arm around my shoulder.

"Yes." John's eyes were moist. "Our little Emma Mae is finally here. Come. Jo would like to see everyone."

When John turned, motioning for everyone to follow, I nudged Luke in the ribs. We'd had a bet whether it was a boy or girl. Luke's wrong guess meant he'd be doing dishes for a week.

Josephine, my aunt and somewhat adoptive mom, had invited me to be a part of the birth and initially I had agreed until I found out she was going to give birth in the hospital without drugs. There was no way, with that much pain, I'd be able to compose myself and not let everyone in the room know my talent—the secret ability I'd acquired at age five, right after my mother's mysterious disappearance. Though I didn't actually feel the pain itself, it seemed real enough to overwhelm me. Pain, of all the emotions, was very distracting. Later, after watching a documentary of a real birth in Health Class, I had to gently tell Jo I didn't think I could handle it. She was disappointed, but understood.

I figured, *if* I ever had kids of my own in the future, I'd definitely get drugs just in case someone in the room next to me decided to go without like Jo did. I wanted to avoid that kind of pain at all costs. But with a half-vampire as a boyfriend, even if we did get married someday, I didn't know if having children would be a possibility.

"Jo did so well . . . without any drugs . . . her nurse kept saying she was a natural at it," John said breathlessly, as he padded down the hallway in his slippered feet.

Part of me was glad to hear everything went well, but another was annoyed he kept telling the details—her story. I just wanted him to lead us and keep his mouth shut.

We arrived at her door and walked in. Jo looked slightly tired but gushed a beautiful sea of love while holding a little pink bundle in her arms. Her eyes were glistening as she invited us to come in.

I got to Jo's side first, wringing my hands awkwardly, unsure if she'd let me hold Emma. Without a word, Jo passed me the baby. I smiled down at my new cousin.

Emma's peace surrounded me instantly while she slept, taking me to a utopia I'd craved all night sitting in the waiting room. Faintly, in the background, I heard Jo fill her sister-in-law, Erin and Dad in on what happened. Luke stood by John, slightly grossed out at the details.

A little tuft of black hair stuck out from under Emma's hat, framing a wrinkled forehead. Tiny lashes rimmed closed eyes, rosy cheeks surrounded a button nose and little puckered lips,—she looked like a cherub. I remembered back to the first time I'd felt Emma's emotions. Sometime during Jo's second trimester, Emma's contentedness began to compete with Jo's general motherly woes. Emma loved her sanctuary within the protection of Jo's womb. Only yesterday did I sense something new—a growing disquiet. I wasn't surprised to hear after I left, Jo's water had broken.

"Five more minutes," a heavy-set brunette nurse called through the open doorway. "Then you'll all have to leave."

Erin's agitation increased and I sighed, gently passing Emma to her. She'd been anxiously awaiting her turn. Without Emma's sweet aura to hide within, I suddenly wanted to go. Hospitals drained me.

As if sensing my discomfort, Jo's hand caught mine and she pulled me into a hug. The embrace comforted my spirit.

"How are you?" she asked quietly.

"Me?" I laughed while shaking my head. "Uh, you just gave birth. How are you?"

Jo squeezed my hand a little tighter. "If only I could share how wonderful I feel."

I glanced away and grinned. I already knew.

"—but I want you to remember, while Emma is my real child, she's not going to replace you or your brother. I still consider you both my children too, you know."

"I know," I whispered, leaning into her shoulder.

She'd become our mother when Dad moved us from L.A. to Scotts Valley after our real Mom disappeared, shortly before my sixth birthday. But, unbeknownst to any of us at the time, she hadn't disappeared; she was murdered. I'd just learned the truth a few months ago, when Nicholas saved me a second time from an unseen stalker—a vampire. The first time, I was lucky while my mother was not. Nicholas, too late to help her, prevented the bloodsucking vampire from taking my life as well. In his guilt, he vowed to secretly protect me always.

But with my second encounter, Nicholas was no longer able to keep his presence or his identity a secret after I learned the truth. We'd been dating ever since.

Jo kissed the top of my head. Her loving tenderness covered a multitude of longing and sadness for my mother.

"So proud of you, Jo," Dad called across the room. "Emma is beautiful."

A general murmur of consensus rang through the group. Being

between two ecstatic parents and a contented baby put me in the perfect Bermuda triangle of love. Everything seemed perfect until *Attila the Hun* came back.

"Visiting hours are now over," Attila said in a gruff voice. "My patients need their rest."

I rolled my eyes, said a quick goodbye, and waited for my family in the hall. I wanted to text Nicholas and tell him the good news anyway. I'd been keeping our relationship a secret from my family. Nicholas believed, even though I wore a vampire-warding talisman, anyone I loved could still be in danger of retribution since Nicholas was a hated vampire slayer. Luckily, and completely puzzling to us, none of the leaches had returned after the last attack. Whether Nicholas' reputation preceded him or they were off wreaking havoc on easier targets, we didn't know. Even still, he wanted to be extra careful.

Within two seconds his reply text came back.

- **Congrats. Leaving soon?** <
- **Yes. 30 mins. 3**
- **Great. Sleep tight.**

I bit my lip to stop the huge grin from forming upon my lips. Sleep tight didn't mean good night; it was code for us to meet outside my bedroom window on the roof ledge later, something we did almost every night. The < from his text and the 3 from mine represented a heart when put together, reminding us of the one I'd carved into a piece of symbolic wood that brought us together, but broke when I carved it, both of us keeping a half. For sometime, I'd suspected my dad frequently checked my text messages online, so we'd resorted to code.

I read his messages several times before deleting them—another precaution I decided to take after the last attack. If another vampire ever stole my phone again, they'd never know who I consorted with.

I rested my head on the back of the seat during the drive home, relieved to finally be free from the birthing tormentors. Dad and Luke wordlessly sat in the front, all of us emanating a tired peace. I held the talisman that hung around my neck, anxious to get home for my good-night kiss. Our nightly roof-top meetings were risky, but I was confident that I would feel if someone had awakened, and was close enough to catch us.

Dad parked in the garage and I feigned needing something out of my car so I could see if Nicholas was here yet. The crisp night air refreshed my tired senses as I walked across the dewy grass. Once I rounded the corner, I felt a tiny bit disappointed when I discovered he hadn't arrived. I wondered what might be taking him so long when my phone vibrated.

-**Give me 20.** <

-3

I grinned as my heart beat a little faster, knowing the wait was only 20 minutes more. Maybe he had a surprise for me.

Just before I opened the front door to go inside, I noticed movement in the shrubs next to the porch swing. I knew it had to be an animal, since I couldn't sense any human emotion.

"Aladdin, is that you?" I whispered, keeping my distance, worried to get too close in case it was a raccoon. I squinted to see evidence of our tuxedo cat, Aladdin, when another cat appeared—pure black with icy blue eyes.

One I knew. One that wasn't really a cat.

I froze.

"She's back."

Chapter Two

"E*nigma, nice to see you again,*" I spoke internally, my words laced with sarcasm. "*Let me guess, I can't say anything, right?*"

"*Correct,*" she said in my mind.

"*And if I do?*"

Her tail twitched ever so slightly. "*Disastrous consequences.*"

"*For who? You? Or me?*" I asked tempestuously while staring daggers into her little kitty face. "*Because when Nicholas finds out I've been lying this whole time, he's not going to understand. I'm putting everything in jeopardy to keep your secrets.*"

"*Not for me—*"

"*Really? Really!*" I let my air out forcefully in preparation of my well-rehearsed speech. "*I'm only giving you grace because you saved our necks last fall, but my patience is running thin, especially since all you've told me is to keep quiet, then you disappear, and even now, you're leaving me in the dark.*"

"*I have my reasons. In time, this will all make sense.*"

"*Yeah, right.*" I leaned up against the porch pole and folded my arms. "*I should take you to the Pound.*"

She arched her back, bristled the hair across her spine, and tightened her cat-eyes.

"*You lack manners, young lady. I'm older than you can fathom. I deserve your respect for that at least,*" she hissed.

My eyebrows shot up at the revelation, stealing away all my bravado. In human form, she only looked a little over twenty-five.

"*Your job is to help Nicholas find Alora before she finds you, but he's going to need his father's help first.*"

With a slouch of my shoulders, I leaned my head back. Yet again she insisted on more impossible things. Alora was the meanest and most cunning vampire I knew, who, unknown to Nicholas, narrowly escaped after he defeated her coven. Enigma made me vow I wouldn't mention I knew of her until it was time. But getting Nicholas to admit he needed help, let alone ask, was never going to happen—especially when it came to his father.

Lovely.

"Anything else?" I asked haughtily.

I heard a guttural snarl. *"Stop trying my patience."*

Humph. I let my lip curl a tiny bit. It was nice to feel like I'd had some control for once.

Enigma, a mind-reading shape-shifter, was used to having the advantage whenever we ran into each other, able to ruthlessly sift through my secrets. But now that I wore the talisman, my thoughts were shielded against her invisible grasp. She could only read what I wanted her to, leveling the playing field since I couldn't read her emotions while she was in cat form.

Before I could lay in another retort, a waft of my dad's confusion floated over me, distracting my concentration.

"Julia?" he called while he poked his head out. "What's taking you so long? It's late."

"Sorry, Dad," I said quickly. "I was looking for Aladdin."

"Pretty sure she's upstairs," he said and stepped onto the porch to usher me inside. "Come on."

I looked over my shoulder to give the cat one last angry reply, but she'd already disappeared.

Figures.

Enigma's words echoed in my mind while I lay on my bed, cell phone in hand, trying to figure how to warn Nicholas with nothing coming to mind. He was somewhere in the city, patrolling the area like always at 2:20 in the morning. If it were under any other circumstances, I'd have chuckled, but I worried he'd run into Alora without me and meet the demise a fortune teller predicted to me a while back.

Crap. Crap. Crap.

- **Miss me?**

The surprising buzz of the phone made my anxious hands jerk, almost dropping it on the floor. The relief was instantaneous; he was still okay. Nervously, I punched the keys to reply.

- **Yes. Where are you?**

I held my breath.

Please be close.

- Long story. Sleep tight. Talk to you soon.

I smirked at the secret code he used to throw my dad off. Whatever happened was going to be interesting.

Since there weren't any vampires to rid the city of, Nicholas had become the resident incognito superhero, minus the costume. He'd document the crime in process via film, catch the bad guys, and leave them cuffed at the precinct where they'd be found (usually in the alley). It was reported Nicholas had said, "Do you feel lucky today, Punk?" which coined him *Dirty Harry* in the Sentinel. Tonight must have been more intricate than usual.

I began to pace, knowing he'd arrive on my roof at any moment and I didn't feel ready to talk yet. The hospital left me shaky from the barrier I tried to create during those three long hours, and now, with Alora back, I knew he'd hear the worry in my voice.

If we could just touch first, his soothing spirit would relieve my tension in a second. The tap on the window made my insides jump even though I'd already felt his presence.

"You're here," I said after opening the window. I leaned out so he could reach me.

His strong hands gently cupped my cheeks and his green, electric eyes focused on mine. The energy zinged from his fingertips down to my toes and weakened my knees. His lips met mine and were firm, yet gentle. My eyes closed as I submitted to his kiss. The only thing that mattered anymore was us being together, and I crawled out of the window into his waiting arms.

"Are you doing okay?" Nicholas asked while he stroked the back of my hair.

"I am now."

I stayed firmly planted into his side, not wanting to move, and wondered if we could just stay like this forever—then nothing bad would happen.

Pride swelled inside Nicholas and he chuckled.

"What?" I said quickly and pulled back to look into his grinning face.

"One of the guys asked if I was *Dirty Harry* after I tied them up."

"Oh?" The kiss had made me forget all about his escapade he'd mentioned earlier. "So, what happened?"

"I caught them trying to jack a car. So I tied them up, put them in the trunk, drove it down to the precinct, and parked out front."

"Aren't you afraid the cops will see you?"

"Not really," Nicholas said and wrapped his arms tighter around me.

"But the bad guys saw you."

"I gave them the look."

"The what?"

Nicholas hesitated. In his excitement he'd revealed more than he wanted.

"I let the demon out."

He'd always referred to his vampire side as a demon fighting to overtake control. I'd regularly felt the wall he'd stuffed all the hate behind, unsure what really lay there. Even during the most recent attack with Bettina and the rest of her vampires, he'd managed to keep it under control. The thought of what Nicholas would turn into if the animal within was allowed to emerge frightened me.

"I'd show you, but I don't want to scare you," he said apprehensively.

Inside him, I felt the excitement of something new, something separate from the man I loved. It wanted to frighten me. It wanted all the control. I sensed the urge tempt Nicholas' desire to quench my curiosity before the feelings vanished, stuffed back into Pandora's Box.

"Um . . . better not then," I said with a nervous twinge in my voice.

He hugged me tighter and nuzzled my hair gently with his nose. He'd told me several times he was addicted to my scent—a cross between cotton candy and a fresh rain storm. I felt the same about his—earthy yet ocean-like.

"I've been meaning to tell you," he said with caution. "This whole vamp hiatus has got me a little worried. I need to go see someone in L.A. to find out what's happening, and it might take more than a day."

My anxiety jumped. I didn't like the idea of Nicholas being so far apart from me, especially for so long.

"Why?" I said while pulling away.

"It's okay, Julia," he said and grabbed onto my hand. "It's just my arms' dealer. I need more stuff anyway; plus, this tank-top is getting a little ripe."

"What are you talking about?"

All the time we'd spent together and he'd never mentioned an 'arms' dealer' or a tank-top. Nicholas dropped my hand and undid the top buttons of his shirt. Underneath was a thin, yellowish undershirt.

"This," Nicholas said, "protects me from getting staked."

I furrowed my brow.

"It's soaked in vampire venom. We've found you have to fight immortals with immortal properties. Without the talisman I needed extra protection."

My mouth fell open. "That's nasty!"

"Better than blood. Venom doesn't reek as quickly."

Blood? I wrinkled up my face in disgust. "Wait, so you wear—" I full-body-shivered "—a venom-drenched undershirt because it protects you from being staked?"

"I do."

I remembered back when Nicholas told me he was protected and not to worry. He never elaborated on the details, though I'm sure it was because it was gross.

"Who's venom?"

"My dad's."

I processed the information quickly, seeing my moment of opportunity. If I could tag along, maybe I'd get a better handle on Nicholas' relationship with his father. And I'd be able to keep an eye on him as well. The problem was leaving without my dad's knowledge.

"Hold on."

I jumped up and crawled through my window towards my beloved ocean scenes calendar on the wall. The timing couldn't have been more perfect. Dad was supposed to be leaving Friday for a weekend technology conference in Tulsa. I could go and tell Luke I was spending the night with Sam.

"What are you doing?" Nicholas called softly from the window.

I whirled around with a smug smile. "I'm going with you."

"What?" Nicholas whispered emphatically, "No. I forbid it."

"Why?"

"First, your father would never let you go. And the people I'm visiting are . . . dangerous."

I put a hand on my hip. "Any more dangerous that what I've encountered already?" I tapped my finger lightly against the talisman.

"Yeah, well—" Nicholas turned and leaned against the siding of the house. His aura brimmed with anxiety.

I ran over to the window and poked my head out.

"My dad will be out of town this weekend, so I don't even need to tell him. And I'm wearing the talisman. Your vampire dealer dude won't be able to hurt me."

"It's not him."

"Your father?"

Nicholas ran his hand through his hair.

"I'll wait in the car," I said quickly "They don't even have to know I'm with you."

"They'll know," he said and closed his eyes.

I leaned against the window frame. I'd already felt the decision before he spoke it. There was no convincing him. The sigh slipped through my lips.

"Julia, I'd love to take you, but it's not a good idea. Besides, I don't want to cause any issues between you and your dad. After everything, he trusts you again."

"Well," I said while pushing back the cuticles of my thumb with my fingernail, "not completely."

Darn it!

"And, you need your rest. It's very late now."

I looked at the clock. If I happened to fall asleep right at that moment, I'd get three hours of sleep before I needed to wake up for school.

"Come here," he said, arms outstretched.

I climbed back onto the eve and wrapped my arms around his torso. His sorrow enveloped my soul and left me guilty for secretly plotting against him. Maybe his absence was what I needed so I could find Alora first.

The nagging foreboding made me think differently.

Chapter Three

"You need me to cover for you? Why?" Sam asked while we stood closer to each other than left and center fields during P.E., hoping we wouldn't get in trouble for abandoning our positions.

"I'm going away this weekend with Nicholas," I said casually.

"Holy crap. No way," Sam said with big eyes. "How?"

"Oh, come on. It's no big deal." I cocked my head to the side. "He's visiting his dad and I want to go with him—totally innocent. My dad won't be home anyway, but I need you to keep my phone."

"Your phone? Why?"

I sighed. This proved to be more difficult than I wanted it to be.

"My dad activated that GPS tracking thing, so I need you to keep it and answer it if he calls. Tell him I'm in the shower or something."

"Oh . . . wow . . . um. A tracking thing?"

Her hesitation surfaced. Sam didn't lie well, which wasn't a bad thing, but her reaction made me suddenly wonder if I should have come up with another alternative.

After my friend Phil, a recent transfer to our high school, died in a fire downtown, my dad's been overprotective of me. Little did he know that Phil was actually a recently immortalized vampire and part of Alora's coven. Phil happened to be staked by Nicholas when he tried to turn me into a vampire too. All that remained was his teeth, so we staged a fire.

"I guess with everything that happened with Phil, he's just being a concerned dad," I said quickly. "I mean, I'm not going to do anything. I just know he won't let me go if I ask. I doubt he'll call. Seriously."

My aggravation flared as the night I'd figured out he'd added the service replayed through my mind. I'd lied, saying I was at work when really I was on a date with Nicholas at the Boardwalk. Right as I stepped into the house, he called and grounded me for three weeks—all from Chicago. Baffled by his new psychic abilities, I hammered Luke to tell me how he knew, but he didn't have a clue, so I tried—unsuccessfully—to figure it out myself, until I saw the GPS advertisement on TV. Once I checked online, I realized he'd clamped on the electronic leash.

"So you're not going to . . . you know," Sam said sheepishly, full of curiosity.

My cheeks flushed in response. I loved Nicholas with all my heart, but I wasn't ready for anything like sex just yet. There were too many girls I'd known who'd rushed into it. Their disappointment and pain, especially if the guy dumped them right after, was immense and long lasting. Plus, I wanted my first time to be really special and when I was married. And not everyone was having sex like they bragged they did anyway.

"No," I said defensively. "Not even thinking about it."

"Really?" she asked and kicked a dandelion puff, knocking loose its wispy seeds.

Sam was a virgin too, but Todd had been putting pressure on her. She'd alluded to maybe going all the way, but I affirmed our pact to wait. If he cared, he'd accept her decision. She worried if she didn't, she'd lose him. I worried he'd break her heart.

I stuck my pinkie out. She looked at it and laughed.

"We haven't done that since the 6th grade," she said and reached out her pinkie to meet mine.

"Pinkie swear, double dare," we said together while doing our secret handshake. "Best friends we'll be, for eternity."

At the end, we bumped fists and did what we called "The Explode," where our fingers shot open and drifted apart from each other. Our act bolstered her resolve. For the moment, Sam was going to keep her ground.

"Heads up!" Mandy called from first base.

I ducked with my mitt over my head and Sam moved forward to catch the ball, missing it. We both watched as it landed right between us with a thud, which sent some of the fallen dandelion seeds floating back up into the air.

"Ahh!" Alexis, the third baseman called out. "What the heck are you twits doing? Throw the freaking ball!"

I picked up the ball and, with my best effort, threw it forward. It sailed straight up and lobbed over, only to fall a few feet in front of Alexis. With ease, she scooped up the ball and chucked it to the second baseman for the third out.

Our team cheered and ran into the dugout. Sam and I exchanged relieved glances, thankful for Alexis' recovery—she was on the Varsity team after all. But I dreaded the next part of the inning. My batting skills made my catching look brilliant.

Later, in the locker room, Alexis' homerun made her forget all about my error in the outfield and my strike-out, but I still avoided her while we changed out of our gym clothes.

"I wanted to tell you," Sam said under breath. "I'm worried about Katie."

"What do you mean?" I asked while pulling my shirt over my head.

"Have you noticed her whole schedule changed this quarter?"

Katie mentioned something about how she'd been transferred into some Senior classes this term, but she'd been tight-lipped about how.

"Yeah, so?"

Sam leaned in. "Well, she's been taking college courses at night and I think it's because she's trying to graduate early."

"That's ambitious of her," I said.

"But she's doing it to be in the same classes as Tyler."

At Sam's suggestion, the correlation clicked. All her classes were now conveniently with Tyler, but it didn't change the fact that Tyler was still unavailable and deeply in love with Mandy.

"Hmmm, interesting," I said as we walked out of the locker room. "Did she tell you that?"

"Not in so many words. Lauren, the office TA, told Megan about her college credits, who told Emily, who told me—all in confidence of course."

This meant the whole school knew. Katie did seem to be keeping to herself lately and, come to think of it, I hadn't heard her mention

Tyler at all. Even though I felt she still had a thing for him.

Before turning the corner of the hall, a sudden burst of anxiety bowled me over and I scanned the area to find the source. Off to the side, Tyler and Mandy stood close together. It didn't take an emotion-reader to know they were fighting. My eyes locked with Sam's in surprise while we wordlessly took our books out of our lockers for History.

"What do you mean you don't know who this text is from?" Tyler said quietly with a scowl and handed Mandy back her cell phone firmly.

"I don't know anybody named James," Mandy said, face flushed, fear flooding out around her. "It has to be a mistake."

"Mistake? He seems to know you pretty well. Where were you last night anyway?"

"I was home like I told you," Mandy said emphatically as her eyes began to water. "You can even ask my mom."

Katie slid in between us. I felt satisfaction play across her aura though her face looked concerned.

"What's going on?" she whispered.

"Stop gawking," I said quickly. I closed my locker door and motioned for her to move out of my way. "Apparently a mis-understanding."

"Oh?" Katie stated, still watching from the corner of her eye.

"But you obviously gave *James* your cell number," Tyler said behind us.

"I promise, Tyler, I don't know who this person is or how he got my number," she said in truth. "I'm *your* girlfriend."

We watched as Mandy reached out to touch Tyler's arm, but Tyler pushed her hand away.

"I don't believe you," he said quietly, his eyes angry but glistening, expressing the hurt he obviously tried to hide.

"I promise. I do not know who this person is."

"Yeah, right," Tyler said, glancing away, putting on his sunglasses. "Don't pretend you don't flirt when I'm not around. I've seen you with other guys, with Cody."

"Cody? You're jealous of *Cody*?" she said, her voice astounded.

Tyler must have been pretty desperate to assassinate her with a flirty accusation tied to Cody, of all people, the widely known school flirt and class clown.

After taking a moment to process the rejection, Mandy took a step back from him, as if she'd been slapped. The tears streamed down her cheeks as she gave him one final look, which he ignored. Then she turned around and ran down the hall towards the bathroom. Tyler slammed his locker shut and headed in the opposite direction as the warning bell rang.

"Oops, late for Calculus," Katie said and quickly darted off in Tyler's direction. "Catch ya later."

Sam mouthed "wow" while pulling open the door to Mr. Marshall's room. I walked past her with a look, feeling the same shock. If it weren't for my gift, I might have been on Tyler's side. But Mandy's innocence was clear and I couldn't ignore Katie's smug enjoyment of the altercation.

I took my seat and watched the news spread from person to person—the curiosity heightened with each retelling while Mr. Marshall lectured with his back to the class, oblivious to the fact he'd lost control of his classroom, again.

Sam passed me a note.

"I can't believe that just happened."

I hid the paper under my textbook and wrote back.

"I know, totally weird. Do you think K might be involved?"

Shock registered across Sam's face as she read my words. She glanced at me, pupils dilated. Her pencil scrawled something quickly back.

"You don't think she would, do you?"

"After what you said, I wouldn't put it past her."

Mr. Marshall turned from the whiteboard and suddenly noticed no one was paying attention to his lecture. His fury ignited.

"I believe it's time for a pop quiz," he said gruffly. "Books away. Take out a sheet of paper."

Everyone collectively groaned as papers shuffled throughout the classroom. Out of the corner of my eye, I saw Sam stuff the note in her bag to keep from getting caught. Completely deflated, I took out my own sheet. I'd almost recovered my grade to a B, after my huge distraction with Nicholas last quarter, and this zero would quickly undo all that hard work.

By the end of fourth period, there wasn't anyone in the school who didn't know about the break-up. Mandy, unable to deal with the pressure, left school with a sudden illness. My heart went out to her and I wished we were better friends—most people took Tyler's side and she needed someone who implicitly believed her side of the story.

"She's obviously up to something," Dena said while picking apart her sandwich, only eating microscopic bites.

"And finally got caught," Morgan said, finishing Dena's statement.

"Maybe, but I was there when it happened and it didn't look like that to me. Right, Sam?"

"Yeah, it seemed like the text was a mistake," Sam said. "Tyler should at least give her a chance to explain."

I glanced over at the table where Tyler sat. He was doing the macho thing with his buddies, pretending not to be upset while a greedy group of cheerleaders flittered in the wake, looking to give consolation. Any one of them could have sent the text to sabotage the relationship.

"I just never thought they'd break up," Dena said. "They were like the perfect couple. Well, almost . . ."

Dena interlaced her fingers with Morgan's while looking adoringly into his eyes. The gesture made me miss Nicholas until the heart-rocking reminder Alora was back overshadowed everything. I internally steadied myself by realizing I'd let the drama cloud my plans of finding her. After school I'd need to start scouring the city and look for her unique bloodlust. There couldn't be too many places she'd be able to hide uninvited.

"Hey guys, what's up?" Katie said, out of breath, a smile plastered across her face.

I gave her a puzzled look while she sat down.

"You didn't hear?" Cameron questioned.

"About?" Katie said, feigning innocence. "Oh, yeah that. I was there actually. Too bad. They were such a nice couple. Are you going to eat that?"

Katie pointed towards Cameron's apple on his tray.

"Help yourself," he said in bewilderment while Katie took a bite.

"I have news," Katie said with a mouthful. "I've been accepted to Texas A&M."

"You have? So soon?" I asked.

Katie's pride swelled. She'd successfully managed to keep this juicy secret from everyone until now.

"I've been taking college courses to graduate early," Katie said. "And with Mrs. Peet's recommendation I applied in January and was accepted."

"You've been taking college courses?" Dena said in amazement. "When?"

"At night and during the summer."

"But you've always wanted to go to UC Santa Cruz," I said in confusion.

"Yeah, well . . ." Katie's nostalgia flickered. She'd wanted to be a Marine Biologist since our fieldtrip to Marine World in the fourth grade. "Texas A&M is a really good school and I need to get out of here anyway."

"But do they have a Marine Biology program?" I asked.

"I've changed my major," Katie said quickly. "I'm going to study Business instead."

"Since when?"

"Since I've found out there are no jobs in that field and I wanted to check out Texas."

Something triggered in my mind when she mentioned Texas again. I felt the recognition from Sam at the same time.

"Didn't Tyler get a full ride to Texas A&M for football?" Sam said in wonder.

The corner of Katie's lip curled for a brief second before she covered it up. Her plan had been unveiled.

"He is?" she said, bluffing her ignorance. "Oh cool. At least I'll know *someone*."

I coughed and exchanged glances with Sam. She could fool Dena, Morgan, and Cameron, but not us.

"Actually, I need to talk to Mrs. Peet so she can add me to the college acceptance board," Katie said before she darted out of the cafeteria with a "Toodle-loo!"

Confusion still lingered from the others as we watched her leave.

"See, I told you," Sam said under her breath.

"Yeah, I see what you mean. I'll talk to her later."

When I said later, I meant after my weekend with Nicholas. I had bigger problems to deal with than a conversation about the coincidence of Mandy's text from "James" and being accepted to the same college as Tyler. It would still be there on Monday.

The bell rang for fifth period and my brain went into problem solving mode. Not math problems, but how to systematically find where Alora hid during the day.

Under my desk, I scrolled for an iPhone app with a mapping function. I wanted to track the ground covered as I drove around the city later. I'd have an hour after school today and possibly tomorrow which wasn't much considering the zig-zagging pattern I'd need to perform. If I could find her before we left Friday night, arranging a sunset drive-by where Nicholas might be able to feel her presence (safely within the sanctum of his vehicle of course) would be ideal.

- **How's it going?**

The text startled me, interrupting my search. I was mad until I saw it was from Nicholas.

- **Good. And you?**

- **Hoping you'd be free after school for a quick bite.**

I smiled at Nicholas' humor. To some, if they'd known he was half-vampire, the word "bite" might have left them wondering—or horrified. Even still, the idea, no matter how awesome, interrupted my search plans.

My fingertips hovered over the touch-screen.

What to say? What to say?

- Sure.

Even though I knew figuring out Alora's hiding place was more important, being with Nicholas sounded better. The day had already seemed too long, and watching Dena and Morgan together made me want to see him sooner.

Chapter Four

Friday evening finally arrived and the little time I'd spent searching for Alora was a complete bust. I'd have to resume the search after *our* weekend, once I was able to invite myself along of course.

I rushed to put together what I needed—my jeans, underwear, pink T-shirt, black hoodie, toothbrush, deodorant, hairbrush—only the basics I could fit in my backpack. Any second he'd be here to say good-bye and I had to be ready to go.

My heart skipped a beat when I felt his sweet aura, nervous but refreshing, like an evening breeze. I acted busy when he rapped on the pane.

"Hey," I said after opening the window. "Fancy meeting you here."

Unable to cross my threshold, per his request, Nicholas, being part vampire, was unable to touch me until I came outside.

I could only wait a fraction of a second before the glint in his smiling, sea-green eyes made my knees turn to Jell-O and I couldn't clamber out of the window fast enough. But before I'd even got one foot on the awning, he'd lifted me by my waist and brought our faces level with each other. The sudden tense pause made me hold my breath before our lips touched. We brushed our mouths in sync while his sweet breath tickled my nose.

Several moments later, I was able to tear my lips from his. I melted into his embrace and enjoyed the euphoria, not wanting to breach the forbidden subject of me tagging along.

"I should leave more often," he said after a few more kisses.

"Well, I wanted to talk to you about that."

"Am I forbidden to go?"

I giggled. "Yes and no."

He gave me a puzzled look.

"Yes, you're allowed to go," I said with confidence. "But not without me."

Nicholas closed his eyes slowly, keeping control of his frustration, and released my waist.

"Julia, you know I'd love you to go with me—I can never get enough time with you, but I don't think your dad would approve." He paused to give me his most endearing smile—the one he knew I couldn't resist.

"Well, that's why I'm not telling him. He's out of town this weekend so he'll never even know. I won't even be lying. I'll just be withholding the complete truth. Come on, please?"

"What if something happens while we are gone? How would you explain that to your father? He'd forbid you from seeing me ever again. I can't risk that. I need you more than you'll ever know." The pained look on his face was enough to nearly stop my argument, but I was determined to carry on.

"Well, if something did happen, we could always tell him a little more about you. If he knew what transpired with my mother –his wife—he'd trust you without a doubt and let us date. Heck, he'd probably give us his blessing," I said in my defense.

I could see him waver, considering my argument, but he didn't look convinced. It was time to put on the pressure.

"And . . . I want to see my grandmother."

Nicholas' eyebrows pressed together. "Your grandmother?"

"Yes, she's in a rest home in L.A. and I haven't seen her since my mother's disappearance."

"Julia . . ." Nicholas said with a sigh, his face still like stone.

My request put a chink in his armor, but I wasn't done with my bag of tricks yet.

"And . . ." I said slowly, "I want to visit my mother's grave."

Internally, the wall of bricks fell in to expose his wounded heart. How could he deny me this request when he still blamed himself for how it happened?

"Not fair," he said, face crestfallen.

"How is this not fair?" I said quickly and looked up at him with puppy-dog eyes. "Like I said, this is the perfect weekend. My dad is away and everyone thinks I'm going to be at Sam's. She even has my phone. We can drive stealth there and back."

"You have this all planned out, don't you?"

I wrapped my arms around his torso and waited. The battle within him ensued. Fear verses guilt, but the guilt was winning.

I felt bad for twisting his arm, but I knew things he didn't and the thought of being that far apart from each other when I knew nothing of his L.A. life scared the tar out of me. Come what may, I needed to be in the wings just in case, and use my unknown talent to save him before the prophecy could come true.

"Okay," he said in a final huff. "But— you will do as I request once we get to L.A., promise?"

"Scouts honor," I said. "I'm already packed."

"Fine, let's go."

His peaceful presence relaxed me the instant we hit the highway. All his angst against me coming along had melted. He must have felt better because he could still keep an eye on me, conveniently placing the blame on my persistence when it came to the sticky details with my dad. But I felt okay about it because the whole trip was purely business. We'd be home before anyone could miss us.

His *stealth driving,* as he called it,—speeding as fast as the car would go with the headlights off—shot us like a slingshot towards Los Angeles. I sank into the soft leather seat and let the serenity of the jazz music that floated from his speakers pull my eyelids shut. Suddenly the fog cleared and I found myself walking down a dark corridor, looking for Aladdin. She'd jumped from my arms and scurried into a crack in the wall of the abandoned structures towering around us. Rickety, rusted-out siding shot up from the ground into the sky so far up I couldn't see the top, or the sky. I only heard her anxious meows echo off the walls, unsure where the cry came from. I turned the corner of the growing metal labyrinth, losing my sense of direction, frantically calling her name. My spidery senses were tingling and all I wanted to do was leave. But the bloodlust found me, coming from behind and I already knew I was trapped.

"Welcome home, darling," Alora said as I spun around. Her mellifluous voice turned my stomach. I prepared to run in the other direction, but my feet stayed rooted in their spot. "I've been waiting."

I startled awake.

"Bad dream?" Nicholas said while rubbing the back of my neck, still *stealthing* past tall, blurry buildings unfamiliar to me.

"Um," I said and blinked my eyes to clear the fog. "Yeah, something like that. Where are we?"

"We'll be there in about ten minutes."

The general unhappiness hit hard. Even in the car, I realized Los Angeles was a gigantic city filled with lots of confused and hurting people. My mind whirled as I watched the traffic, the lights, the architecture, and signs to the endless interlocking maze of freeways, wondering what made this place so miserable. I'd forgotten the oppression such a huge populace could bring—only hanging out in my small beach town.

"Are you tired? I got you a room," Nicholas said in concern.

"You're not —" I gulped "—you know, staying with me?" I asked sheepishly, unsure of his intended plans.

"Well, I figured while you slept I'd run my errands and then tomorrow we could go see your grandma, if that's okay with you."

The thought of being in a weird hotel, with unknown strangers in rooms all around me, doing God knows what, and Nicholas far away, freaked me out.

"You're going to leave me there?"

The panicked look in my eyes must have been pretty evident as Nicholas' sudden concern sent out shock waves.

"I was, but not if you don't want me to."

I shook my head. I'd already planned to stay glued to his side, or wait in the car—whatever, just as long as we were together. And, I didn't have my phone, so Nicholas would always need to be within screaming distance.

Nicholas' shoulders slumped as he grew quiet while deeply concentrating on something. It was apparent he didn't want me coming along wherever he had to go.

"I'm sorry," I said quickly. "I just get freaked out at the thought of being alone in a strange place. I don't mind waiting in the car. I won't be any trouble. I promise." I sat up straighter to check my reflection in the visor mirror, and wiped away smudged mascara. "I'm ready to do whatever . . . I'm not tired."

I tried to give a convincing smile when I didn't feel like my speech helped.

"I'm not sure that'll work."

"Why?"

"Because where I have to go . . . you'll wish you waited back at the hotel."

"Oh." I bit my lip. "Some scary vampire-ville?"

Nicholas chuckled. "No, though every town usually has a few. Actually, Harry doesn't live in the best part of town."

"Harry?"

"He makes my weapons."

"Isn't that your nickname?" I asked with a smirk. "Or should I call you *Dirty* and him *Harry*."

Nicholas let out a snort. "More like call him *Dirty Harry*. And please don't tell him my newspaper nickname. He'd never let me live it down."

I giggled. Harry sounded like my kind of dude.

"A couple of things. Harry's blind but don't let that fool you. He's very intuitive and uses all of his other senses well. Also, he's a big fan of Clint Eastwood—you'll see what I mean when you meet him."

"Does he look like Clint Eastwood?"

Nicholas' enjoyment of my statement felt refreshing, otherwise toning down his overall tension.

"Not exactly. Let's just say he's watched a lot of *Dirty Harry* movies and picked up some bad habits. I'll ask him to curtail the colorful adjectives in your presence."

We pulled off the highway and Nicholas flipped on his headlights which sent the underground life skittering. The general heightened oppression and fear on the street made my heart hammer faster. I grabbed Nicholas' hand in response, instantly infused with his confidence, creating a bubble against the bombardment.

"Don't worry," Nicholas said and squeezed my hand back. "I grew up on these streets. No one's going to bother us."

Still keeping an even pressure on my hand, I felt the sweat pool under my palm. I believed him, but would feel better once we were driving away from this place. This wasn't what I'd call "home."

The signs on the dilapidated buildings were in a language I didn't recognize. The people on the street appeared hard, ready to do real damage if you looked at them wrong. Nicholas maneuvered through the streets with ease, feeling a sense of fondness. Like this part of the city really was his home.

"Is Harry an uncle or something?" I finally asked.

"Not . . . really," he said. "More like a guardian. Someone had to keep an eye on me during the day."

"But he's blind?"

"With ears like a hawk."

Nicholas turned into a dark alley and the walls swallowed us whole. He pulled into a shadow of the building and parked.

"I'll be out in a minute."

My eyes grew big in response, until I caught the smile.

"Kidding. Harry would kill me anyway if I left you out here."

I fell back into the seat, filled with relief. His talent for hiding his emotions happened at the weirdest times.

We exited the vehicle and approached a worn iron door. Nicholas rapped on the metal while I stood glued behind him. There was a flicker in the peephole and then happiness burst forth as the door opened.

All I could understand was "Nicholas" before a string of what I believed to be Vietnamese.

A small-framed woman, a little over five feet tall, dark hair, heart shaped face, attacked his neck in a hug. I marveled at how love in any language all felt the same.

Nicholas spoke back with the same sentiment. Her curiosity piqued once she noticed me.

"Girlfriend?" she asked in broken English.

Nicholas' smile reflected the effervescence of his eyes as he nodded. I'd never been introduced as The Girlfriend before. The title made me feel special, giddy.

"Hung," he said while motioning to me. "I'd like you to meet Julia."

"Namaste," Hung said sweetly with a bow, her hands pushed together in a prayer pose. "Happy to meet you."

"Likewise," I said, but before I could bow in return, she grabbed our arms and pulled us across the threshold.

"Don't like evil spirits," she said while waving her hand in the air. She gave the alley one last look before slamming the door shut.

Once the iron collided against the frame, she proceeded to flip three locks followed by some ritual with a circular jade amulet that hung off the wall.

Nicholas touched her shoulder and spoke gently—conveying something so she'd stop worrying. She responded back in Vietnamese, still spooked. Her chocolaty brown eyes caught my concern and she shot me a warm smile.

"You eat? Hungry?" Hung asked while she rubbed her stomach. "Come." She padded down the hall in her beaded slippers and motioned for us to follow.

The kitchen smelled amazing and was covered with little vials of herbs. A large pot bubbled with an exotic soup along with a pan simmering with stir-fried meat. Fresh vegetables covered her work area and dough lay thinly rolled out for some sort of pastry.

She forced us to sit and began to pile plates with sticky rice, dried fish, and fresh spinach. I was glad she forced us to eat because I was actually very hungry. After she'd been satisfied we'd eaten enough, we were finally allowed to see Harry.

Hung escorted us to the back of the house, bowed, and left us in front of the closed door.

Nicholas knocked.

Muffled cursing could be heard from within, full of irritation. Nicholas coughed loudly to cover it up right before the door flew open to reveal a small Vietnamese man. I almost gasped, not expecting his appearance. Harry's ivory skin tone matched his opalescent eyes, bushy white eyebrows, alabaster beard, and the ring of straw-like milky colored hair that circled his head which left the top bald. His anger quickly faded to surprise, then elation.

"Nicky, my boy, good to see you, you fine—"

"Harry," Nicholas said quickly. "Sorry to interrupt you, but I have company—female company."

"I thought I smelled something better than your ugly mug," Harry said with a deep, scratchy voice and emerged from the dark room with his hand forward. "Freesia and wild apples. Where are you, Nicholas' lady-friend?" Harry's raspy voice seemed completely opposite of his actual appearance. I suppressed a giggle and reached out to meet his hand.

"Hi, Harry," I said meekly. "I'm Julia."

"Hello," he said and patted the top of my hand before he turned to Nicholas. "She's a pretty thing, I can tell." I blushed before he turned back to me. "Don't listen to anything he says. He's full of b—"

"Harry," Nicholas interrupted with a warning in his tone.

"Unbunch your panties, Son; I was going to say baloney."

"Yeah, sure you were."

Nicholas entered the office while Harry held my hand, leading me inside to a chair, removing a few things off of it first.

"Grab the light Nicholas, you know where it is," Harry said. "And don't touch anything. I finally know exactly where everything is."

"Harry, I'm not ten anymore."

"You still do it though—you little scroungy pain in the— It took me months to find my things after you left the last time. Just don't move anything and I won't have to yell at you!"

Nicholas huffed and flipped the light.

The illumination revealed the vast immenseness of his Organization System which astounded me. Harry left my side and followed along the path of boxes that led from the chair to a large oak desk covered in stacks of books and sat down. Behind him, lining the wall from floor to ceiling, were more books along with glass canisters filled with weird things—hair, bugs, herbs, gold-colored liquid with floating oddities, rocks, and bones. I gasped when I saw the pickled snake.

"A delicacy," Nicholas said quietly.

My body went into full tremors. I hated snakes. No matter where I stood, dead things watched helplessly back; the unrecognizable stuff freaked me out even more.

"So, Sonny, got something for me?" Harry asked while holding out his hand, then after taking a sniff in Nicholas' direction, wrinkled his face. "Ever heard of soap?"

"I ran out of venom. I need another shirt," Nicholas said in a low tone and dropped a small satchel into Harry's hand.

"I'd say you do." Harry opened the bag and poured out the shiny white stones into his other hand. "What's this? Skimping out on me? Or have you been busy playing Romeo with Julia?"

"The vamps are staying away for some reason. I was hoping you'd know why."

"How the he—heck would I know? Maybe the beacons are working," he said while scratching his beard with one hand and fondling the rocks with the other. "Or maybe it's your reeking shirt."

Nicholas pursed his lips. "Well, they've been up a year, and the hiatus started only four months ago."

"Beacons?" I asked quietly.

"Hollowed out limestone carvings filled with vamp blood etched with a warning in Latin. I've placed hundreds of them to encircle the town."

"Well, there are only ten sets of teeth here. I'd say that is quite a dry spell or you've lost your touch."

"That's unlikely."

Harry put one of the sharp rocks to his nose and inhaled. "Interesting. These bloodsuckers were very old." He spun around in his chair to face Nicholas. "Were they talented? What powers did they have?"

"Shape-shifting, mind-reading, flying—" He snorted after he said "flying." "Let's see . . . linguistic." He turned to me. "Remember anything else?"

I blinked, feeling a little tongue tied.

"Got to see the suckers first hand, did ya?" Harry interjected.

"She even staked one," Nicholas said with pride.

"Way to go, Annie Oakley," Harry said and tipped his invisible hat in my direction.

I just smiled and touched the emerald stone that hung around my neck. The necklace was the real hero and somehow helped me throw straight at that precarious moment when Justin threatened my life.

"One had blue eyes."

"Ah," Harry grunted. "From the Della Greca branch. Haven't seen one of them in a long time. They're usually very gifted. You know, you're from the Della Greca branch, Sonny."

My mind whirled. Alora had blue eyes as well and seemed very powerful.

"Nicky, in the box over there are some new stakes with a lighter alloy core. Try them out."

Nicholas took out a wooden stake and inspected it before chucking it towards the dummy in the corner. The sudden loud thwack surprised me, effectively jolting me out of my memories with my responsive yelp.

"Nice," Nicholas said and picked up two more, handing one to me. "The crosshatch design is new."

The spike's heaviness deceived me when Nicholas let go and I almost dropped it on the floor. The wood seemed denser than most. I noticed fine slivers of metal threaded along the sides of the shaft joining at the tip to make a sharp point. In the side, a miniscule brand of the cross was etched—the same one Nicholas had tattooed on his arm.

"Can't lose these, Nicky my boy," Harry said in complete somberness. "They'll penetrate your defenses—look."

Over on the floor, in a heap, a couple of tank tops lay. Nicholas picked one up and inspected the hole through the middle of the shirt.

"Using my clothing for target practice?" Nicholas said to be funny, but I could feel his nerves.

Harry's hand shot out to grab Nicholas' arm.

"I mean it. You account for every one."

Nicholas removed Harry's hand and clapped him on the back. "Got it, Harry. I'll be careful."

"You better," Harry said and rose from his chair. "I'm starving. Who wants ice cream? Hung. Hung! Where's that woman?"

Harry shuffled out of the room while calling her name.

Nicholas shot me a look of concern as I sat, wide-eyed.

"Why don't I wear the shirt and you, the talisman," I suggested quickly.

Nicholas softened. "Julia, no shirt is going to prevent a vamp from biting you. I wear the shirt to prevent getting staked, remember?"

"Yeah, but these are like—like those cop killing bullets, only for vampires," I said while shaking the stake in the air at him. "I thought you said nothing can get through the venom?"

"The metal has been infused with the vampire's teeth, ground down and put into the molten ore. It apparently gets through the venom vampire element—like scissors against paper."

"The teeth?" My mind was swimming with details.

"Yeah, teeth—that's what I just gave to Harry."

My bottom lip quivered. Nicholas was suddenly at my side, his arms wrapped tenderly around me.

"Hey," he said and tipped my chin up. "No tears. This is a good thing. I've got the stakes, the vamps don't. And they don't know our secrets either. Remember, we've got the advantage."

"Yeah, but—"

Nicholas put his index finger tenderly up to my lips to stop me from speaking. "We don't let others call our fate. We live our lives honorably, and when it's our time we accept it."

I sighed while a single tear fell and splashed on my pant leg. Nicholas knelt down, placed my chin between both of his hands, and held me for a second. His piercing eyes melted my soul.

"No fear," he whispered before he kissed me.

My eyes closed as we kissed, a few more tears spilling forth. The sweetness of his mouth mixed with the saltiness of my tears. I entangled my hands in his hair, demanding more. The thought of anything happening to him was too much and he responded with the same intensity. I almost completely lost all awareness of where we were until a sudden surge of embarrassment interrupted our passion.

"Holy mother of— Get a *room*," Harry said and slammed down the tray of ice cream before leaving abruptly. "Call me when you two are finished."

I heard a few expletives under his breath as he shuffled down the hallway.

"No, Harry," Nicholas called out while standing up. "Come back."

Alone, I took out a pocket mirror from my purse to examine my eyes. Red, like I expected. I powdered them before I heard them coming back, then remembered Harry was blind and snickered at my vanity.

I jumped up, grabbed a dish, and began to eat before they entered the room.

"This is good, Harry," I said with a mouthful. "Thank you."

"Sucking face does work up an appetite," Harry said gruffly.

"Sure does," Nicholas said while making a face. I stifled a chuckle which relieved my own awkwardness. "Okay Harry, enough chit-chat. Let's get down to business."

Chapter Five

I tried to concentrate while Harry and Nicholas talked, but ended up falling asleep in the chair. When I opened my eyes we were in the car driving again.

"Where are we?" I asked, sat up, and yawned. The freeway seemed extra desolate at three in the morning.

"Just left Orange County."

Nicholas reached over and put his arm over my shoulders. Still feeling sleepy, I snuggled into his chest and inhaled the glorious scent of his body mixed with his leather jacket. My eyes closed while he lightly rubbed my neck and shoulders. I loved that I still got butterflies from his touch.

"You're tense," he said and applied pressure to my trapezius muscle.

"Am I?"

Of course I was.

Because of my manipulation, I'd dangerously run away with Nicholas to L.A. while Alora staked out her camp in my town with intentions to find and capture Nicholas, the wanted vampire slayer. Enigma, being ambiguous as usual, said our success in defeating Alora included eliciting help from someone I didn't know, and who Nicholas despised—his father. And then somewhere in the mix I was supposed to destroy all the vampires because of a prediction from a now deceased fortune teller with an unknown gift that could mean the ending of Nicholas' life. All because he was part vampire. Not to mention, if my father ever caught word I'd left town without permission I'd never see the light of day. I had a lot on my mind.

But Nicholas temporarily took away the worry as I melted under his touch, relieved to be anywhere but the bad part of Orange County. The environment, still discontented, felt somewhat palatable with Nicholas' peace blocking it, like icing on top of a burnt cupcake.

"I'm sorry to drag you all over at such an insane hour. Harry's an insomniac and most congenial late at night."

I snorted. Of all the words to describe Harry, congenial wasn't one I'd pick. If that was Harry being congenial I'd hate to see what he was like during the day.

"I begged to come. Remember?" I reminded. "What's next?"

I actually hoped a pillow would be in our near future.

"One more quick errand, then we'll check into the hotel. You've got a big day tomorrow."

Suddenly the realization of being alone, together in a hotel room *with a bed* brought a blush to my cheeks and my heart quickened. My shoulders reactively tightened, undoing any benefit the massage might have brought.

Nicholas responded by kneading deeper. His calm worked its magic on my tattered body and I realized, with slight disappointment, he had no intentions of seducing me. His role—forever the protector—trumped any of his other desires. It'd been this way since the beginning of our relationship. I wasn't sure if I should be flattered or frustrated.

At the moment I was too tired to care. I snuggled deeper into his chest and pushed the doubt from my mind. He loved me and that was all that really mattered—not the fleeting feeling of lust.

When I opened my eyes again we were parked in front of a three story Victorian house in an established neighborhood. The maple trees stretched far into the night sky, which effectively blocked out the moonlight and left ominous dark shadows over the manicured lawn. Cement stairs led up to the porch flanked by two unlit lampposts. Somewhere beyond, I assumed, was a door.

Nicholas glared towards the house, full of disappointment and bitterness, unaware I was awake. His head flicked a fraction upward and I followed his gaze. The curtain fell into place, as if someone had just peeked around it.

Then I saw him; his face glistened in the moonlight, arms folded, leaning up against one of the posts. A vampire. A very sad and lonely vampire.

The standoff made me anxious.

When I shifted in my seat Nicholas' hand enfolded mine.

"Who's that?" I asked in a whisper, but I'd already suspected who the stranger was.

"Meet Pastor Preston Kendrick," he said without emotion. "My father."

My jaw dropped. I had no clue Nicholas' father was a pastor.

"I'll be back in a second. Promise," he said with a kiss on my temple.

I felt him squeeze my hand before he disappeared. While my eyes closed to blink, he'd opened the car door, closed it, and breezed into the house. If I hadn't heard the car door shut I'd assumed he'd vanished into thin air.

I waited anxiously, feeling the atmosphere inside—stiff, unemotional, strictly business. Preston didn't feel like the other full-blooded vampires I'd met, which was surprising. His thirst was minimal, but the guilt was overwhelming—something Nicholas struggled with frequently as well. I knew Nicholas' stemmed from the regret of being late to save my mother, and for putting me in harm's way by being romantically involved with me. But I didn't have a clue why Preston would feel guilty. Maybe his grief from losing his wife in the traumatic birth of Nicholas strained their relationship. Or he felt responsible since the pregnancy was his doing, unaware he wasn't sterile as believed in the vampire world.

At the same time, Enigma's words rang through my mind. We needed Preston's help in order to defeat Alora, and somehow I was supposed to facilitate Nicholas' asking for it. The thought of just knocking on the door and blurting out what I knew came to mind, until I imagined the outcome. Nicholas would feel betrayed, and possibly mortified I'd begged his father, of all people, for assistance with information I'd kept hidden from him through lies. And Preston might not even want to get involved with our petty situation. He could possibly become upset that Nicholas allowed his initial relationship with my mother to blossom into a romance with me. Not to mention his irresponsibility in giving me the talisman.

Whatever happened would need to be handled delicately, and

possibly without Nicholas' knowledge. Coming back at another time or writing Preston a letter seemed a more reasonable option. I glanced back at the house and noticed a faint address etched in the cinderblock at the bottom of the stairs. It read 612 Elm. Using Google maps later would give me the city and zip.

My eyes focused on the nearby houses. They seemed charming, but not kid friendly. I wondered if Nicholas was even allowed outside to play growing up. My assumption was he'd spent a lot of time with Hung and Harry, getting more of a loving upbringing from them on the hard streets of Orange County.

The door slammed shut and I jumped. Nicholas threw a brown leather satchel in the backseat and started the car. His hands moved so fast I couldn't register what he was doing until we were zigzagging down a maze of side streets. Once I realized we'd left I sat quietly and allowed Nicholas to process his thoughts all the way to the hotel.

"If you'd feel more comfortable I can go in and get the keys," he said when he pulled into the driveway of the Beverly Hills Hilton.

"I want to stay with you," I said, feeling like it was my turn to heal his tattered spirit. I grabbed his hand and massaged it.

Nicholas parked, grabbed our gear, and opened my door in seconds. I only saw a blur. He usually reserved that talent for when we were in danger, but he was clearly rattled from the visit with his dad.

"You okay?" I asked while searching his eyes.

"Yeah," he lied and looked away. He held out his hand to help me out of the front seat. My eyes were drawn to the large padded case that hung over his shoulder.

"What's that?"

"My guitar," Nicholas said nonchalantly.

"You—you play the guitar?" In six months he'd never mentioned he played.

"I'm not that good; I just didn't want to leave it in the car—it's special to me." For the first time I saw Nicholas blush.

"Will you play something for me later?"

Nicholas glanced sideways with a coy smile. "We'll see."

We walked hand in hand quietly through the vacant lobby. A preppy college guy at the front desk wasn't too eager to help us since we interrupted the movie he'd been watching on a DVD player. He suddenly became very professional after Nicholas handed him his VIP Hilton members card.

"Welcome back, Mr. Kendrick. Would you like your regular room?" Preppy Guy asked after he swiped it through the machine— his nervousness suddenly surged to epic proportions.

Nicholas nodded. I furrowed my brow as I watched him from the corner of my eye, curious at the use of "regular room."

"Very well," Preppy Guy said while quickly clicking a few keys on the keyboard. He ripped off the printed receipt and slid it forward for Nicholas' signature. I almost thought I saw a bead of sweat glisten on his upper lip as he handed over the room keys. "Enjoy your stay."

Nicholas squeezed my hand, as if to convey there was nothing to worry about, and led me towards the elevator.

"What was that all about?" I peeked back at Preppy Guy who smiled enthusiastically at me.

"Let's just say I'm a very special guest to the Hiltons."

Inside the elevator Nicholas inserted his card and the light to the 23rd floor illuminated. He pressed the button for the Penthouse Suite.

I gasped. "Are you kidding me? That's got to be so expensive."

"Not really. It's on the house." A teasing smile finally flickered across his beautiful lips.

"So you're not going to tell me?"

"My father saved Barron Hilton's life once. We are invited to stay whenever we'd like."

When the doors opened I stared, unblinking, for a second in disbelief. The foyer led to a giant room with vaulted ceilings, exquisite artwork covering the walls, lush burgundy couches, and floor-to-ceiling windows that overlooked the city. The famous HOLLYWOOD sign loomed on the hillside beyond the buildings.

I pointed and looked at Nicholas with wide-eyes.

"It's the real thing," he said smugly.

Inside, I meandered left, through a doorway, and entered a mint-green bedroom. A lavish headboard canopy hung over a King-sized bed adorned with downy pillows. I ran, jumped, and buried myself in the heavenly linens with a squeal. After composing myself, my eyes drifted to the attached bathroom. An intricate black-and-white marble floor led to a powder area, shower, and Jacuzzi tub. I sighed and made a note to soak in there before leaving.

"There's more," Nicholas said as he studied me, his effervescent eyes gleamed with satisfaction.

He stood, leaning one arm against the doorway, and looked absolutely adorable. I removed myself from the downy goodness of the bed and moved past him, trailing my hand across his irresistible chest. He caught me and pulled me into his arms while he nuzzled my hair. I giggled and our lips touched.

"How could there be more?" I whispered, smiling at his delight.

He nodded and led me to a dining area so fancy I didn't feel I could ever eat there, afraid I'd spill something and stain the upholstery or carpeting. French doors led to a deck, a hot tub, and the perfect view of the city. I was just about to check it out when I noticed another set of unopened doors. I turned the handle, expecting to find a kitchen, and walked into another mint-green bedroom and bath.

I looked up into his face and smirked. "I guess this solves my question of who's sleeping where, doesn't it?"

"Well?" His eyes caressed my face with tender care and he wrapped his arms around my waist.

Always the gentleman.

"Doesn't this make you wish you'd just taken my advice and waited here while I talked with Harry?" Nicholas said with a playful tone.

"Hmm. I remember the word *room*, not *penthouse suite*, as my choice."

"Ah, true."

I snickered. "Although, it would have been mighty tempting, considering Harry's neighborhood and some of its creepy inhabitants. I'd still choose to be with you," I said with a smile. "Hands down."

Nicholas sighed and rested his chin on the top of my head.

"You're too precious, Julia," he said softly. "More than I deserve."

No, you're more than I deserve.

Chapter Six

The morning sunlight filtered through my closed eyelids, signaling my brain to wake up. My backpack lying on the luxuriant carpeted floor reminded me where I'd slept the night before. I yawned and looked at the clock with a gasp. It read 11:38 AM. I'd slept most of the morning away. To my surprise, next to the lamp, a single pink gerbera daisy sat in a vase with a note attached.

Enjoy your soak in the tub.
I'll be back soon with breakfast.
_< Me_

Holding the note to my chest, I swooned while reaching out for Nicholas' presence in the next room and didn't feel him there. My stomach growled as I imagined what he was picking up for us. I stretched, dangled my feet off the bed, and curled my toes into the fluffy carpet that reminded me of kitten fur.

Moseying over to the bathroom I expected the floor tiles to be cold, but they felt warm under my bare feet—another lavish mystery. A vast array of French bath gels were perched on the tub ledge in a decadent display. I flipped the tap on, adjusted the temperature, and sifted through the different bottles, smelling each one. The sandalwood fragrance won the sniff test. The rest would be going home with me in my bag and used in the near future.

I sank into the tub until the hot water was up to my chin, pressed the buttons on the side of the tub, and felt the Jacuzzi jets spring into action. The pampering sprays melted the tension in my body—until I remembered I was going to visit my grandmother today. Nervousness rattled my insides like fall leaves fluttering in the wind. Would she remember me? Could she help me put together the pieces of my broken childhood?

I imagined a bitter old woman, deeply hurt by the fact her only surviving family members never came to visit her, or worse, her mind was riddled with dementia unable to remember the past or even who I was. I decided to stop worrying over something I couldn't control. Whatever was supposed to happen today would and our conversation would help me; it had to.

I sank further into the tub until the water level reached my earlobes. Bursting bubbles crackled in my ears and reminded me of the song Nicholas played on the guitar the night before. Our romantic evening in the living room lasted all of ten minutes before I so rudely fell asleep. The fire, his song, the comfy couch, and his peace were a deadly combination for my exhausted state. I remembered fighting with all my might to stay lucid, but my humanity won out, and the sleep that overtook me never felt so good.

Suddenly, Nicholas' happiness floated through the door and surrounded me with love. I flipped the drain open and crawled out into a cozy floor-length terrycloth robe, anxious to see him. Wrapping my wet, dishwater blonde locks in a towel, I sat at the powder table. As I quickly applied mascara, I wondered what Nicholas ever saw in me. I felt so plain—boring hazel eyes, heart-shaped face, small simple stature. There was nothing remotely sexy about me.

After dressing I grabbed my flower and headed into the living area. Nicholas sat at the table drinking coffee and reading the *L.A. Times* behind the rest of the gerbera daisies that were nestled in a huge arrangement. I blinked and he disappeared, but in the next instant I felt my body encased in his arms, his lips inches from mine.

"You took too long," he said warmly. His sweet breath tickled my nose and melted my knees. "I missed you."

I leaned in and caressed my lips eagerly against his, unable to wait any longer. He wrapped me into a tight hug and nuzzled my ear.

"If you start that—" Nicholas said playfully while kissing my temple, "—we'll be here all day."

"So," I purred and wiggled into his chest. "I don't mind."

Nicholas snorted and I went in for the kill with a kiss that made us both dizzy. When we came up for air I swayed a little. Nicholas, with a wanting gleam in his eye, quickly ushered me to the table, struggling against his inner desire to take things further. I smiled. It was good to know that under all his hardcore chivalry was a man—a man who felt real, manly feelings.

Heavenly mouth-watering smells wafted from under metal lids set before me. Nicholas placed his hand on the small of my back and guided me to a have a seat. I reached over to discover what was beneath the closest one, but he stopped me.

"Coffee first." He placed a paper cup from my beloved Starbucks within my palms, which I took and held ardently. With a sly grin, he waited a second before he revealed the first dish. "Here we have eggs Benedict, fresh peaches with cream, and turkey sausage." I let out a yum sound. "If you're still hungry after that—" he removed another lid, "there are waffles with blueberries or biscuits and gravy. Your choice."

"All for me?" I asked, stretching my neck forward to gape at the delicacies.

"I already ate," he said, expelling happiness—obviously because he'd pleased me. "After dragging you all over last night, I figured you'd be starving."

He was right. I nodded, unsure which morsel to feast upon and decided to tantalize my taste buds with the waffles first. Nicholas sat down and watched me eat each bite.

In embarrassment, I wiped the trickling blueberry juice off my chin and pointed to the abandoned newspaper.

"What's going on in the world?" I asked before stuffing a fork heaping with decadent peaches slathered in heavenly cream into my mouth.

"I was looking up the surf report."

"Oh? Are you planning to go surfing today?"

Nicholas grinned. "No. But this vacation has me thinking I need to do more things I enjoy, like surfing. I miss it."

"Why don't you go more often?" I asked while I assembled the perfect bite of egg, crab, and English muffin doused in hollandaise sauce on my fork. "This crab is yummy by the way."

"Lobster actually." He winked, then looked longingly out the window towards the ocean. "Dawn is the best time to hit the surf, but I'm usually wrapping up a very long night at that point. Going during the day hurts my skin without the talisman."

Guilt swept over me. I hated the fact that after he gave me the talisman, he had to give up so many things he'd enjoyed since childhood.

"I wish there were two necklaces." I looked down at my half-eaten waffle.

Quickly he reached out and tilted my chin up. My eyes met his intense gaze.

"Don't you dare think this is your fault. I don't need a talisman," Nicholas expressed with fervor. "Especially to do something like surfing."

I melted, fighting back my tears.

"I know . . . I . . . it would just be easier for both of us if you did."

"Julia, stop carrying this burden. I'm fine. I can handle this," Nicholas said, digging deeper into my soul with his stare. "What's really bothering you? It's hard for me to believe you're so distressed just because I don't go surfing as often as I used to."

"Nothing," I lied, and shoveled another bite of peaches into my mouth.

"Is it that psychic's prediction?"

My cheeks bloomed bright crimson and I tried to move my head. Nicholas stopped me from turning away. His hands held my face towards his and the heated electricity in his touch burned me to my core. I whimpered under the intensity and a tear fell. His hand caught it and absorbed the moisture, his touch lingering a second longer.

"I'm not leaving you, Julia. I will be here to protect you forever. Nothing will change that. I promise."

I sniffed, holding back a sob.

"Yes, but—"

"The talisman allows us to be together, remember that," Nicholas said passionately. "I treasure that over everything."

"Okay," I whimpered.

He gently pulled me from the chair and into a hug. I relaxed into his arms. He'd dealt with worse problems before, and vampires like Alora were all the same: nasty, greedy little cowards who ran at the first sign of defeat. If we conquered Alora this time the threat would finally be over. It was just a matter of when. I had nothing to worry about.

"We make our own fate," Nicholas whispered into my hair while nuzzling it. "Mmmm . . . I like this shampoo, what is it?"

I pulled away in surprise. "Something from the bathroom." I grabbed a lock and sniffed it. "I don't know. It's written in French."

"I'm getting you more. I really like it."

I laughed and shook my head.

"Did you eat enough?" Nicholas asked, shifting back into task mode.

"I think so," I said sheepishly, looking over at the half-empty plates.

"Then grab your things, we've got a busy day."

I felt weird carrying the oversized floral arrangement through the lobby—almost like we stole it—but Nicholas insisted we bring it along. I figured we'd need to leave it at Sam's once I picked up my phone later because I couldn't explain where they came from to Luke or Dad.

"Mr. Kendrick, please wait up." A woman's voice spoke behind us.

I walked faster towards the exit, but Nicholas turned and held a cool exterior. We were caught for sure until Nicholas brimmed with recognition.

"Miranda. I almost forgot." He took an elegant Hilton bag from her hands with a nod. "Thank you. And please call me Nicholas."

"Yes, Nicholas," she said with a blush. "Did you enjoy your stay?"

Miranda stood before us looking just like a Barbie doll, in a fitted black shift and heels with an exorbitant amount of makeup. She gave me a haughty once over, surprisingly seeped jealousy. I clutched the flowers tighter.

"We did." He put his hand around my waist. "Didn't we?"

The twinkle in his eye made my legs weak and I nodded back as heat crept up the sides of my cheeks. I didn't appreciate the way our night had been presented—nothing happened though Miranda was led to believe otherwise.

"Thank you, again." Nicholas led me out of the refined foyer.

"What's in the bag?" I asked, once we walked outside and my cheeks had a chance to return to normal.

"A present for you." He opened the bag so I could see two slender bottles with French wording on the outside.

I blushed again, a little shocked he remembered. "Thank you."

Once in the car Nicholas plugged the address I'd given him into the GPS and I became quiet. I wasn't looking forward to going to a rest home, and was still worried about what Grandma's reaction would be to my surprise visit.

When we arrived at Wilshire Rest Home for seniors and parked, a knot formed in my stomach. The grounds of the four-story building—pristinely decorated with fountains, manicured shrubberies and lawns—seemed welcoming; the inside was another thing altogether. Like all rest homes I'd visited, loneliness topped the charts for the highest ranking emotion. Depressing despair ripped at my heart—such an unfair way to live out the end of one's life. I gripped Nicholas' hand tightly as we walked across the path and entered through the automatic double doors. The overall weight of sadness and the antiseptic aroma hit me at the same time. My shoulders tensed.

"You okay?" Nicholas asked softly.

"Yeah," I said and took a deep breath. *Let's get this over with.*

An older woman with curly, short brown hair, and mauve-rimmed glasses encrusted with fake diamonds, sat behind the counter of the reception window. Her kind almond-shaped eyes turned downward to meet the creases of her cheeks when she smiled to greet me.

"Hello, how can I help you?"

"I called yesterday about visiting Grace London," I said timidly.

"Oh yes, I remember. Julie, right?"

"Julia actually," I said with a lump in my throat and looked down, fidgeting with the paper on the sign-in sheet clipboard.

"Oh, right, pardon me. If you'll sign here I'll have Charlie take you to her room."

She pointed for me to sign the guest list then provided us with clip-on visitors' tags. Charlie, noticing the mention of his name, stopped mopping the hall and waited for us to give him eye contact before he proceeded down the hall. Unsure what to do, we quickly caught up with him, but he offered no conversation.

The stench of loneliness overwhelmed me and I hoped, maybe once we got to Grandma's room, we'd take our conversation outside. Nicholas' calm—exuding from his hand into mine—soothed me and I focused on staying within the folds of it, imagining we hid under an umbrella deflecting the stormy unhappiness. It worked temporarily until the feelings managed to sneak under and hit me sideways like hurricane rain.

I tried to stay calm until we arrived at her door. Charlie knocked gently before pushing it open, and my heart thumped a little faster.

"Gracie, you awake?"

Following behind Charlie, I watched him pull back the pastel colored curtain. Grandma sat on her bed while staring at the silent TV with a cordless earphone gadget hanging around her chin. Grandma looked like I remembered, except a few more wrinkles and a fluff of purplish-white hair instead of blonde. I wondered if she'd even recognize me.

"Gracie, you've got guests."

Grandma turned with a blink, pulled the contraption out of her ears, and smiled. A glimmer of hope entered her blue eyes and I felt it.

"Hi, Grandma," I said. I rounded the corner of her bed, took her weathered hand, and was relieved she wasn't angry. Her skin felt soft, but her grip was weak.

"AnneMarie," she whispered in relief. "You look just like AnneMarie."

"No, Grandma, it's me, Julia."

She smiled with understanding. "I know, sweets. Look at you. You're all grown up."

I blushed at the misunderstanding. "Yes, Grandma."

"How refreshing young love is," she said with a wink. "Thank you, Charlie."

As Charlie slipped out of the room, I suddenly felt Grandma's feelings disappear and my head whipped back around to study her eyes, worried she'd just breathed her last breath. Grandma squeezed my hand in response.

"Grandma?"

How did she go completely emotionless? I'd never encountered anyone who could hide from me, except when Enigma was in cat form.

"I'm here, Love. And speaking of love . . ." she said with a gleam in her eyes; her glance danced between me and Nicholas. "Who's your friend?"

I shifted nervously and realized she had uncanny powers of her own. My heart quickened, unsure of the extent.

"This is Nicholas, Grandma."

Nicholas walked over to shake her hand. I moved out of the way and sat in a chair by the wall, concerned what she'd say next.

"Nice to meet you, Mrs. London," he said.

"Grace, please," she corrected with a smile. "You're a strong one. And *youthful* for your age . . ."

I cocked my head to the side. How could she know he was older than he looked? My eyes flickered to Nicholas' as his gaze tightened on her. I felt his concern too. He did have a lot of hidden secrets and her insight upon just meeting us seemed too accurate for my comfort.

"Just like your mother you are, Julia. Like me. And the gift goes on . . ." she said, trailing off in a sing-songy voice.

Nicholas looked bewildered for a brief second.

"Nicholas, dear? Would you be so kind as to give me a moment alone with my granddaughter?" she asked sweetly.

Nicholas nodded his head. "Of course." His eyes caught mine. "I'll wait for you in the hall."

I nodded and smiled reassuringly as Nicholas left the room. She'd read my anxiety correctly.

"Is that better?"

I bit my lip and shifted in my seat.

"What do you mean, Grandma?"

A knowing smile crossed her face. "The ability of empathy is nothing to be ashamed of, dear. What we can do is actually very handy," she said softly. "Don't you think so?"

"Uh," I stammered, while staring at the tile floor covered with various handmade rugs. My mouth became dry and I swallowed hard.

Most of the time I hated my ability. It only came in handy when I was being hunted by a vampire, or needed to know if someone was lying or not.

"You haven't told Nicholas?"

My eyes flicked up to hers. "I haven't told anyone."

"I see," she said in a very neutral tone.

Right now would be an ideal time to read Grandma so I could know where she was going with this, but she blocked my attempts somehow.

"Have you figured out how to control it?"

I snorted, holding back my retort. *Control? Are you freaking kidding me?*

"Well then, let's give you your first lesson," she said and patted the space next to her on the bed. "Come sit down here."

Reluctantly, I got up and sat next to her.

"Okay, now close your eyes."

Filled with suspicion, I closed my eyes. Since she did manage to make her feelings vanish on me she obviously knew a trick or two.

"Visualize yourself looking down onto us sitting here in this room."

I sighed, rolling my eyes under my closed lids, feeling very silly, but followed her instructions anyway.

"Now envision the entire floor of the building. Concentrate to find the sources of the feelings. Do you see the clouds that make up people's auras?"

I shook my head no. All I saw was a murky, impenetrable green soup enveloping the entire floor, making it difficult to locate anything.

"Okay, let's start simple. Find the closest person to us and will the emotion to stay within their personal space."

I focused on the closest person to me: someone in the next room. Their toxic despondency spilled out, ran through the wall, and surrounded me with wispy talons.

"How?"

"Imagine pulling something tightly around them to trap their feelings in. Like a blanket."

With rapt concentration, a blanket magically appeared and fell over the top of my subject's head. And, like Grandma promised, the emotions were captured and stayed underneath. I exhaled, then smiled, excited to think this trick might actually work, until I moved to the next person. Once I tried to encapsulate someone new, the first person's emotions broke through, like a rambunctious two-year-old merely being held by tissue paper.

"Ugh. I can't do it," I yelped in frustration.

"You're trying too hard, Love," she said, her tender eyes peering into mine. "Let's try this instead. Close your eyes."

Grandma took both my hands.

Suddenly, she was with me inside my body and we watched simultaneously out of the same pair of eyes in a collective mind— hers and mine. I gasped, not sure if I liked the sensation.

"It's okay," she whispered, squeezing my hands. "Relax."

I inhaled and let her float us over to the first person. Out from my grandma's fingers spun a colorful parachute of fabric that shot over their head. The edges magically fell to the floor and cinched up around the recipient's feet. The feelings fought against the barrier, trying to punch through the tough fabric, but once the corners were securely fastened with elastic, its misty hands disappeared and could no longer weave around my head to taunt me.

Internally I did a little happy dance.

"See?" she said. "Now try one by yourself this time."

"Okay."

I floated to the next person and visualized the same parachute. Though mine wasn't as colorful as Grandma's, it still did its job; it mystically fell down around the feelings, cinched at the bottom, and kept them in place.

"Keep going . . ." she whispered.

One by one I worked over the floor and compartmentalized everyone in multicolored fabric. The ward began to look like a patchwork quilt. After I bundled up the last one my eyes flew open. The relief was instantaneous. The barriers stayed between me and all the faceless inhabitants, stopping the previous mental tug-of-war.

The tears began and I threw my arms around Grandma's small frame, hugging tightly, but careful not to crush her.

"Now, now . . . don't cry. What will your beau think?" she said while holding me.

I didn't care. I was finally free. For once I could actually be in this horrible place and not feel it. I was practically normal.

We released our hug and I looked into her crystalline, clear sky-blue eyes. Since the other, more powerful emotions were gone, I could genuinely feel her tenderness flowing around me like a cool spring breeze.

"Grandma, do you know how long this has been tormenting me?" I asked through broken sniffles.

"I know dear, I'm so sorry. It's too bad you didn't visit sooner. Practice though. In times of stress, it's not so easy to do. Those little buggers crave attention and hate to be tied up, I guess you could say."

I wanted to jump for joy, sing, dance, and scream. The jubilation I felt was so incredible. My grandmother's face mirrored my emotion.

"Sorry," I said, suppressing a giggle. "I can't help it."

"No please, continue. This is the most fun I've had in a while."

The thought of a radio announcer asking me "Julia, you've just contained the feelings of everyone around you. What will you do now?" rang through my head, and I chuckled.

"But how do you take on another's feelings?" I asked quickly.

"Practice this task first, Love. You'll figure out the other things with time."

I already felt like I knew. Whenever I held Nicholas' hand his confidence infused me and I felt braver. He also could act as a shield, like he did earlier when we walked down the hall.

"Grandma," I said wistfully while hugging her neck again. "I've missed you."

"Me too, Dear, but you need to go now. Nicholas is antsy," she said quickly. "Just promise me you'll come back soon."

The blame swelled within me. I knew we should be leaving soon, but I couldn't help feeling like I'd be abandoning her.

"No need for that, my dear," Grandma said in a motherly tone. "We have enough guilt around here already. Keep the love instead and go have fun with your beau." She winked.

"Are you sure?"

"Yes," she said while getting off her bed. "I've got bridge in a few minutes anyway. Promise you'll come back soon and bring your brother."

I traipsed after her as she grabbed her cane and left the room with speed I didn't expect. Nicholas gave me a quizzical look once we both entered the hall.

"You two have fun," she said without stopping. "I'm off to my bridge match. I can't lose my championship title."

I shook my head in amazement and grinned, watching her purple fluff disappear around the corner.

"I guess it's time to go?" Nicholas asked, completely confused.

"Yeah."

I grabbed Nicholas' hand and hugged his arm the entire way out, refraining from skipping.

Chapter Seven

As we drove away I leaned back in the seat with a smile, opening and closing the invisible barrier around Nicholas and anyone driving close enough for me to isolate. I fought a giggle each time I silenced everyone's aura, marveling in my new buffer. It almost seemed easier to just throw the blanket over myself than encapsulate people individually. Nicholas sat in quiet, full of caution.

"You seem happy," he finally said, glancing in my direction with sunglass-covered eyes. "Did everything go as expected?"

I removed a portion of my feelings' blanket to seek him out. I'd expected him to be curious, but he wasn't.

"Yes," I said with suspicion. "You didn't happen to over-hear us by chance, did you?"

"No."

A lie. It was the first time I'd sensed a lie from him—he flowed out guilt and regret, I could feel that he hated lying to me.

I looked at the floorboard. How stupid of me to forget his eagle hearing. With heated cheeks, I replayed through the conversation with Grandma. We'd revealed it all, leaving nothing to interpret. He knew. He finally knew.

I began to feel his growing fight. His regret told me he wished he either didn't lie or didn't listen. Either way, he waffled with his dilemma. He wanted to tell me the truth, I sensed it.

"She helped me with a problem I've been dealing with for a long time," I finally said.

"I'm glad." He struggled to be emotionally void; his vulnerability prominently evident.

I struggled too. Should I tell him? Verbalize my biggest secret even though he probably already knew? Why was I so afraid to? Did he still love me even though I was a genetic freak?

His hand interlaced with mine and I closed my eyes. With a huge gulp, I hesitated before opening my mouth. My heart began to pound faster.

"I can read other's emotions," I said quickly before I could take it back. "I've been able to since my mother's death."

Nicholas' shoulders relaxed while he traced his thumb alongside mine. A quick peek revealed the hint of a smile on his lips. His compassion enveloped me, softening me, encouraging me to go on.

"Apparently, it's something my mother and grandmother could do, but I thought I was the only one. It's also the reason I knew someone, not a mountain lion, stalked me the night you saved me when I fell off the cliff. How I knew to question your story."

Nicholas silently processed my confession, seeping understanding and enlightenment.

"I can feel them—the vampires. They have a distinct hunger, not like everyone else has. It's icky and all consuming. Though it's sickening, I see why they enjoy what they do so much. It's also why I have a hard time making friends. Why I've never really dated anyone. Why I'm so emotional all the time. Why I like being alone."

"And maybe why we're so good together," Nicholas finished. "Our differences compliment one other. I'm glad you have this ability because whenever I'm with you, you bring me contentedness I never feel with anyone else."

My heart warmed. I loved feeling and hearing the admission at the same time. "I like feeling that from you too. It centers me."

"Kind of a perfect storm," Nicholas said with a chuckle. "So what am I feeling now?"

I smiled. "Compassion and love and—you lied just a minute ago."

Nicholas' right eyebrow twitched under the corner of his glasses.

"It's okay; I forgot your hearing is—"

"Your grandmother—she was so insightful. I had to know how she could sense all the things she did," he said quickly. "For your protection. Not all people are entirely human, you know."

"You thought my grandma wasn't entirely human?" I snickered. "She's good looking, but not in a *vampire* way."

"Just being cautious," he said in slight embarrassment.

"Sorry. I know." I looked down somberly, wanting to confess my own secret sins. "I've practically been lying this whole time by not telling you . . ."

Nicholas remained silent. There was no blame, only a twinge of disappointment.

"I've wanted to . . . for a long time," I said, leaning into his shoulder. "I was afraid you'd leave me or something."

Nicholas rested his chin on the top of my head and sighed, still keeping an eye on the road. "Never, Julia," he said in earnest. "You're stuck with me whether we're together or not."

I took a deep breath, letting my eyes fall shut. The confession brought a bigger sense of relief than I expected. I just wished I could lay everything else out on the table—about Enigma, Alora, and how we needed his father's help. I hoped, when the other secrets came to the surface, Nicholas would still have the same sentiment, and my keeping quiet didn't put him in danger.

When Nicholas parked, I opened my eyes. Somehow in the discussion, I'd not paid attention to where we drove.

"Where are we?"

"Here." The somberness of his voice and his heart told me where *here* was.

Ahead of us stood an orchard of olive trees, knotty and overgrown with weeds. A surge of grief weakened my limbs while the flashback of walking through the same field ten years ago hit me suddenly. This was the place. The place that had been haunting my dreams. We were about to visit my mother's grave.

I sat up, sucked in a deep breath, and clutched Nicholas' hand to my chest. The fault of her death wasn't his and I wanted him to know I didn't blame him. His grief and guilt flooded me with a rush anyway and I worked to contain it, failing miserably.

"Stop," I said forcefully. "This. Here. All of it. I don't blame you and it's not your fault. Please, let it go."

Nicholas' jaw tightened, but his feelings remained the same. He struggled for a minute so I dropped his hand, half in anger and half in frustration.

"Stop reading my emotions and let me fight my own battles." His voice was laced with annoyance.

"Yeah, well . . . I can't help myself . . . like you can't help overhearing my conversations."

We sat for a minute, both stewing in aggravation. I loathed that the situation brought out the worst in both of us. Unable to gain a hold of my own emotions, let alone block his, I opened the door and got out. My legs went into autopilot as I stumbled forward through the trees. The path led down into a ravine with a creek. I traversed over the smooth boulders and headed for the meadow. Wild flowers of every color covered the field and I stopped, unsure where to go.

Nicholas appeared silently behind me; the heat of his body radiating outward mixed with his remorse. His hand slid gently along my arm to rest on the outside of my wrist; his nose nuzzled my hair.

"Sorry," he whispered in my ear.

I leaned into his chest. "I'm sorry too."

His hand hooked around my waist and brought me toward him. With gentle eyes, his gaze swept over my face. He kissed my forehead and I felt his love heal the gaping hole where the memories had poured out. In his other hand was the bouquet of gerbera daisies.

We walked, hand in hand, through the flowers for a ways before Nicholas stopped at a spot that looked unremarkable to me, but by the distraught look on his face I knew this had to be the place—my mother's unmarked grave. My hands shook as I slowly knelt down, placed both palms on the ground, wishing I could feel her one last time.

"Mom," I whispered. "You have no idea how much I've missed you." I tried to go on, to tell her all the things I'd been holding in for so long, but I knew that whatever I said would send Nicholas into a pit of despair—he already carried around enough unnecessary guilt. Instead, I spoke my wishes internally.

"Mom, I'm sorry I wasn't able to come sooner. If you're watching me, then I guess you know why. It's been horrible that there's never been a place to visit you—a place where I can be with you. Being here

now fills the longing I've had since 'he' took you from us. I've missed you so much.

"Nicholas carries a lot of guilt for your death. He thinks it's his fault that he didn't arrive in time to save you from the . . . well, you know. It's been really hard on him . . . on us. But in the end, he's given me the best gift which is himself and a piece of you. And now that I know where your resting place is, I can visit more often.

"Nicholas has been watching over me all these years since you've been gone. I feel like I've had a guardian angel protecting me, but he's so much more than that, Mom. He's like my other half—the half that I didn't know I'd been missing until I met him. It's strange how fate has a way of turning your life around in crazy and unexpected ways.

"To think that you and Nicholas had become friends right before you were killed. At least something good happened because of it. Your short friendship led Nicholas to me. And this all brought my destiny to light too. I promise, Mom, I'm going to do whatever I can to make this right. To stop 'them' from ever ruining another family again. To put an end to the heartache we've needlessly felt.

"So thank you, for sacrificing yourself in an attempt to save me, and for bringing Nicholas into my life. I love you. We all love you. I hope you know that."

A cool breeze whipped around my hair and tickled my face. Somehow I knew she heard me and felt at peace. Nicholas sensed I was finished and laid the flowers on the top of the grassy mound of dirt. I kept a buffer between us so I could focus on my own grief.

"Your mom liked flowers," he said with a scratchy voice.

I looked up into his stricken face and noticed a tear falling down his cheek. Since my dad never spoke of Mom, there were so few things I knew of her. Especially her likes and dislikes. I studied the bouquet and then the cornucopia of varieties draped across the meadow.

"I wanted to be sure she'd always have them around her to enjoy."

"Thank you," I whispered.

He nodded and turned, casually wiping his face with the back of his hand.

The day she died replayed through my mind. We'd come to the park at dusk to pick up Nicholas, my mom's newly adopted troubled teen. I was only five at the time. The vampire appeared from nowhere and grabbed her before we could run. Nicholas—late because he'd gotten into a fight with his father about becoming too friendly with mortals—came right after, only in time to stop the vampire from taking my life.

Nicholas and his father, needing to cover up the incident for fear of discovery, chose to ditch her car in the river and bury her body in this once desolate meadow. Nicholas anonymously returned me to my porch the next morning. I'd only just remembered the whole incident after another vampire tried to take my life this past fall, and Nicholas had no choice but to reveal himself to save me.

It was then I discovered he'd been protecting me from vampires ever since. That was a good thing, because for some reason I was a vampire magnet. Hunting, fighting, and killing vampires was something he did to deal with his guilt. Being the only half-vampire in the world was a double edged sword. Blessed with super human strength and hearing, but yet he still retained a conscience unlike most vampires. He loathed the wanton murder his full-blooded kind did to humans on a daily basis. His actions forced him to always look over his shoulder looking out for vengeful immortals who wanted nothing but to take him to their leader as a trophy or torture those around him as punishment. He purposely remained alone to prevent putting others in danger.

With the talisman, I was the only one allowed to break that rule.

I pulled myself out of my memories and realized Nicholas no longer stood by her grave. He'd slipped away, and since I hid under my feelings' shield I didn't feel his absence—something I'd have to get used to.

I spied him standing a little way off, leaning against a tree that overlooked a valley filled with clumps of sky scrapers interlocking like a puzzle all the way to the sea. I walked over and stood next to him.

"Beautiful," was all I could say, trying desperately to keep from losing it. More than anything I wanted to toughen up and stop being such a bawl baby.

"Yes," he said.

He still oozed with guilt, so I remained within the folds of my barrier. I didn't need to add to my pain.

I hoped coming here would help me with closure—to accept the truth and say goodbye. But the reality left me bruised and broken. I missed my mom deeply and felt cheated of something I deserved: a loving, doting mother. I loathed vampires everywhere for doing this to me—to us.

"I'm ready," I said, wanting to leave.

He nodded, took my hand, and we walked wordlessly to the car.

Chapter Eight

"I think I need to get another cell phone," I said while trying to figure out what crops grew in the fields next to us as we cruised down the highway towards home.

"Are you planning on losing the one you have?"

"No," I said with a slight smirk. "I want to get my own. I'm sick and tired of having to do cryptic texts all the time. I want my privacy but I'm not old enough to get one by myself."

"Ah," Nicholas said, "I should just add you to my plan."

A shared phone plan.

My heart flip-flopped. Something about hearing him suggest we share made me excited, like we were taking our relationship to the next level.

"Could you?"

"I don't see why not."

"Oh wow," I said, my mind suddenly drooling with the possibilities of cell phone freedom. "How about a miniature one, like this size." I held up my fingers a few inches apart to demonstrate.

"We should get you a watch phone. So you don't get caught with it accidentally."

Oh! Even better.

My mind started turning, partly in a bad direction. I imagined something sleek and James Bond secret-agent like.

"You could help me with algebra," I said, my words flowing incredibly fast in excitement. "I could take a picture of the test page and you could send me the answers."

Nicholas looked smugly back. "Nice try."

I faked a laugh while lounging back in my seat. The nagging dread of getting caught interrupted me every time I started to have fun. And now that we were nearing home, the feeling seemed to heighten, causing my heart to twitter and my foot to shake. I imagined Dad at home, in the doorway with his arms folded, anger shooting from his eyes like fire.

"Hey, can I call Sam to let her know we are on our way? I want to make sure everything's okay."

Nicholas handed me his silver Motorola Ming with a clear cover. I opened the phone with an *oooh*.

"Don't get any ideas," he said teasingly. "You're getting the plain watch model—no camera."

"Funny."

I scrunched up my nose at him, then punched in her number and waited.

"Hello?"

"Sam, its Julia—"

"Crap, Julia. Your phone's been ringing off the hook all morning. Where are you?"

"What? Who's calling me?"

"Some unlisted number, and Luke a couple times. I didn't answer. I didn't know what to say," Sam gushed out in a total panic. "You know I'm lousy about lying and stuff. Geez, Jules. When will you be back?"

"In about . . ." I looked to Nicholas and he mouthed *two hours*. "Two hours."

"Two hours? What the heck am I supposed to do for two hours?"

"I don't know, stall or something. I'll get there as quickly as I can."

"Yah, you better. Crap, there it goes again."

I moaned, listening to my symphonic ring. Getting caught could ruin our perfect weekend, our budding relationship, my life. The phone beeped with a message.

"Wait, I want to listen to what he said."

"Okay . . . hold on." Sam jostled her phone and suddenly the sound seemed to echo. "Can you hear me?"

"Yeah."

"I put you on speaker. Okay, let me play the messages."

My heart swam in fear of why Luke would be calling when the annoying message lady started speaking. "You have three new messages. First message . . ." Luke's voice rang clearly through the speaker, filled with concern. "Julia, call me as soon as you get this."

I shivered. Luke never called. He usually just sent a text.

"Next message . . ." You didn't need to be an emotion reader to sense the panic in Luke's voice this time. "Dang it. Where are you? Call me."

"Next message . . ." I closed my eyes. "If you don't call me back," Luke all but yelled. "I'm coming over to Sam's to get you."

Sam gasped. "What do I say? What if he's coming over right now?" Her breathy voice fit the image I had of her dancing around her room, flipping her hands in hysteria.

"Calm down, Sam. I'll call him right now. Don't worry."

"But your return number. He'll know you're not using your phone."

I looked towards Nicholas and he nodded with radiating confidence. He obviously listened in with his super hearing and knew what to do.

"I'll figure it out and call you back."

I flipped the phone shut, silencing Sam's next whimpered concern. Nicholas held out his hand for the phone.

"What's your brother's number," he said.

I repeated the digits from memory and Nicholas added a few of his own.

"Are you ready?" Nicholas' finger hovered over the send. "Don't worry, I've masked the number. Tell him you were out with Sam and left your phone at her house by mistake."

"Won't your number show up?"

"It'll show your number, not mine."

"Really? Okay." I gulped down my own fear, imagining myself crawling under Nicholas' confidence instead. Infused in his spirit, I nodded my head.

My heart didn't even pick up in tempo once the ringing started.

"Hello?"

"Luke, it's—"

"Julia! What the heck? Where have you been?"

"At the movies and forgot to bring my phone. What's going on?"

"Dad," Luke said in a breathless stream. "He's . . . okay now, but he was rushed to the hospital with chest pains. They thought it was a heart attack, but now they aren't so sure."

At the news, my own chest began to hurt—no amount of calm feelings radiating off of Nicholas could mask this panic. "Is he okay? Where is he?"

"He's fine. He's in a hospital in L.A."

"L.A.?" My eyes grew big. "But he's supposed to be in Tulsa."

"He came home early. He wasn't feeling good. It happened when he was trying to get to his connecting flight. They took him to the closest hospital."

"Oh, wow." I felt the tension run along my spine. Part of me wanted to insist Nicholas turn around. "So, now what?"

"He's coming home tomorrow. I'm picking him up from the airport." Luke sounded agitated, fearful. "But man! I need to be able to call you in an emergency. You never know, you know? This . . . this was completely ridiculous trying to get a hold of you."

"Yeah, sorry," I said quickly.

And I was.

"Come home, okay?"

I didn't need to be near him to sense how much he was hurting, the pain radiated from his voice and nearly knocked me breathless. Luke didn't want to deal with this alone—our worst fear could have come true. We'd survived Mom's disappearance, but to lose Dad too? That would be unimaginable.

"Yeah. I'll be home in a bit."

When I clamped the phone shut, Nicholas' sudden acceleration slammed me back into my seat, taking the air out of my lungs. I responded with a gasp. He reached over and held onto my free hand.

"Just needed an excuse," he said while turning on his radar detector, completely at ease. "Hold on."

I grabbed the handle above the door and did just that. I didn't mind him speeding, but the weaving in and out of traffic, and occasionally driving on the shoulder, frightened me. In the rear view mirror, the flume of dust trailed behind, and I shuddered as the alarm of nearby drivers ping-ponged around our vehicle. Internally, I dove under Nicholas' shield of focus to get relief. At least staying there and watching the road would keep me from getting carsick.

"It'll be okay," he said reassuringly, peeking sideways out of his sunglasses. "Your Dad's going to be okay."

"Okay . . . yeah. But we may not be," I said nervously with a point of my finger. "Eyes on the road!"

He nodded and smiled his sweet adorable grin. My knees weakened.

In forty-five minutes, we were pulling up to the front of Sam's house. I jumped out and stumbled forward to the door, feeling like I should have been moving faster.

"You're here? What happened? You didn't call," Sam said, relieved to see me at the door. "I couldn't call you back." She held out my dreaded phone like it was cursed.

"Sorry, I meant to." I took the phone. "If Luke asks, we were seeing *Knight Angels*, okay?"

"Huh?" Sam asked, partly annoyed.

"I told him we were at the movies."

Sam looked deeply into my eyes. "I don't like these kinds of secrets, Julia."

"I know and I'm really sorry. It'll be the last time. I've learned my lesson."

She let out a huff. "What was the big deal anyway?"

I looked away to avoid her flustered stare. "My dad had a heart attack scare."

Sam's jaw dropped. "Oh my gosh. Is he okay?"

"I'm not sure, but I have to go. I told Luke I'd come right home."

"Oh, of course." Sam's emotions tumbled around her like clothes in a dryer: relief, frustration, worry, aggravation.

We exchanged a quick hug. "Thanks." I felt badly for causing her so much drama. With a wave of my hand, I ran down the walk towards Nicholas' car. "I'll make it up to you."

"You better call me later—" Sam yelled behind me.

I smiled and shut the door.

"I'm a horrible friend," I confessed to Nicholas. "Totally horrible."

Chapter Nine

In the car, I checked my texts, worried about any other drama that might have happened while the phone was in Sam's care. Dena sent me one Friday—just to say hi. Katie sent one too; hers particularly baffled me though. She asked if we could get together after school on Monday "to talk." We rarely spent time out of school just the two of us, so I wondered what was so important. Even still, the timing worked for me. I wanted a private opportunity to talk some sense into her and make sure her Tyler obsession didn't involve anything serious.

Before I could mention it though, Nicholas slammed on the breaks, suddenly bursting at the seams with rage. He jumped out of the door, leaving me and the idling car on the side of the street. Stunned, I yelped for him as he disappeared.

When he didn't return, I sat up on my heels and frantically looked out of the windows, unsure what to do. He'd never done anything this drastic before. "Nicholas?" I called out the open door.

Within seconds though, he had some guy pressed onto the hood of his car and yelled, "What do you think you're doing, punk?"

The kid—with disheveled hair and an oversized dark raincoat—looked like he was just about to pee his pants in public while he whimpered that he didn't know. Nicholas, unsatisfied, leaned over and whispered something close to his ear. The kid cried out "No," but stubbornly continued to lie in his answers, even while he feared for his life.

With rapt attention, I watched the altercation in amazement, feeling sorry for the kid, even if he was a criminal. Who was he? He couldn't have been a vampire since he was unaffected by sunlight. What did he do to make Nicholas so angry?

Nicholas pulled him up by his collar, ripped off his jacket, and shoved him in the direction of the alley. For a brief second I saw Nicholas' face contort into something wild, animalistic even. His incisor teeth lengthened as he snarled. I gasped. The kid did too and tore out of sight.

"I better not catch you again," Nicholas yelled after him. "I'll be watching."

He pawed through the coat and swore. He'd found some vials of drugs or something. I blinked and, within that tenth of a second, Nicholas returned to the car and took off down the street towards my house, fuming, but quiet.

"What was that all about?" I asked in astonishment, looking behind us to see if anyone saw what just happened.

"I've seen him before . . . caught him before, but today—" he said through gritted teeth. "Today, I smelled he was selling something different."

"What?"

"Immortality in syringes."

"He's what? As in—" I sucked in a deep breath, not wanting to breach the subject. "How's that possible?"

"All you need is a little venom in your veins and you'll join the undead." Nicholas chuckled darkly and shook his head. "Incredible."

"How can he?"

"He must have a donor who needs money."

"A vampire?"

"Yeah, but that's not all. When we came back into town, I felt the energy shift." The evil side of Nicholas, ever so slightly, shuddered in delight. "Look over there." He slowed long enough for me to see two guys in a fist fight.

"The darkness the evil brings tempts the hearts of men. It's so much bigger than us—than just protecting your life. It's a battle of souls. It always has been." He spoke more like he was talking out loud than to me. Like he was reciting something he'd heard a million times.

"I'm confused," I paused. "And you're kind of freaking me out."

Nicholas interlaced his hand with mine and squeezed, coming back into focus. "Sorry. During that whole fiasco with Bettina's coven, I didn't realize how dark the presence had been when it lingered over the city. Their absence has shown me a drastic difference now that they are back again."

"They're back?" I whispered. My response was partly an act, but mostly I was relieved he knew and could finally be on guard.

"Yes, but this time the evil is stronger. It's been calling to me, wanting me to join its side ever since we hit the edge of town."

My eyes widened, feeling his inner turmoil. I was speechless, terribly aware he could cross over if he had a moment of weakness.

"I'm glad I stocked up on my supplies," he said to cover his distress.

"Well, I'm not leaving you. I can't afford to *lose* you . . . lose you to the dark side."

Nicholas chuckled. "Sounds like *Star Wars*."

"I'm serious. I sense your struggle, remember?"

"And how would you stop me if I chose to?" Nicholas clenched his jaw. "Why don't you trust me?"

"I do, but . . ."

"But nothing. This happens every time. I've got it under control."

I scowled. "You said it was stronger this time."

"And so am I. I have a better incentive to stay on the good side now. I have you." He tightened his eyes and gave me a harder look. "Have faith."

I placed my free hand on my chest; the talisman lay silently beneath the folds of my shirt, shrouded under my palm. I hoped the necklace would glow with warmth to indicate things would be okay, but it didn't.

Nicholas pulled the car around the corner and parked out of view of my house.

"Let me deal with Luke, then I can meet you on the roof. If you're going out tonight I'm coming with you."

"Julia." Nicholas' voice lowered an octave, followed by a deliberate tilt of his chin, completely disappointed in me.

"No. I mean it," I said, my voice firm.

I looked beyond Nicholas and towards the house. A girl with blonde hair and long, tanned legs in a short skirt stood in front of a

BMW with her back to me. Some guy's arms were wrapped around her torso. The way her head moved told me they were making out—passionately, and my cheeks flushed in response until I noticed she was smacking on my brother.

"Uh," I groaned as my voice caught in my throat.

Nicholas turned to see the source of my distress. I blocked his aura instantly. I didn't want to know what he thought of this revolting display. "Looks like you're not the only one with a secret relationship."

I smirked. Having a girlfriend none of us knew about was one thing, but making out in the front yard was another—completely tacky. I glanced again over Nicholas' shoulder as Long Legs drove off and Luke disappeared into the house.

"Yeah, guess not." I paused with my hand on the door handle. "Are you meeting me on the roof?"

Nicholas softened. "I will . . . in a bit."

"Okay." *You better.*

Inside, I found Luke, recovered and cool, lounging on the couch watching TV in his usual place. Luke typically didn't hide his girlfriends from me, so I wondered why this one was different. I dropped my backpack on the floor.

"How's Dad?"

"Better." His gaze flicked over to meet mine. "He'll be home tomorrow. How was the *movie*?" He reeked of suspicion.

"Okay," I said, not breaking eye contact until he looked away first.

Suddenly, his courage swelled. "You weren't at Sam's this weekend, were you?"

"Why would you say that?"

"You didn't drive your car over there—"

"She picked me up," I interrupted.

"She didn't drop you off. That guy did. The one who brought you home that night." Luke snapped his fingers a few times. "Nicholas, yeah, that's his name. I recognized the car. Is he your boyfriend now?"

I glared, happy for the showdown. "You should talk big brother."

He smirked back, still radiating confidence.

"You practically had your tongue down Goldilocks' throat just a minute ago."

A slight wave of shock registered across his face for a brief moment; the emotional stun lingered longer. I couldn't help the side of my lip from curling up in victory.

"A *friend*."

"Yeah right." My eyes fell into slits. His cell phone sat on the coffee table—closer to me than him—vibrated with a text. I lunged and snatched it up before he could.

"Hmmm, who's texting you?" I flipped open the phone. "Amber says she had fun last night. Fun, huh? What did you do?"

"Give it back!" With flushed cheeks, Luke stood up, grabbed and twisted my arm so I'd let go. I winced in pain and dropped the phone into his waiting hand.

"Stay out of my business," he said after checking the text.

"Of course." I held up my hands in surrender. "Just stay out of mine."

"Yeah, whatever." He slumped down on the couch again, turning up the TV to an uncomfortably loud decibel.

I flung my backpack over my shoulder and charged upstairs to my room, slamming the door behind me. We typically kept our secrets between the two of us. Since when did I have to resort to blackmail?

Maybe seeing me with Nicholas brought out his brotherly concern? I had my reasons for keeping Nicholas a secret from Luke, but I thought we were close enough that he'd tell me about *Amber*.

I ran to the window, but didn't see or sense Nicholas nearby. My fists clenched into a ball. He'd managed to use this to escape me. I whipped out my phone and shot him a text.

- **Where are you?**
- **Got some errands to run, be by later.**
- **What errands?**

I waited uneasily, repetitively glancing at my phone. The longer the silence, the more my nerves jittered.

He better not be planning to do anything rash.

Thankful the sun hadn't set yet, I unpacked my backpack in an effort to stay busy. The note he wrote fluttered to the floor. I smiled, snatching the pretty paper up and rereading it again before hiding it under my mattress. Happy memories of the suite played in my mind, along with Nicholas' song, breakfast, and the shampoo incident. A twinge of sadness followed thoughts of visiting my mother's grave. I wished I could talk to Luke about it. The buzz of my phone transported me back to reality.

- **I have to pick up my dry cleaning.**

I rolled my eyes.

- **Funny. See you soon?**

- **Give me an hour.**

The relief came abruptly and I fell back onto my bed, quickly dialing Sam as promised. An hour would be plenty of time to fill her in on my incredible weekend. Afterward, Nicholas and I could discuss how we'd rid the world of the vampires in town: AKA Alora and her evil new followers.

Chapter Ten

Completely exhausted, I drifted to sleep easily after Nicholas kissed me goodnight. He promised to stay close by after I freaked out about the vampires being back in town. I also convinced him that by using my emotion-reading power we could find the coven's hide-out in the daylight, so he could surprise attack them at dusk when they came out. Nicholas was open to the idea considering how difficult it was to find them the last time they were here. Vampires with the ability to fly leave virtually no scent to track.

Morning came too quickly though. After slamming my hand against the alarm clock to stop its incessant racket, I rolled over and wished for a few more hours of sleep. If I'd gone out with him the night before like I wanted, I would've been seriously wasted.

At school, I compartmentalized myself into my own personal force field, completely separated from everyone's drama. I almost skipped down the hall in my new found independence. People responded differently to the uncontainable smile plastered across my face. But in History I accidentally drifted off to sleep and the emotional tsunami came crashing in, waking me up with a start. Mr. Marshall wasn't amused. At lunch, I wished for a caffeinated beverage, cursing the powers-that-be who took out the vending machines, and bought my usual milk carton and a pizza pocket.

"Yo, yo," Cameron said when he saw me walking towards him at our usual table.

"Yo yourself." I punched him lightly in the arm before sitting down, amused at his sudden transformation from geek to chic. Instead of his usual science camp T-shirt, he wore a plain grey crewneck with a button-down shirt over the top, and faded jeans. Something completely out of character and trendy. Plus, he'd had his curls straightened, resulting in hair that now swooped across his forehead in a very emo fashion.

"How's it do?" he asked.

"Okay," I said, biting into my pizza pocket and hiding my grin. "I like your hair cut and your new shirt."

Cameron's cheeks flushed. "Thanks."

For a brief second I allowed myself to enjoy Cameron's pride swell before I clamped the wall back down when a group of cocky jocks walked by.

The rest of our clique quickly joined us. Dena gracefully flitted up to the table under Morgan's arm; her hands held *their* lunch tray. Sam followed behind, saying a quick goodbye to Todd—her boyfriend—who ate with his linemen buddies and the cheerleading squad instead of us outcasts. It always hurt her feelings, but today I didn't have to sense it. Katie seemed to be missing in action.

Cameron was technically the only single guy at our table, but, if his transformation stuck, I suspected that wouldn't last for long. A nearby group of freshmen giggled as one redhead slyly eyed him. They'd be cute together with their matching red locks.

Only Sam knew of my relationship with Nicholas. I'd kept it a secret to avoid Katie's incessant questioning, and to protect them from retaliation in case some vampire got clever and decided to read their minds to find out our lives.

"Where's Katie?" I finally asked, unsure since she wasn't in any of my classes now.

"Who knows," Dena said with a little more candor than usual. "She's been so unpredictable lately—like she's too good for us."

Morgan agreed with a chuckle.

"She wasn't in Calculus," Cameron added while trying to keep his cool and eat his Doritos at the same time.

Sam shrugged after I shot her a look.

"Maybe she's sick?" I pulled out my phone and sent Katie a text to check.

- Are you at school? We still on for later?

"Did you see my new toe ring?" Dena pulled her foot out of her flip-flop to show Sam and the rest of us. "Morgan got it for me this weekend."

"Cool," I said, still slightly worried about Katie. She may have been a rebel, but grades and attendance were two things she took seriously.

Dena continued to share about their weekend at the beach. Sam appeared to be listening, but kept peeking over at Todd as he carried on with his buddies. She scowled when Eliza, the hot new transfer, touched his shoulder. With nothing to share, I stayed silent, waiting for Katie's return text.

The conversation shifted with the current rumors haunting Mr. Brewster. He'd apparently had no qualms in denying Mr. Walentine's request for microscopes in Biology while new furniture and a very expensive painting showed up at Mr. Brewster's office. But once the school district got involved, he magically produced proof he'd paid for the items out of his own pocket. A week later, the microscopes showed up without question. I laughed, just hearing the story for the first time. The incident was totally Mr. Brewster's style.

I scanned the lunchroom and noticed Mandy hadn't returned after leaving with sudden flu-like symptoms in first period P.E. class. Tyler wasn't too disturbed by her absence as he flirted blatantly with Amanda, the head cheerleader. I assumed they must still be broken-up.

At the warning bell for fifth period, my phone buzzed with a text from Katie.

- **Yeah, let's meet at Mr. Pickles on Front Street at 6:30.**

I knit my brows together and punched a text back.

- **Where are you?**

- **Tell ya later. Super busy with stuff to do.**

- **Okay.** *I guess*

I nudged Sam on our way to Algebra. "Katie and I are still meeting later."

"Why isn't she at school?"

"Who knows? She said she's doing stuff. I'll get the scoop tonight."

We walked into Algebra and my heart sank.

Fractions again. Ugh!

The first thing I felt when I got home was my dad's concern rushing through the house like a rough wind.

"Dad?" I called through the hallway.

"In here, Jules." His voice floated from the kitchen along with something that smelled really yummy. I followed my nose to find him at the stove with a spatula in hand, grilling cheese sandwiches.

"Don't scare us like that, Dad." My words caught up in my throat as he turned around. A bandage covered his forehead and a row of stitches trailed down his bruised cheek bone.

I gasped. "What happened?"

Dad grazed his black-and-blue eye with his knuckles. "It looks worse that it is," he said quickly in embarrassment. "I'm fine."

"Fine?" I walked over to get a better look at his wounds. "Luke said you'd had chest pains."

"I did." He wrapped me up into a hug. "And fell down some stairs."

"What?" I pushed away and looked at his wounds. He suddenly appeared older to me and a tad bit thinner. "How did that happen? Are you okay?"

"Ah, it was nothing. I wasn't looking where I was walking." He rested his hands on my shoulders, seeping irresponsibility. The fear and doubt added to the flurry around us. Something else had to be wrong. "I'll be fine; don't worry."

Partially true.

"Really, Dad?" Whatever the news, I wanted it straight.

"My doctor wants to do a few more tests to be sure. They let me go, so it can't all be bad." Truth. "But the good news is I'll be home for a couple weeks."

I wrapped my arms around his chest again and listened to his heart beat, willing it to keep going. He always seemed like the rock of our family, infallible and unbreakable. Looking up into his grey eyes surrounded with laugh lines, I saw he wasn't. His health issues also came at the worse time with all the vampire drama coming back into town. I'd have to be more careful under his watchful eye so I didn't add to his stress level.

"Don't worry, Jules," he said softly. "This is just my body's way of telling me to slow down and take better care of myself."

I sighed as my own concern swirled around me and bit my lip to stop the tears from welling up.

"I'm going to be here a good long time," he said, returning to his griddle. "Are you hungry?"

"Yeah. Sure." Actually, I was starving.

After we ate and caught up, I ran upstairs to change. Dad thought I was going to work at the deli tonight and meeting Katie afterward for a late dinner. Instead, Nicholas and I were going to scout for vamps and already planned the whole evening out, including a brief intermission with Katie.

On the drive to Mr. Pickles, butterflies darted around in my stomach with the anticipation of seeing Nicholas again. I pulled into the parking lot and smiled with glee when I saw his car. He got out and the sunlight danced on his brown hair, highlighting the copper strands. The light continued to illuminate his neck and shoulders, making him look so kissable. He turned to look at me with sunglass-covered eyes and my pulse raced. His smile made me weak in the knees. I fought the urge to run towards him, walking slowly instead.

He pulled me into a tight embrace and kissed me tenderly. I wanted more, but he rarely showed affection in public. Today was different, though. Deep down, he really missed me.

"Hi." I stood on my tip-toes, attempting to steal another kiss. He kissed my nose instead.

"I have a surprise. Come on," he said with a familiar gleam in his eye. He led me by the hand towards the strip mall. At the end of the line of stores was a cell phone shop.

"Seriously?" I asked, raising my eyebrow.

"Seriously."

I squealed and hugged his torso, tempted to skip through the open doors.

Adding me to Nicholas' account was easy, but getting the watch phone that didn't look so obvious was the problem. We opted for a smaller version I could attach to my keychain instead. I was happier with the choice until we discovered they'd just sold their last one. Replacements wouldn't be delivered for another week. Total bummer.

"Sorry," Nicholas said as we exited.

"It's only one more week." I tried not to appear disappointed. "I can wait."

"That's my girl." He rested his hand on the small of my back, giving me chills, and guided me towards the passenger side of the car. "We've got to get going, not much time before dusk."

It was a lucky thing Katie didn't want to meet earlier.

"So," Nicholas said, sliding into the driver's seat and starting the car. "I've covered most of the west side today and figured we'd cover the east together. I ran through it last night, but any hint of scent would have dissipated after they evacuated their hide-out. I'm hoping they'll stick to their familiar territory."

"Me too," I agreed, too distracted to watch the road while studying his jaw line, wanting to attack it with kisses. He was so adorable when in hunting-mode. "Have you run into *that guy* again?"

"Which guy?"

"The one who was selling the venom?"

"No," he said with a twinge of disappointment. "I think he's too afraid to show his face around here again, though it was stupid of me to overreact. I should have followed him to the source. That's my next project after we deal with this coven."

I smiled at the fact he said "we."

"How's your dad?"

I took a deep breath and Nicholas took my hand. "Okay, I guess. Just a chest pain scare *they* said. Dad's supposed to take it easy, so he'll be around for a few weeks." I decided to leave out the fact he fell down the stairs too.

"That's good, right?"

"Yes, but not the *being around* part. Kinda hard to get away with anything when he's there, checking my cell phone GPS and stuff."

"You put your phone in your car, right?"

"Yes," I said, not appreciating the parental overtones of his question, but knew he was just trying to keep me out of trouble. "Of course."

"He loves you, Jules. That's why he's doing this. I'd be upset if he didn't seem concerned."

"I don't need him to worry. I've got you."

Nicholas squeezed my hand and brought it to his lips. "That you do." He smiled crookedly and I blushed.

Nicholas drove us down to the industrial center of town. We passed the burned down building Nicholas fought Phil and the rest of Alora's vamps in a few months back, and I sensed Nicholas' satisfaction. We drove by the other building a few blocks down—the one they lived in—and I took a deep breath. The building looked just as ominous during the day as it did at night. Nicholas studied my countenance.

"They're not here," I said, knowing he was curious to see if I'd sensed anything. "I imagine they're smart enough to find a new place."

"It's not easy finding refuge being a vampire. You must be invited within if it's been occupied recently by humans or vampires."

"I know," I said, feeling a little perturbed. I didn't mind being under his protection, but I remembered the details of the curse rules.

We drove a few blocks further down the street in silence when I sensed it. Like the putrid stink of a skunk—the hunger, the longing, the craving for power and blood swooped upon us in a thick fog. My pulse raced.

"Stop," I whispered.

He slowed down and parked, watching my reaction intently. I scanned the buildings towering over us. They all seemed abandoned with broken-out windows and graffiti on the walls. I closed my eyes to search the source. The feelings ran the gamut as usual, but not completely the typical animalistic kind I'd felt in the past.

"Are they here?"

"Maybe," I said, trying to pull more from my senses. "There

seems to be a group of people inside, but only a few vampires. Why would people be hanging with vampires?"

"Are you sure?"

I began the exercise Grandma taught me. I started with the ones discharging typical human feelings and began to encapsulate them. After separating about ten or so, I ended up with only two vampires. One was definitely Alora.

"This is so confusing." I put my hand to my head.

"I guess there's only one way to find out. Wait till dusk."

I opened my eyes and turned towards Nicholas. "I'm waiting with you."

"But you have a date with Katie."

"Screw Katie, this is serious." I raised my right eyebrow.

Nicholas' eyes crinkled. "And what are you going to do to help?"

"I don't know. Throw stakes?"

He pursed his lips. "Julia, it's almost impossible for me to concentrate and do what I'm supposed to do with you nearby."

"Then I'll stay in the car."

"I don't plan to park anywhere near here."

I grumbled.

"Julia, you said there are only two vampires among ten or so humans. I can handle two vamps. Remember, I've killed hundreds."

Nicholas started the car, turned it around, and headed back to town.

"Where are you going?" I said with a raised voice.

"To Mr. Pickles, so you can meet Katie."

"No, I'm canceling with her right now." I felt my pockets for my cell phone. "Crap . . ."

Nicholas pulled the car to the side of the road.

"Look at me." He leaned forward and shot his magical green eyes at me, sending an electric jolt to my stomach, melting my core. "I can't do what I do best with you there. It puts me in danger because I *worry* about you."

I looked back, wringing my hands. *Yeah, but you don't know Alora.* "I want to be with you." *To save you.*

"I know, and I'll come pick you up as soon as I'm done. It'll be quick. I usually am."

"But . . ."

He put his finger to my lips. "Please understand and let me do this my way. I bet those humans are going to be their next recruits. I need to save them before anything else happens, don't you understand?"

"I guess so." I sighed heavily, feeling fear prickle down my spine.

"Meet with Katie and I'll be right back."

I looked down at the floor. "All right," I said softly.

"Thank you." Nicholas tilted up my chin and his lips met mine.

This time I wrapped my arms around his neck and kissed him back so deeply his whisker scruff hurt my lips. The worry I'd never see him again pushed the fire behind my passion. Nicholas didn't seem to mind and responded to the intensity.

He pulled back and pushed the hair out of my eyes, wiping away a tear.

"I love you," he said, his emerald eyes twinkling.

I was too choked up to respond, only nodded.

Nicholas put the car into drive and headed towards Mr. Pickles. I held onto his hand the entire way and he caressed my fingers with his thumb.

Once we arrived, the pit that formed in my stomach took my breath away. It required all my effort to open the door and climb out without falling apart. Once outside, my legs quivered. Everything inside me screamed not to let him go. I held the talisman for support, but it lay dormant under my fingertips.

"Be strong," he said, excitement surging from his pours. "I promise I'll be right back."

I only nodded, sniffling.

He leaned over the passenger seat and we kissed one last time before I closed the door. I wanted to heave right there on the sidewalk as I watched his car drive down the street and out of sight. The prophecy—like a warning siren—kept blaring through my mind.

". . . the one to save us all from them."

I stumbled to my car—pushing through my urge to follow him—and took my phone out of the glove box. No texts from anyone.

I walked down the street to Mr. Pickles and decided to wait outside on a nearby bench. The pickle cut-out, complete with a white chef's hat, taunted me with his welcoming smile. I looked away and my attention drew to the horizon. The setting sun displayed the most incredible colors across the horizon. My heart sped up, knowing at any moment Nicholas would meet Alora for the first time. I clasped my hands together and asked God to protect him, even if Nicholas was a half-vampire.

I chewed on my fingernail while waiting, trying not to check the time every five seconds—the last being 6:38 PM. Just like Katie to plan the time to meet and be late. Unable to wait any longer, I started to text her when another came through.

- **My car battery is dead. Can we meet another time?**

What?

My anger erupted. She probably just figured out her car wasn't working and didn't even have the audacity to let me know she was already running late.

The thought to punch back a retort took a back seat as the overwhelming urge that Nicholas needed my help flooded my body. I rushed down the sidewalk to my car instead. But when my car was in sight, I heard someone call my name.

Automatically, I turned to find the source. A weathered-looking buff guy covered in tattoos ran at full speed towards me. I bolted, but he was too close. His hands clamped around my arms and mouth. My phone toppled out of my hand to the ground; the plastic shattered.

My muffled scream rang through the street, but no one noticed as he drug me to a nearby van.

Chapter Eleven

A mixture of feelings expelled from the people inside the van—happiness, excitement, greed, fear. But the unique one, the one I feared most, was the one with the bloodlust. It had the same intensity like Phil's after he'd become a vampire: completely insatiable.

The van door slammed behind me as the ruffian dropped me to my knees onto the floorboard, and bound my hands behind my back.

"Nice work boys," a female voice said. One I recognized.

I turned around and squinted so my eyes would adjust to the dark interior faster. Sitting in the seats in the back were two husky guys with Katie between them.

"Katie?" Her name slipped out of my lips in a gasp as I crawled back into a sitting position. I quickly assessed who the vampire was. Only Katie had the dark eyes, the flawless pale skin, and the radiating youth.

"Hello, Julia," she said, mawkishly sweet. "Sorry, but food no longer appeals to me." She turned and placed her hand on the shoulder of the guy to her right. "Actually, I'm craving something different. Tony?"

Willingly he held out his wrist. Several red crescent shaped wounds lined the inside of his forearm.

"Slice or bite?" she asked seductively.

"Bite," he purred, his eyes lighting up.

She grinned and brought his wrist to her mouth. I mashed my eyes shut, but felt his discomfort from her teeth piercing his flesh anyway. What followed, I hadn't anticipated.

Her pleasure exploded like a firework, starting from her stomach, radiating out through her extremities, launching her and me into fluffy comforting warmth, free of any worries. I gasped as Katie let out a groan. Tony enjoyed the same euphoric heaven as his eyes rolled back into his head.

She pulled back and licked the blood off her lips, her thirst not entirely satisfied.

"Better than a hit," she said with a grin. "Well, you wouldn't know about that." She eyed me like I was some innocent child.

Wide-eyed, I tried to catch my breath, wanting her to bite him again so I could experience the feeling, instantly addicted. My cheeks burned as I tried to look disgusted.

"You've done drugs before?"

"I drink a guy's blood in front of you and you ask if I've done drugs? Honestly." Katie laughed, throwing her head back. "I didn't think it was true when she told me you already knew."

I glared at her, feeling stupid for not acting more shocked. Out of the corner of my eye I watched Tony for the signs—at any moment he should start to burn from the venom in her bite, his body fighting from undergoing the *change.*

But Tony just covered up his wound with a bandage from his pocket and left the wrapper on the floor.

"Isn't he going to . . .?" I stopped, realizing I revealed more than I wanted.

Katie snickered. "He wishes," she said, giving him a knowing look. "No, he won't from me. I'm a hybrid."

"A hybrid?"

"A non-venom producing vampire. Sterile."

"How is that possible?"

"Questions . . . questions." She clucked her tongue while running her hands through her crimson-streaked hair. "You're the one who needs to answer our questions."

I remained tight-lipped.

"Oh, don't be so coy. You've already met our illustrious leader before. She's so fond of you and your boyfriend."

I hated the taunting tone to her voice, like I was Alora's little puppet. My eyes formed into slits as I tried to inconspicuously wiggle out of my restraints.

"Where are you taking me?" I demanded, trying to divert the conversation, nervous because the windows were blacked out.

"You never told me you and Nicholas got back together."

"I have no clue what you are talking about."

"Psscht. Knock off the act." Katie put her hands together in a prayerful pose, resting them lightly against her lips. "I'm actually here to help you. I could arrange for your transformation, instead of whatever *she's* got planned. Just—you know—tell me what Nicky's deal is."

"His name is Nicholas," I said with a glower.

"Now see? We're getting somewhere."

"I'm not telling you anything."

"Look, Jules," she said while leaning forward in a whisper. "You don't want to become a blood slave. It's bad. Just tell me *like* . . . where he gets his cool weapons, and I'll make sure you get a vampy makeover like me."

"As if," I said with a smirk.

Katie smirked back, radiating smugness. I cursed internally at myself for again revealing too much.

"She'll get it out of you whether you want to tell her or not, so there's no protecting you after that."

I'd spent enough time with Alora to know she'd neither care nor appreciate what Katie could deliver if she could acquire it herself. Again, Katie's agenda was to get in good with her new *Queen* and nothing more.

"Never."

"Your funeral." Katie waved her hand, looking bored now. "Gag her."

"No. Katie, seriously, I know her. She doesn't care about you. You don't have to choose this life. I can help you. You wanted to go to college. You were pursuing Tyler."

The wicked smile flashed across her face. "Who says I'm not going to get him?"

I gaped right before Tony put on the gag.

"Blindfold her too."

In the dark, I listened to the four of them talk. Katie spoke too softly for me to hear what she said. I kept wondering when the van would start and then panicked. If they knew Nicholas was going to return, were they just waiting to capture him?

Then I felt Katie come towards me, her lips close to my ear.

"Enjoy the trip," she said.

I heard the door open and close; the blood lust faded away. Then the van started, moving erratically away from the curb. The sudden acceleration and sharp turn toppled me over and I flopped like a fish onto the floorboard.

Nothing much was said during the drive. I tried to memorize the many turns and stops, but finally gave up. Eventually the van slammed to a halt and the engine died.

"We're here," one of the guys said. "Get her up."

Someone drug me to my feet and led me towards the door. Outside, the ground felt uneven and the air smelled of the sea. Sounds of a rollercoaster ride and shrill screaming could be heard in the distance. We were somewhere near the Boardwalk.

"Come on," my handler said, slightly annoyed, after he slammed the door shut. A scuffle between the other guys happened next to us. "Just leave him in the van, Tony. I'll explain what happened." I felt someone take my arm and lead me away from the van. "She doesn't like to be kept waiting," he yelled over his shoulder.

"No," a deeper voice said back in anger. "Help me carry him, Evan."

I heard a loud groan and a shuffling against the ground far behind us.

"Whatever," my handler said under his breath, tugging for me to move faster. "I haven't got all night."

We walked for a little ways and I tried not to trip on the trash scattered on the ground. It seemed vampires liked to hang out on the dirty outskirts of society. We eventually ended up on a sandy surface before stopping.

I cringed as I was greeted with an impatient frustration coupled with a unique, controlled bloodlust before the loud squeak of door hinges signaled we were entering a building of some sort. My captor's anxiety spiked as he walked me over the threshold and inside.

"Bring her to me," a familiar, melodic voice spoke from the back of the room, sending chills up my spine. I remembered the voice well, a voice that haunted my dreams. Alora.

The guy pushed me forward and I stumbled, only to be caught by someone's strong grip. Her lust for power infused me while she held my arm, helping me catch my balance. The memories hit from when I experienced her feelings for the first time, when Phil, her newly sired vampire, had brought me to meet her.

I'd suspected she was trying to read my mind in the process, so I repeated over and over "I'm not telling you" to keep from thinking of anything else. She let go with a chuckle.

"Very nice," Alora said, but not to me. "Where's Katie?"

"She stayed behind, my queen."

I sensed a silent exchange happening behind me. Someone felt excitement followed by a revelation. Shortly thereafter, the door clanged as the others—extremely annoyed—shuffled in.

"Come on," my handler said from further behind me, closer to the door.

"But what about Aden?" the husky male voice asked.

"Leave him over there," he replied.

There was a ruckus of movement and someone snorted, then the door clanged again. I listened as footsteps retreated away, leaving me in silence. Someone was still in the room with me, snoring lightly and very much at peace. Alora was here too, wallowing in her self-love. I shifted in the direction of the door.

"Now, now, where do you think you're going? The show's about to start."

She lifted the blindfold from my head and I blinked back into her pale-blue doe-eyes. She looked the same. Her red, smooth tresses fell down over her shoulders, framing her delicate, angelic features. She smiled her usual sweet, non-threatening smile. I gritted my teeth on the soggy gag, wanting to spit in her face.

"If you'll be quiet, I'll remove the gag."

I nodded. She touched me before removing it. I felt her smugness change into frustration, then anger as she continued to rest her hand on my shoulder.

"Interesting," she said in a low voice while she untied the knot. Her eyes studied my neck. Out of nowhere, she grabbed my shoulders and held my body sideways.

"Hey!" I barked as the talisman slid out from under my shirt, dangling from the chain around my neck.

Alora's eyes reflected the blue gem, and revenge flickered ever-so-slightly along with it. "A family heirloom?"

"From my boyfriend," I said. My heart beat fiercely, half in excitement and half in terror. Did she know of the powers behind the necklace?

"I see," she said, letting go of my shoulders. "It's very lovely."

The corner of her lip jutted up for a millisecond before she turned away from me and moved towards the body slumped on the floor.

With one glance, I concluded we were in a storage facility for the Boardwalk. Broken carnival equipment lay strewn around the edges of the walls. Next to me stood the old sea captain that used to stand at the entrance of the water ride. He'd lost an arm and the paint on his black jacket had peeled away, revealing a reddish color underneath.

In the corner were cages from the western days last summer when you could pay for someone to be arrested and they couldn't leave until the time was up or they'd raised enough bail—all for charity, of course. Large stocks stood in front of that. Ironically, I'd been locked up in those same stocks for pictures.

The ceiling was a mesh of metal with large holes along the edges of the beams. I could see the night's sky beyond. Wherever this place was it wouldn't keep out the sun come morning. Obviously, the vampires had to be living somewhere else.

Alora cursed after mopping the sweat from Aden's pale brow.

"Is he dead?" I asked out of impulse.

"No," she murmured. "Just a little more spent than usual. He'll recover." She bent over and whispered in his ear. "Aden, love. Wake up."

Aden rolled over and put his hands to his head, pushing on his temples. "I feel . . . dizzy."

"I know," she said, steadying him to a more upright position. "Katie had too much fun with you, didn't she?"

Aden giggled like a child, appearing half-asleep. She offered him water which he drank wholeheartedly.

I sighed, anxious for Nicholas to come find me. I didn't like waiting around for whatever they had planned.

Out of nowhere, courage surged through my veins. "Why are you keeping me?"

Suddenly, Alora was in my face and the talisman froze against my skin. "No one addresses me without my title," she seethed, her honey-breath wafting gently across my face. "I'll be patient since you don't know the rules. Next time, I won't be so inclined."

Like I'd ever call you Queen.

Her hand hovered at my neck, just over the medallion. The iciness radiated off the stone, giving me chills. I willed her to injure me, eager to see her hand burst into flames. That type of pain would take the sass out of her evil smirk and put her in her place.

"What are you going to do, choke me?" I asked with my legs firmly locked beneath me, my blood rich in adrenaline. "I bet you can't do it."

Alora wavered. She must have read something in my mind to know she couldn't hurt me. I'd called her bluff. "But that would end things too quickly. I have plans for you," she finally said.

"Plans?"

"Yes," she hissed. "And you *will* start respecting me."

"Whatever." I rolled my eyes.

Her anger magnified while her hand blurred through the air and froze next to my cheek. I flinched anyway. The muscles in her neck constricted, the tendons jutting out from under the surface of her delicate skin. But the talisman warmed, calming my pulse. With a grunt, Alora's hand shook, but she couldn't come any closer.

A deep, cleansing laugh burst forth from my belly when I felt her irritation follow.

"There's nothing stopping me from ordering Katie to hunt down your father, your brother, your best friend, even Nicholas," Alora spoke with her index finger in my face.

I clamped my lips shut to stop myself from calling her a bad name and wiped the smirk off my face.

"That's better." The malevolence played across her tone. "I've come to get something that's been stolen from me. It's only fair, don't you think?"

"How does that involve me?"

"You, my little pussy cat," she whispered while using her finger to trace along my chin line to hold my jaw up so she could cast a burning glare into my eyes, "*unfortunately* are the key to everything."

Why am I always the key?

"Aden," Alora said while snapping her fingers. "Aden!"

He'd fallen over again and slept on a pile of fish nets next to a bald mermaid.

"Forget it. They'll be here soon." She recovered into her calm, angelic self, smiling her innocent smile. "Get comfortable. You're going to be here a while."

I gulped, unsure what she meant. But before I knew it, she'd ushered me to one of the cages, locked me inside, and left the room.

In the dark corner I stood with my eyes glued to the door—the one Aden lay drooling next to—awaiting my doom.

Chapter Twelve

"I invite you in, Nicholas," I whispered ever so slightly through the hole in the metal siding next to me, knowing that in order to cross a vampire's domain you must be invited in. "Come get me, please."

All I could see outside was a cement wall topped with curled barbed wire stretching out of my view. I sobbed and crumbled into a heap on the ground. Now that I was alone, my bravery diminished to practically nothing. Hot tears began to pour down my cheeks and splashed on my pant leg.

For once, since the fortune teller's prediction, I feared for my own life. If they left me here the talisman would do me no good. I could die of thirst or starvation before Nicholas could find me. And without my phone, there was no GPS locator for my dad to come to my rescue either—not that I wanted him to be drawn into the vampire lair.

I'd have to try to escape or get someone's attention, which was very unlikely considering our desolate location. The general mixing of the beach-town carefree emotions was all that could be felt beyond Aden's peaceful slumber and Alora's thirst for power.

The jagged edge on the metal hinge of the door caught my attention. While leaning my back up against the grate, I placed the rope gingerly along the edge and tugged. In my haste, the rope slipped and the metal sliced my hand instead. Fiery pain shot up my arm. I sucked the air in quickly between my teeth and tried again.

With more care, I was able to break the rope free. Blood gushed down my arm and pooled in the crook of my elbow. To hide the scent, I licked the blood off and put pressure on the wound with my sock. The rusty-tasting substance turned my stomach and I gagged, completely puzzled at how becoming a vampire made blood taste like liquid heaven.

Holding the sock on my wrist, I clambered to my feet and yanked on the door. The lock was new and held the frame solidly in place.

"*Enigma, if you can hear me, tell Nicholas where I am. Have him come get me,*" I begged mentally in desperation. "*I invite you, too.*"

"I invite everyone," I said out loud in anguish.

I scanned the floor for a nail or something to pick the lock, without any luck. Aden snorted.

"Aden," I whispered. "Aden, can you hear me?"

He grunted again and stirred slightly.

"Can you let me out?"

"Huh?" he asked with half-opened eyes. "How'd you get in there?"

"I'm supposed to do something for Alora but I'm trapped," I said with a hushed voice. "Do you have a key?"

"Don't use her name or she'll get really *peeved.*" Aden sounded like he had marbles in his mouth. He reached his hand into his jean pocket, fumbled around, and extracted a set of keys and a can of chew. "Is this it?"

I wasn't sure, but I hoped one would unlock the door.

"Yeah."

He half-heartedly tossed the keys, just missing my outstretched fingertips. They fell to the ground in a jangling heap just out of my grasp. "Aden, I can't reach them."

"Oops." He snickered and slumped back over again.

"Aden? Aden!"

I grabbed the bars and shook them. Aden continued to snooze away soundly, ignoring me. I folded my hands up under my chin and leaned against the cage in defeat.

God, if you're up there. Please send someone to save me.

The minutes ticked by and turned into an hour, then possibly two as the keys sat and mocked me. I nervously paced and waited for the others to come back. Alora's lust-for-power trademark wasn't within my radar anymore. *Why did she leave?*

Now would be the opportune time for Nicholas' gallant rescue since I wasn't being guarded. But how would he know where to look? Thoughts of him returning to Mr. Pickles and not finding me there, along with my unanswered texts sent my nerves ablaze. He'd always been so level-headed, I imagined he'd return to my house before panicking. Maybe my scent lingered in the air leading up to the sidewalk where I was taken. Maybe my broken phone still lay on the ground where I dropped it, alerting my capture. That could make him go mad with worry.

Yelling for help crossed my mind and I almost did when the atmosphere changed. An unknown number of people, including vampires, were on their way back to the building. My pulse began to race in expectation of the entourage's arrival. I gathered the rope and wove it around my wrists behind my back, sitting in the shadowed corner.

The door opened and Katie sauntered in with the two other guys from the van. They carried another poor soul in between them, supported by their shoulders.

"Where is she?" Tony's voice was full of excitement—a child with a surprise for his mother.

"She'll come." Katie dusted off her hands on her pants and straightened her black fitted-top.

"Do we have to wait long?" Evan asked with a grunt. "He's kinda heavy."

"Shut up, you big baby," Katie snarled. "If you want immortality, you'll do as she wants without whining. Keep it up and maybe next time I'm thirsty I won't stop."

Evan spat on the ground, internally covering up his loathing hate. The man between them mumbled undecipherable threats and jerked, pulling Tony and Evan off balance.

Katie pivoted around and lifted up his head by his hair, still blocking my view of their captive. "Quiet down, Nicky, or I'll have to do something more drastic."

At the mention of his name I shrieked and rose to my feet. "What have you done to him?"

"Now, now, Julia," Alora said, suddenly appearing in the room. "You promised to behave."

"Not to this!" I grabbed the bars between us and shook with all my might. "Let him go!"

Alora pursed her lip and eyed the bloodied sock next to my feet.

"Tony, she's apparently escaped her restraints. Silence her."

With a satisfied smirk, Tony heaved Nicholas onto Evan, grabbed the gag off the floor, and headed my direction.

I eyed the dirty rag and put my quaking hands to my side. "I'll be quiet." My chest heaved as I tried to center myself. My escape would be easier without being gagged and tied.

"You'd better," Alora said, no longer interested in me, but inspecting her new specimen. "Katie, what happened to him?" Her voice and eyes hardened in anger.

Katie's aloof demeanor dissolved into a bumbling child. "I'm sorry, my Queen. One dose wasn't working, so we had to do . . . three."

Out of nowhere, Katie's body flew into the air and hit a nearby wall. She yelped in pain as the sound of the collision reverberated throughout the room.

"Good grief, Katie," Alora barked. "Your haste has almost cost me two of my servants tonight. I've entrusted you to handle my affairs properly and all you've done is mistreat me."

"I'm sorry, my Queen," Katie whimpered and kept her distance in the corner.

Alora turned her attention to Nicholas. "My poor darling. Let's get you fixed up." She glanced towards Katie with disdain. "Get Alexandra, now."

"Yes, my Queen." Katie bowed.

"Untouched," Alora added.

"Of course."

Katie's animosity inflamed as she straightened up and calmly flitted out of the room though her face didn't show it. Effortlessly, and with great care, Alora took Nicholas from Evan and carried him into the cell next to mine. She gently laid him down on a cot; something my cell seemed to be lacking.

My heart pounded in my chest like a sledge hammer against my ribs. Now was the time my secret power needed to emerge. I couldn't stand here and watch the love of my life die when it was my destiny to save the world from the retched blood-suckers in the first place. I gritted my teeth and willed for a miracle with all my might, but nothing heroic happened.

Then Nicholas' eyes rolled back into his head. The consuming suffocation he felt pulled me under, as if we were both trapped within a wet wool blanket.

"He's dying!" I screamed out, watching him gasp for each life-sustaining breath.

"It'll all be over shortly." Alora spoke, her gaze attentive on his face. She pushed back his damp bangs. "I promise."

With rapt concentration, I tried to break the connection from his all-encompassing aura. What Grandma said about the distancing being more difficult during times of stress couldn't have been more accurate. The severing tore at my chest and left hollowness in its place as I focused to put up a mental barrier. Once I was free, I studied his face to make sure abandoning his side internally wasn't going to make the pain worse for him.

What I felt afterwards was surprising. Out of Alora's cold heart flowed genuine concern for Nicholas, like a mother's love for her son. I furrowed my brow. Her feelings didn't make sense at all. Phil had said she wanted him for the reward. The higher-ups didn't like vampire assassins roaming free and had ordered his capture.

"The one thing I've learned about family skeletons is that they always have a way of finding the light of day and ending up at the neighborhood garage sale," she whispered.

I helplessly watched in horror, as the time between each breath grew longer my hatred for Alora increased with each second.

"You're insane. I thought you had to turn him in alive," I spewed. "His death will do you no good!"

"Oh, but I have grander plans for Nicholas than fulfilling his warrant. But I wonder . . . did Nicholas ever mention his mother's name?"

I shot Alora an ugly look. What a crazy question to ask? Why did it matter if he ever did or didn't tell me her name? Nicholas was dying.

"Please help him," I whispered, watching his skin turn grey, his breathing almost at a complete stop. More than anything, I wanted to throw the necklace to him or do something. Maybe being in contact with the talisman would save his life.

"Don't fret, Julia."

"You heartless witch," I blurted. "You're doing nothing but talking—look at him, he's going to die!"

The door opened again. Katie brought in a girl, younger than me with a serendipitously happy grin on her face, towards the cell.

"Thank you," Alora said to Katie, taking the girl by the hand and leading her inside.

The girl pursed her lips in contained excitement.

"Thank you, my dear, for your gift."

My eyes opened wide, wondering what "gift" meant.

With a flick of Alora's fingernail, blood gushed from the girl's arm and she cried out. I gasped, expecting a sudden feeding frenzy. Instead, Alora patted the girl on the back and motioned for her to do something. The girl smiled and willingly held her arm over Nicholas' mouth.

"What are you doing?" I ran to the edge of my cage.

Nicholas spit red bubbles as the blood poured into his mouth.

"You'll suffocate him. He needs water!" I exclaimed and fell to my knees, tempted to beg them to stop.

He fought the liquid, shaking his head. I lifted my feelings barrier just as the huge internal struggle erupted inside him. The vampire within wanted to claw its way out and actually drink the blood. His eyes rolled back into his head and he groaned, trying to control the urge.

"Stop!" I screamed, afraid of what would happen if they didn't quit.

Alora gave me a joyful look while smoothing back Nicholas' hair and sang a little tune.

The animal inside him exploded through the tight container Nicholas hid him in. His eyes burst open and his face contorted with a snarl; he took the girl's wrist and yanked it to his lips— wanting more. The girl moaned in delight, followed by a sigh, then fell down next to his body.

"We must be gentle and no biting," Alora warned, like Nicholas was her pet. "Blood bestowers are to be respected."

Unable to stop the flood of yummy mind-numbing glee, my body began to tingle as the sensation hit me too. I fought to stay composed, but the euphoria took over and I crumpled to the floor, relishing in the delight.

"I see you're experiencing it too. Wonderful," I heard Alora say, her ethereal voice dancing around in the sudden vastness of my head.

And at that dangerous moment, all I wanted was to become a vampire and feel the rush whenever and wherever. With grave disappointment, I felt the bliss suddenly cease. A lion-like roar brought me back into reality and I opened my eyes.

"Sorry. We don't want to expend her." Alora ushered the sappy, smiling girl into the waiting arms of Tony. "Take her back."

"I want more," Nicholas growled and lunged forward with a snap of his teeth.

Blood still clung to his lips. Dizziness caused him to sway and sit back down. He watched like a tiger deprived of his catch as Tony left through the door with his tasty snack draped in his arms. Then Nicholas' eyes locked with mine. I gaped at his contorted, animalistic face that hid any resemblance of the man I loved.

Alora patted his arm.

"The next course will be in a second," Alora said, shooting a glance sideways at me. "We need to talk first."

Chapter Thirteen

Nicholas had other plans as I felt his drug-induced stupor begin to fade and his body increase in strength. At any moment, fueled by a ravenous hunger, he was about to claw through the bars between us to get to me.

"Look at me," Alora demanded, placing her hands on his cheeks forcing him to stop gawking. He looked into her eyes and her touch doused the flames of his burning want, clearing his focus temporarily.

"That's better," she said in a wispy tone and joined him on the cot, mussing with the front of his hair. "I'm here now. I'm going to fix everything."

He grabbed her hand by the wrist, tightening his eyes, then opened them widely, strangely emanating recognition.

"Mother?" he whispered in disbelief, his voice slightly hoarse.

"Yes, Son," Alora answered, with a mixture of love and loss, bringing his hand to her heart. "I'm here."

I gasped, almost falling over at the confession.

"How is that possible?" Nicholas pulled his hand away. "He said you died when I was born."

"Oh, did he now?" Alora's disdain and nostrils flared outwards. "Makes sense. Preston hid you from me after we disagreed on the finer points of parenting. I've been looking for you ever since."

Nicholas pressed his hand to his forehead and closed his eyes. Anger, grief, disappointment and shock rose up into a full blown whirlwind. "I don't understand."

"After you were born, I hemorrhaged. Preston told me it would be the only way to save me and keep our family together."

"He lied?" Nicholas mouthed, still excreting doubt.

Alora tilted her head, her shoulders sinking down. Both of them exhaled at the same time.

"I'm sorry, Son." She rested her hand on his shoulder.

Nicholas opened and closed his mouth a few times. Confusion

encompassed his body.

"So this whole time you were just *looking* for me? You're not turning me in for all my slayings?"

"Of course not," she said with a chuckle, clasping her fingers over his clenched fist. "Well, I might have misled the others into thinking it was my intention—" The corner of her lip curled up.

"What others?"

"You don't remember? My sweet Bettina, her sister, their mates and Phil. Oh, how I enjoy Phil." Her eyes twinkled at the mention of his name.

"It was *you* that was in charge of their coven?"

"Julia didn't tell you?" Alora asked, faking her surprised expression. "I met her with Phil, the same day you defeated my coven. She seems to get around, doesn't she?"

I returned her phony astonishment with a glare, suspecting she'd known all along I'd kept our meeting a secret, twisting yet another situation to turn Nicholas against me.

"You've met Julia?" Nicholas shot me a wounded look, which pierced my heart like an arrow. The distrust that followed crushed it into tiny pieces. I wanted to die.

"I did. It was delightful."

Please remember you promised we could explain situations like these. Please remember, Nicholas.

"It wasn't like that . . ." I stammered, a plausible excuse eluding me while my lip trembled.

"But yet you trusted her enough to give her *my* talisman," Alora said, in disgust.

Nicholas looked off to the side, his mind elsewhere. "Your talisman," he echoed.

"Yes," she said softly. "I gave it to you, when you were born, to protect you from the both of us. A foolish and weak decision that I now regret. The truth is your father couldn't bear to live without me, his precious and perfect human wife. He thought if he changed me, we would continue to be a happy little family. He didn't account for what I'd want after becoming a servant of the night—

and it wasn't being a docile homemaker, hiding in the house, denying my thirst.

"I shouldn't talk disrespectfully about your father, he did liberate me. But he didn't do so well in raising you," she said, laced with irritation. "But soon you'll see how being a vampire slayer isn't really your place. But, I want my necklace back."

Her flip from sweet to evil, with only one goal of retrieving the necklace, left me cowering in the corner. Only Nicholas had the power to remove the necklace beyond my will. Without it, I'd be a free lunch to any vampire that wanted me.

"No," I whispered, watching Alora remove her hand and with it, the shelter she'd temporarily placed over him which dissolved to practically nothing.

Nicholas didn't answer. The freedom from the absence of her touch finally allowed the evil leniency to push towards the surface and gain control, swallowing up the clear-headed side. What was left were cold and empty eyes like a great white shark, hungry for blood and determined to fulfill its murderous desires.

"I'll leave you two to talk," Alora said with a knowing nod, standing up. "Do with her as you want, Nicholas, just collect my necklace."

"Yes, Mother," he said and his eyes locked on my neck.

"Daylight will be upon us soon. Katie? Evan? Grab Aden. Let's go." She snapped her fingers and the group followed her command and scattered.

I shivered, finding that Nicholas and I were suddenly alone.

My eyes welled up with tears as the panic enveloped me. The prediction said I'd save the world with a hidden talent, that unfortunately still eluded me, and apparently without the talisman's protection. Fulfilling the destiny under these circumstances seemed downright impossible.

Reasoning with him or becoming like him were my only two viable options. If I resisted, he'd snap me like a twig. But if I were to change, I'd have to commit suicide to defeat the vampiring world.

He moved to my cell door, effortlessly destroying the lock. I grasped the talisman with both hands, my arms shaking, unsure what he'd do next.

"You don't want to do this," I said quietly. "She's our enemy, remember?"

The astounding hunger sparked his eyes, electrifying the viridian flecks, making my head dizzy. I backed up into the corner, holding the bars behind me for support.

"Nicholas, please."

He walked in gradually, growing stronger with each passing second, watching me without blinking. I stared back, searching through his madness for the man I loved. Some shred of goodness stopped him from just tearing into me like an animal.

With all my courage, I stepped forward and turned my head to expose my neck. "If you won't spare me," I said boldly. "Make me like you then."

He exhaled, oozing satisfaction. I felt his hand move my hair from the nape of my neck and with his finger, he lightly traced the chain lying on my collarbone.

My heart began to pound while ice poured down my spine. He ran his nose along the side of my cheek and inhaled. I swayed.

"What are you doing?" I asked, in a whisper, feeling excited and petrified.

"I'm savoring you," he said, his breath hot against my ear while he nuzzled my skin.

The power of our emotions intermixed together, clouding my judgment. At the same time, his hands moved up the sides of my torso to the back of my neck, unclasping the chain. The talisman slipped off my body and fell into his other hand with a clink. I stiffened, feeling the tension within him coming closer to snapping.

The absence of the necklace made me feel naked, raw, and vulnerable. In response, I wrapped my arms around my torso, hugging myself.

With a velvety touch, Nicholas pulled away my T-shirt so my shoulder was exposed. His arms fastened around me, his breath dewing the hairs on my neck while he rested his lips on my skin, a simple kiss before the inevitable. My chest heaved in anticipation of the pain, already knowing what it felt like. I could no longer separate myself from his aura. The want encompassed me and all I longed for was to tumble into the bliss with him forever.

"Never forget I love you," I breathed before surrendering limply to his body.

"Hold up, Nick," a male voice called from behind us.

Suddenly, I was free and Nicholas' body haphazardly sailed away from me towards the opened door. The talisman fell perfectly into my hands. My fingers gripped the stone in thankfulness before a blurred figure grabbed me as well, our bodies moving in the same direction.

Outside, we zinged upwards, hovering twenty feet in the air while Nicholas rolled over from his sprawled position on the ground.

"What the heck?" Nicholas cried, looking up at us. I also turned to discover the identity of my rescuer.

"Phil?" My voice teetered up an octave.

"At your service, Ma'am," he said with a smile, fanged teeth gleaming in the moonlight. "Uh, hold on."

Our bodies lurched up higher into the sky as Nicholas lunged to grab Phil's ankle. I couldn't help the déjà vu from flooding my senses. The last time I saw Phil, he was just about to sire me into a vampire and Nicholas impaled him with a stake just in time, turning him into dust. I had no idea vampires were capable of coming back from the dead.

"But you . . . he . . . that night . . ." I choked out.

"I'm supposed to be dead?"

"Uh, yeah?"

"I was—I mean technically I still am, but I'm back. Long story," Phil said with a snort. "Good thing, isn't it?"

We jerked higher into the air each time Nicholas found something new to catapult his body off of.

"Hang tight, Nick," Phil said, throwing him a bag with red liquid inside. "Drink this."

Nicholas grabbed the bag and sank his teeth in. I took a deep breath and clung to Phil, feeling another rush overwhelm me.

"What's up with you?" Phil said, suddenly concerned. "Are you feeling all right?"

"Um, sorta," I breathlessly squeaked out, relaxing into Phil's embrace, reveling in Nicholas' ecstasy.

"Whoa, girl. You need to hang onto me." He let out an ear piercing whistle as if to call in the calvary and held me tighter. "I need to get you home."

From the corner of my eye, I drunkenly caught a flash of black bolting across the sand towards Nicholas. I squinted to make sure I wasn't seeing things. The object morphed into a woman with jet black hair and fair skin, dressed in all black.

"Enigma?" I asked in a whisper, not wanting to recover from Nicholas' drunken blood-engorged stupor.

"Enigma? That's a new one." Phil laughed. "That's Scarlett, though she is quite the enigma, that's for sure."

"Her name's Scarlett?" My head finally started to clear as Nicholas finished drinking the contents in the bag.

"Yeah. We just met. She's totally rocking." Phil's aura brimmed with confidence, like the first day I met him in the cafeteria at school.

"I'm so confused," I mulled out loud.

In slow motion, I watched as Scarlett tackled Nicholas to the ground, the sensation feeling like a punch to my own gut. I groaned.

"Yeah, I think we need to go," Phil said quickly, smoothing back my hair like it was fur. "You got it, Scar?" Phil yelled down to the beach.

Scarlett looked up and nodded. Nicholas struggled, but remained pinned beneath her.

"Scarlett," I mumbled, curling up in Phil's arms.

He launched into the air and I welcomed the cool wind, rushing against my face. At that moment, I didn't have a care in the world.

Chapter Fourteen

"We have to go back," I demanded and pounded my arms against Phil's chest as he landed on the lawn in front of my house.

"Shhh." He put his finger against my lips. "Someone will hear you."

I looked over his shoulder. The lights in the front room were still on and my dad happened to be awake, worried something fierce.

"Crap." I gritted my teeth.

"What?" Phil turned to find the source of my discomfort, grimaced and came forward, about to grab me. "Do you need me to sneak you to your room or something?"

"Whoa. Hang on." I placed my hands against his advancing body and felt the pectoral muscles beneath his shirt tighten. For a moment I struggled not to get distracted. "You've got a ton of explaining to do first."

"Parker, you've got to smooth things over with your dad and then we can talk."

I bit my lip, invisibly feeling him out. Phil had no bad intentions for once, which was surprising. "Um, I guess I could use a lift to my second story."

He didn't allow me to finish my statement before he sprang up like a gazelle to my window and set me down softly on the ledge of the roof.

He turned his ear awkwardly towards the house. "He's downstairs in the kitchen. Go get a drink of water and act surprised when he questions your whereabouts. Tell him you've been asleep this whole time."

"Uh, okay." I wrinkled up my forehead. "But what about my car?"

"Where is it?" Phil reached out his hand and flicked his fingertips forward, obviously wanting the keys.

"Downtown, by Mr. Pickles." I fished for them in my pocket, pausing before dropping them into his hand. He shot me his adorable half-smile which melted me.

"I'll take care of it." He disappeared and only the rustle of the leaves on the nearby trees gave away his exit.

I steadied my arm against the house siding for a minute, stunned. *How the heck could Phil possibly be alive?*

The memories of him burning up into a pile of ash flashed vividly in my mind followed by his funeral shortly after. I was grateful to see he was back, but totally confused and wondered if what I saw was real or not—or some horrific trick played by a very believable actor.

Wake up, Julia.

I bit my knuckle almost drawing blood when another burst of my dad's angst hit me. Rushing inside, my stomach did a somersault when I realized the hour—one-fifteen in the morning. I didn't waste any time changing into my jammies and mustering up a believable sleepy-face. The sack over my head and windy ride had done wonders to give the perfect bed-head effect.

Taking a deep breath, I stumbled down the stairs to the kitchen in my bunny slippers and robe.

"Young lady," my dad barked, suddenly confused after giving me a once over. "Where have you been?"

"Upstairs, asleep. Why?"

He scowled. "Since when?"

"Since earlier this evening?" I crinkled up my lip feigning confusion while rubbing my eyes to add to my act.

"Your phone is off."

"Oh, that . . ." I put my head down and moved towards the cabinet for a glass. "I actually dropped and broke it. Sorry."

"Another one?" he groaned, scrubbing his hand against his forehead. "But where's your car?"

"It's not out front?" I rushed to the kitchen window, prepared to freak if Phil hadn't returned yet. Sure enough, my car was parked on the side of the house where I normally left it. My dad walked up behind me flowing more confusion than ever.

"It's there, Dad." I put my hand on his forehead. "Are you feeling okay?"

"It wasn't there earlier," he said with a grimace and pushed my arm away.

I yawned to cover my smile, feeling Phil's enjoyment waft down from upstairs, evidently listening in.

"I'm really tired, Dad," I said while filling a glass up with water, relieved I'd avoided getting caught. "Big day tomorrow: math test, history report due. I'm going back to bed."

With a shrug, I headed for the stairs.

"Next time, check in," he said, his voice gruff but his interior bewildered.

I grunted a yes and purposefully meandered slowly upstairs. Once I closed my bedroom door, I ran to the window.

I threw open the blinds and opened my window. "That was so close."

"You did amazingly well," Phil said with a twinkle in his eye. "A little too good, perhaps."

"Not really," I said with a guffaw. "You told me what to say. How did you know?"

Phil chuckled, leaking a twinge of nostalgia. "Years of practice with my own parents." He raised his eyebrows and nodded his head.

"Yeah, well." I sighed, and slumped onto my window seat. "I've had to lie a little too much lately. I feel horrible about it."

Phil stood at the window, his jet-black eyes were filled with compassion. In awe, I gave him a once over. He looked the same as before: blonde hair, pale skin, surfer build, breathtakingly beautiful. But his aura no longer excreted consuming selfish desires for blood or my conversion to the vamp side. He'd returned to his former human self: compassionate, fun, carefree, brave, though a tiny hint of bloodlust gave away what he really was.

But once the adrenaline of averting lifetime grounding dissipated, the world stopped as reality resurfaced. Nicholas, the love of my life was evil now; the switch caused by my immortal enemy—his mother. The thought had me seething. Alora never intended to capture Nicholas and Scarlett knew this all along and didn't tell us, for fear of what he'd do. And now that he was solely fueled by his vampire side, his new goal was to take the talisman from me and give it to her. I burst into tears and sobbed into my hands.

"Oh, geez, Parker," Phil said in a panic, "If you are going to cry, at least invite me in."

"I . . . I don't know what to do," I sniveled. "This whole thing is insane. He's lost . . . gone . . . one of them now. It's hopeless and *over*."

"Jiminy Christmas," Phil said with a grunt I couldn't ignore.

I looked up to see his hands pressed against the space between us, like a mime does against the air. He pushed the invisible force field with all his might to no avail.

"Don't you think I'd have bitten you by now if that was my intention?" he complained, repeatedly jabbing the corner of his shoulder against the barrier. "Please, just let me in. This is killing me."

"Fine, you can come in."

Phil fell forward, but landed gingerly onto my floor like a cat. His tender arms scooped me into a hug, encouraging me to lean up against his body. I curled up and closed my eyes while he placed his chin upon the top of my head and stroked the side of my cheek with his thumb.

"It's like a bad dream," I whimpered. "I just need to wake up."

"If it is, I don't want you to," Phil said softly.

Any other girl would have swooned and thought she was in utter bliss being held delicately in his arms. But the fear he put out gave me the chills, squelching the unintended insulting comment.

"What do you mean?" I sniffled and tightened my eyes.

"It's nothing. Never mind."

"What? What happened?" I pressed off his chest, just to be corralled back in again by his arms.

"We'll talk about it later. Just hush," Phil said and shoved the fear back down.

"No," I said, pushing away to study his face. "You didn't die? You went somewhere else, didn't you? Where?"

Phil's eyes flashed in terror. "Where do you think?"

I blinked and tried to figure out what he meant.

"Well, I didn't go to heaven," Phil said darkly.

"Not . . .?" I asked in a gasp, unable to say the word "Hell".

"I don't want to talk about it," he said and his anxiety erupted like a geyser.

I back peddled internally, fighting all the questions bubbling to the surface. "How did you get back?" I finally blubbered out.

"Alora did it somehow. One minute I was *there*, the next I was lying on the ground on a bunch of burnt two-by-fours, naked."

I imagined the scene and blushed. "I . . . I didn't know that was possible."

"Me either, but thank God it was," Phil said and pulled out a very small book from his pocket. He kissed the black leather cover. "We don't have to tonight, but sometime soon, we need to compare notes."

My mouth fell open. "Is that . . . a *Bible*?"

"Yeah, so?" An impish grin spread across his lips. "Look, I've got to get in good with *The Man*—and fast. I'm totally running on fumes right now, it's not even funny."

I stared in bewilderment at his cute, yet very serious expression.

"Come on," he said, palms open. "I'm a changed man. Reborn, but not in the way I think I'm supposed to be."

I rubbed my hand across my forehead. This couldn't be real.

"I'm . . . " I couldn't finish.

"Yeah, speechless, I know. Scar did the same thing. But we need to get to work. Alora has got to be stopped. I need to know everything about Nick and why she's so keen on him anyway."

All I could do was look at Phil with wide-eyes.

"I know you miss the old sexy wanna-bite-you Phil, but he's long gone now. Sorry."

I suppressed a chuckle. How could he be making jokes at a time like this? "Who's Scar?" I finally squeaked out.

"Scarlett. Were you not there a few minutes ago? She's the one who's with *your boy* Nick. She'll get him off the *stuff*, no doubt. She's got *skills*."

I didn't like his tone inflection when he said she had "skills."

"Really?" My eyes narrowed. "How?"

"Mind trick him basically, like she did me. I came out of Hades with a hang-over the size of Texas, itching for a fix something fierce. She just talked me through things and after a few days, sure enough, I felt better. I'm four days sober so far."

I let out a gust of air, unsure what to think.

"It's going to be okay," Phil said and lifted my chin, demanding eye contact. "Just tell me what happened before I showed up."

I glanced away, then zoned out. The memories hurt, making a lump form in my throat. The moisture brimmed in my eyes. "Alora is Nicholas' birth mother apparently."

"Really?" Phil said confounded, before growing somber. "Whoa, didn't see that coming." He became guarded, like he knew things he didn't want to tell me.

His change worried me.

"What's she going to do to him?" *And me*? I looked into his eyes for support.

"Um, wow. Does that make us . . . half brothers?" Phil's eyes darted away from mine, effusing an inkling of disgust.

"Focus, Phil," I said and put my palms on his cheeks to bring his awareness back to the severity of the situation.

He blinked once he looked into my eyes and fondness radiated outwards. I let go.

Phil cleared his throat. "She's just assembling her group of followers, preferably ones she doesn't have to sire. All to play into her power trip I think. She barely gave me permission to change you, but I told her I wouldn't stay if she didn't."

My cheeks flushed as my heart warmed at the gesture. I still liked, in some weird way, that he chose me out of all the girls at school until the word *change* registered in my thoughts. The sound of a record player needle ripping across an album zipped through my head.

"Did you just say *change me*?" My voice was harder than I'd anticipated.

"Calm down. I lied to her. Believe me. I have no intention of doing that." Phil said emphatically.

"How can you lie to a mind reader?"

"She wasn't touching me then, so . . ." He grinned, showing all his teeth including his sharp canines. "I'm convincing."

"So, if you're supposed to *change* me . . ." I studied his vampire teeth. "And Nicholas is too . . ." *And take the talisman.* "I don't get why? She doesn't even seem to like me."

"I don't think it's you in particular, though it is strange she's authorized both of us to change you. We really can't share you . . ."

"N-no." I shook my head.

"I think you know too much, so you're collateral damage. And she's fine either way if you're changed or not, but . . ."

"Do you even think she suspects we'd all defect?"

"Probably not. I've already accepted I'm going to have to run because I can't kill her." He made a slicing motion across his own throat in jest to hide his concern.

I'd forgotten the rule that if Alora was killed, all her sired kin died too (along with Phil) because their lifelines would be severed. This made me worry. Even if we got Nicholas back from the dark side, we couldn't just kill her and be together. He'd never agree to that in the first place but I'd never want to be responsible for sending Phil back to Hell. We—including Phil and possibly Scarlett—would have to always be on the lookout for her. *Forever.*

"Why does she want faithful followers anyway?"

"Why do evil people want what they want?" Phil rhetorically asked with a snort. "World domination, ultimate power, I don't know. She keeps to herself a lot but says she wants to be in charge and do things her way. She's actually pretty brilliant, but . . . I don't trust her."

If she had the talisman, would she be invincible?

Everything started to fit together. Not only did she want the talisman, she wanted her sons, Nicholas and Phil, to be part of her elite little group and me too, apparently. With the necklace, she'd be able to do whatever and no one could kill her, and quite possibly be unaffected by the sunlight.

"This is totally insane." I pressed my head into my hands.

And I'm the key to stopping it.

I let out a cackle of hysteria, louder than I should have and gaped at Phil with huge eyes. He listened while I telepathically sniffed out any emotional disturbances from my family. When they continued to sleep soundly, we both relaxed at the same time.

Phil teasingly punched me in the shoulder. "Shush already."

"Ouch," I whispered, while rubbing my arm, realizing the talisman should have prevented him from bruising me. Then I remembered I'd forgotten to put it back on after Phil's rescue.

Pulling the necklace from my pocket, I glanced at the stone and panicked. The gem had turned black and lifeless in my hand.

"What's that?" Phil asked, reaching forward.

Suddenly tongue tied, my hand froze unable to stop him. He removed it gently from my fingers. Nothing happened.

"Wow. It looks really *expensive*," he said, handing it back. "Is it yours?"

"Um, yeah," I mumbled.

Our eyes met. With shaky fingers, I clasped the chain around my neck and waited for the stone to glow with welcoming warmth and turn blue like before. But the talisman remained the same.

I continued to freak out on the inside, trying to think back to what Nicholas had said about its powers. The protection worked when the talisman was freely given and if it accepted its new owner, it changed color. If not, the stone turned black and burned the unwanted recipient. But it wasn't burning me or Phil.

What's wrong with it?

"Quick, try to bite me," I said in desperation and thrust my neck towards Phil's mouth.

He jumped off the seat and backed up. "Whoa there, sister. Didn't you just hear me a minute ago? I'm trying to avoid the delectable red nectar. You becoming a vamp isn't going to help things."

"No, I mean, *try* to bite me. Don't actually do it."

Phil twisted up the side of his face into a grimace. "What?"

"It's an experiment."

"Look, you're tempting enough as it is," he said and kept his hands up, increasing the distance. "Imagine being absolutely starved and someone puts your favorite food in front of you and says, 'Here, take a whiff, but you can't eat it.' "

"Oh." I ran my hands through my hair and grabbed a handful, wanting to yank a chunk out. "That would be cruel."

"Heck yeah." Phil watched me like I was a lit firecracker that hadn't gone off, unsure if I was safe to approach.

"Never mind. Sorry, I didn't think about that."

I slumped to the floor, overwhelmed with grief and information. My room swayed as new tears welled up in my eyes. The gaping hole where my heart used to reside felt raw and empty. I wanted to curl up and die. Then, my stomach lurched.

Oh, please dear God no.

I choked down the bile and squished my eyes shut, willing the contents of my stomach to stay inside. A sheet of glistening sweat burst across my goose-bumped skin.

"You okay?" Phil asked sweetly and put his arm over my shoulder.

His kindness and the fact I didn't actually puke lessened the embarrassment, but I still felt like someone had punched me in the gut. From nowhere I completely lost all composure.

"I can't do this," I said with my palms against my face, suddenly overwhelmed with haunting memories of Nicholas' cold hard green eyes. "I guess it all makes sense since he's evil now, to fulfill my destiny but . . . but . . . now you're all *unevil* so why would I kill you too?" I asked in mumbled sobs. "And the talisman is broken, my friend is a blood sucker, my boyfriend is addicted now. It's completely a mess and utterly impossible . . . "

"Parker," Phil whispered while pulling my hands off my eyes. "Parker! Look at me."

I sniveled and glanced up into his face. The calming darkness of his eyes invited me to come inside and relax within their satiny comfort.

"Nicholas isn't lost, he's just confused. I'm sure, after he's had a chance to get off his blood-high and work with Scar, he'll figure out he doesn't want to follow Alora's wicked plans. You'll have him back in no time."

I whimpered and nodded.

"Just take things one day at a time. I'll watch your back and we'll get this all straightened out." Phil sat closer next to me and rubbed my back and shoulders.

"But," I said, voice quaking, "I'm supposed to."

"Supposed to do what?" he whispered behind me, close to my ear.

"Scarlett's former psychic boss said my destiny was to wipe out all the vampires."

Phil laughed. "Oh, really?"

I pursed my lips. "She could see the future and I believe her. So does Scarlett."

Phil swiveled me around by my shoulder so I faced him. "Listen to me. No one really knows the future, except for the *Big Man* upstairs, so don't let *their* opinion wig you out right now." Phil had a harder edge to his voice.

"I have to. It's true," I whispered, looking downward.

"Okay, so maybe it is true, but don't you think, if you are the Chosen One that when it came time, you'd have all the tools you need to kick everyone's ass?"

His choice of words made me smile. "I guess so."

"Great. So, let's worry about that when the time comes. Right now, you need sleep. You've got to go to school tomorrow and also keep your dad's suspicions down. We don't need him freaking out anymore."

"I don't think I can sleep."

"Well, I've accounted for that. Here, take these—" Phil put two pills in my hand "—and everything will be okay. I'm hanging out with you tonight anyway. I need a place to crash."

"What are they?"

"Just take them and things will be clearer in the morning. Promise."

I flipped the little white pills over in my hand and judged his aura. He smiled his knee-melting smile that I found difficult to resist. When I knew I could trust him, I popped them in my mouth. Within seconds, the world became fuzzy, taking away all my cares instantly.

"They work quickly," I mumbled, feeling my body crumple to the floor.

"I know."

Something lifted my body up and from there I floated under a rainbow towards paradise.

Chapter Fifteen

"Julia? Julia!"

The muffled voice of my father boomed from heaven, breaking apart the sparkly cloud I floated on. With all my might, I clung to each piece, trying to hold the fluffy filaments together.

"Ugh," I muttered. "Leave me alone."

"Julia, wake up."

His agitation yanked me back into reality. Unwillingly I opened my eyes. Just beyond my father's panic-stricken face the clock read 3:30 AM.

"I'm sleeping," I said, yanking my covers over my head. "It's flipping three in the morning."

"Yes," he said with a gruffness that made me cringe. "Maybe you should tell *that* to the police officers who are downstairs asking to speak with you."

I sat up in my bed, instantly awake. "Police officers?"

"Julia." He held me firmly by my arm and I flinched, the bruise from Phil's playful punch still tender at the spot. "If there is something you need to tell me, I suggest you do it now." He looked at me with worried eyes.

"No, Dad." I shrugged off his grip. *I hope not.*

He stood up, angry, fearful, frustrated, exasperated. "Put on your robe."

As we filed downstairs, the cockiness of the occupants in the foyer seemed to be a bit much for our little house. I knew whatever conversation about to take place would be interesting and probably twisted against me.

"Officers," Dad said with a nod. "Let's go into the living room."

I scanned the two faces, neither of which I recognized.

"We just need to ask some questions," the taller one with jet black hair and a cleft chin said.

"And we can do that in the living room," Dad said firmly, holding out his arm to direct them towards the couch. I followed behind the shorter one who happened to dispense the most attitude.

They sat down after we did.

"We're looking for this young lady," Cleft Chin said, producing a photo of Katie. "Do you know of her whereabouts?"

The photo opened the floodgates of despair, Phil's sleeping pills temporarily buried, confirming this whole nightmare to be real. I took a deep breath and fought the barrage of memories that threatened to drown me. The whole torrential storm of missing friends and worried parents from last fall flashed before my eyes. I'd completely forgotten the aftermath would happen again with Alora back in town.

While folding my arms, I refocused on the officer to try to remain calm and act like I had no clue where she could possibly be.

"Is she missing?" I asked, my eyes flickering between them.

"Possibly."

I grabbed onto my dad's hand so I wouldn't fidget, faking I needed his support.

"We were supposed to meet at Mr. Pickles tonight," I said with forced worry in my voice. "But she sent a text and told me her car wouldn't start and cancelled our plans. Did . . . did she leave and not come home or something?"

"When did you see her last?"

A little bit ago.

I bit my tongue before I admitted the truth, thinking back to the time before tonight.

"Um . . . Friday, at school," I finally said. "You didn't answer me."

"Yes, Ma'am. Miss Kennedy has been reported missing," he said trying to convey warmth, possibly fearing I'd start freaking out. "Do you know where she was today?"

The two appeared to be watching my every move, but I felt their boredom instead of the intended intimidation. This must be routine questioning for all missing persons cases. Good thing this time I'd be dismissed as a suspect.

"No." I looked away and tried to muster up a few tears. *Why can't I cry when I want to?*

"Has she done anything suspicious lately?"

Like kidnapping me or drinking blood from some guy's arm? I'd say heck yeah! I fought a smirk that wanted to form on my lips. "No."

"Do you know where she might have gone?"

Alora's hideout maybe? Or stalking Tyler's house? My heart thudded a few hard beats thinking of him. He'd definitely need some protection; I'd have to ask Phil later, if it wasn't already too late.

"No." I shook my head and took another deep breath, trying harder to cry.

"When did you receive your last text from her?"

"I'd tell you the exact time, but my phone's busted. So, I don't know. Some time around six?"

Cleft Chin shifted in his seat, dissatisfied. His suspicion alerted me my act wasn't winning any Emmy's. I took another deep breath and refocused my energy on Phil's funeral, imagining the look in Phil's mother's eyes. The memories came back like it happened yesterday. Katie's mom would feel the same distress, but unlike Phil's mother, she may never get closure unless we killed Katie. The realization sent shockwaves down my spine and like magic, the tears burst freely from the corners of my lids.

"Can you think of any information that might help with this case?" Cleft Chin asked, his demeanor softening.

"No." I looked down, sniffling and wiping away the now endless flow.

"Well, okay then," Cleft Chin said, rising to his feet.

The short, cocky one snapped to attention and stood as well. "Thank you. Here's my card. If you hear from her, or find out anything about where she might have gone, please give me a call."

I remained on the couch, slobbering in my snot while my dad took the card and nodded.

After the cops left, my dad returned to the couch and put his arm over my shoulder. My tears stopped, but the worry, regret and anxiety snaked around us, threatening to form a lasso and choke our necks.

"I hope they find her," he finally said.

"Me too," I said in an effort to give him some hope.

My heart hurt knowing Katie was as good as dead to me now and I needed to separate myself from caring anymore. She was no longer my friend, but a ruthless killer, unless Phil could show her the light. And then maybe Phil knew of a way we could stop this much easier than last time. I just hoped the whole "we need to move away from here" talk wouldn't come up again.

I rubbed my eyes and leaned into my dad's shoulder for comfort. The last thing I wanted was for him to worry, especially in his fragile condition.

"Katie's been acting weird lately," I said. "Maybe she just snapped and took off. She's prone to do crazy things every once in a while."

"And not call you?"

"Maybe she did call. I don't have my phone."

"I'll get you one tomorrow. You'll need to pay for it though."

"I know."

I closed my eyes and tried to push a little peace my dad's way. It seemed to work, clearing up the emotional clutter. After a few minutes, I heard him snore somewhere within my own dreams. We'd managed to fall asleep.

"Whoa," Luke said, standing in the doorway. "What's with the slumber party?"

Dad woke up with a snort.

I groggily looked at the clock. "Oh, crap."

I was supposed to be leaving in ten minutes for school.

Darting up the stairs, I flew into my room to find the shades drawn, blocking out the morning sunlight. The hall light illuminated Phil sitting patiently on my bed, a goofy smile plastered on his face. He jumped up and put his hand over my mouth to muffle my startled scream.

"Shhh," he said quietly, shutting the door behind me. "I came back last night and you were downstairs with your dad. Looks like everything's on the up and up. Nice work."

"Not exactly," I muttered, scrambling blindly in the dark to find something clean to wear. My heart rate returned to normal but my vision was a few seconds behind. "They know Katie is missing, so today is going to be interesting."

"Who?"

"The cops. They must have come sometime after you left," I said, looking at Phil. My eyes had adjusted to the dark and I tried not to notice his dimples.

I scooted into the bathroom to change, flipping on the light. "It's like your disappearance all over again," I said softly from behind the cracked door.

"Oh?" Phil questioned, seeming far away and lost in thought, like he'd returned to that time in his mind.

I shimmied out of my jammies, brushed my teeth, threw my hair up into a pony tail and put on jeans and a tee shirt. "The school is going to be wallpapered in missing fliers and I can't say anything."

"Well, I'm kinda stuck here until tonight but we'll figure something out."

I came out of the bathroom and glanced around my room. Not much for a vampire to do all day.

"On my bookshelf is my romance novel collection, or if you want, you could write my history report." I gave him a cheesy smile.

"I'd rather read romance."

"Your funeral." I threw my backpack over my shoulder. "I'll get you something from the library later. Be good." I gave him a stern motherly look along with a firm point of my finger.

"Trouble is no longer my middle name. I've been reborn," Phil said, making the sign of the cross followed by two fingers for scouts honor.

I rolled my eyes. "You're a dork."

The dewy air rushed my nostrils as I squished across the grass to my car. Phil had successfully earned my trust again and I felt confident leaving him unattended in my house, until I could return.

Coach Hoffman hated tardy students and often made them run the whole class period instead of detention (which I'd take over running any day). I couldn't be late. But once I arrived, I found the entire class sitting on the bleachers engaged in a discussion. Kara was sharing about Daisy, her Chihuahua dog, and how she'd run away and its affect on her trust of animals ever since. Once someone saw me walk in though, the whispers started along with a rumbling of empathy.

"Oh, Julia," Coach said getting up and holding out her arms for a hug. "I'm so happy you came to class today. We were worried you'd stayed home with the news of Katie."

At the mention of her name, three girls burst into tears. I caught Sam's glance and noticed worry etched across her face.

"Yeah," I grunted, suffocated from the pressure of her bourgeoning bosoms, waiting for the hug to be over with.

More than anything I wanted to sit by Sam, but Coach walked me over to sit between "huggy" Maya and "cryie" Beth. It took all the effort I had to endure their concern and affection.

At the end of class, I bolted to history to avoid the mob and buried my face in my book.

"It's happening again, isn't it?" Sam asked, sitting down next to me. "The mysterious disappearances, the dea—" Her sudden distress finished the statement for me.

The desire to tell her the truth burned in my stomach, forcing bile up my throat.

"I don't know." *If Phil and I can stop it fast enough, no.* "Maybe."

"Katie's mom called last night after she didn't come home. I mentioned you two were meeting up. How did that go?"

"We didn't. She cancelled and said she had car trouble."

"She called you?" Her eyebrows knit together.

"No." I looked away. "Texted me. I was the last to hear from her I guess."

"Oh. I was hoping she didn't, like, kidnap Tyler and head for Mexico. He's not at school either."

"He's not?" My voice echoed throughout the classroom, creating an avalanche of curiosity behind the eyeballs peering back at me.

"Keep your voice down, Miss Parker," Mr. Marshall said, looking up over his glasses with his beady eyes. Fortunately, class hadn't started yet.

"Geez, Julia. Chill." Sam puckered her lips as her cheeks reddened. "Tyler's got the flu. I was kidding about the Mexico thing."

Internally, I breathed a sigh of relief. He'd have to stay home and indoors until he was better—hopefully for longer than the usual twenty-four hours. "I didn't know that."

"Miss Parker," Mr. Marshall said, motioning me to the front of the room. "Come forward."

I gulped once I saw Sarah, the T.A. from the office, standing next to him, relishing in her importance. Begrudgingly, I walked to the front, while students stared at me like I had some contagious disease, though spewing great interest in my business. The last time I was called to the office, Mr. Brewster torturously interrogated me over Phil's disappearance. I didn't think I could endure that again. Luckily, this time, the cops had already questioned me and I wasn't the last to be seen with her like I'd been with Phil.

But the only thing Sarah handed me was a note.

Please come straight home after school.
I have important things to tell you.
Uncle Phil

I looked up in relief and stuffed the note in my pocket.

"Everything okay?" Mr. Marshall asked, actually showing some concern.

"Fine," I stated and swiveled around to return to my seat.

I kept my gaze forward only to catch Sam's eyes, which were big as golf balls. "It's from my dad telling me to come home," I whispered when Mr. Marshall turned to write on the board. "My phone's busted, so he can't call me."

Sam formed her lips into an O shape, accepting my lie with disappointment. She obviously hoped for something juicer. After that, I kept my head down and my feelings' radar in neutral. I was *so* done with everyone's nosiness.

"Do you think Katie's really missing? Or just—I hate to say it—pulling a stunt or something?" Dena asked while slowly nibbling tiny bites of her potato chip. "'Cause lately, I don't really trust her. And pretending to be missing just isn't cool, you know?"

"I doubt she's faking," I said as my tummy unhappily gurgled, resulting in me pushing my half-eaten salad away. "The cops showed up at three this morning to ask questions. It doesn't look good."

"Really?" Cam asked. "What did you tell them?"

"The truth." *Sorta.* "I said I didn't know anything. She did flake on me for dinner, which was weird." *Kinda.*

"Wow," he responded, pushing his straightened red hair that normally was a mountain of curls out of his eyes.

"So . . . say she *is* faking, where would she go?" Sam asked, while taking a sip of her coke. "Her car and all her clothes are still in her room and her mom says her bank account hasn't been touched at all."

"I don't know," Dena said. "Maybe she met some rich guy online and ran off to Jamaica."

"Seriously?" Sam scrunched up her face. "I doubt it. She's done some crazy stuff, but nothing extreme. I'm worried she's in real trouble."

"I agree," I insisted. "It's not like her to blow off a dinner date."

"Did they ever catch the gang that—you know—with Phil and Justin?" Cam asked, avoiding mentioning the obvious.

My gaze went straight to Sam, whose fear rang out like a gunshot.

"I think so," I said cautiously, trying to convey reassurance with my expression. "Maybe we should be careful, just in case."

No one except Sam seemed to be phased by my concern, probably because I wasn't very convincing. Tyler was the only one on Katie's radar and if she couldn't sire anyone, then he'd be safe for now. And the vamps had faithful blood donors, so no unnecessary killings *should* happen. But I'd been around them enough to know, vampires couldn't be trusted and I still didn't know Alora's lethal intentions beyond recruiting Nicholas and taking the necklace. My only hope was Phil and I would figure out how to stop them before they hurt anyone else.

"She'll come back," Dena said with confidence, her gaze lingering into Morgan's electric stare just before giving him a kiss. "And have some exotic story."

Dena's lack of concern bothered me, but their display of affection sliced like a razor across my heart, reminding me of Nicholas' change.

Would he ever look at me that way again—not just because he wanted my blood?

My eyes welled up in response.

"She will." Sam patted my back, noticing my sudden emotion, though misunderstanding who I was worried about.

"Yeah," I said, stuffing back the pain. "So, what's new?"

Dena quickly filled in the silence with recent gossip and I tuned her out, pretending to listen. I'd never felt lonelier in my life than at that moment. The insurmountable problems of Nicholas and Alora boomeranged around in my gut giving me a dull stomachache. More than anything, I wanted to wrap myself up in someone else's aura and escape this nightmare, but the only person who came to mind was Phil. Hot, irresistible, reborn Phil who was waiting for me in my bedroom right now.

Then my stomach lurched for real and I straightened up ready to dash to the bathroom.

"What's wrong?" Sam looked at me with concern.

"I'm not feeling so great all of a sudden." I gulped back the next wave of nausea.

"Yeah, you don't look so great." Dena grimaced.

"Can you get my assignments?" I slowly stood and averted my eyes from my half-eaten lunch only looking at Sam. "I'm going home."

"Yeah, sure." Sam nodded.

With that, I made a beeline for my car.

Chapter Sixteen

"Oh hi," I said to my dad half-heartedly as I walked in the house, shocked to find him still at home. He looked back, just as surprised, with his keys in hand.

"What're you doing home?" His parental gullibility alarm shot out like water from a snaking hose turned on full blast.

"I don't feel good," I said and folded my arms tightly around my midriff and felt a sheen of sweat gloss across my skin. "Can you call school and tell them I won't be back to class?"

"You left class and didn't let your teacher know?"

"I left at lunch because I almost got sick in front of everyone, so I just came home. Please call." *Please?*

"Are you telling me the truth, young lady?" Dad asked, the infamous sleeper-wave scowl prominently displayed on his brow.

"Yeah." I gulped, suddenly unsure where this anger and doubt stemmed from when I really was telling the truth for once.

Did Nicholas show up looking for me? Did Phil do something? Did the cops call with more information about Katie's disappearance? For a second, I wished for mind reading abilities, cowering under the pressure of my dad's fierce stare.

Dad finally put his hand to my forehead and hummed in acknowledgment. "You do seem warm."

"I'm not faking."

"All right," he said, finally emanating genuine concern but still keeping a gruff exterior. "You should probably go lie down."

I nodded my head in agreement then glanced at the keys in his hand. "Are you going somewhere?"

"Just shopping. Do you need anything? Medicine? Soup? Gatorade?"

"Don't talk about food." I pressed my hand to my mouth to stave off the queasiness as I ran for the toilet.

"Are you okay?" I heard Dad ask uncomfortably through the bathroom door.

"Yeah," I mumbled and flushed the toilet, overwhelmed with weak limbs all of a sudden.

"I'm . . . leaving . . . I'll be right back."

I grunted and stayed on the floor, not wanting to move. Phil was around somewhere, curious and quiet.

After I heard my dad's car back out of the driveway I wondered where Phil was hidden and was surprised he hadn't checked on me yet. Maybe he knew why my dad was so furious at me.

"I know you can hear me," I said feebly. "I'm sick."

He appeared magically—startling me—covered from head to toe in a black robe, looking like the grim reaper.

"Do you want to go upstairs?" His voice was soft and comforting, making me thankful that my dad had left—he'd done a great job raising us as a single dad, but barfing was something he just couldn't stomach.

I frowned at Phil's strange appearance, but felt too drained to ask, only nodded.

Carefully, he lifted me off the floor, and instead of walking, he flew me upstairs, cradled within his arms. I laid my head against the folds of his robe, inhaling the odd aroma of mothballs. He touched down lightly and pushed aside the books on my bed before he laid me down.

One particular notebook caught my eye then disappeared. I blinked to make sure I wasn't seeing things; the embarrassment Phil gave forth told me otherwise.

"You read my diary?" I asked as my chest tightened, slightly turning my head on the pillow to meet his gaze.

"No," he lied, flipping the hood off his head to reveal a sheepish grin playing on his mouth. A really sexy mouth that I remembered kissing not too long ago.

"Sure you weren't," I muttered with a deep inhale, contemplating if I should pummel him or just try to put on pajamas or not.

"I was really bored."

"Bored? Maybe no one ever taught you this, but it's never okay to read someone's diary!" I screeched before giving him another once over. "And *what* are you wearing anyway?"

"You like it?" As Phil turned in a circle, the black folds of the fabric billowed outwards. The ensemble looked like he was ready to go live in a monastery. "Found it in the closet."

"Do you realize you're wearing my brother's Halloween costume?"

"Really? I wondered. But it's a good thing. I have to protect my pretty skin from being singed and sunscreen always gives me such a *nasty rash*," he said in a snarky tone, then stripped off the robe and threw it on my desk chair, covering up the white *Scream* mask that lay on the seat.

I couldn't help but laugh. Thank God he didn't wear the whole costume, or I might have had a coronary.

He sat next to me with a syrupy grin, but I glared back, annoyed he'd practically snooped through every inch of my room. I wished Nicholas were here to take care of me instead. He'd never disrespect my privacy.

"You're *so* hilarious." I powerlessly attempted to kick off my Converse, but quickly gave up and curled limply on my side. "Why would my diary be of any interest to you anyway?"

Phil ducked his head and helped me take my shoes off all the way. Then he tucked me under a blanket. My anger diffused and my flu-ridden body collapsed.

"I only wanted to—" Phil gulped down his apparent discomfort, "—get a handle on Nick's story, so we could help him. But you didn't say a whole lot about him. Though you did say some nice things about me, I might add."

The satisfaction ebbed from his self-contented smile. I rolled my eyes but fire hit my cheeks anyway as I remembered I'd gushed about how beautiful he was over several entries. Back in the day, when I didn't know Nicholas had feelings for me and Phil was still human, I did mention I fantasized about kissing him.

"Remind me to edit those pages," I said with as much contempt as possible. "I didn't mention him for good reason. I *have* had vampires steal important things with vital information and use them against me in the past as you may recall."

Phil snorted while I gave him my most convincing evil eye, trying feebly to be threatening. My newly acquired green complexion and inability to lift my head off the pillow surely made my attempt pretty laughable.

"That was the old Phil," he said with a compelling smirk.

He pulled the blanket up to my chin and something golden flashed from his neckline—a cross. My mother's cross.

"What's that?" I asked with a gasp, pointing towards his chest.

"I . . . I planned to ask you. Only to borrow it," he said, flashing puppy dog eyes.

His fear erupted and rolled over me, making my stomach hurt again. I clutched my waist and closed my eyes, too exhausted to fight him.

"You need to get one of your own. You can't borrow this one. It's . . . special," I mumbled into my pillow.

With a feather-like touch, Phil took a hold of my hand and placed the necklace within my palm, curling my fingers around the chain. I brought my hand to my chest, thinking of her and experiencing his apology at the same time; his regret made me feel reprehensible.

"I'm sorry. I just feel like crap and don't want to do anything but sleep."

"No. It's my bad for not asking."

I opened my eyes to meet his. For a moment we watched one another. Phil reached over and moved a wayward strand of hair away from my cheek. My breath caught in my throat for a second. If I wanted, all I needed to do was move slightly upward and a kiss would happen, easily.

I immediately forced my eyes shut and wallowed in my guilt. He grew disappointed and faded into the background, somewhere in my room, struggling with his desire to be near me.

The urge to say something plagued my mind: to define our relationship again, to ask what else he snooped into today. But I chose not to. Though I liked Phil at one point, I loved Nicholas with all my being. And whatever it took, I would help Nicholas recover from this addiction so we could be together again, forever. And Phil already knew this.

I tried to sleep, but couldn't. As soon as I'd drift off, Phil's longing would flood in and distract me, waking me up. We were stuck in my room, torturing each other, neither able to leave.

"I can't sleep," I finally said, slowly rolling over to face him. "Do you have any idea why my dad was super mad at me when I got home?"

"Oh, that," Phil said, smoothing his blonde hair back with his hand, eyes plastered to the floor.

"What happened?" I asked with more urgency and sat up on my elbows, immediately anxious due to his sudden disquiet.

"Let's see . . . your dad checked further into whatever you told the cops about Katie standing you up and figured you were probably with someone instead of her and grilled Luke about it. He kind of 'fessed up to your secret relationship with Nick."

With each word my heart beat harder, sending electric jolts down my legs. The blood drained from my face, changing my complexion into a horrid shade of ghost white.

"And your dad also turned on the GPS to your car, so . . . yeah, you're in a lot of trouble."

I fell back into my pillows, feeling an entirely new sickness wash over me. With a moan, I covered my eyes with my hands. "Crud." I wanted to say something a heck of a lot stronger. Phil moved next to me and rubbed my shoulder.

"But you don't have to worry about that because you've got me. And so far . . . " He patted himself down with his free hand. "I'm GPS-less, so you could still *sneak out* if you wanted."

In spite of how horrible I felt, I glanced up into his darling eyes and chuckled. It was either that or cry, and I was afraid if I cried, I'd never stop.

"But, hey, I've checked on our man Nick and he's on the up and up."

He faked a smile and I knew he'd stretched the truth even without feeling it. I looked away, not wanting to seem upset. How could he lie to me at a time like this?

He acted like he wanted Nicholas to get better, even going so far as to call him "our man" but I sensed he hoped the opposite. Without Nicholas around, I'd become a free woman with options. And a part of me was still super attracted to Phil, taking all my effort to keep from encouraging the attention he gave me. Plus, I didn't have a clue what Scarlett's intentions were or even why she'd want to help cure Nicholas. I could be playing right into the enemy's hands.

Asking pointed questions would delve into Phil's lie, helping me flush out his deception. The problem was, I wasn't sure if I really wanted to know the truth. Deep down, I needed to believe Nicholas really was getting better because I didn't know what I would do if he didn't. And I wouldn't accept failure without a fight. Once I got my strength back, I'd be on a mission to find him.

"You could show a little bit more enthusiasm." Phil moved into my direct line of sight, breaking my internal struggle.

"Yeah . . . good news." I tried to turn up the corners of my lips. "Can I see him soon?"

"Sure," he said, seeping a tiny bit of resentment.

I hid my face under my arm, trapped in this never ending rollercoaster called my life. My stomach felt like it was about to pitch another fit.

"You okay?" Phil asked in sudden uncertainty.

"I need sleep, but I can't." *Until you stop telling lies and turn off your hormones.*

"Want another pill?"

The suggestion sounded mighty tempting but I didn't trust him until I could hide my diary in a more secret place. "Uh."

"I have a better idea," he said with his adorable cocky grin. I held my breath anxious for what his surprise would be. "Did you pick up any books from the library?"

I chuckled inside for being so silly with my anticipation. "I did. Check my bag."

For a brief moment, he disappeared then reappeared with the

stack of books in hand. I cringed as he flipped through each one. His disappointment was disheartening when I had tried so hard to find good *guyish* novels.

"Oh, I love this one." He produced the weathered copy of *Jurassic Park*. "Have you read it?"

I faintly smiled in response. "No, but I saw the movie."

"Oh, then we have to read this together," he said and got comfortable at the foot of my bed. "The movie doesn't *even* do the book justice."

His plan worked as his amorous feelings faded, brimming with intrigue instead and I closed my eyes to listen. The sound of pages flipping was music to my ears. I hadn't been read to since I was a child.

Phil cleared his throat. "The InGen Incident. The late twentieth century . . ."

I hummed before sleep slowly took over my senses.

Chapter Seventeen

At first I giggled, nestling myself in the thick satiny blanket of clouds, marveling in the fantastical escape, enjoying the soft breeze playing with my hair. Here, I didn't have to feel anything other than my own feelings, which seemed to be reflective of the magical carpet floating beneath me.

I eventually crawled to the edge and peered down, my chin resting on top of my hands, amazed at how solid the cloud felt beneath me. Below, the streams of water flowed from epic mountains towards a sparkling never-ending sea. The luscious landscape undulated with breathtaking untouched beauty of forests, meadows, and sandy beaches. I rolled over and let the sun warm my skin. In the distance, birds sang and the waves crashed, creating the perfect lullaby.

Firm, yet gentle hands scooped under my shoulder blades, lifting me up. I opened my eyes to peer into the dark outline of Nicholas; the sun hung in the sky perfectly behind his head, leaping rays of light from the ends of his tousled brown hair.

The air bounded out from my lungs, escaping with it all the tension I'd stored as I collapsed. Gratefulness flowed through my body and I finally felt free from the nightmare. I wrapped my arms around his neck and brought my mouth to his; his breath was the most delectable fragrance of dew and freshly baked cookies. Our lips floated back and forth in harmony across one another's, playing a sweet song I longed to compose. Then he took my face between his hands and pressed his lips onto my skin, kissing away the tears of happiness I didn't realize I'd wept.

"I love you," he whispered in my ear. "I've always loved you."

We rolled over, cushioned perfectly by the clouds, and I found myself laughing, snuggling into his chest. With a soft touch, I caressed his angelic face and brushed my fingers over his lips as he kissed them.

"And I love you," I replied.

Everything seemed utterly flawless until the warmth grew into unbearable heat. I looked over the edge to find the landscape had changed into a desert, void of any greenery or life. We panicked, using our hands to paddle back towards the utopia. But our motions seemed to cause the cloud beneath us to break apart. We clung to the dissolving cottony shapes, but this time, I didn't wake up. Once the last puff disappeared, we fell downward from the sky into the mouth of a volcano.

Anticipating we'd sizzle to our deaths, I screamed and closed my eyes. But we stopped and floated in the scalding air, barely above the smoldering aperture as the fiery smoke licked at our feet. In shock, I gaped at Nicholas, who stared back at me with shame covering his countenance, as he flew us safely away from the danger.

"You can fly?" I asked in amazement.

"I have a secret," he said, verdigris eyes resonating something dark beneath. He reached behind his neck and pulled his hair, ripping off a mask in one fluid motion to reveal he was actually Phil underneath.

"Phil," I mumbled in a gasp. "It's you."

"Forever at your service," he said, his lips curled up on one side of his mouth. "I'm sorry, but I knew you'd never accept me for me, but now you know you do love me."

I blinked in wonderment, but felt unfazed by his deception. He was right. And, actually I was terribly relieved and the overwhelming desire to kiss him flooded my body.

I leaned in, lips puckered when Phil let out a gasp of pain and panic filled behind his eyes.

"Never," I heard Nicholas shout from the ground.

"No," Phil screamed as his body started to become consumed in fire. My scream followed after his as our bodies tumbled downwards towards the ground.

"No, Phil, no!" I felt the super-heated air suck all the moisture, leaving my throat parched. My lips cracked and started to bleed. I shuddered just before hitting the ground, waking up in a ball of sweat.

"Water," I choked out.

Within seconds, a cool glass of water appeared before me in the dark. I took it and sucked down the liquid in three large gulps. The water washed away the reprehensible feeling lining my gut for wanting Phil so badly.

"Nicholas?" I asked, in a groggy stupor.

I waited, judging the aura in front of me and realized it couldn't possibly be him. Not only had he insisted I never invite him inside my house, he'd never exude jealousy at the mention of his name.

"No," the silhouette washed in moonlight said. "It's me. Phil."

"Oh." I looked away, embarrassed, reality and my vision coming into clearer focus. The clock beyond him read 2:20 AM. "What day is it?"

"It's Tuesday, well, Wednesday actually."

I sat back into the pillows and tried to make sense of my surroundings as visions of the dream remained at the forefront of my mind. A horrid taste laced my mouth and my stomach felt like a washer spinning a load of rocks. "You didn't go out tonight?"

Phil got up from the corner of my bed and sat down at my desk chair, oozing disappointment. "I came back early. I was worried about you. You've been thrashing around, talking in your sleep."

Soft light streamed in and frolicked across the naturally blonde streaks in his hair, illuminating his pale skin. The sight was angelic like my dream. For a brief second, the same attraction I experienced in my dream rose up again inside my chest.

"Oh," I said, looking downward, feeling majorly embarrassed, unable to handle his radiating countenance. "What did I say?"

"Well," he said with humor in his voice. "I think you were professing your love for me before something horrible happened."

"Did not," I quipped quickly, wanting to hide under my covers in utter humiliation.

"Sounded like it to me . . ." He coughed to cover his laugh, reveling in his glory. "Our secret," he said with a wink.

I hardened my lips. "But I wasn't . . ."

He chuckled. "Feeling better?"

"Kind of," I said meekly, feeling rather uncomfortable from sleeping in my clothes. Slowly, I peeled my body from within my sheets and touched my feet to the ground. "You didn't have to come back so soon." *And overhear my embarrassing dream.*

"Well . . ." He melted into the playful Phil I knew well and adored. "Believe me, I wasn't excited to go back and get the whole twenty questions thing. This was the perfect excuse."

"Go back?" I stopped to give him a puzzled expression before stooping to get my pajamas off the floor on my way to the bathroom.

"Yeah, and give an update. It's hard to keep secrets when you report to a mind-reader," he said with a snort.

I swiveled around a little too fast and had to use the wall to steady myself. "Whoa, you're supposed to be spying on me?"

"Well, yeah. Why else do you think she brought me back? I'm the mole." Phil held up his hands quickly. "I mean, don't get me wrong, I'm totally on your side. Luckily she can only read what I'm thinking the moment she touches me. And actually—" he smirked "—after the last hand meld, she's not touched me since."

I continued on towards the bathroom and rubbed my eyes, wondering if I was still dreaming. His honesty was the only thing reassuring me I could trust him, but his casual candor muddied my brain, making my head thick with gunk.

"Hand meld?" I said from behind the cracked door with a toothbrush in my mouth.

"You know, she touches you and melts into your head."

Suddenly, I remembered all too well, flashing back to when Phil—a newly sired vampire—took me to meet her for her approval, after he'd kidnapped me.

"But how can you avoid thinking about stuff she wants to know? Especially if she asks questions point blank?" I asked and came back out, headed directly for my bed happy to be in my comfy jammies.

Phil raised his left eyebrow. "I show her where I've been instead. It's a reality she really doesn't want to face, believe me. None of us do."

The word *Hell* ricocheted through my mind. I wasn't sure if I could handle an in-depth discussion of *that* place, wanting to forget it existed as badly as Alora did.

"Oh," I said, holding my temples and pressing inward with my fingertips. "This is a lot to take in."

"It's okay, Parker . . . Seriously. No worries."

I slid under the covers and closed my eyes, hoping to just fall asleep again, wanting to avoid everything while Phil grew wistful. He apparently had something serious he wanted to talk about. Internally, I willed him to wait until the morning, when I knew I'd feel a little more level headed, but his courage burst like a bubble and I braced myself for the onslaught.

"I wanted to ask you something."

My eyes flicked open to catch his gaze, the seriousness thick between us. In the blue light, I saw a glitter of a tear in Phil's eye and felt my stubbornness dissolve. "Yeah?"

"Are my parents still . . . *looking* for me?"

I took in a quick breath. "No," I said serenely. "Nicholas burned down the building you were in. They used dental records to identify you from the teeth they found—both yours and Justin's. They held a service after—it was really nice. A whole bunch of people came. I had a hard time though, because I felt responsible."

"Oh," Phil said somberly. "I passed by the house. My parents have moved."

"I—I didn't know. I'm really sorry. Maybe it was hard, living here, knowing you'd—" I couldn't finish.

His longing hurt exposed the pain I'd felt all these years missing my mom. I couldn't imagine being on the other side, dealing with the knowledge people who loved me still mourned my death when I was very much alive. "I bet they went back to Los Angeles. I could help you find them, if you want."

"And what would I say? 'Hi Mom and Dad. Sorry for the misunderstanding, but I'm alive. Except I've got this disease where I want to drink blood, I never age, and I can't go out in the sun. It's also made my eyes black.' Not likely."

"Well, even if you can't talk to them, you could visit from a distance."

"No. I'd rather not risk it. It's better they think I'm dead anyway."

My heart continued to ache alongside his and I didn't know what to say to fix it."I wish I knew of a cure," I finally said.

"Me too." Phil shook his head then suddenly stood to his feet with hardened eyes on my bedroom window. He inflated with sudden hostility. "Oh, crap."

I glanced at the window too, sensing the animalistic loathing attached to whoever was outside. Apparently another vampire that Phil didn't have a good relationship with had stalked us and intended to do God-knows-what.

"Who is it?" I whispered.

Phil crouched down and hid behind my bed, but not because he was afraid. His sudden feelings of protection radiated out.

"Hide," he whispered back.

I pulled the covers up to my nose and disappeared under the pillows, only peering out of a small crack between them. The hate from the unknown predator riddled my body with nervousness, though I knew they couldn't enter uninvited.

Someone hit the windowpane and I squealed, expecting them to crash through.

"Get out here, Parasite, before I rip this house down," Nicholas growled through the window, his green eyes full of fire.

My breath accelerated once I recognized him and I burst out of my protective 300 thread-count barricade, scrambling to go to the window. "Nicholas?"

Phil jumped up from behind my bed and grabbed my arm to stop me. "Calm down, Nick, you need to think about what you're doing. Julia's family can hear you."

"I am calm and I don't like you around my girl."

I pulled against Phil's restraining hand and swooned because Nicholas called me "my girl." Everything inside me wanted to throw my arms around his chest and hold him tightly. That would be all he needed to take the pain away.

Phil moved quickly and created a barrier in front of me, puffing out his chest with a guard-like stance. He firmly kept his hand on my arm, trapping me behind his body. "Until you can be trusted, I'm protecting her."

Nicholas' brutish expression tightened, his glare locking onto Phil, consumed with revenge. "That's my job, you two-time traitor. Step. Outside. Now."

"Dude, you're just *jonesing* for a fix. Calm down and hang alone for a while," he said ardently. "The urge will pass."

Nicholas' feral eyes flicked towards mine as I peered over Phil's shoulder. "You can't hide in there forever," he seethed directly at me.

I knew the bad part of him was speaking; only interested in retrieving the necklace. His true suffering crushed my spirit and left me helpless as I watched the viciousness hold full control, torturing any goodness within him. From inside my being, I did the only thing I could do. From my heart I beamed out all the love I could muster, hoping he'd feel it somehow. Hoping it would help with his agony. Hoping he'd back down and think rationally.

Miraculously, for a second his carnal expression softened and behind Nicholas' exhausted human eyes was a glimmer of hope. He roared, consumed with affliction before he vanished.

I stood, gasping for air and broke free of Phil's hold. In desperation, I ran towards the window. Nicholas was nowhere to be seen. I turned around, concerned my family might have heard Nicholas, to find Phil stunned. The panic filled up behind his eyes.

"Dude, we need to see Scar, and quickly."

Chapter Eighteen

"Do I really need to go?" I asked, silently refusing to put on the sweatshirt Phil had just handed me. I watched him look for my other shoe. If I was going anywhere, it would be to find and help Nicholas. Not to see Scarlett.

"Um . . . yeah." He hesitated.

"Why don't you go and I stay here?" I asked, tempted to crawl back under the covers, lacking any energy whatsoever to even move.

Phil sat next to me and helped me put each arm into the sleeves. "Because I don't know where to go."

"What?" I turned my head slowly towards him, jaw partly open. "You said you checked up on him."

"I did, indirectly. He wasn't with Alora, so I figured he was good," Phil said, while finding my missing Converse under my bed and putting both shoes back on my feet.

"Good?" I clenched my hands into fists, trying to keep composure and not scream at the top of my lungs, waking my family. "I wouldn't say what Nicholas just did was *good*."

Wrestling my foot free, I kicked him away with my last bit of energy and curled into the fetal position. With closed eyes, I began cursing at myself for putting all my trust in Phil and Scarlett without even checking to see if they knew what they were doing.

Phil touched my shoulder. "Scar said she'd take him to his place, so we just need to go and get her preferably before dawn, or else—"

Phil made a sound that resembled something exploding into a ball of fire—the juvenile noise boys made when playing war. I sighed, annoyed at his inappropriate humor. Dawn meant something entirely different for me, including my life being taken away. And pretending nothing bothered me while my crazed boyfriend roamed the streets, threatening to stalk me. All packaged up with a pretty little bow of another sleepless night.

"Shoot me now," I said, my voice laced with disdain. "Oh, and Scarlett's not coming here, so don't even ask."

"I don't get why you hate her so badly."

I opened one eye and gave him the *"don't even ask"* look to which he held up his hands in disgust.

"I have school tomorrow," I rolled my back to him and mumbled in my pillow. "I need to sleep."

"I doubt you'll be going."

"Since when are you my keeper?" I barked, refusing to agree though I knew he was right. "If I'm not well enough to go to school, I'm not well enough to go now."

"Scar's in trouble and may need our help."

"I hate that you keep calling her that. It sounds like you're referring to the bad lion in *The Lion King*."

"There's a bad lion?"

"Never mind . . . geez, I can't believe this is happening." I tangled my hands in my hair. "You think you can just waltz in here and charm me—"

"I'm not trying to charm you. I'm trying to help. We've got it under control—"

"Under control?" I spit while trying to contain my unamused laughter. "Excuse me, but didn't you just see our apparently perfectly-fine Nicholas a second ago? He's far from being under control and is running around somewhere, angry and upset, thinking we are—" I gulped back the sudden pain emanating from the gaping hole where my heart used to be and took a deep breath. "He needs me. I should really be looking for *him*, not Scarlett. Why did I leave him? Why did we let him go?" I was standing now, flailing my arms at his rock-hard chest.

"Parker, if I would have left you there, with him like that, you'd be like me now—but evil or even dead. Don't think the *power of love* or whatever you guys think you have would have changed that fact."

"As if." I turned to glower at him before collapsing on my bed and put my head back into my hands. "I'm so sick of this." To keep from yelling, I slowly rocked back and forth. More than anything I wanted to be alone and far away from him, preferably in Nicholas' arms. "I don't think I have the energy to do it."

"Look," he said quickly "I'll carry you there and back, wrapped up in a blanket like a burrito if you want, but you have to come."

Suddenly, it dawned on me I didn't have a clue where to go. Nicholas had never taken me to his house. I rolled over, putting my back to Phil and moaned.

"Please," he begged. "It's important."

I laid there in exile trying to figure a way to avoid telling Phil the truth, assuming once he found out, he'd laugh his ass off. Every piece of me was on fire with embarrassment.

I forced my eyes shut and thought really hard. Nicholas had once told me he lived in a desolated area, in the Santa Cruz Mountains. My mind whirred, trying to figure out how I could find his exact address without alerting Phil, when the solution popped into my brain.

The cell phone receipt.

Luckily, I wore the same jeans I'd worn the night we'd purchased the phone. Of course, the contract must have required his personal details. Discreetly, I pulled it out and sure enough, Nicholas had written his address at the top.

"It's Bear Creek Road," I breathed in relief. "1217."

"Where's that?" Phil replied innocently, not paying attention to what I was doing.

Crap. "Um . . ."

Phil snickered. "I don't have a satellite link to Google maps, you know."

"I know," I stammered, feeling stupider by the minute. If only I had my iPhone to look it up. The computer downstairs seemed so far away. "It's up on the ridge."

"What's that in your hand?" Phil asked with amusement.

"Nothing," I said while trying to shove the paper back into my pocket, but Phil snatched it from my hand before I could.

"What's this, Parker?"

Phil's shock, wonder, and slight envy played through his mind, like he'd just rapidly flipped the dial through a barrage of radio stations while my cheeks must have blazed fire-engine red. I waited for the dial to land on a smug note, but Phil felt bad instead and handed me back the paper.

"I've never been to his house," I barked. "Happy?"

"Easy there, it's not a big deal," he said, backing down instantly. "Let's just get the directions."

A part of me wanted to spit out all the reasons why I'd never been there, all pointing towards Nicholas' honor of course. But another part, the one that felt Phil clearly still had feelings for me, wanted to let the moment go and spare him the embarrassment like he'd spared mine.

"Yeah, good idea," I said softly.

Phil volunteered to get the directions and disappeared downstairs to use my dad's computer while I waited in my room, slowly putting my shoes back on. A big part of me suddenly wanted to go and see where he lived, giving me a burst of hidden energy.

But mostly I wondered where Nicholas ran off to, confused why he didn't just stay outside and wait for us to leave in order to nab me or fight Phil when the opportunity presented itself. But, mysterious or not, we had to take advantage of his sudden absence.

Looking again at the receipt, my finger grazed over his signature, causing moisture to well up in my eyes. Just a few days ago when he signed this, he was normal—normal and wonderful—and we had such plans for our future.

I bit my lip and pushed my anguish down, wiping away a tear with the back of my hand as Phil returned. I pretended to be tying my shoe laces.

"Got the directions," he said in excitement. "You ready?"

I nodded and gulped down the rest of the tears threatening to cascade down my cheeks, forcing my lips to smile when I noticed a black box by my door.

On the top was a little yellow post-it from my dad.

Hope you are feeling better soon.
Love Dad.

Inside I found a new iPhone with a pink cover, my favorite color. The gesture warmed my heart. He wasn't as mad as I thought he was after all.

The phone felt sleek in my hands as I turned it on, happy to be reunited with my connection to the world. The screen illuminated and flashed a beautiful sunset, similar to the one Nicholas and I watched regularly on our beach, making my heart feel heavy in my chest. I pushed back the grief and touched the screen to check my text messages instead, to which I had none.

Phil paid no attention and rushed to the window, standing on the ledge while I turned off the phone and pocketed it. I slowly moved to the window, a little less eager. A rough breeze blew against me, making me shiver. I zipped up my sweatshirt.

"Is he out there?" I asked, sensing nothing beyond Phil's curiosity and slight hesitation.

"Nope," he said with a whisper. "Come on."

Disappointed, I climbed onto the roof and stood next to Phil, noticing a twinkle in his eye when I turned and looked up at him. Suddenly, I found myself wrapped up in his arms, flying up into the night sky. The massiveness of the full moon stole my breath away but all I wished for was to be in Nicholas' arms instead.

My mind drifted towards protecting Phil and giving him a heads up about the venom T-shirts until I remembered Nicholas' super-power stakes. And I wasn't sure if I could reveal the secrets without Harry's permission. Maybe a chain mail shirt of teeth could defeat the stakes, though it would take a lot of vampire deaths to make one.

"What are you thinking about?" Phil finally asked over the wind, his voice pulling me back into reality.

"Protecting you," I said reluctantly.

"From your boyfriend?" Phil chuckled. "Cute, but completely unnecessary."

"I think you should be leery of him. He is a vampire slayer you know."

Phil laughed, refreshingly. "He can't hurt me."

My eyes tightened. "Don't you remember what happened the last time?"

"He can't do it twice. Double jeopardy. I'm invincible against him now."

"You're what?" I stated with a stutter. "How?"

"It's just one of those things Alora figured out. Apparently you can't kill a vamp twice. She *is* the brains behind this whole resurrection operation after all. Plus she likes me, another reason why I made a good candidate to bring back."

My heart quivered at the gravity of the situation. Thinking about Bettina, Angelia, and the rest of the vampires coming back in revenge, protected with sudden invincibility made me shudder. Nicholas would have to rely on me to defeat the ones he'd previously killed and vice versa. Yet another step towards the prophecy coming to fruition.

"How did she do it?"

"Bring me back? I don't know," he said calmly. "Like I said, I woke up naked and mighty grateful."

"This is insane," I said under my breath. "How am I supposed to defeat her? All of them?"

"You won't need to do that," he said sympathetically. "Scar and I have a plan, plus you'll recruit Nick to our side. He just needs a little time to regroup."

More than anything I wanted to believe him, but after what happened and the doubt emanating from Phil, I was left with a sour taste in my mouth. I appreciated his desire to console me but even Phil knew the likelihood Nicholas would choose to be on Alora's side over mine. That meant Nicholas was lost to me forever unless I was changed—again—making the prediction painfully clear. He would die along with the rest and apparently at my hand. Fate drove a hard bargain.

We arrived above his street, Nicholas' house hidden within the thick cover of redwood trees. I scanned the area for him, coming up blank. More than anything I wanted Nicholas to be nearby to steal me away; wake me up and tell me this was all a bad dream.

Phil touched down and gave the surroundings a once over.

"It's safe," I said, pushing past him towards the house, no longer wanting to pretend like I didn't know.

Phil studied my face quizzically. "You've got that psychic connection with him don't you? I forgot."

I snorted. "Yeah, kind of," *but unfortunately, it's with everyone.*

Phil shrugged and caught up with me easily, grabbing onto my hand. For a moment, I didn't want him to but his confidence fused into my being, making our task seem less daunting. Together, we walked up the path to the wooden porch.

Nicholas lived in a small rugged log cabin nestled in the forest. I marveled at how charming it was, just like I'd imagined.

Phil reached forward and instead of knocking, pushed against the wooden door, swinging it wide open. Scarlett sat inside on the floor, her arms wrapped around her legs, her head propped against her knees. I silenced myself against her deafening defeat.

Immediately, I dropped Phil's hand, almost expecting to find Nicholas inside. It stung that he'd never taken me to his place before.

Nicholas' living area was simple and immaculate, yet sterile; almost like a hotel room except boxes lined the walls. On one end of the room, in a nook, stood a queen sized bed with an end table and a lamp. Next to it was his dresser, bare except for a solitary framed photo. I walked over and picked it up. Alora—human and very lovely—stared back at me with green eyes. She stood in a kitchen, wearing a white sundress and laughing, holding wild flowers out to the person behind the camera. The talisman caught my eye—bright crimson—catching the light of the flash.

I grimaced while setting the picture down, instinctively cradling the talisman with my fingertips. The stone still remained dead beneath my touch.

I continued to look around, noticing the surf boards propped in the corner. The guitar though—abandoned on the couch—did me in. I walked towards the instrument and traced the frets with my fingers, hoping to draw closer to Nicholas somehow. He'd been there, recently playing. Pieces of paper with handwritten lyrics sat on the coffee table. The title read "My Pretty Little Flower." It took all my concentration to keep from bursting into tears.

Phil coughed from the doorway. I glanced over and realized he couldn't come in.

"You're invited," I whispered.

Phil nonchalantly moved forward and put his hand on Scarlett's shoulder.

"He's gone," Scarlett said breathlessly, without looking up.

"Is he doing okay?"

She shook her head. "I tried. The evil is strong. He's been suppressing that side for too long. It's now raging out of control. He's not slept or eaten anything since the change. He . . . he got away."

"What's that on your arm?" Phil said, turning over her wrist. Two purple curved scars lined the inside of her delicate forearm. "Did he . . .?"

"It . . . was an accident." Scarlett looked away, pulling back her hand, ashamed. "I . . . it's tied us together."

"What?" I exclaimed, coming out of my fog, feeling very disturbed they shared that type of euphoria together and were connected somehow because of it. "What do you mean you're tied together now?"

"I sense what he senses and I think he senses me too."

Anger washed over me, leaving nothing but jealousy in its wake. "I can't believe you let this happen. You—" I pointed my finger at her, "—this is all *your* fault!"

I rushed her, climbing over the coffee table with fists drawn. Phil stepped between us, holding me back. "Whoa there, Parker, calm down."

"Let me at her!" I barked, wishing he'd give me just one second to land a much deserved punch. Phil firmly sat me back down on the couch. I struggled, frustrated I was still weakened from my flu, withholding the horrible names I wanted to call her.

"Do you think, by telling Nicholas about Alora, things would have been different?"

"Yes," I said indignantly. "We could have been better prepared. I could have told him what he'd be up against. Warned him. Been truthful and upfront."

"He would have gone after her," she said darkly. "You know he would have. The coincidence that she had the same name as his mother would have been too ironic."

My eyes burned into hers. I didn't want to agree. I wanted to hate her, blame her, scratch her face off, call her ugly names, but I couldn't. From within her heart flowed sincerity, grief and exhaustion.

"It's in the past now," Phil said, loosening his grip on me. "We need to figure out a new game plan so we can stop her."

Ignoring Phil, I gritted my teeth. "Where'd he go?" Jealousy ravaged my bones, disgusted they shared a special blood-bond, almost like he'd cheated on me.

Scarlett looked off to the side. "He's alone for now, wrestling with himself."

"Where? I should be with him."

Her eyes darted back to mine, concern glittering out. "No, it's not safe yet."

"Of course you'd say that. You're always calling the shots whether or not it's the best thing!" I bellowed.

"Parker, she's right." Phil squeezed my hand. His calm melted into me from his body to mine, relaxing me though I fought it. I scowled and pulled my hand away, wanting to stay mad.

We were all suddenly quiet—but only on the outside. When I felt both Phil and Scarlett's agitation rise at the same time, I knew they were telepathically talking to each other.

"Quit it you two! If you have something to say, say it out loud," I growled.

"We—" Phil radiated nervousness, his eyes dancing between the two of us, "—think he needs more time, that's all. What he's going through right now is very *complicated*."

"I love that I'm the one now being kept in the dark." I let out a sarcastic howl. "He needs help, he needs someone who can understand him, he needs—" *me*.

Suddenly, I thought of Harry, his hero and father figure. Then I pictured him dead, unaware of Nicholas' change. A horrific hiccupping noise followed after I sucked the air into my lungs too sharply. Katie had specifically asked about the weapons when she kidnapped me, making everything painfully clear. Alora not only wants the necklace, she planned to get her hands on the weapons too–Harry's weapons. Maybe even Harry himself. "Oh no."

Scarlett's curiosity followed a shiver that ran along my hairline, radiating across my scalp. I instantly remembered, without the talisman's power, nothing stopped her from canvassing my mind. Internally, I bolted and fastened myself under Phil's feelings, hoping to confuse her, which it did.

"Knock it off," I said with a glare, getting up off the couch and moving to the other side of the room. "You have no business in my head."

I wanted to throw the talisman on the ground and smash it into tiny pieces for all the help it was doing.

"I—meant no harm," she said apologetically, laying her head down upon her knees again. For a moment, she looked vulnerable, like an abandoned child, lost and broken. I felt sorry for her for a second. A very *brief* second.

"I'm not helping anyone." Scarlett said and let out a long sigh.

I snorted in agreement. Phil's frustration erupted.

"Look," Phil's eyes burned into mine, "I need the *both* of you to knock this off and get along. This is huge and, believe it or not, we must work together as a team in order to survive."

"I'm not thrilled with the arrangement," I interrupted, glaring at Scarlett who'd turned her head away from us.

"Well, you don't have much of a choice," Phil said coolly, pulling me off to the side.

"She's a freaking mind reader," I whispered.

"And she's on our side, so I say suck it up, because it's the best weapon we've got to defeat her Highness and Minions

Incorporated. Don't you think?"

I folded my arms and pouted.

Phil put his arm around my shoulder and percolated compassion, "Come on, Parker. Scar's cool. She's always had your back since the beginning."

"Yeah, but she told me not to tell Nicholas about Alora and look what's happened?"

"No one is to blame except Alora about how that all went down. Scar's right. If you'd have told him earlier, he'd have gone after her and ended up in the same place. The reunion was bound to happen. At least now, you have an opportunity to help."

I grunted, refusing to agree.

"Even still, Jules. Why'd you just freak out a second ago?"

Phil was more concerned than he let himself feel. This time, the "Jules" told me more than my gift did.

"I—" I wanted to tell him enough but not everything just in case. "Nicholas has someone he's fond of in L.A., like a Father figure. He could help and is super knowledgeable about vampire stuff, but he's unprotected now. I need to warn him."

"Okay." Phil nodded. "Where in L.A.?"

"Somewhere in Orange County."

Phil groaned. "Really?"

"Why? What's wrong?"

"Um—nothing. I can take you," Phil said apprehensively. "If I have to."

"I'll take her," Scarlett interjected, obviously eavesdropping, her voice suddenly soothing.

"You'll need to rest up first," Phil said over my shoulder, shooting her a look of concern.

Scarlett exhaled in exasperation. "I'll be better by tomorrow."

"I don't need either of you," I said quickly, turning around to face her. "I'll go alone."

Invisible warnings rung like sirens from the both of them.

"No," Phil said, while shaking his head. "That's not an option."

The tension escalated in the room while the three of us squared off, all wanting to do something different. Phil had already made up his mind and enforced domination over our motley crew even if it killed him.

"This is the deal," Phil finally said in determination, "Scarlett, you need to rest up and get your strength back. Julia, you'll stay home tomorrow and when Scar's better, she'll escort you during the day."

"Escort?" I let out a loud guffaw. "Not likely."

"Don't give me grief, Parker," Phil said, eyeing me firmly. "She'll be able to protect you when I can't."

"Protect me from Nicholas? Oh, brother," I said with an eye roll. "He isn't going to hurt me."

"We don't know that," Scarlett said in my mind.

"Shut-up," I spewed back. "You both seem to think you know how to handle this situation—how to handle Nicholas—but so far, you've majorly failed. I'm all for this—" I waved my hands in the air, trying to come up with a likely word to describe our group "— team *thing*, but I want to handle what happens with Nicholas. I can bring him to our side."

"No," they said simultaneously.

But before I could argue, darkness descended on Nicholas' house the moment someone crashed through the door, framed by Scarlett's scream. Her cry initially sounded more human than cat-like and echoed inside my head.

Chapter Nineteen

Phil's sudden movements were a whir. The rough grasp of his arms took my breath away as we catapulted upward. The sound of shattering glass followed a bellow from the living room. I craned my neck to see but, like a bullet, Phil climbed through the overshadowing redwoods into the moonlit sky, me in one arm and Scarlett, in cat form, in the other. I shook tiny broken pieces of glass and redwood twigs from my hair, watching them tumble out of sight with a shimmer. Phil had draped his arm over my head and pressed my face into his shoulder to protect me from injury when he'd broken through the ceiling.

"What happened?" I whispered in his ear.

"*Nicholas returned,*" Scarlett said.

I looked down as my heart agonized to be with him and caught a blur of movement beneath us, too quick for my eyes to focus on.

"*He's following,*" she said as if to confirm my suspicion, though I didn't let her back within my mind. I'd remembered to stick close to Phil's aura. "*We need to get back to your place before he does.*"

The increasing g-force pulled on my cheeks, sucking the moisture from my eyes. I leaned into Phil's chest and snapped my eyelids shut, wanting the ride to be over. "*What does Nicholas want?*" I asked Scarlett.

She remained quiet, terribly quiet.

"*I know you know. Tell me!*" I internally yelled.

"*The necklace, your blood, your life, what else?*"

Grief surrounded me, pulling me under the suffocating water of agony as the air ripped at my hair. He wasn't there to steal me away because he cared for me like I hoped. All he wanted was the talisman for his God-forsaken vampire mother.

If only I could press rewind and go back to the time when Nicholas was sane, so we could run far away from the nightmare of the future. But the lies that created this chaos had taken over, leaving nothing but destruction in its path. The insanity made me chuckle like a mad woman. Here I was, being flown through the cold of night at four in the morning with a fever while my blood-crazed boyfriend chased us, all over a piece of jewelry. I should have been in bed recovering.

Our bodies descended and I opened my eyes just enough to see we were back. Phil headed for the open window but when we entered, he stopped with a jerk, and I tumbled out of his arms onto the floor. With a loud crash, I plowed headfirst into the nightstand and knocked the lamp off the table.

My hand went to my brow, expecting blood to start trickling down my forehead while flashes of white lights skittered across my ceiling. Phil remained half-inside and out of the window, trying to bring Scarlett inside.

"I invite you," he whispered in determination.

When it didn't work, he cussed; still trapped at the frame with his body inside and Scarlett's out.

"Invite her!" he bellowed, his face stern.

I swiveled around, steadied myself with my hand, and flooded with a new sense of satisfaction. An evil smile crept on my lips.

"No," I said plainly. "She can finish what she was supposed to do earlier."

Phil wouldn't let go or stop trying to bring her inside. "Julia, don't do this. She has no strength to get away and Nicholas is almost here."

Scarlett leapt out of Phil's hands onto the ledge, her legs wobbling beneath her.

"No, you can't, Scarlett," Phil said, looking directly at her, as if she told him to leave her be.

I gritted my teeth and remained silent.

"I'm invincible but she's not," Phil implored. "For me, *please*."

I stared at both of them, feeling the anxiety grow to unbearable heights, amused their frustration didn't bother me. But when Phil's bravery burst open like a dam and he stepped outside and retrieved Scarlett, ready to confront Nicholas, I crumbled. Besides a debacle of that magnitude would surely get me grounded for the rest of my life.

"Fine, come in."

Phil darted through the window with Scarlett in his hands right after I felt Nicholas' loathing outrage.

"You better be potty trained," I mumbled, giving her a glare.

Scarlett hissed.

No one seemed to care I was injured on my bedroom floor. For a brief second, I contemplated escaping out the window myself. Phil brooded, watching out the window. Scarlett stayed perched next to him, still in cat form. When nothing happened, I finally got up and went to the bathroom to inspect the damage, noticing a large goose-egg forming just below my hairline.

Within minutes, on the other side of the bathroom door, Scarlett's concern swirled about, signaling she'd returned to human form. Their fretful emotions ebbed and flowed like a school of fish, echoing each other in a colorful rainbow of variety—telepathically discussing things, privy to Nicholas' mind now. Instead, I chose to canvass the exterior of my house and found Nicholas close by, acrimoniously plotting as well.

I wanted to reach out and remind him I loved him. When I projected my feelings earlier, the evil hold on his heart weakened. But with Flotsam and Jetsam guarding me, I didn't know how I could sneak away.

Unless . . . .

I pulled out my cell phone and quickly texted Nicholas.

- <

As I waited, my heart began to beat faster with each passing second, hoping the change hadn't erased his memories.

Please respond.

- 3

The buzz of the phone sent shivers of joy through my body. At the same time, a disturbance happened in my room. I reached over and quickly locked the door.

"Parker, what do you think you're doing?" Phil demanded quietly as his hand tried the knob.

"Fixing my head," I snipped. "Remember the gash I got because you threw me into the table earlier?"

"That's not what I mean."

I chuckled caustically. "Why do I need to tell you? Ask Ms. Nosey. She'll fill you in."

"Julia, you're playing with fire. Open the door and give me the phone."

- **I'd like to see you.**

My heart continued to pound at the words of his return text.

- **Me too.**

- **Is it too early for coffee?**

My lips crinkled into a knowing grin. Coffee cryptically meant he wanted to meet at our secret beach.

- **I can't. I'm sick.**

- **You are? What's wrong?**

I melted into a puddle, his concern slathering salve on my wounded soul.

- **The flu, I think.**

"Julia, don't make me break down the door," Phil said in a controlled voice.

"If you break down the door, I'll un-invite you," I seethed.

- **I wish I was there to be able to take care of you.**

I swooned in glee. Nicholas *was* back. My actions earlier gave strength to his good side and overcame the evil, bringing this whole nightmare to an end. I could kick Scarlett and Phil out forever and replace them with the man who I wanted to be with, the one who loved me unconditionally.

"He's trying to trick you into inviting him in," Phil said softly, brimming with distress. "Be careful what you say."

My hand froze over the keypad of my return text. I'd planned to say, *"I wish you were here too."* Indirectly, it was an invitation to come inside. A bead of sweat rolled down my temple when I realized Phil was right. I'd been ignoring how he really felt, so desperate to have him back in my life.

"I un-invite you Nicholas," I breathed just in case, my throat thick with heartache. Then I turned off my phone.

My lower lip quivered as I reached out to find him in my front yard. The sinister workings of his evil side gave me the chills. Phil and Scarlett had been right all along. There was no way I could be alone with him and not become his victim. He was solely fueled by manipulation and lies, aimed at taking back the necklace no matter the cost. I curled up on the floor, wishing I could pass out and escape.

"Julia," Phil said kindly, his hand rocking the door knob again. "Come out."

I pressed my eyes shut, keeping the tears inside. "No," I choked out. "Not when *she's* out there."

"Scarlett doesn't want to see you suffering either," he said calmly.

"Yeah right." I balled up the corner of the rug and squeezed as hard as I could. "She just wants to ransack my mind and use my secrets against me."

"Not at all," Phil said sweetly. "She's a good and decent person. We all misjudge situations. It's normal. We're both very sorry about all of this. Really."

I rested my head on my arm. The cold tiles pressed against my aching body, sending a chill across my skin. I didn't know how long my stubbornness would outlast my humanity and glanced at the cupboard for any extra towels. There were none.

"Please?" Phil begged. "I feel really rotten out here."

The last thing I wanted to do was walk out and admit defeat, but I started to shiver. A hot shower seemed like a better idea, but I'd forgotten to grab the clean towels out of the dryer. If Dad heard the water running at this time of night, he'd know I was awake—my actions adding to his already massive arsenal of suspicion. Resigned, I stood up and pulled up my sweatshirt hood.

Phil got out of the way when I unlocked the door. With my eyes down, I brushed past him, and headed straight for my bed. Even though I knew my behavior was juvenile, I pulled the covers up over my head anyway.

Phil sat next to me and rubbed my shoulder. Normally, I would have pushed him away but the massage felt soothing.

"Just rest," he said. "Nick's gone for now and Scarlett's sleeping."

I peeked out just enough to see her curled in a ball in the corner—the cat version again.

"She's really exhausted and I don't expect her to wake for a while, so close your eyes too."

I looked up at Phil through my bangs, knowing I'd never be able to sleep with his affection floating about.

"Do you want another sleeping pill?"

"No," I mumbled. I wanted to be lucid just in case something else happened.

"How about if I read to you some more?"

Jurassic Park would be a sufficient distraction. I nodded. He'd think about something else long enough for me to be lulled to sleep by his soothing voice and I could shut my brain off long enough to hopefully fall asleep.

"Great." He retrieved the book and flipped to where we'd left off. "Can't get enough of the veloci"crap"tors; can you?"

With a roll of my eyes, I laughed. "Guess not." *Among other things.*

If he wasn't so darn adorable, they'd both be tossed outside on their heads.

Chapter Twenty

When I woke up, Phil was sitting in the same place, staring at me intently. I looked away feeling invaded, then worried about my morning breath.

"Hi," I said awkwardly, sensing his boredom bloom into happiness.

"Hi," he said with a smile in his eyes. "Sleep well?"

"Yeah." I slowly picked my head up off the pillow to sit up.

The pounding pain radiated in all different directions. I didn't know what was worse, the beginnings of a caffeine headache about to slam sledge hammers in my temples or the dull throbbing ache from the bruise on my forehead.

"Oooh." My voice made a funny whoosh sound as I carefully touched my wound.

"Yeah," Phil said with a wince. "Sorry about that. You've got a nasty bruise."

"I bet. It really hurts."

I glanced around the darkened room to search for Scarlett, noticing the sunlight trying to peek around the curtains Phil had obviously drawn them to protect himself. But Scarlett wasn't on the floor where she'd fallen asleep the night prior.

"Where's the fleabag?"

"Easy girl." Phil pursed his lips. "She needed to eat. She'll be back."

"I hope she's not eating Aladdin's cat food." I smiled, maybe bigger than I should have. "Breakfast of champions?" Phil glared at me. "Sorry, I'm not cordial until I get my caffeine," I bit my lip and dangled my feet off the bed, taking my time to stand. "Is my dad still home?"

"He just left, but your bro's here—still sleeping though. Does he ever do anything?"

"Apparently not." I stifled a chuckle. "His activities circle around Amber his secret girlfriend, college classes at night, and now tattling, but that's about it. Did you happen to hear if my dad called school to tell them I'm sick again?"

"He did and he checked on you too. I think he left a note."

Phil didn't *think*; he knew (the little snoop). I'm sure being locked up for seven or so hours, even with the riveting stack of books I brought him, would make anyone stir crazy.

Phil made me sit back down. "Here, I'll get the note and a cup of coffee for you. Okay?"

I looked into his sparkling eyes and let out a sigh of thankfulness.

"That would be perfect," I said sheepishly, ashamed after being so cruel the night before. "Everything should be easy enough to find. The coffee beans are in the fridge."

"I got it." He pulled on his black robe and disappeared out of the door.

I stood and walked to the bathroom, desperate to brush the fuzz off my teeth. The light hit my eyes, worsening the pain in my head. I fumbled in the cabinet and found some Advil, taking two pills before examining the battle wound. The bump looked better than it felt and could be hidden under my bangs, if I styled them just right. I'd definitely need an excuse for this whopper though, if anyone saw it.

Upon leaving the bathroom, I ran directly into Phil, who stood smiling with his arm outstretched. He held a pink painted "It's good to be Queen" mug in his hand. I smiled back and took the hot mug between my palms, inhaling the rich aroma. But before taking the first delectable sip, I cocked my head, and wondered how he brewed the coffee so quickly. Obviously he was trying to hide something.

"Okay, I didn't make it," he confessed. "Your dad left some in a thermos downstairs and . . ."

He shyly handed me a crumpled note.

Julia,
Out to run errands. Call if you need anything.
Enjoy the coffee. Love Dad.

"Makes sense," I said with a generous laugh. My dad did brew some stellar coffee. "I didn't think you could make coffee *this* good."

"Thanks for the vote of confidence. It couldn't be that hard, right?" He laughed.

I smiled. Little did he know the disasters an amateur barista could invoke upon a helpless little coffee machine.

"Truth or dare?"

I crinkled my brows together. "Did you just say you wanted to play 'truth or dare'?"

"Yeah." Phil raised his right eyebrow and got comfortable on my bed, with a coquettish smile. "Wanna play?"

I snickered when images of Phil skipping through sprinklers with women's clothing on or knocking on my neighbor's door to ask if his refrigerator was running floated through my head.

"You must be incredibly bored."

Phil nodded, fortified with intrigue. I squinted my eyes in return, just as curious to know his deepest secrets as he obviously was of mine.

"With ground rules, I will," I said confidently.

Phil gave me his sexy smirk. "Okay. What rules?"

"Nothing painful, illegal, dangerous, noisy or embarrassing," I said quickly.

"Pfft. No fun."

I tilted my head to the side. "Seriously—"

"Fine, but this is going to be boring." Phil faked a yawn, fanning his mouth. I punched him in the arm with my right hand, which he grabbed, swirled me around and pinned me against his body.

"Truth or dare," he whispered, his lips dangerously close to my neck.

My body electrified, feeling the warmth of his breath, and I swallowed hard, trying to ignore his strong chest behind me. I liked being within his arms and the thought scared me.

"Truth," I squeaked out before wriggling out of his grasp.

Phil let me go and sprawled out across my bed, evidently prepared. "When did you and Nick start dating?"

I gained composure and sat on my desk chair, looking at the floor, holding my mug for security.

"Uh . . ." I stammered, wanting to talk about the subject delicately. "Not officially until after the incident at the warehouse. Nicholas was worried about vamps finding out and thought someone might come after me to get to him . . . you know?"

My eyes darted back up to his. I hadn't quite satisfied his question.

"I see," he said, deep in thought, radiating a smidge of envy. "He lacked faith in his ability to protect you."

"No," I defended. "He was just being precautious. He's had other situations that ended poorly."

"All those broken hearts . . ." Phil clucked his tongue.

My anger welled up. "Not exactly," I said, my tone terse. "My mother was murdered."

Any color Phil possibly had drained from his cheeks. "Dude, I'm sorry."

"No worries. Your turn," I said, trying to cover up the uncomfortable situation. "Truth or dare."

He paused for a minute, still feeling horrible when enlightenment suddenly danced from his eyes.

"Dare." He licked his lips.

I wanted so badly to choose something that would knock the sassy off his adorable face when the little stream of late morning light caught my eye, highlighting the frolicking motes in the air besides us.

"What would happen if you put your hand in the sunlight?"

Phil's eyes grew big, his angst heightening. "Imagine putting your hand on the burner of a stove—"

I gasped.

"—times a thousand."

"Oh." I cringed. "Never mind then. Definitely breaks the danger rule." I bit the corner of my lip and tried to think of another dare.

"I can think of one," he said, full of ardor.

"I bet you can." I felt flustered and tried to appear unfazed.

Deep down though, if he did try to kiss me, I knew I'd let him because I really wanted him to. In nervousness, my hand unconsciously made its way to the talisman which yanked me back to reality. Nicholas loved me enough to give up the one thing that protected him in his dangerous job. To allow a kiss, even an innocent one would disrespect that sacrifice. Though the stone was dead—why I didn't know—it still symbolized his concern for my safety and love for me. "Um . . . how about . . ." I continued to fidget. Nothing was coming to me. "Crap. I can't think of anything."

He got up and walked towards me with a shameless expression, turning on the charm. "How about . . . a nice back massage? Or—"

"How about cleaning my toilet?"

His charisma faded into disappointment. "Yeah, sure."

Literally ten seconds passed in which I heard something swipe the bowl and the water flush down the drain. He returned, humbled, and smelling of Pine Sol.

"Done. Your turn."

My heart beat a little faster. I gulped, unsure what to choose. "Um . . . Truth?"

"Are you sure?" The flicker in his eyes drove me crazy. I couldn't help but enjoy his undivided attention as our chemistry naturally sent invisible sparks flying across a room, healing a part of me that felt vulnerable and wounded. The fact that we could be together so easily made me worry my attachment to him was growing into something I might not be able to live without if Nicholas never recovered.

"I don't trust you with a dare."

"Really?" His dark snicker gave me shivers, but in a good way. His bravery spiked and I knew this question was going to be a doosey.

"If I hadn't gotten staked by Nicholas, would we have had a chance?"

Please don't ask that.

I sucked in the air too quickly and worked to control my exhale, unsure how to answer. Back then, he'd used his power to confuse me and the cells of my body—like now—they cried out, begging for his touch.

"Maybe," I said with intentions to keep from leading him on, still deeply in love with Nicholas. "It wasn't a choice I had to make and now I'm with Nicholas. So, I—I don't know."

"Things change," he mumbled.

"Your turn," I interrupted. "Or do you want to continue playing?"

"Yeah. Truth."

I tightened my lips together, prepared. "So, when you took off to L.A., you said you—you know—had a situation with your girlfriend. What happened?"

"With Lauren?" He sighed, feeling tremendous shame. "Yeah, I should still be rotting in Hades forever for that and everyone else I—you know. I loved her with all my heart and she threw it away on Jack. I was an impetuous heartless killer without a conscience back then. They deserved better."

His anguish made me regret I asked. "Sorry."

"It's all my fault and I need to suffer the consequences. I was a fool to let her string me along and over-reacted when I found out differently. Such a fool . . ." He sighed and put his head in his hands. No longer did he seem like a vicious killer, but a troubled soul infected with immortality. The guilt swept up and washed over me, leaving me anxious to find Nicholas and help him before the same thing happened to him.

I got up and sat next to Phil, putting my arm over his shoulder, unsure what to say. "You didn't know—"

"The thing is, I did know, but I can't change the past."

I closed my eyes and held tight to Phil's shoulder—Nicholas' half-vampire brother—wishing somehow I could help him make amends. Nicholas, many times, breathed the same words to me, trying to get over his torment of being too late to save my mother's life. Nicholas' love for me seemed to be the only thing that helped him move beyond the past. But the lives Phil took weren't the same.

"Are we going tonight?" I asked as a distraction. "To L.A.?"

"Sure." His hesitation sent out tremors.

"Why don't you want to go?"

Phil fidgeted, rubbing his knuckles over his chin. "I've been told never to return."

"What?" I snorted. "That's absurd. By whom?"

"The vamps that run that town," he said matter-of-factly.

"Oh." I tightened my eyes. "When?"

Phil took a deep breath. "After the incident with Lauren, I went a little crazy and ran into some locals there. It wasn't pretty considering how territorial they are and how sloppy I was. They warned me never to come back or they'd turn me in."

"Turn you in?"

"To the council, where they wanted to take Nick."

Nicholas had mentioned the Royals. Maybe they were one in the same.

"Who is this Council anyway?"

"The big wig vamps that run everything and Alora totally hates them. She complains they're so *old school*—"

For some reason, I couldn't picture Alora saying "old school" and had to smile.

"But—" Phil tisked "—the L.A. vamps have got that place wired so they'll know I'm there, no doubt about it."

I pushed my hand through my hair, unsure what to do. "You don't have to take me then."

"I have no choice. You can't drive with Daddy monitoring the GPS, now can you? It'll be okay." His teeth gleamed through his conniving smile. "They can't fly."

The infectiousness of his danger-craving made me grin too. And actually, the escapade started to get my spy juices bubbling. Maybe we could sneak in and out undetected. We had to try. "I'm going to have to go back to Nicholas' place and see if he's got the address, or even a phone number. Maybe I can just call."

"Yeah sure," he said, slightly disappointed. "We'll go back after dark when your dad thinks you're sleeping, or we can send Scarlett over to Nicholas' now."

"No." *The last thing he needs is the mind shrink snooping through his personal things.* "I'd feel better if I did it."

"Sure thing, Boss."

I stuck out my tongue. "Brat."

Deep down, I didn't want Phil to get in trouble, but there wasn't any other way to get to L.A. and back without alerting Dad. We didn't have a choice—Harry had to be warned.

"What are you thinking about?" Phil asked, his face pensive.

"I'm just wondering, since Nicholas is a half-vampire, why he didn't mention having trouble with a vampire gang and you did? He grew up there after all."

"Heck if I know. His dad's a vamp, right? Maybe he's part of the gang or they don't even know he's a vamp. When I first met him, he didn't give off the vibe, so I didn't have a clue who or what he was. Just a mutant or something. Now I realize he's part vamp." Phil touched his nose. "Maybe my rebirth has sharpened my senses."

"Maybe," I said, knowing full well why Phil suddenly could sense him.

When Nicholas and Phil met initially, Nicholas was wearing the talisman which rendered him undetectable and invincible. Now, since he didn't have it on, other vamps would naturally sense his heritage.

My fingertips grazed the talisman and wondered, with it not working, how I could keep the necklace from ever getting into the wrong hands. The smart thing would be to hide it some place where no one could find it. But I didn't want to take it off, hoping, somehow, when Nicholas returned to his former self, it would flicker to life and begin protecting me again.

"Hey, do you want to go watch TV or read or something?" I said, really wanting a mind-numbing distraction.

"With you? Always, Parker."

"You'll be able to hide if my dad comes home or Luke wakes up, right?"

"Yeah, I'll take off. No worries." He flashed his million dollar smile before we filed downstairs.

Chapter Twenty-One

I couldn't remember the last time I'd had so much fun doing nothing. Our day consisted of hiding in the dark, eating bon bons and making fun of cheesy Soap Operas and idiots trying to lie to Judge Judy. When nothing good was on, we read out loud some more and dined on grilled cheese sandwiches and chicken noodle soup. Phil ate like it was the last meal on earth, which made me feel like an accomplished cook. By the afternoon though, I finally got the courage to turn my iPhone back on. To my disappointment, I found Nicholas hadn't texted me back.

To distract myself, I shot Sam multiple text messages so she knew I was still alive, but her return texts were mostly about the growing anxiety at school surrounding Katie's disappearance. Guilt crept up and several times I almost told her the truth. Phil stopped me though and insisted I kept what I knew a secret. Painful as it was, we didn't need to taint Sam's world unless we had no choice.

When Luke finally got up and made an appearance, Phil had fun acting like a ghost, hovering silently behind him.

My gasps and anxious behavior freaked Luke out and he left shortly thereafter. I felt rotten because I wanted to make up after our fight, sensing the tension lingering, but Phil wouldn't stop goofing around.

Sometime after four, Dad finally came home with a ton of groceries, forcing Phil to remain upstairs while I put on my "sick" song and dance. Dad kept mostly to himself, seeming distracted while he made dinner. I was surprised he didn't grill me or even mention he knew about Nicholas, given the opportunity.

But right before he finished cooking my favorite dinner—garlic mashed potatoes, fried chicken and sautéed green beans—I pushed down my ravaging hunger and said I needed to lay down. Dad, taking the bait, must have thought I was practically on my death bed to pass up his cooking. In fatherly concern, he checked on me shortly thereafter and brought a plate to my room. But as soon as he left, I had to fight Phil with my lone fork, which he promptly stole from me.

"You're dad is a really good cook," Phil said after shoveling the first bite of mashed potatoes into his mouth. "Does he always cook like this?"

I hummed after Phil finally fed me something with the fork we now shared and fanned my fingers right after so he'd give me another bite. "He does when he's home."

"Smart thinking to get dinner in bed. This is a total score plus he must think you're super sick." He dove into the green beans, stabbing them one by one, filling up the tines. "Maybe we shouldn't eat it all and leave something on the plate."

"Naw," we said at the same time before bursting into laughter.

I wiped the fried chicken grease from my lips and smirked.

"Jinks, you owe me a coke," he interrupted.

"That's so old; I can't even believe you said that!"

"But doesn't a coke sound really good right now?"

"Or a tall glass of milk."

"Or a nice warm neck . . ."

I gasped.

"I mean, a tall glass of . . . beer," Phil put down the fork. "Bad slip."

I frowned. His angst was more heightened than usual. "Are you safe to be around? Should I uninvite you?"

I tried to sound like I was teasing.

"NO!" Phil straightened his back, his eyes fiercely tensed. "Don't. That'll force me outside and it's not quite dusk yet. I'm completely under control. Honest."

"Has that ever happened before?" I glanced at the darkened window shade; the orange sunset peaked through at the corners.

"No, but I don't really want to experiment right now."

I nibbled on my fingernail and watched him through my bangs. "I guess you really trust me then, don't you."

"Like you trust me." The corners of his lips lifted as he put down the fork. "I mean, if you had an addiction to chocolate but knew every time you ate it, someone died, you'd give it up. Right?"

"Of course." I bit the inside of my cheek. "Is that what it's like?"

"A million times better but still, I'm not going to do it. No matter how tempted."

Suddenly disinterested in food, I used the abandoned fork to push around the last few beans on the plate. I wanted to stop the awkward tension, but drew a blank. "Are you finished eating?"

"Dinner was amazing, don't get me wrong." He pulled his lips into a straight line. "I just always feel unsatisfied."

"I know," I murmured and got up to move the plate out of the way, placing it on my desk.

Just beyond, the clock read six-thirty. Luckily, my pajama day would be coming to an end after sunset. I craved a hot shower and normal clothing.

"I don't know how you do this," I said, realizing the daily burden he endured. "Don't you get bored waiting for the sun to set?"

"That's what I miss and hate the most—the sun," he said wistfully. "But like always, it's easy to take the simplest things for granted until they are taken from you."

Like Nicholas' protection and love. "True." I said pensively. "I've been wondering . . . do you sleep?"

"I do sometimes, but technically, I don't need to do anything extra to survive. I'm frozen in time and will stay like this forever as long as I don't get staked or burned up."

"You sure gobbled up dinner like you were starving."

"I am, in a way. Haven't you ever been hungry for something particular and no matter what you eat, you can't make it go away?"

"Yeah," I said, realizing I'd been subconsciously encapsulating his bloodlust so I didn't have to worry while we were together.

His was still there, irksome as ever, like a piece of glass you feel hidden in your foot but you can't seem to get it out.

The vampire life suddenly didn't sound sexy anymore. I couldn't imagine never being able to lay out at the beach, nor watch another sunset, besides being starved for blood all the time. And Phil's change after experiencing Hell was almost like he'd grown a conscience, not wanting to give into merciless killings anymore. Would Nicholas suffer like that as well? Though, with the talisman, if I ever ended up with a vampy make-over, I wouldn't have to worry about being burned up—if it started working again. But what really perplexed me was how the change would affect my decisions. Would I get all power-hungry like Alora? Or stay myself and be bloodless like Preston?

"It's not so bad, as long as you have the right company," Phil said with charisma, pulling me from my worries, melting me with his obsidian eyes.

"I guess not," I said, darting mine away to look at my fidgeting hands. "So now what?"

"I'm going out to find Scar. You need to get *the home front* all squared away with good ole Dad and make your bed to look like you're sleeping in it. Oh, and put on something very warm and dark colored. I'll get a wig."

"You'd look really hot with blonde hair with highlights," I said with a giggle, unable to help myself.

"I bet." He smirked. "It's for your sleeping corpse. I'll be back in an hour."

Phil reached over and tapped my nose. His anxiety spiked just as the sun started to set. My body responded, pumping a bit of adrenaline in my blood, unsure if we should take this chance. I almost backed out when Phil spoke.

"I'm off." He winked before he vanished.

The curtain fluttered ever so slightly in his wake. I walked over, pulled up the shades, and scanned the dark yard, hoping to feel Nicholas close by. The fact he didn't come around the entire day bothered me.

I pushed the anxiety down, took the dirty plate and left my room to tell Dad goodnight. He was preoccupied in his office and when I mentioned I was going to bed, he didn't even move to hug me. Maybe because he thought I was still contagious. He only recommended some Theraflu to help with my discomfort. I agreed and headed back upstairs, thankful he didn't want to fawn all over me, but curious why he'd let the entire night slip by without one word about dating Nicholas.

Once I showered and changed, I had nothing to do until Phil returned. The beaded dusty pillows suddenly came in handy for making a makeshift body and the oversized teddy bear became my head and shoulders, shrouded under the sheet. All I needed was the wig and my stunt double would be set.

I paced, hoping Scarlett wouldn't come back with Phil. I already had a plan to keep her here just in case she wanted to tag along. Tyler needed protection from Katie, naturally, and Scarlett would be the perfect guard until we returned. I'd even written down the directions to his house as a back-up.

I texted Sam to say goodnight right before shutting off the phone, wanting all my actions to look normal in case Dad checked my records. Worried I'd drop the phone from five thousand feet during our flight, I waffled whether or not to bring it along. Common sense won out and I placed the phone within a zipper pouch on the inside of my backpack. I didn't think, with it off, the phone transmitted a signal. But if I were ever stranded, at least I'd have a lifeline to society to solicit help.

The only ski hat I had was bright pink. Luke owned the only black one, but I didn't know where he kept it. Hot pink or not, *a hat* was better than freezing my ears off so I stuffed it in my backpack along with my scarf and gloves.

I flipped off the bedroom light and went to the open window, peering outside, checking for Phil again. The serenade of crickets greeted my presence over the void of emotion within the trees. I wished for Nicholas to come kidnap me instead, sending out a silent beacon, hoping he hadn't beaten me to L.A. already. My dad was the only one that registered in the night, who seemed to be doing something tedious—I'm sure for work. I shivered from the cold air and decided I might need another sweatshirt for the journey.

Unsure how long the trip would take, I took one last bathroom stop. When passing by the mirror, I glanced at my reflection noting the fresh application of makeup, not understanding why I bothered to put it on.

Am I trying to keep Phil in the wings just in case Nicholas and I don't work out? My heart ached at the thought of losing Nicholas forever. I shook my head, shut off the light and turned, running right into Cousin Itt.

Completely startled, I yelped.

"Shhh!" Phil peeled back the blonde curtains of hair to reveal his sparkling black eyes. "It's just me."

I scowled, annoyed my feelings radar was a second late to warn me, suddenly picking up his radiating smugness loud and clear.

"Nice hair," I said, removing the blonde wig off his head and placing it on the teddy bear instead.

"Are you ready?" he asked behind me, suddenly feeling very enticed, and not in a way I wanted.

I stood up quickly and swirled around, watching his eyes glance from where my booty once was, giving me a once over that sprung my heart into overdrive.

"Nice leggings," he said with a throaty tone and a half curled smile.

The heat radiated outward from my collar bone towards my ears, leaving a nice crimson trail in its path. Bending over in front of Phil with tight leggings on, ultimately giving him a peepshow wasn't what I intended to do.

"It was the only thing I had that was black," I said sheepishly, pulling my jacket down over my hips with my eyes glued to the floor. "I'm ready when you are."

Phil quietly gawked a moment longer, then chuckled while I died of embarrassment, my cheeks heating to blistering levels. I finally looked up at him and pursed my lips.

"Okay, let's go," he said, holding out his hand which I took. He led me out of the window.

"Where's her *Highness*?"

Phil tilted his head in disapproval, though enjoyment played across his thoughts. "Let's be nice, shall we?"

I smirked and fastened myself next to Phil's aura again, trying my best to keep away from her prying tentacles.

"I have catnip as a peace offering; do you think she'll like it?"

"*I'll pass,*" she said with disdain.

I withheld my laughter. "Guess not . . . so, what's the plan? Is the coast clear?" I was anxious to get on our way, noticing Scarlett below within the bushes peering up at us.

"So far so good. Scar says he's running around in the forest, working off some steam."

Phil talked casually like Nicholas was out doing his usual workout, completely ignoring the fact Nicholas—the love of my life—suffered alone.

"Oh," I mumbled, my face crestfallen. "Is that good?"

"Well . . . the fact that he's not committing mass causalities is positive. Look . . . he needs to work out his anger where he can break stuff and yell. The forest is a good place to do that."

"Yeah, I guess so."

Phil felt more assured this time and I tried to take that as a good sign. Before I knew it though, we were off again, me and my dark Superman zipping along in the night sky.

"Once we get the address, how long will it take us to fly to L.A.?" I asked in his ear.

"You never whisper anything sexy," he said with a pouty face.

I punched his arm. "Stop. I'm being serious."

"Okay, *Miss Serious.* An hour or so," he finally said with a grin in his voice. "Happy?"

"Yes."

Our plans seemed too easy. We'd fly to Orange County, warn Harry, then jet home, all before daylight. The worst that could happen would be Phil running into the vamps there and having to abort the plan. "She's still going to be escorting you at school tomorrow, you know," Phil said, interrupting my thoughts.

"Who? Scarlett?" I huffed. "No-o," I said in a whine.

"She's the only one who can. Nicholas totally wants to get you alone. Don't think he doesn't have motive to either turn you or just bite you for food."

"Yeah, yeah, I remember." I snickered in disbelief.

"You don't want to become like me. I promise."

"You're like a walking billboard against the lifestyle: 'Besides the sunlight, being a vampire sucks,' " I said with a Transylvanian accent, busting up laughing at my play on words.

"Cute, Parker," he said. "You should go into advertising."

I stuck out my tongue.

Just like before, when we arrived, Phil scanned the area before touching down.

"It's clear," Scarlett said, running underneath us towards the house.

"Whoa there, Betty Page, this is my job," I barked. "You two stay outside."

She turned and hissed slightly, but sat on the top step. I marched past her and walked to the door, turning the knob. But the knob didn't turn.

"Key's under the flower pot," Scar said it in a flat tone.

I wanted to ignore her but the impulsive "thank you" squeaked from the lips of my mind anyway. I wasn't sure if she actually heard it though, since her emotions were dead to me in her cat form.

The quiet of his house eerily surrounded me as I walked in and shut the door, glancing around. The guitar was gone, along with the love song on the table. In the ceiling, the hole where a skylight used to be was covered with a blue tarp revealing Phil's escape the night before.

The gesture, no matter how minute, showed he wasn't completely gone and cared about the small things, like water and other damage to his place.

I naturally gravitated to his dresser only to find clothing. I took out his blue shirt—my favorite—and smelled the fabric, rubbing the cottony goodness against my cheek. He always looked so handsome in this color, one that naturally brought out the viridian flecks in his eyes. I could see him in my mind the last time he wore it—on our beach—telling me about how he once used his powers to paddle faster so some local wouldn't steal his wave. I smiled at how real the vision felt, being intoxicated by his scent.

"Julia, you need to hurry," Scarlett warned.

I snapped out of my daydream and snarled, noticing her kitty face peering at me through the window. Would it be so bad if he showed up now? Reluctantly, I got back to work and headed towards his bed, which had nothing under it.

Nicholas' house was very immaculate but empty, almost like a summer rental. Nothing lined the counters, no pictures decorated the walls, very few dishes or *even* food was stored in the cabinets. The bathroom only had basics: toilet paper, razors, shaving cream, soap, toothpaste and a solitary toothbrush. It was as if he'd packed up everything that wasn't a necessity, preparing to move soon.

I sat on the bed and sighed, feeling defeated. I'd failed to find anything with even his name or address on it. His desk had pens, paper and a small empty filing cabinet. His trash basket was empty too. The last place to check was his nightstand.

I grabbed the handle on the drawer and tugged, finding it stuck. I yanked harder and the drawer tumbled free onto the floor with a clunk. Well, two clunks actually.

I picked up the drawer and shook it. Something shifted, like there was a secret compartment inside. But when I ran my hand along the seam, there wasn't any way to pry it open. Tempted to bust the drawer in two, I turned it over. Underneath, two small diagonal cuts dissected the groove the drawer slid against. The wood was darker and worn between them. I ran my finger over the groove when the area depressed inwards.

Like magic, a panel on the inner side of the drawer popped open, releasing the hidden contents that fell to the floor. I froze at the discovery. Lying at my feet were some letters addressed to Nicholas, official documents, some bills, and a journal.

My hand gravitated towards the letters, opening the first one. Inside, the words were unfamiliar, decorated with accents and tildes. I recognized the syntax and guessed the language to be Vietnamese. My heart quickened as I turned over the envelope for the return address, which was blank.

Full of disappointment, I flipped through a few more of the letters hoping one would list where it came from, the ink over the stamp displaying Orange County. The bills gave no clues either and were due the next month: gas, water, and electricity. He'd paid them all on time the month prior. I opened another document to find the deed to a house. The buyer was "Clint Eastwood" with an Orange County address. My hands began to shake once I realized the house belonged to Harry. I almost bolted off the floor and out the door with my fantastic find when my eye caught the journal.

I hesitated, unsure if I wanted to violate his private thoughts. I grazed the leather cover with my fingertips, wanting to use osmosis to pull the feelings from the silent cover. The strap prevented it from accidentally opening when everything fell to the floor.

"I love you," I whispered, caressing the cover. "Come back to me, please."

I turned on my phone, plugging in Harry's address for the directions and quickly shut it off, hoping it didn't alert my dad. Then I shoved everything back into the drawer, kissing the top of the journal before placing it back into its home when I noticed a corner of a picture peeked out between the pages. Half in hesitation, I delicately worked the picture free, to find a candid photo of myself, one I'd never seen before.

The shot was a close-up of the side of my face turned downward, looking at something unseen with the wind blowing back my hair, the sun shimmering on my blonde-locks. I couldn't be sure, but I must have been standing on the cliff over-looking our beach. But my hair was longer, meaning the picture was taken last summer, before I'd chopped several inches off: before we'd ever met. I gasped.

"*Are you done yet?*" Scarlett asked, her voice laced with impatience.

"*Almost, give me a second.*" I replied sharply. "Geez."

I stared at the photo a little longer. Nicholas must have wanted this picture an awful lot to risk having something tying us together in his possession. I ran my fingers over the top then flipped it over to find "absolutely breathtaking" written on the back. My stomach flip-flopped at the words, taking my own breath away.

All I wanted was to stay there, crawl up into his comforter and wait for him to come home. I didn't need to go run off to L.A., or do anything else. The key to breaking Nicholas' addiction was me and our love, plain and simple, and I no longer wanted to be part of the Phil and Scar duo. I almost kicked off my shoes when Phil opened the door.

"Did you get the address?" he asked, looking at me peculiarly, possibly because I was taking so long.

"Yeah, let's go," I said, giving up on my heavenly dream.

I stuffed everything away and scanned the room one last time, feeling very nostalgic about Nicholas and his *supposed* home, simple yet barren. Even here, where he should be able to be himself, he stayed distant with nothing to cling to. His personal effects lay hidden in a little eight by ten box from his enemies—from me. His only decoration, a picture of his (thought to be) deceased mother showed the reality of what he really wished for. I welled up at the thought and brushed my hand against his pillow, on my way out.

My heart hung heavy in my chest as I left his house, following behind Phil, hoping I could change his paradigm and give him something more than a façade of a life, knowing if I failed, I'd lose him forever to the dark side.

"Are we leaving?" I asked Phil, pulling out my hat and gloves, wrapping the scarf tightly around my neck.

"Cute," Phil said, his eyes flickering up at my hat. "You got it?"

Phil radiated concern but stayed silent, wrapping me within his arms, preparing for take-off.

"Oh." I reached in my pocket for the slip of paper on which I'd written Tyler's address on and turned towards Scarlett. "Can you check on Tyler for me? Katie's bent on recruiting him to be her bloodsucking boyfriend."

"*Where?*" she asked.

I read the address to her, realizing without hands, holding the paper wasn't actually feasible.

"I know where that is. I'll check on him," she said reassuringly. *"Don't worry."*

I stood there—watching Scarlett twitch her tail gently—still afraid to let her inside my head, but something tore at me, wanting me to let my guard down. The long day of agonizing over Nicholas and keeping up a bristly exterior against her, exhausted me. It seemed convenient to blame her for everything but I finally started to realize she'd only tried to protect the both of us from the inevitable: a truth I wanted to refuse existed.

We'll find him and bring him home," she said full of empathy.

I melted at her words. *"Thanks."*

She purred happily and pounced off into the bushes. Phil turned and smiled. "Good to see you two getting along."

I smirked. *For now.*

Chapter Twenty-Two

"I brought you something," Phil said, producing an oversized backpack of some sort, layered in straps and buckles.

I wrinkled up my nose. "What's that?"

"It's what parachuters wear when they jump tandem. Thought it might help for the trip."

I looked at the complicated webbing attached to the metal contraption. "Do you know how to put it on?"

Apprehension sprung from his pores, revealing he had no clue what he was doing.

"Yeah," he said, stepping into two of the holes, shimmying the harness up his legs. He fed his arms through two other loops and clipped the buckle into place. The part my body might possibly fill hung partially behind and in front.

"Where do I go?'

Phil's eyebrows pressed together as he tried to get the remaining straps untangled and opened far enough for me to climb in. I suddenly didn't feel comfortable being strapped into this web like labyrinth.

Walking over to him, I batted my eyelashes. "Do you really think we need this? I was hoping you'd just hold me close to you in the air."

Shock and happiness rang from his body, beaming outward like a beacon, energizing his eyes.

"Oh," he said in elation. "I—I guess I could. Sure. Let's go."

The harness fell to the ground the instant he grabbed my waist and swooped me off my feet, launching us briskly into the air.

I finally exhaled, happy to be on our way and curled in the natural curve of his shoulder, feeling a rush when our bodies moved from a vertical angle to a horizontal one from the wind pressing our legs up and back, both of us looking down upon the city.

"Remember the first time we did this?" Phil snorted, holding my waist firmly. "You totally hated it and screamed the whole time."

I laughed at the memory, enjoying the wind ruffling the hair poking out around my hat. "I guess I did." I glanced up at him from the corner of my eye. "But you freaked the crap out of me."

"I was a recent aviator back then. I've since mastered the art."

"I would hope so. But where are the drinks? The snacks? The in-flight movie?"

Phil made a crackling sound with his mouth, like a walkie-talkie. "Thank you ladies and gentlemen for choosing Phillip D'Elia Air. Please keep your hands inside the vehicle and your seatbelt fastened at all times. I also highly recommend you don't wander about the cabin either. In case of a water landing—once you've stopped screaming of course—please use your neighbor as a flotation device. We are now at cruising altitude and it looks like smooth sailing from here on out."

Phil suddenly started wiggling his body erratically. I shrieked and dug my nails into his arms.

"Whoa, please remove your talons. I was joking."

I eased up for a second after he stopped jerking about. "What was that?"

"Turbulence, of course."

I elbowed Phil in the chest. "Knock it off. That's not even funny!"

He burst into laughter so hard his whole body shook.

"Shut up," I said, crossing my arms over the top of his, fuming but wishing he'd hold still. "It's not like I have a parachute."

"I would never let you fall, Parker," he whispered in my ear, his lips grazing my skin, kissing my temple. "Ever."

His immense devotion zinged through my body and I shivered. For a moment—though we didn't speak—our bodies chemically responded, igniting a blazing heat between us, producing warmth as if we stood next to a camp fire. I didn't mind actually. The temperature noticeably dropped as we ascended, leaving the exposed parts of me defenseless against the elements.

"How much longer?" I asked with chattering teeth, pulling my sweatshirt hood up over my pink hat to insulate my head, hoping for a break from the frigid wind. Somehow, over the last half hour,

Phil stopped radiating the heat back to me. He pressed his cheek against mine and I pulled away when it felt like ice. "Ack! Don't do that."

"Sorry," he said apologetically. "My body temperature acclimates to the climate. We'll be there soon though. Hang in there"

"W-what else am I going to do?" In complete misery, I waited, wishing for one warm spot to cling to, rubbing my gloved hands together and blowing on them. Each inhale froze my nostrils, making breathing painful. I shifted, curling into a fetal position, feeling the icy blast shoot air through my jacket across my neck and shoulders. I anguished when I thought of the return flight home.

"H-h-hot ch-ch-chocolate," I murmured. "Hot c-coffee, camp f-f-fires, the s-s-sun."

"Are these your wishes?"

"Y-y-yes. Nothing against the acc-c-c-commodations, but I'm officially a p-p-popsicle now."

Phil chuckled before descending and the air changed, feeling a tiny bit warmer. "Isn't hypothermia fun?"

"A-a-awesome. Are we there yet?"

The heightened alarm from Phil and general unhappiness from the city hit me like a sonic boom. I rolled over so my stomach faced downward again and looked for identifiable landmarks.

"So where do I go?" Phil asked.

I took off the glove to fumble for the directions in my pocket. My numb fingers made grasping the paper difficult. The first attempt revealed an old chewing gum wrapper.

"Okay, we need to follow the 110 and get off at 108th Street."

Phil guffawed. "How am I supposed to tell where the 110 is?"

"Didn't you live here once?"

"Yeah, but without signs, I don't know all the freeways. Los Angeles is huge, as you can see."

"Well, what's that freeway below us?" I pointed to the shining row of headlights roaming like ants headed towards their home up the mountain slope.

"Um . . . it could be the 405, the 110, the 710 or the 605. I can't be sure."

"Argh," I groaned. "Then get closer so we can read the signs."

"I can't. If *they* sense me, it'll be all over once we touch ground. We need to drop in without alerting anyone—including humans, remember?"

"Oh, right," I said tersely, looking at the ground. "So how far up in the air do we need to stay?"

"Well, like a mile or so."

"So, if you can't fly lower and I don't have a map, what are we supposed to do?" My frozen mind wouldn't work to help me solve the puzzle.

"Doesn't your phone have GPS?" he asked, feeling ingenious.

"Yeah, but my dad's monitoring the GPS."

"That too?" Phil coughed. "Geez, Parker, what did you do to get on his bad side?"

"Hung out with *you* and got called into the principal's office when you disappeared. Before that, I didn't need constant watching." I huffed with malice.

Phil wasn't going to pin the blame on me for my father's over-protectiveness when he started the snowball of mistrust in the first place.

"Well, we have one thing on our side. Right now, he thinks you are very sick and in bed sleeping."

"I'm *not* if I turn it on," I said indignantly. "He'll know."

"But, I'm pretty sure he'd have to be monitoring the website at the time you *do* turn it on."

"But what if it keeps track somehow?"

"Electronics can go haywire, especially if you magically showed up in Los Angeles when he knew you were upstairs sleeping. Just lie about it."

Lying got me in all this trouble in the first place. "Can't we ask for directions?" I asked.

"Not unless you want to fly somewhere remote and get a map."

Somewhere remote meant more time freezing and I had to defrost before I started losing limbs.

"Fine," I said, too cold to fight. "I'll just tell him something's wrong with my phone and it's not turning on."

"There, see? No harm, no foul."

Whatever. Reluctantly, I tried to plug in the address but my finger tips wouldn't register on the screen.

"Ack," I cried out.

"What's wrong?"

"My fingers are too cold."

"Try putting them in your mouth."

"What?"

"I'd do it," he said, his voice sexier than normal. "But I'm not warm enough. Just suck on them."

I grumbled, feeling totally juvenile. With a roll of my eyes, I put my index finger in my mouth, trying not to worry about germs. Phil moaned in delight.

"Shut up," I mumbled.

After a minute of defrosting I touched the screen. Like magic the phone worked. I quickly input the address. Suddenly, the GPS lady's voice chirped out of my speakers and I turned up the volume as high as it would go. She sweetly barked out orders and we zigzagged accordingly, following her every command.

"This is cool. I've never done this before," Phil said in amusement.

"Well, if you go the wrong way, she gets very upset with you."

"Really?" Phil's curiosity peaked.

"Don't even think about it. We can play with it later, let's just get there so I can defrost, pee, and turn off this *blasted* phone," I barked.

Phil sobered up and stopped wasting time. Within minutes, we were hovering over Hung and Harry's house. I shut off the phone, hoping for a miracle.

"That's it." I pointed to show Phil. "How do you want to do this?"

"Well, let's land and knock on the door. I'll wait until you are safely inside, then I'll hover up here until you are ready to go."

"And what if someone sees you?"

"I'll deal with it. Ready?"

"Yeah." I held my breath and Phil descended into the alley.

With anxious hands, I rapped on the door. Inside, the general uneasiness resonated outward. I tried not to look frightened when the peephole became darkened from the eyeball peering at me.

"Hung, it's me, Julia," I assumed.

Recognition rang out and the sound of the locks unlatching one-by-one filled my ears. I finally let my breath go.

"She'll let me in," I whispered to Phil. "You can go now."

Phil stiffened, radiating an ocean of fear right before the alley filled with a cornucopia of lustful sundries—power, revenge, and desire for blood.

Before I could see them, Phil was in front of me, sandwiching my body between his back and the wall. My heart hammered in my chest as twin sets of black eyes attached to ferocious blood-sucking beings stepped into the alley entrance, their beautiful bodies illuminated. On the left stood a buff guy in a white tank top sporting an orange Mohawk that shot upward like flames. Next to him was a buxom blonde curled tightly with snakelike arms onto his shoulder. I might have been a little more confident if I knew Phil had more experience in fighting.

"I come in peace," Phil said with a voice full of courage though his insides rattled like chains.

"You've been warned, fledgling, never to return and yet here you are—with a human no less," the buff guy said. His arms were covered with tattoos decorating his skin like clothing.

The cackles bounced off the walls around us as two more vampires appeared from the shadows like cockroaches behind them. A dark-haired, heavily made up Emo girl sauntered forward accompanied by a black-haired Goth boy, both dressed in black.

"Listen," Phil said, holding up his hands. "I've broken no rules. I'm here on a mission of mercy. To make amends for my past."

Blondie, who wore tight leather accentuating her assets, removed herself from Mohawk man's shoulder and crept forward, closing the small space between us.

A sly smile crossed her crimson lips. "Look, Slide," she said, her voice gruff yet sexy "He's trying to be *honorable* now. Is that what you tell all your pretty little snacks?"

My fingers gripped Phil's shoulder tighter on their own, ready to jump on piggy-back if he needed to shoot into the sky.

Phil shifted his weight, concern swirling around him. "I'm serious."

"And so are we," Slide said firmly.

I stood plastered to Phil's back, trembling, recognizing the V attack formation from the fight I'd witness with Nicholas in the past—someone distracts while the others spread out with a surprise attack. Phil remained poised, ready to spring into the sky at any moment, maneuvering his arm closer to my waist. With our botched arrival, we'd managed to lose our only opportunity to warn Hung and Harry about Nicholas and managed to attract nasty vamps into their alley instead, putting them in more danger.

"Let's go," I whispered with a shaky voice, hoping our retreat would lure them away.

Suddenly, I felt hands, warm and inspired with courage, grasp my arm, and jerk me backwards.

I yelped and disappeared within the walls of the structure, watching Phil's face twist into a panic. He shot his hand towards me only to bounce off the invisible force field between us and the door jam. I reached back only to be quickly separated by Hung who closed the door. She turned and greeted me with terrified eyes, sighing in relief as she flipped the locks one by one.

"Safe now," she said with wild eyes and a ghostly pallor, followed by a string of Vietnamese and hand gestures. The one I understood all too well—the pointing towards the alley and making like she had fangs—translated perfectly.

"Yes," I said, nodding my head. "I know there were vampires in the alley. But the one I was with was good." I made the sign of the cross. "He's good . . . Phil, he's my *friend*." I touched my heart. "Friend."

She turned and brushed her hand across the circular jade pendant hanging off the wall, repeating the familiar rhetoric from before.

I got up and touched her shoulder. "It's going to be okay, don't worry."

She frowned, expelling confusion, still guarding the door. I didn't know what else to do, so I invisibly pushed my comfort towards her through my hand. She responded by relaxing, percolating more peace.

I closed my eyes, reaching with my mind into the alley, no longer feeling Phil nearby. He must have been successful at getting away due to the lack of a clear confrontation and struggle. There were still two stragglers in the alley, confused and agitated, meaning the other two had left. Possibly trying to follow him.

"Hung, is Harry home?"

She peered into my eyes, worry etched into her weathered skin. "No. No Harry."

"Where is he?"

Hung lowered her head. "Harry no here."

"Did Nicholas come here? Did something happen?"

"Nicholas." She shook her head rapidly. "Yes, Harry go Nicholas." She made a hand gesture of a bird flying in the air.

"He went to Nicholas or did Nicholas come here?" I pointed to the ground.

"Nicholas," she shook her head. "Harry go." She closed her eyes and wiped away a tear, erupting tremendous grief. "*Tôi đang lo lắng.*"

I took her hands. "What happened?"

Confusion lingered. We weren't communicating at all. She opened her brown eyes as far as they could and began speaking feverishly, flapping her arms wildly.

"I . . . I don't understand, Hung," I said to try to convey she could stop trying to explain.

She continued a little longer then waited, as if for an answer.

"*Vâng?*" she asked.

I looked back somberly, wishing I could understand. Something horrible happened and I didn't know if Nicholas came and took

Harry, forcing him to make weapons under duress or something worse. "I'll find him, both of them."

Hung finally smiled, her tense shoulders dropping. "Come, eat."

Chapter Twenty-Three

Filled with nausea, I sat in Hung's kitchen and pushed my food around with a fork, while Nicholas' new self kept flashing before my eyes. I had no way—without Harry to interpret—to convince her to un-invite him so he wouldn't come slaughter them in their sleep. Where was Harry anyway?

Earlier, I'd gotten the brilliant idea to write a note until I remembered Harry was blind. The internet could have helped translate, but then again, the only access I knew of was on my phone. My eyes swept the book shelf for a translation dictionary but I couldn't read the spines. How was I to tell her?

Hung watched me quietly with rapt attention, thirsty to communicate. I'd mentioned Nicholas' name and made the vampire fangs gesture again. She stared back, completely bewildered. Why would she believe me that Nicholas had changed? I gave up the charades after that.

But our language barrier wasn't my only problem. I literally had no way to get home without Phil, unless I accepted getting into *mondo* trouble and called my dad. How the heck would I explain how I ended up in Los Angeles of all places?

The uncertainty, coupled with two dark chocolaty eyes watching my every move, stole the very breath from my lungs, making me feel claustrophobic. I needed Harry. *Now.*

Something crashed to the floor in the other room and Hung darted towards the debacle, leaving me alone. My heart beat wildly unable to feel who the intruder was.

Hung yelled something inaudible as a flash of white shot past the doorway towards the back bedrooms.

I let my breath go, realizing their cat had knocked something over.

If only it was Scarlett.

My mind wandered to how horribly I'd treated her the past few days. She could have helped in this situation, if I'd let her come along. I sighed, hating that I actually missed her.

"*I'm here.*"

I straightened my shoulders and whipped my head around to find the black cat associated with the voice in my mind. "*Where are you?*"

"*Outside,*" Scarlett replied.

I looked towards the window and locked on the blue eyes framed in obsidian fur peering through the glass. "*Is Phil will you?*"

"*No, but I'm here to take you to him.*"

"*Is Phil okay?*"

"*Yes, for now. There isn't much time.*"

I got off the chair and picked up my backpack. "*But what about Hung?*"

"*Tell her goodbye. I'll do the rest.*"

Hung entered the kitchen with a dustpan full of white broken ceramic pieces, mumbling angrily under her breath as she tossed them into the trash. Whatever the cat broke seemed sentimental.

"I'm leaving now," I said while putting on my backpack and pointing towards the door.

Hung straightened up from leaning over the garbage and pressed her eyebrows together. "Go?"

"Yes," I pointed towards the clock. "It's late," *almost midnight.* "I need to go home—sleep." *Hopefully.*

Hung emanated distress but tilted her head in a gesture of understanding as if everything suddenly made sense. But one thing was for sure, she didn't want me to leave.

"I'm sorry. Tell Harry I was here." I grabbed a piece of paper and scratched out my phone number. "Have him *call* me." My fingers formed a phone.

Hung took the paper and nodded again; a warm smile formed on her lips. We'd connected finally.

She walked me to the door and looked out the peep hole before opening it. In overwhelming concern, she grabbed my arm. "You—" Her hands formed around an invisible steering wheel, rotating back and forth.

"Yes," I answered, wanting her to think I drove.

Relief flooded her tiny frame as she drew me into a tight embrace. Surprisingly her maternal tenderness enveloped me, giving me a connection of what Nicholas must have experienced growing up. She'd been his true mother, raising Nicholas into the wonderful man he was today, and I grew angry, determined not to let the red-headed tyrant ruling our town receive any benefit from Hung's devotion. Hung and Harry—if anyone—deserved his loyalty implicitly. I planned to remind Nicholas of just that, if I ever got another chance.

My chest ached once we let go of each other, feeling like a vulture sat on it, slowly pecking away at my dying heart. How would we ever handle it if he never returned to us—to me? After all, Alora's image sat on his dresser, not Hung's.

"*Don't worry. He'll come back,*" Scarlett whispered ever so slightly, prickling the back of my subconscious.

I gritted my teeth, recognizing her intonation instantly, figuring she was cleverly trying to manipulate my thoughts so I'd be more compliant. Having to fake a smile, I returned Hung's bow.

With my lips pressed tightly together, I turned and walked into the alley, searching for the nuisance. Scarlett sat perched on top of a dumpster.

Fitting.

"Goodbye," I said, waving my hand while Hung eyed the darkness and me in disquiet. I disappeared out of her sight.

"*Okay. Where is he?*" I stared at Scarlett, keeping my mind blank, unable to hide myself within anyone's aura.

She jumped off the dumpster and morphed into a woman, dressed in a snug black jacket, tight jeans and leather boots. The ensemble contrasted against her pearly skin and blue eyes.

"Would this suit you better?" she asked, radiating compassion.

"Yeah, whatever you want to *be.*" I looked at the filthy ground and kicked a rock. Even though her human form allowed me freedom to finally read her emotions, growing my confidence, her beauty quickly counteracted it, leaving me filled with insecurity.

"Can we go now?"

She nodded and walked towards the neighboring street. I followed closely behind, unsure of our surroundings and kept my personal radar on a heightened alert. Thankfully, we blended easily into the shadows with our dark ensembles. But my eyes darted back and forth, feeling the environment with each step we took.

"Where is Phil anyway?" I whispered.

"On the outskirts of town, trying to stay incognito. He'll find us soon," she said gently in my mind.

"How did you know where we were anyway?"

"I followed you." She spoke plainly, like her feat was no big deal.

"You followed us?" I let out a quiet chuckle of amazement, imagining her as a cat scampering at lightening speed over the Grapevine. *"But what about Tyler?"*

"He's fine for now," she said matter-of-factly. *"Katie has another mission to regain favor so Alora will fulfill her promise and allow Tyler to be sired. Her hope is to find Nicholas and assist in helping him come back to the coven—quite unsuccessful so far I might add."*

I shuddered at both the fact she stalked Nicholas but also that she hadn't given up on changing Tyler. *"Does she know where to find him?"*

Scarlett snickered. *"Katie's not even looking in the right place."*

My shoulders relaxed. Good thing Nicholas was smart enough to elude the venomous snakes that turned him into what he'd become. Scarlett's dual aura distracted me though. She'd mentioned that she and Nicholas were connected by blood because of the bite and this still infuriated me. I pushed aside my jealousy and concentrated on finding the place where the connection lived. Buried deep within her being, was overwhelming anguish, loathing, and insatiable hunger that had to be coming from Nicholas. I grieved at the discovery.

"He's suffering," Scarlett said, reading my intentions, responding greatly with disgrace. *"I'm afraid the taste of my blood has made things terribly worse for him."*

"How?" I balled up my fists. *"What did it do to him?"*

"A vampire's blood is the most decadent substance on the planet, and you already know how wonderful a sensation human blood can give."

I closed my eyes and remembered the euphoria all too well, secretly craving it myself.

"Wait? You're a vampire?"

"Half—like Nicholas . . ."

I gasped at the confession. In all my interactions, I hadn't suspected her powers came from a vampire lineage, never sensing her bloodlust. Suddenly everything made sense. Did she have similar circumstances as Nicholas? Who were her parents?

"I don't know my parents—I was adopted. But that doesn't matter. What I'm concerned about is his battle. He needs to overcome his desires and choose which side to give allegiance. I fear your presence could push him over the edge and we'll lose him—and you forever."

I didn't want to believe her. *"What do you mean?"*

"It would be much easier for him to sire you and join Alora than to deny and overcome his desires."

"Why do you even care?" I stated in malice, amazed she'd been so careless with him to allow such a disastrous blunder.

"I care like Nicholas cares. We both abhor the lives we've been given, living in the middle between good and evil. But it's not our fault our lot was picked for us by our parents, as naive as that may sound. Most vampires do not choose their lives either. But unlike most of them, I've retained my soul, therefore I ultimately want to see good prosper."

I pursed my lips, secretly agreeing. That was the only fine, thin thread that bonded us together—our desire for good to win over evil. *"And if Nicholas doesn't pick the good side?"*

"Actually, it doesn't matter. We'll all be destroyed in the end anyway."

My throat suddenly became dry. How dare she? Not if I can help it.

"They aren't my rules. It's the laws governing the universe. Your destiny."

"And it doesn't bother you that I'm supposed to eliminate all the vampires?" I asked, feeling very indignant. *"Even you?"*

"I'm prepared to meet that fate. Being immortal, tied to the evil one, isn't all red carpets and fanfare. I suffer the curse daily and choose to deny it." Scarlett meant every word she said—radiating actual happiness that my destiny meant the end of her life. *"But in the end, it's actually better for everyone."*

"That may be fine and dandy for you, but I know for a fact Phil does not want to return to Hell. And what about Nicholas?"

"I do not think any of us has a choice."

Something shifted in the street behind us followed by a catcall. My feet stumbled forward, rushing to get away from the source and closer to Scarlett. I'd kept my feelings-monitor so close to her aura that I'd not sensed any danger lurking around us.

"Argh," she grunted with disdain. *"Men sometimes!"*

I let go of my bubble to experience—for a second—the lasciviousness of the man meandering into the street behind us.

"Hey, Baby," he called in a slur. "Why don't you two come over here for a little fun?" His mind obviously raced with things he wanted to do to us—exciting to him, but bent towards evil.

My mind raced as well. I knew Scarlett could kick this guy's ass in a heartbeat, but if there were more like him close by, how would we get away? I suddenly wished for Phil's magic carpet ride.

"Don't worry. This will only take a second."

She turned and raised her chin, lifting out her arms. Suddenly, the man screamed and wilted to the ground, sobbing like a baby.

"I'm *sorry . . . So sorry,*" he whimpered over and over. "I'll never do it again. Please . . . *spare me.*"

My mouth gaped. Scarlett felt nothing of malice, or anger. She only radiated something ethereal in nature, holy even.

She smiled at her handy work then her maternal glance swept across my wide-eyes. "Ready to go?"

I glanced at the man who cowered prostrate on the ground in a growing puddle of liquid. "What did you do to him?"

The corner of her lip curled ever so slightly. "Introduced him to his maker."

"His what?"

"His *worst* fear. I probed his mind and found he's deathly afraid of God—well, actually His wrath. He fears the judgment he's going to receive for all the evil things he's done."

"How did you figure that out?"

Scarlett looked back at the pathetic man and clucked her tongue. "The inebriated are the easiest to control. They'll tell you anything you want to know . . . if you know how to ask." Her eye twinkled with satisfaction.

I stood, speechless.

"I was able to change my appearance through his thoughts. I saw the picture of what he believes God to look like and amplified it, projecting the image through his eyes onto myself, like an illusion."

The man remained on the ground, begging for forgiveness and mercy. For a second, I felt sorry for him.

"This vermin does not deserve your sympathy, Julia. He's a horrible man who needed a good fright to change his ways." Scarlett tugged at my arm. *"Let's go."*

I let her lead me away from the scene, my eyes unable to stop gawking at the change the man undertook. One minute he was a sexual predator, the next, a repentant naked soul. My mind began to swirl with the potential of Scarlett's gifts, gathering courage in her abilities. *"Why haven't you done that to Alora? Probed her mind and scared her into submission with her greatest fear?"*

"I can't snoop into her mind without her knowledge like I can humans. Plus, I can only read the current thoughts, not the past. Strong minds are often difficult to manipulate."

I fastened my mind within a nearby sleeping street-person so I could really ponder on what I'd witnessed. Every time Scarlett danced on the fibers of my thoughts, I knew she was there. Before, the talisman gave me complete protection which meant I could let my guard down. Without it working properly, my only alternative was to tirelessly jump from aura to aura to elude her.

"So that's it? You're giving up?" I asked, tired of mind talking.

Scarlett sighed with apathy. "There's nothing to hold onto. It's a losing battle. I've accepted it and the sooner you do the same, the better off you'll be."

"Killing Alora is not an option," I stated, almost rhetorically.

"Because of Phil?"

"Yes! You may want to live a death sentence, but I will not let you send him back to Hell prematurely. How can you even pretend to be his friend?" I folded my arms over my chest and wished I didn't need her protection, wanting to scream Phil's name for him to find me.

She shook her head in frustration as displeasure wafted out in shallow bursts. "Answer me this. As we wait, how many more will die or be changed under her leadership? Innocents pulled into the fight? Those exactly like Phil?"

"Then we must capture her."

"And then what?"

"Keep her." I cringed at how ridiculous my suggestion sounded, wanting to take it back.

Scarlett sniggered. "That is neither a reasonable nor humane option, Julia."

"Then we present our problem to Harry . . . to Preston." I wouldn't accept this outcome blindly. Vampires were innately evil, but apparently could be swayed for good with the right motivation.

"Even still, you're future is to bring all of this to an end. Forever. That means that all vampires *die*, period."

"For Nicholas and Phil's sakes and even yours, I don't accept that. There has to be another way."

"There isn't and fighting against your fate is only going to prolong the inevitable."

I screamed in my head, once again upset I'd lowered my guard and let her inside, blackmailing me with a stupid prediction.

Regardless of what she believed, I would not accept it. There had to be another way. I'd sacrifice myself before I'd let Nicholas die at my hand.

"Then why pretend? Why not just go kamikaze and take out

those around you and just get it over with?"

Scarlett puckered her lips, emitting disappointment. "Because I care for Phil, like you do. And . . ." Admiration and longing trickled out.

My cheeks burned. I hated that she knew my struggle to keep my feelings for Phil under control.

Scarlett straightened up and turned her head. Her long flowing black hair shimmered like a dark waterfall in the moonlight. "Murdering innocents is no better than what *they* do. I'm only here to help the prophecy come to fruition. *Your* destiny."

I huffed and folded my arms over my chest. "Nice. I get to do the dirty work." *Whatever.*

Chapter Twenty-Four

We walked for several hours, dodging headlights and the freaky nightlife. Scarlett—most of the time—mentally created distractions or blended our figures into the surroundings, keeping out of the watchful eyes of the local riff-raff. The few she toyed with did give me a healthy dose of satisfaction until one guy shamelessly cried for his mother.

Every block or so, I'd successfully found a lifeless soul to hide within to keep Scarlett from intruding on my thoughts. Each jump required intense focus in order to keep balanced on the high wire of their psyche. One wrong thought of sympathy for them would topple me into their never ending pit of sorrow and despair. My feet and back were another story. They ached something fierce from my illness.

"Are we there yet?" I asked again, perplexed that with all the power she encompassed, she still couldn't notify Phil and give him our location. Or seduce a taxi driver and have him drive us there.

"*I do have limitations. Walk faster,*" she said in my mind.

"*Are you serious? I just got over the flu and it's two in the morning. I wasn't prepared to walk ten miles tonight. I am human.*" I balled up my fists. "*Give me a flipping break.*"

"*He'll catch our trail . . .*"

"*Catch our trail? You mean he's not waiting for us somewhere?*"

"*We must keep moving.*"

I threw my hands up into the air and laughed. "This is the plan? And if we don't meet up, then what? Because I have to be home before morning or I won't be saving anyone from anything. Do you realize that my father *will kill me* if he finds I've left without permission?"

"I'm quite aware of the situation, Julia. There's no need for theatrical drama," she said bluntly out loud.

"Really? Really! Because the only people who seem to be picking up our trail are the perverts and drug dealers who think we're hookers."

"Which you've thoroughly enjoyed, watching them get what they deserve."

I pressed my eyelids shut, refusing to agree. "I want to take a hot shower and crawl into bed—my bed—at home. I can't believe I let Phil talk me into this. Harry isn't even here and I'm stuck in L.A.— with *you*—and the clock is ticking. I bet my dad has already called the National Guard by *now*."

"*Teenagers*."

"I heard that."

Scarlett quickly exhaled. "I *could* carry you on my back."

I whistled. *Oh whoopi-do.* "I'll pass, Wonder Woman."

"*Pride cometh before the fall . . .*" The words echoed slightly in the back of my thoughts, provoking my anger because they were not my own.

"Knock it off!" I twisted my eyes into slits and glowered at her innocent expression. "You should talk." I folded my arms across my chest, refusing to speak as we continued to walk down the semi-deserted street.

We finally rounded the corner between two abandoned buildings and I hoped we'd finally reunite with Phil, when Scarlett sent out another twinge of frustration and disappointment.

"Let me guess," I said with contempt. "This is the place."

She hesitated in slight confusion. I let out a sharp exhale and turned my eyes toward the night sky, hoping my gift deceived me and his black silhouette would magically show up at any moment.

"He'll come. I'm sure he's just . . ." She didn't finish. Instead, the dust swirled up around her morphing ankles as her skin grew a coat of black fur.

"What are you doing—?" I didn't finish either.

I turned to face the deluge of oncoming gluttony as my blood ripped through my veins. My voice froze within my windpipe.

"*I needed to change to hide,*" she whispered.

"*What about me?*" I asked in fear, trying to sound brave as I backed against the wall. "*Aren't you going to hide me too?*"

"They've seen you—they sense you. Just do what I tell you. I'll do the rest."

This time, I didn't argue. Whether I liked it or not, I had to trust her. She clearly had some plan, though I couldn't confirm her confidence, unable to read her aura any longer. I just hoped the plan didn't involve abandoning me.

"I wouldn't think of leaving you, Julia."

"Okay," I squeezed out, relieved for this one time she could read my thoughts.

My hands shook as I watched the dark archway, knowing at any moment *they'd* be revealing themselves in the moonlit corridor. For a second, I kicked myself for not taking a stake or two when I was with Hung earlier but recanted that thought once remembering my feeble human abilities. Without the power of the talisman, my aim would only put the weapon into my enemy's hands.

Like before, they appeared in a V formation. Slide, Blondie, Goth Boy, and Emo Girl were all present and accompanied by two new additions. My eyes drifted to check out the newbies: disheveled Biker Dude, who reminded me of a hyena, nervously fidgeted and cackled every couple of minutes, and Hulk-Man who wore a black do-rag on his head and sported an insanely ripped body. Even his muscles had muscles. They anxiously paced, hungrily licking their chops. Their combined lust for blood hit me like a wall of fire.

The six pairs of black viperous eyes locked onto me, a lowly mouse searching for a crack to escape into. Every cell in my body screamed to run, screamed for Nicholas to come save me.

"You're awful brave to be roaming this part of town alone, young lady," Blondie said, tilting her head to the side. Her birdlike movements reminded me of the velociraptors Phil and I just read about.

I swallowed hard and tried to keep a stony exterior. "Who says I'm alone?" My voice shook more than I wanted it to.

"With your gnat of a friend gone, I'd say you are . . . unless your cat does tricks."

I worked hard to control my smile from forming into a smirk.

Little do you know.

"*Phil has eluded them . . . Keep talking,*" Scarlett interjected.

"He'll be back," I said with more confidence.

"Will he?" Slide asked. Hyena dude snorted behind him, his laugh eerily tainting the ambiance.

I shifted my weight to my left foot, reminding myself to keep breathing and not lock my knees. "I know you didn't kill him."

"If that's true then where is he?" Blondie pressed her lips outward into a pucker, then tisked her tongue. "You know what I think? I think he ran home to Mommy and you've run out of luck."

Again, more creepy laughter permeated the air, sending shivers across the back of my legs.

"He's not the one you need to worry about—"

"*Go with it,*" Scarlett confirmed, pushing me to continue with my bluff.

"My boyfriend—Nicholas—won't like the way I've been treated here in his absence."

"Really?" Slide stepped forward, the name ringing familiarity but no real concern. "He should know better than to allow his *girlfriend* to roam freely in *our* town."

More snickers bounced off the building walls.

"Yes, but if I don't return safely, he'll find you . . ."

"Let him," I heard Hulk say with a Spanish accent, radiating contempt. Emo Girl and Goth Boy felt a little bit more reverence and shushed him in unison.

"He'll hunt each and every one of you down. He doesn't abide by the *rules* you know," I said with growing bravado.

"Pity," Blondie said apathetically. "Neither do we."

The bass from the growl that ripped from Hulk's lips reverberated in my chest, spiking my heart rate to a dangerous level.

"*Scarlett,*" I said inside with a timid voice. "*Do something.*"

"*You're doing great,*" she interrupted, her voice now brimming with excitement. "*Keep it up.*"

Doing great? Holy freaking crap!

I looked each vampire in the eye, knowing my mad-dog stare

bubbling anxiety didn't interfere.

"What's wrong?" I whispered, finding my voice worked a tiny bit better, my face still buried in his comforting leather coat.

"It's Scar . . . I need to rescue her too."

My chest shuddered as I forced my eyes open, not meeting the green eyes I wanted to see. Instead, charcoal colored eyes stared back at me with concern. The tears came from nowhere, falling shamelessly down my cheeks.

"What's wrong?" Phil asked, in confusion. "Are you hurt?"

I closed my eyes, willing the anguish away, shaking my head from side to side. I couldn't tell him the truth, not after I knew he was falling in love with me.

"I'm—I'm just thankful," I finally said, looking away—anywhere to avoid the depths of his searching eyes.

Below us on the ground, Scarlett danced around, fighting the six vampires like a ninja. She seemed tireless, though I sensed her growing distress.

"She needs our help," I stuttered out, trying to take the attention off myself.

"I know. Are you ready?"

I looked back into his eyes for a second, sucking up my disappointment and heartache. "Yeah, let's go get her."

Phil gently turned my body so we faced the same direction, tucking his arm around my waist before barreling down towards the ground, screaming "Cowabunga." The vamps looked up, suddenly filled with indignation, and poised themselves in a prepared ambush.

Filled with amusement, Phil darted in a different direction at the last second, away from their line of defense and towards Scarlett who magically appeared from nowhere. He scooped up her newly formed cat body into his arms and let out a whoop of satisfaction. The vamps turned around, stunned at first then erupted with furious cussing and threats, too late to catch him.

"See you later, suckers," Phil called down, while arching up into the moonlit night sky, laughing hysterically. I knew, if his hands weren't full, he'd be giving them *the bird* to seal the deal.

"That was terribly close." Scarlett's voice trembled, her exhaustion clearly evident.

"Sorry I took so long, girls," Phil said, emanating valiant excitement.

The talisman dangled from my neck, reminding me of it's awakening earlier and I frantically looked on the ground, searching for Nicholas. I hoped even though Phil had come to my aid, Nicholas was nearby and affecting its powers. To my horror, the stone was black again.

"Where were you?" I asked as chills from Scarlett's confession rippled over my skin, realizing if Phil might have been a little bit longer, I might have been killed.

"Sorry, I was detained, but no worries. Scar had it all under control. Didn't ya, babe?"

"Under control? Bah!" I barked, practically spitting with animosity. "I almost had my throat crushed!"

"I couldn't stop him mentally like the others. He blocked my abilities."

"Geez. Couldn't you have just morphed and crushed him like a bug?" I used slow and deep breaths to calm myself down so I wouldn't reach over and strangle her neck. "Always an excuse, isn't it?"

"I'd successfully used their fears and doubts against them so they'd squabble and distrust one other . . . it worked, for a while," she said, her voice growing fainter each word she spoke. *"It's tiring to concentrate and manipulate so many minds at once."*

"But where's Nicholas?" I asked, worried we were getting too far away and abandoning him to deal with the local vamps alone.

"Nick is here?" Phil said, in a panic.

"He's not here, Julia. Your necklace lighting up was an illusion I created."

Her words turned my stomach over in a somersault. How could this be? *"An illusion?"*

"I knew if I'd brought the necklace back to its former self, your

reaction would help in the deception. It worked, even down to the perceived pain when the others touched it, except on Slide."

"Hello? Answer me, Julia. Where's Nick?" Phil asked, completely unaware we'd excluded him from the internal conversation.

"No," I said quickly. "I thought for a second you were him when you caught me. I . . . I was confused."

"Oh," Phil said plainly trying to hide his disappointment.

"I never meant to cause you any pain. I'm sorry. I know how much you wanted to believe it to be true—that Nicholas was healed and here to rescue you."

The sadness in Scarlett's tone tore at my reasoning, but all I wanted to do was punch something.

"Screw you," I huffed in my mind, mashing my eyelids tightly together to hold back the tears. *"How dare you use those feelings against me."*

"It saved you," she whispered. *"Saved us."*

"Phil saved me, not your pathetic illusion."

I turned my head away from her and dove into Phil's aura—one filled with contentment and relief. The bitter cold began nipping at my body again and I shivered, not looking forward to enduring the freezing journey again.

"Here," Phil said, passing over Scarlett towards me. "Hold Scar. She'll keep you warm."

Unable to explain the reason for my animosity towards her, I just crossed my arms over my chest and refused. Warm or not, I would never hold her willingly.

Phil grew frustrated. "Look, I know things didn't exactly go as smoothly as we'd all hoped, but you're cold and I want to fly faster to get you home on time. So unless you want to literally freeze your ass off, you'd better hold her."

I scowled, still unwilling to take her from Phil's other arm.

"Take her now!" he barked. "And, if you even think about dropping her, I'll drop you. Got it?"

Though his feelings told me he'd never follow through with his threat, I was crushed he'd even have to warn me. I despised her, yes, but I wouldn't let her fall to her death.

"Fine," I huffed, taking her small but dense body into my arms.

Instantly, Scarlett's delightful fur flooded my body with radiating warmth. And the irresistible softness made it impossible to stop kneading her tantalizing coat as she tucked herself into a ball. Her purr simultaneously soothed my hurts and numbed my pain.

"I'm . . . so . . . sorry," she mumbled, as if she were falling asleep.

"I know," I thought, washed over with my own guilt. *"I know."*

Chapter Twenty-Six

Deep in twilight—the place where one isn't really sleeping, but not totally awake either—the wind rustled my hair while I snuggled deep within the comfortable goodness of my sleeping bag. Aladdin lay nestled next to me under the downy covers, purring like a lawn mower. We'd just left the drive-in theater and Dad let me and Luke stay in the truck bed for the ride home. The rumble of the engine had lulled me to sleep.

"We're here," I heard him say, but not in a tone I was familiar with.

I pried my eyes open and awoke with a start, staring at the world from a few thousand feet.

"Whoa," Phil said, gripping me tighter. "I've got you."

My nails became talons, clawing into his arms as I blinked several times to clear the fogginess from my brain. The drive-in wasn't real, but a fading dream sparked by a childhood memory.

I cleared my throat to stifle my scream.

Phil spoke soothingly, squeezing me a little tighter. "It's okay, Parker. You fell asleep."

"I . . . I did?"

"You did," Phil replied, pleasantly amused.

My hands relaxed off his arm and grazed over the lump in my jacket where Scarlett, a ball of heat, lay tucked within my coat. Phil's arms wrapped around my waist, keeping her secure next to my body. The recollection of putting her there slowly resurfaced. My arms had gotten tired and Phil suggested I store her in my coat while she slept. Good thing we did because I might have accidentally dropped her when I fell asleep myself.

"She's like a little space heater," I said jokingly.

"Yup."

I sensed his smugness, thankful he didn't follow with an "I told you so."

My house slowly came into view and I braced myself for the

onslaught of fear and worry but found nothing. Apparently—once again—I'd avoided suspicion and successfully snuck out of the house without consequence.

"Looks like things are okay," Phil said, just before landing on the roof ledge, relieved. "The *fam* seems to be sleeping."

"I guess so," I said with a shrug, unzipping my coat and lifting out the limp bundle of black fur.

"She's totally spent," Phil said, petting the top of her head. "Mind stuff always wears her out. Why don't you let her crash here while I go back and give the fake scoop to the *Empress*." He made a fluid sweeping motion with his hand and bowed.

I chuckled then frowned, realizing he wouldn't be staying with me tonight. I'd enjoyed the time we'd spent together . . . maybe a little too much and didn't prefer Scarlett as his replacement. His growing attraction was starting to make things difficult.

Phil spotted my frown. "She'll be hanging with you tomorrow anyway, so it'd be cool if she could just stay," He tapped his finger lightly against my pouting lip. "Smile."

I scrunched up my face. "Do I have to?"

"I like it when you smile."

"No," I smirked. "I mean, have Scarlett escort me to school? I can handle it. Really."

"No. We don't need anymore accidental makeovers." Phil wrapped his arm around my shoulder with one arm and mussed up the front of my bangs with the other hand. "And besides, you two are becoming such good friends."

Little do you know. "Whatever." I stuck out my tongue.

Phil laughed with a wink then leaned in towards my lips. For a brief second, my heart palpitated. Instead, he gave me a peck on the cheek and whispered in my ear, "Miss me."

Stunned, I teetered backward after he let me go and sat on the window ledge, unable to stop the butterflies his mischievous grin gave me. A huge part of me was going to do just that—miss him— and I didn't like he was going back to the den of vipers, even if he was our spy. Instead of asking him to stay though, I crawled inside and dropped the fluff of fur gently onto the floor, desperately trying to act like his departure didn't faze me.

"Yeah," I said with a fabricated chuckle, peering out of the window. "Miss me too."

"Always." He winked again then disappeared.

At his absence, my smile faded and all the tension from the night came out in one big exhale. The last thing I wanted to feel was disappointment that he could leave so easily. But I did.

The room looked the same as when we left earlier but the ridiculousness of the blonde wig made me chuckle out-loud. My pseudo-body couldn't have possibly fooled anyone, especially my dad. I pushed everything onto the floor, set my alarm, and crawled under the covers. The day had been one of the longest in my life and everything ached, especially my neck.

My head hit the pillow and my heavy eyelids drooped, begging for sleep, but I had to take a moment to deal with the ever nagging gaping hole that longed for Nicholas' presence and touch.

A huge part of me wanted to give in and send out an open invitation, hoping he'd make the decision easier for me. If he could only sneak in and partake of my blood while I slept we could just run away together under the shadow of darkness and never return. The thought sounded blissful until I remembered my dad. I could never leave him like that.

"I love you," I whispered, lifting my hand in the direction of the window. "Come back to me." Utterly exhausted, I let it fall and drifted instantly into a deep sleep.

"Wake up."

Something heavy lay on my chest, nudging its wet nose against my cheek.

"Stop it, Aladdin," I said and rolled over, knocking her off in the process. I pulled a pillow over my ear to stop the blaring music. *Who's playing music so loud at this hour?*

"Your clock is. Get up."

The weight came back, this time on my hand. I ignored the

obnoxious pressure until sharp pins pricked into my skin, shooting pain up my arm.

I yanked my hand away with a yelp, tempted to swat away whatever hurt me, finding myself glaring back into exotic-blue cat-eyes. "What the heck?"

"Turn off that racket."

The fog cleared as I realized a cheesy love song blared from *my* alarm clock. "You can't press snooze?"

"I've been pressing it but it starts playing again," Scarlett said, animosity lacing her tone.

I reached across her body and flicked the switch to the off position, inspecting the time—a little after seven. "Oh crap."

Shoving her and the covers off my bed, I leapt up and headed towards the shower. "Why did you let me sleep this long?"

"Let you?" Scarlett snarled, walking out from under the comforter, fluffing her fur to get it back to its luminous splendor.

"Forget it," I said while slamming the door of the bathroom, separating visual contact. I shrugged off the clothes I'd slept in and turned on the tap. The warm water felt amazing, washing away the worries from the night and bringing hopes for a new day.

"I guess you'll be coming with me?" I asked. *"Scarlett?"*

She didn't answer.

I toweled off and caught a glimpse of the black talisman that hung lifeless around my bruised neck in the mirror. Today would have to be a turtleneck day.

Darn you, Slide.

With a sigh, I caressed the stone, wishing my touch would encourage it to wake up. Something inside told me unless Nicholas and I mended our relationship, it would forever remain dormant. I turned away from the mirror and tried to ignore my logic, brushing out my wet hair instead.

After leaving the bathroom, I noticed Scarlett wasn't in my room any more. For a second, I wondered if I should find her, or steal a peak at my text messages away from her prying mind. The phone won out and I retrieved it from my backpack. The screen flickered to life as I held my breath.

Six new messages lit up my inbox, all from Sam. I let out my breath in a noisy lip flapping trill and scrolled through her comments, all from this morning.

- **You coming today?**
- **I can't handle another day of History without you.**
- **Hey! You alive? Text me back.**
- **OMG! Major news! Call me!!!**
- **Holy crap! Tyler saw Katie last night!**
- **She's alive, but all vamped out. Weird.**

The last text sent me into a panic to get to school. Quickly, I pulled on my clothes and bolted downstairs to grab coffee and a bagel, although something else super yummy wafted from the kitchen. Tasty or not, I had to ignore my hunger and get in the car before the scheming cat returned to escort me.

I burst into the kitchen and skidded to a halt, phone in hand, just about to call Sam when I saw them.

Scarlett and Aladdin sat side by side eating tuna from the same bowl on the floor. Dad stood at the stove with his beloved spatula in hand and turned at my arrival. A welcoming smile formed across his face to greet me.

"Good morning, Pumpkin. Good to see you up and back to your old self today."

"Dad!" I barked, giving him the eye and pointing to Scarlett.

"What?" Dad shot me an innocent look, reverberating annoyance at me. "She seemed hungry, so I fed her."

"Next I'm having pancakes," Scarlett said with a purr.

"Like heck you are," I spouted out loud, temporarily forgetting the *faux pas* of her secret identity.

"What did you just say?" Dad asked, now trickling a little anger.

"Never mind." I smoothed my jeans with my sweaty palms and sat down at the table, glowering at Scarlett. "What I meant to say was you shouldn't have. We don't know who she belongs to."

Dad walked over and scratched the top of Scarlett's head. "She seems tame enough and don't forget how we got *Laudy*. Who knows, they might be in need of companionship. They seem to like one another."

Scarlett responded with a meow, arching her back as my dad scratched along her spine.

"Knock it off. This wasn't part of the deal!" I said acidly.

"I'm not denying the hospitality of your dear, sweet Father. He has such little joy in his life and I'm starving."

"He has plenty of joy without you. Get out of his head this instant," I spat, finally at my wits end.

"It's unlike you to be inhospitable towards animals, Julia."

"She's—" My glance bounced between Dad's frown and Scarlett's smug kitty lips, considering exercising my right as a resident in the home.

"Don't even think about it," she warned, the end of her tail flicking ever so slightly. *"How are you going to explain my reaction to your father if I change?"*

"You leave me no choice," I said in glee. *"You better run."*

Scarlett tried darting from the room but froze midway in the air when I mentally uninvited her. She fell, stiff as a board, onto the linoleum with a thud. My dad gasped and rushed to pick her up, holding her awkwardly in his hands.

"She's having a seizure or something."

"Should I call the Vet?" I laughed inside at the suggestion.

"And I saved your life last night." Scarlett sounded pained.

My shoulders dropped; her distress sobered me up. I moved next to my dad, petting her fur lightly. He seemed far away, almost like he was in a trance.

"Dad?" I grabbed his arm.

"Huh?" he shook his head and grunted, dragging his free hand down over his face. "Sorry . . . what did you say?"

"I know what to do." I took her lifeless body from his hands, rubbing fiercely on her ribcage. *"Fine, you're invited."*

Scarlett's limbs softened and I dropped her to the floor. Without a word, she darted out of sight.

"See? She just needed her lungs massaged."

He mumbled something and went back to his pancakes, which were smoking.

"I'm just going to put her outside and go to school, okay?"

"What about breakfast?" My dad's glassy eyes met mine.

"I don't have time," I said with a shrug. "I'm running late."

"No. You need breakfast."

He wrapped up a few pancakes and bacon on a paper plate while I put coffee in a travel mug, secretly grateful. My stomach was growling something fierce.

Before handing me the plate, he looked into my eyes nostalgically, brimming with loving concern. "I love you, Julia."

I enfolded my arms around his torso. "I love you too, Dad."

He hugged back, filled with worry and regret. I had no clue what Scarlett had done to him, but she was going to get it when I found her.

"Just be careful, okay?"

"Of course, Dad," I said, looking up at him through my eyelashes. "Always."

Chapter Twenty-Seven

I hastily closed the door to the house, juggling my breakfast, backpack, and coffee all while cursing at Scarlett under my breath as I headed towards my car. Scarlett sat on the sidewalk and appeared like nothing happened.

"What did you do to him?" I asked bitterly.

"Nothing but a distraction. You left me no choice," she said, her tail held high in the air, tone lackadaisical.

"No choice? I come down stairs to find you with my dad, reading his thoughts like the morning paper and I'm not supposed to be upset? Are you serious?"

"I know you know it wasn't like that."

"Sure it wasn't." I folded my arms over my chest. "Your invitation has been revoked. Do you hear me? I'm so done with this—with you. Done!"

"Contrary to what you think, I do not enjoy this."

I growled, realizing she'd pick-pocketed my brain again and threw my arms in the air, looking towards heaven for a little help, or maybe a thunder bolt.

"You act like you do . . . a little too much actually," I said with a biting tone. Gingerly, I opened the driver's door and put my things inside, careful to set the plate of pancakes upright on the passenger seat.

For a brief second, I was tempted to get into the car and drive off, leaving her stranded at the house.

"I'll just follow you."

I slapped my hands against the sides of my legs. *Grrrr. Of course you will.* "I don't know why I bother speaking to you at all. You never answer my questions; only manipulate me in return to find out what you want to know."

Scarlett moved aside and continued to look up at me, blocking the path of the door. Her silence suddenly felt a little spooky. She, of all people, was the one person I needed to be able to feel out on a regular basis.

From nowhere, the image of Phil's angered face after he'd found out I'd become a vampire—at Nicholas' hand—zinged like a shooting star across my mind. Visions of my funeral and grieving family followed.

I started at the thought. "Is that my future?"

"Possibly," she said with a sneer. *"If you leave me behind."*

I blinked at the idea, tortured by the effect one small decision could have on those I loved.

"Fine." I gritted my teeth. "If you must, get in and leave your fleas outside."

Scarlett leapt gingerly into the car, stepping over my breakfast. She perched herself on the front half of the passenger seat, facing straight ahead. *"Thank you."*

I slammed the car door and turned the key, revving the engine extra hard before throwing the gear into drive, hoping to dislodge her. Scarlett balanced herself perfectly, like a leaf hanging on a branch in a windstorm, using her tail and paws for balance.

"Don't claw my leather seats."

"Wouldn't dream of it," she said in a smooth purr.

I clenched my jaw while gripping the steering wheel and forced my mind to remain blank for the few minutes it took to get to school. To annoy her, I ate my pancakes and only thought of my favorite toppings until my mind drifted to the decadent peaches they served at the Beverly Hills Hilton. I stopped the memory before it played on its own when my phone buzzed, reminding me of Sam's text about Katie.

Scarlett's voice became agitated. *"When did this happen?"*

I wiped clean the slate of my mind. "What?"

"When did Tyler visit Katie?"

I snickered. "Oh, interesting thing. Apparently she happened to visit Tyler while we were gone, which you said was unlikely. I can't wait to tell Phil people at my school have found out vampires exist because you didn't do your job *again*. Kind of ironic."

"Not likely. I'll stop the rumors."

"What? With more mind tricks?"

"Selective amnesia actually."

"Oh, right."

I tore into the school lot and parked. No one paid attention as I rushed from my vehicle. Driving with a cat perched calmly on the front seat was one thing, but having one follow me through the halls would definitely bring attention I didn't want. My only hope was distancing myself from her a little bit so people didn't know she was following me exactly. But honestly, I didn't have time to care. Finding Sam was my highest priority.

Upon entering the bustling hallway, I hid myself in Mary Jo Montgomery's aura so I could think freely. She was naturally smart—more so than Cameron—and kept away from the typical emotionally draining drama. She seemed to be headed towards the gym, which was my direction, eliminating the dizzying challenge of jumping from person to person. Sam slammed her locker, turning in the same direction.

"Hey," I said, lacing my arm within hers, steering her through the crowd behind Mary Jo. "How's it going?"

I hoped she wouldn't happen to notice the cat walking behind us, doing God knows what to my classmates. I was unable to tell since I'd invisibly hid elsewhere. Instead, Sam looked at me through the corner of her eye, eyebrows pushed together. "Geez. A call would have been nice. You aren't contagious anymore, are you? 'Cause like half the student body, including Morgan and Dena have caught this wicked thing and I don't want it."

"Don't think so," I said, unable to wait any longer, feeling pressure to get to the point. "I got your text. What's with Katie?"

"You needn't waste your time. No one is discussing this apparent sighting."

I closed my eyes, and exhaled. *"Waste my time? Is nothing sacred? This IS my conversation. Get lost!"*

"Oh, that," she said unaware of my internal struggle. "He thinks he might have seen a girl that looked like Katie, but she was all gothed out so he doubts it was her."

"But your text said vampire," I corrected.

"Vampire?" she screwed up her face and laughed. "Heck, no. I meant vamped. Doesn't vamped and gothed mean the same thing?"

Inside I breathed a sigh of relief that she wasn't even going there with her thoughts. "Yeah, I think."

My thoughts spun. Maybe he really did see her, and what he suspected to be some crazy goth-girl look-alike was really Katie in her new vampy self displayed in her glory.

She smiled and shook her head, but the sadness resurfaced quickly. "Anyway . . ."

I frowned to mirror her heavy heart. "Yeah, I wish he did see Katie."

"I'll find out. Go straight to class."

"Psscht," I said accidentally, and then coughed afterward to cover it up.

"What?" Sam asked, pulling away from me with a questioning look and anxious to avoid my germs as we pushed open the girl's locker room door.

"Oops," I said and covered my mouth. "Sorry. I just remembered I forgot my gym clothes."

"Oh." She still eyeballed me like I had the plague.

"Seriously, I feel fine, Sam."

"Yeah, yeah," she said immediately. "I know. Germ freak. Sorry."

Sam pouted and walked to the benches to change without me. I gave her a consoling frown before leaving to go sit alone on the bleachers in the gym. Coach Hoffman happened to be at the doors to the gym. I told her my blunder on my way out.

Busy concentrating to find another soul to hide within, I ran smack into Tyler, my radar warning stuck in a jumping limbo.

"Excuse me," I said, almost teetering over. He instantly caught my elbow and helped me regain balance. I stood up and smoothed my palms on my jeans. "Thanks."

"Watch out," he said. His smile covered his hidden sadness.

I bit my lip, wondering how I could have a heart-to-heart about Mandy or even Katie.

"I heard you were sick," I said quickly before he had a chance to dart away to the other end of the gym where the guys assembled to play basketball.

"I got that flu."

"So did I." I smiled, trying to convey warmth. "Felt pretty bad for a few days."

"Yeah, me too . . ."

We locked eyes for a second. His soul cried out to me from behind his copper colored irises: confusion, pain, conflict. I wanted to bring up the subject with a really good question and find out why, but nothing came out of my mouth.

"Well, take care," he finally said, which broke the painful silence and walked away from me across the gym floor.

I grimaced; annoyed I let the opportunity go without even one word about Katie, wishing I had a gifted vocabulary instead of a worthless feeling detector.

"Crap," I mumbled under my breath.

"He'll recover. And Katie did show herself to him briefly, though he's not planning to reveal that to anyone."

I glanced down at my obnoxious shadow, wanting to punt her across the gym floor. *"Nice. When did that happen?"*

"Like you thought. When we were in L.A.."

Of course she did. I snorted softly and walked away from her towards the bleachers. The girls were just starting to file in for volleyball and I didn't want to be associated with the strange black cat. *"What did she talk to him about anyway?"*

"Not sure."

I sighed, completely annoyed that Scarlett only gave me a minimal amount of information, if that. For a mind reader, our conversation shouldn't require me to ask questions verbatim.

"I don't work like that," she snipped.

"OH, I see," I clenched my jaw. *"Fine then, read this. If you don't start telling me what you know right now, I'm going to march right over to Tyler and ask him myself."*

Scarlett sprawled herself out under the bleachers and began

giving herself a bath. *"Go right ahead."*

I scanned the gym and zeroed in on Mary Jo's emotional cloud, only to decide I didn't want to feel her lack of confidence, fusing to Alexis' pompousness instead. If I wanted to be successful with my threat, drawing strength in her arrogance would be a far better choice.

With bravado, I left my comfortable seat and joined Tyler who apparently had a pass to stay out of class today too.

"Hey," I said, eyeballing the spot next to him. "Can I sit here?"

Tyler nodded, studying me with apprehension. "Sure."

I sat down and smiled at his curiosity, fascinated he didn't feel disgust instead.

"Too sick to participate?" he asked uncomfortably.

"I forgot my clothes actually," I said. "One more pass and my grade's going down to a C."

"Oh." Tyler smirked. "My mom doesn't think I should be *over exerting* myself yet so she called Coach to get me out of class and football practice. I told her I should just sleep in and come to second period instead, but that didn't fly."

"That's lame," I said as a cover up, wishing my dad would have done the same for me.

"She just—you know—gets all wigged out about stuff. It's super annoying."

"My dad does too, but in a different way. I've got these stupid electronic leashes on my car and cell phone so he'll know where I am at all times."

Tyler slyly glanced at me while pulling his lips into a tight line, radiating surprise. "Really?"

I sensed he didn't know what to say as trust suddenly filtered around us. Apparently he'd never suspected I'd need constant monitoring.

"Maybe it's this whole Katie disappearance thing," I interjected quickly so he wouldn't spread rumors I was some bad girl. "My dad's super over-protective, you know?"

Katie's name hung in the air, like a soap bubble, ready to burst. I held my breath, hoping he'd talk first.

"She's your friend, right?" he finally said.

"Ever since the 4th grade."

"Has she ever done this before? Run away?"

I kept a frown to cover a smile, realizing his words actually admitted he'd seen her. A confession might actually give him the courage to share his secrets.

"Don't," Scarlett said earnestly.

My eyes found hers to which I raised my eyebrows slightly, purposefully trying to irritate her. She wasn't the boss of me and I wanted to remind her of it.

"Well, not to this degree, but I saw her on Monday actually." I let the confession sink in, and waited, sensing his curiosity peak. "I haven't told anyone yet. She asked me not to."

Tyler's eyes met the floor. The guilt billowed up around us, forming invisible thunder clouds of anxiety. He wanted to tell me. He needed to tell me.

"I . . . um. Well." He looked nervously around the gym and cleared his throat.

I tried to convey a little safety his way with my demeanor, but he remained silent. We sat, listening to the scores called out on the girl's side along with a chorus of grunts, shoe skids and whistle blows from the other.

Then his shoulders relaxed.

"I saw her too," he confessed quietly.

"You did?" I said, scooting closer so our conversation couldn't be over heard, except by Scarlett, who was now sitting at attention, focused on us intently. "When?"

"Yesterday," he whispered. "I was taking out the trash after dinner and she was there, watching me. I thought maybe I'd imagined it or something, you know, from being sick, but she gave me this."

Tyler pulled out a gold locket and opened it up. I gasped. Katie never took off her locket, given to her by her favorite aunt when she turned twelve. She coveted the piece so much; she never showed anyone what was inside. But there they were, a picture of her and Tyler facing each other inside the tiny frames.

"I didn't know quite what to say when she gave me this, but she's *different* now." His voice cracked. "Do you know what I mean?"

Tyler didn't reverberate fear, only attraction—strong attraction.

"Yeah," I said, nodding my head. "What did she say?"

"If you even breathe a word of this, I'll deny it," he murmured, shifting in his seat, eyeballing Matt Henderson who seemed suddenly very interested in our conversation. I caught Sam gawking at us too.

"Oh, of course." I pushed a little peace and confidence against his buffer of uncertainty and he relaxed again, bringing down his defenses.

"I thought I saw her the night before too, when my fever was super high, but passed it off 'cause that's like weird to see girls staring at you from outside your window at three in the morning." He looked towards me for reassurance.

I nodded my head.

"So, when I saw her standing in the shadows by the garbage cans, all pale and ghost like, I wasn't sure what to think, other than I was going crazy. But she smiled."

"Really."

"But she's . . . really . . . *pretty* now. I mean, don't get me wrong, she was pretty before but now . . . um . . . she's just—wow!" His desire sky-rocketed while he cleared his throat. "I wanted to say something, but she only handed me this and said she missed me and that she wanted me to know she wasn't dead. But when I looked up from my hand, she was gone."

He closed the locket back tenderly and held it in his hand.

"Yeah, she seemed very. . . *different* to me too." My mouth couldn't form the words *hot* or even *gorgeous*, afraid the admission would add to his crush. "How's Mandy?"

Tyler looked away, expelling jealousy, and shoved the locket into his pocket. "Heck if I know," he said quickly, skimming across the girls in the gym, finding her then skittering his glance away.

"Doesn't matter."

Mandy had her back to us, serving the ball. She acted as if we didn't exist but on the inside she crumbled to bits. I didn't sense it was over Tyler but something else, something that terrified her.

"Hmmm," I heard, echoing lightly in my mind.

I glanced at Scarlett who apparently had her eyes locked on Mandy as well. *"What do you know?"* I asked.

"There was another Katie sighting—with another student."

"Was it Mandy?" I already knew and didn't really needing confirmation.

Scarlett bobbed her head ever so slightly.

Dang it, Katie. What are you up to?

Putting my hand to my head, I pressed inward on my forehead, waiting for Scarlett to volunteer something insightful. Tyler needed specific encouragement to mend things with Mandy, and Mandy needed to be told she wasn't crazy—her guest visit by Katie probably was very uncordial. "I bet she misses you," I said after momentarily meeting his pained glance to which he rolled his eyes.

"Doubt it."

"A little help please?"

Scarlett's continued silence angered me further. She knew what I could say to help, yet she stayed quiet, only flicking her tail every so often.

"How about—" I fumbled as my brain drew a blank, but his attention shifted towards the debacle in the corner of the gym.

Off to the side, Coach Hoffman stooped like a bird on a perch, pointing to Scarlett with Principle Brewster in tow. He held what looked like a large fishing net and an aura bubbling over with apprehension, like he hunted a tiger. His knees visibly shook. Unable to help it, I stifled a giggle.

"What is he doing?" Tyler asked in amazement.

"Heck if I know," I said, trying not to fall on the floor in hysterics.

"Lovely," Scarlett said and bolted like a flash of black lightening out of the gymnasium.

"Bye." My face sprouted an over-enthusiastic grin. "Stray, I

guess," I shrugged, trying to look unimpressed just as the bell rang.

"Yeah." Then Tyler looked straight into my eyes. "Thanks."

I melted, giving him a consoling smile. "Anytime."

He nodded and walked off to Calculus alone. I stayed in a daze, watching him and everyone else leave for class, wondering where Scarlett fled to. But before she had a chance to return, I darted to History, hoping Scarlett would accidentally get locked out of the classroom. An hour of reprieve was exactly what I needed to process everything.

Chapter Twenty-Eight

"What were you talking to Tyler about?" Sam leaned over and whispered while we acted like we were listening to Mr. Marshall as he droned on about the Battle of the Bulge.

"Oh, nothing much." Sam's huge brown inquiring eyes wouldn't let me leave it at that; I growled at myself while my conscience caved. Unwilling to pull a Scarlett on her, I divulged more details. "I asked him about Katie and how he and Mandy were doing."

"And?"

"He and Mandy aren't talking, and he's not sure he really saw Katie, just like you said," I lied, per his request.

"Oh, really?"

Mr. Marshall stopped talking and gave everyone a menacing stare, to which the class became silent. We both innocently looked down, pretending to scribble some notes. After a minute, he started again.

"Did you see that huge black cat in the gym earlier?" she whispered once Mr. Marshall turned his back.

I withheld my sarcasm, wanting to scream out the truth. "I did. And what's with Mr. Brewster and the net? Was he trying to catch it?"

"I know. What a dork," Sam chuckled. "I guess that cat's been seen all over the school today. But she's like . . . gorgeous. Did you see her fur? It's amazing . . . almost iridescent."

"Yeah, amazing," I echoed.

Out of the corner of my eye, I saw Mikey Leibos sneak into class and a black streak of light shot from between his feet to some boxes in the back of class. Internally, I clung to Sam's aura for solace.

Fancy meeting you here, I spoke in my mind with a forced exhale to which she didn't reply. *I see you've avoided capture.* Dang it.

She still remained quiet, somewhere behind me. I pursed my lips in frustration that I couldn't inconspicuously crane my neck around to see what she was doing.

"*I don't get you,*" I finally said, always feeling like I stood on the fringe of every conversation we had, practically begging for any type of information whatsoever. "*I could have used a little help with Tyler just now. What's your deal anyway?*"

"*I tell you what you need to know, all else is trivial . . . and frankly none of your business,*" she said curtly.

I snorted and kept my eyes straight ahead, aggravated beyond words. Possible detention and dire embarrassment were the only two things preventing me from standing up in the middle of class and revealing her location, feigning I had a deadly cat allergy.

Visions of a sneezing attack seemed like a good idea until I imagined Nurse Nancy sticking me with an epi pen or worse, calling 911. Dad would reveal the truth immediately and the whole event would make me the laughing stock of the school. Scarlett would get a huge kick out of that one. I just had to ignore her and pretend she didn't exist or else I'd go crazy. I decided I'd stop reacting to her and block out her conversations. But that might require enacting mental earplugs to block out her interrupting voice.

"*You already have an advantage reading their feelings. You don't need me to tell you anything more.*"

I bit my tongue, reminding myself of my pact.

"*Besides, I do not use my abilities in that manner. I'm respectful,*" she continued.

Ooof. That's it! "*I'm in History right now, and you aren't shutting up. How is that respectful?*"

Silence followed. I smiled, finally getting reprieve, until Mr. Marshall's beady eyes met mine. I unplugged from Sam for a minute to feel his haughty contempt.

"Julia?" he asked caustically, apparently repeating himself. "The answer please?"

The heat burned out from my cheeks like hotplates as the time slowly passed. I had no idea what to say.

"*The answer is Baltimore,*" Scarlett said, her voice exuding sympathy.

"Baltimore," I blurted out, hoping she wasn't purposely trying to embarrass me more than I already was.

He squinted, slightly shocked. "That is *correct.*"

Disappointed, he resumed his place at the board, pen in hand, blathering on. When I looked at Sam, she blinked back at me, astonished as well. I shrugged. In fact, everyone seemed surprised. Whatever question I answered, no one knew, making me appear smart for once.

"Thanks," I said.

Scarlett didn't say anything more for the rest of the period. The bell rang and I collected my books and headed for English. By fourth period Chemistry my chest ached with the unknown plaguing my mind.

I felt left out, unsure of the plan Phil and Scarlett devised to conquer Alora. If there even was one. And in the quiet moments, my mind always wandered to Nicholas' well-being. Pretending everything was okay and walking through my day like a zombie exhausted me.

I crumpled on the inside, not paying a ton of attention to the make up Chemistry lab I rushed through, one of the many I'd missed when out sick. My astute lab partner, Jessica, happened to be home sick, along with half the class. According to the board, she'd already completed this lab without me. Even still, all I could think about was that Scarlett knew what Nicholas really was feeling, mixing inside me jealousy and despair.

"Stop," Scarlett said abruptly.

I froze, holding the two flasks of liquid in my hands, just about to combine them in the beaker in front of me.

"What?" I yelped, instantly agitated, thinking I was going to blow up the joint.

"If you mix those together, you'll . . ."

A shriek from the corner put everyone on high alert. Mr. Walentine ran over and mopped up the foamy mess, consoling Emily who'd burst into tears, holding two empty flasks. Her lab partner was apparently out sick too. I set down my containers and retraced my steps, realizing I'd measured my liquids incorrectly.

"Thanks," I mumbled.

Wiping the sweat from my brow, I readjusted my goggles and paid more attention to the chemicals in front of me. Twice she'd saved me today and didn't need to.

"So is there any kind of plan at all?" I finally asked after moving to the next lab, a less messy PH testing assignment.

"We have been discussing alternative methods."

"Like?"

"Apprehending Alora isn't feasible and neither is exterminating her. We've agreed a "shock therapy" type of treatment would be effective."

I turned and caught her icy-blue eyes staring back at me from under Mr. Walentine's desk, the only thing shimmering outward to alert her location. Alora getting a nice jolt of electricity put a smile on my face.

"Really? Is that possible?"

"Not with electricity." My disappointment turned my lips to a straight line. *"We believe a healthy dose of Alora's future might sober her up, like it's done to Phil and the others I've recently enlightened. Phil's obviously been inspired to make some new life decisions based on the grander scheme of things. Though, I'm unsure how long her conversion would last, since our session could only be for minutes, not months."*

I let the idea sink in and trembled. The thought of Phil trapped in Hell for months sounded horrific. But he had mentioned Alora wasn't keen on reading his past and avoided mental interactions ever since he'd given her a glimpse. And the incredible reaction from the thugs in the alley made them beg for forgiveness instantly.

"How would you do it?"

"Through touch I could open the gateway of his mind and channel the memories, forcing Alora to see, live, and experience Hell as Phil remembers it. But the experiment wouldn't be isolated. Phil and Alora would experience his past simultaneously in a very real way, which could create emotional distress on Phil.

"He's all for trying it, but his past is very debilitating to him. The vision could be so real, he could believe he'd returned and forget the scenario is only a simulation. If someone could talk to him during the process, it might help him stay grounded long enough to endure it."

"I could do it," I volunteered quickly.

"Yes, but you'd need to stay disconnected. The feelings could pull you under as well."

"Okay," I said, feeling a burst of excitement. If the treatment worked, we could bring Alora to her knees, repentant to only serve the good side. Then Nicholas hopefully would be more inclined to do the same thing. No one would need to die. "And, what about Katie . . . oh, and Mandy?" Controlling Katie seemed like another important thing to worry about.

"She needs to comply, or else."

"Or else what?"

"She's not bound by any bloodlines we are aware of, being the newest vampire. She'll be exterminated if she's a liability."

I gasped. Katie selfishly wreaked havoc with her inappropriate appearances, but that didn't deserve her death. She'd only been drinking from blood slaves as far as I knew and was actually a victim in this whole debacle. "Whoa, we need to discuss this."

"I'll need to alter Mandy's mind too," Scarlett interrupted, ignoring me completely. "She's crippled with fear and it's wearing on her sanity."

"She is? What did Katie do to her?"

"Threatened to hunt her down if she even goes as far as to look at Tyler," Scarlett said somberly.

Oh crap! "Then we need to do a Hell mind-meld with Katie too." And quickly.

"We'll see about that," Scarlett replied. "First things first."

And that we will do. Finally in the "know" of their plans, I could figure out what I needed to do.

Chapter Twenty-Nine

"Where's Cameron?" Sam asked, scanning the sparse lunchroom.

Never mind Cam, where's Scarlett?

I'd darted out of fourth period so fast, I didn't look to see if she'd followed me to the cafeteria or not. The thought of her locked up in the science lab all weekend seemed funny.

"I don't know, he was here earlier." I skimmed across my classmate's faces and under tables, catching Tyler's quick glance to which he smiled, brimming with fondness for me. I blushed and returned the sentiment.

His heartache wrenched my gut as I watched him gaze quickly at Mandy who sat the farthest away she possibly could, her back to him—unknowingly paranoid and petrified. The scene made me vow to stop Katie from using intimidation and vampire seduction to break them up.

"Is that Todd over there?" I said, squinting purposefully in the direction where Tyler and Todd sat between a few cheerleaders.

"Yes." Sam's anxiety bounded forth and she tilted her head down, only glancing towards him beneath the glossy brown curtain of her hair. "Stop gawking at them, will you?"

"What's the big deal? Aren't you guys dating? Let's motion for them to come sit with us," I suggested playfully.

"Uh." Sam's agitation escalated. "No. That's fine. He's hanging with the team. I don't want to intrude."

"He's only with Tyler." I started to stand when Sam's hand caught my arm.

"No, he's busy. Let's have lunch, just you and me today. Please?"

The fact Todd kept their relationship under the radar angered me, conveniently deciding when or if it was appropriate to be seen together. "Doesn't it bother you that he won't eat with you, hold your hand, or even really talk to you while he's at school?"

"Not really," she lied. "He just doesn't like public displays of affection."

"Personally, I think it's rude and he shouldn't treat you like that. Either you are together and he's proud to show people, or you're not."

I stood up and grabbed my tray of half-eaten food.

"Please, Jules. Don't do this." Sam pleaded with her eyes.

On a saving rampage, I waffled, wanting to walk over and tell Todd exactly what I thought of how he treated Sam. But for Sam's dignity, I sat back down and let out an over exaggerated sigh.

"I'm going to talk to him about it tonight actually," Sam said, looking down at the table, her cheeks reddening more by the minute. Her bravery suddenly spiked. "But you're one to talk. Look at you and Nicholas."

"That's different," I said, speaking before thinking.

"Really?" Sam looked me dead in the eye. "Explain to me how hiding your boyfriend from everyone, including your family, is different."

Unwilling to fight with my best friend, and frustrated I couldn't tell her the truth, I caved. I needed to tell someone my heart-wrenching news.

"Doesn't matter. We broke up."

Sam gasped. "What? When?"

The tears bubbled from nowhere. My confession hit harder than I wanted. "Monday."

"After your weekend?" Sam screwed up her face in horror and curiosity. "You didn't —?"

"No. He's a gentleman actually," I breathed softly. "He's going through some rough stuff right now. His mom, who left him at birth, magically showed up and wants him to move away with her." *Among other things.*

I pressed my eyelids shut to stop the tears. When a few slipped down my cheeks, I ducked my head and wiped them away with the sleeve of my shirt. The sympathy of a few neighboring girls wafted over to our table anyway.

"Oh." Sam bit her lip. "Sorry."

"It's not like we kept things a secret because he's embarrassed to be around me, it was for my protection because—" my mind fumbled to find the right words to define his dangerous ties, "—he's a bounty hunter."

Sam blinked back at me with huge awestruck eyes, suddenly enlightened. "No way," she whispered. "As in, hunts down the bad guys and stuff?"

I nodded my head, thankful the rest of the exaggerated story flowed effortlessly. "Remember the Dirty Harry stuff in the newspaper? That was Nicholas actually. So, he had to keep me a secret to protect me from his enemies."

"But he's so young. How did he land a job doing that?"

I licked my lips. "He works with his . . . uncle and he's been training him since he was young."

A huge weight lifted off my chest even though I glossed over the finer details. After holding the vampire secret for over six months, I finally revealed to her a fraction of the truth, receiving some form of moral support for once.

Why hadn't I thought to tell her this rendition before today?

"It sounds really dangerous."

I nodded my head, wondering why Scarlett wasn't interfering with my conversation. She'd be snapping if she knew I was revealing Nicholas' past to Sam.

"Do you think he's in contact with the cops and might know what's going on with Katie?" Sam asked with tears brimming in her own eyes.

I gulped, forcing down my emotions, and hid within a bubble away from everyone so I could keep it together. Any excuse I thought to make—joining a ruthless gang, getting kidnapped, or running away—all sounded unbelievable. We'd known Katie since the fourth grade and though she'd been doing crazy stuff lately, nothing but the truth would suffice in this situation.

"I don't know anymore," I said, putting my face in my hands as the tears flowed freely and my body trembled. I'd been the pillar of strength for so long and didn't want to pretend I was fine any longer, even if I sobbed in the middle of the half-empty cafeteria.

Sam scooted closer and put her arm over my shoulder. "It's going to be okay, Julia." She produced a tissue.

I wiped my nose as the grief, responsibility, and guilt poured from my being, raining down on me and drenching my soul. Sam's concern became my umbrella.

"I'm—I'm so sorry." I snuffled loudly. "Nicholas literally changed overnight and he stopped talking to me."

"I know you cared for him a lot."

I looked down, feeling like a dummy as everyone gawked. "I need to use the restroom."

"Do you want me to come with you?"

Just as I stood, the warning bell rang for fifth period.

"No." I drug my finger under my eyelids to check if my mascara ran. "I'll come in a minute."

"Okay," she said in hesitation.

I forced a smile and shooed her off, then made a beeline for the bathroom.

"*I have to leave,*" Scarlett said, her voice sounding rushed, interrupting my exit.

I skidded to a stop and looked around the room, still unable to find her black furry body.

"*I'll be back at the end of school. Stay in class and on campus until I return.*"

"Wait. Where are you going? Is Nicholas okay?"

My question was followed with silence.

"*Is he?*" I asked in earnest.

I stood at attention as the cafeteria emptied, tempted to run to the parking lot and look for him at the wooded tree line or even worse, text him.

I'd already learned from past experience that I couldn't rely on anyone but myself to do what needed to be done. And now with Scarlett taking things into her own hands, leaving me wavering, I fought becoming completely irrational. Only I had the love Nicholas needed to recover and the bait to lure him in. I just needed a way to talk to him where I was protected and he couldn't leave—like my car. If he crossed a threshold owned by me, and I uninvited him, he'd be frozen.

My jaw dropped at the thought. I'd formulated a plan. One I could control and with my new cell phone, I could call and entice him into the trap.

Scarlett and Phil could work on converting Alora while I helped Nicholas. Perfect.

Chapter Thirty

School couldn't end fast enough. At the bell's shrill, I headed directly for my car and drove straight home. Scarlett would have to catch up with me . . . if guarding me was still a high priority.

No one happened to be there when I arrived, which made my escape easier. I snagged a quick bite of string cheese and crackers, changed for work, and left Phil (and Scarlett, if she was curious) a note on my windowsill explaining when I'd be home. My shift ended at eight and I hoped, since it would be dark, Phil would come back looking for me with reports of what the coven was up to.

The little voice inside suggested I at least needed to let Phil know my plan for trapping Nicholas before moving forward. This, of course required the use of my car, but would be foolproof once Nicholas got inside. Timing would be of the essence to stay inconspicuous to Dad.

While driving to work, my heart skipped a beat as I thought about picking up my new phone and placing the dreaded call—our first conversation in days. Unsure of Nicholas' reaction, I decide to call after my shift just in case. Drama or not, work needed all my focus tonight so my cash register would balance, or I'd be looking for a new job.

Memories flashed through my head as I walked inside the cell phone store, playing hula-hoop with my tummy. I feared with only a receipt they wouldn't allow me to pick up my new phone without Nicholas with me. Luckily the guy who helped us on Monday was working today, allowing for a problem free transaction. When he asked where Nicholas was, I cringed and forced a smile, letting him know Nicholas was out of town. He accepted my story without consequence. Little did he know though, I was on the verge of tears.

With the sleek little phone in my hand, I rushed out of the store across the parking lot to the deli, trying to keep myself together. Besides the acrid odor in the air of burned bread, because Vanessa set the ovens for the wrong time, my shift trundled along as expected. Like a zombie, I took the food orders while the electronic connection to Nicholas burned a hole in my pocket.

As the time drew closer to eight o'clock, my heart began to thump like a jack rabbit's foot. Would Nicholas take the call? Would he be glad to hear from me? The anticipation clung to my bones and my hands trembled while I counted out my cash drawer. Thankfully, I balanced almost to the penny.

When I walked out of the store, I looked around, secretly hoping Phil would be outside to escort me home (giving me an opportunity to practice my "uninviting" trick), but was only greeted with a brisk evening filled with stars. I bit my lip and rushed to my car, unable to appreciate the beauty.

In the safety of my front seat, the cold feelingless air wafted over my damp fingers as I pressed each number deliberately. My throat thickened right before pressing send. I held the device to my ear as my heartbeats shook my body with each heavy thump.

"Hey, *Baby*," a man purred on the other end after the first ring.

I sucked in a quick confused breath. "Sorry, I must have the wrong number."

"Oh, but you don't, Julia. Miss me?"

I hesitated. "Nicholas?"

"In the flesh and at your service." His cockiness rubbed like sandpaper in my stomach.

"How—How'd you know it was me?"

"Caller ID, Love. I programmed this in the day we bought the phone. Remember?"

I thought back, only remembering the nervousness I'd felt instead, anxious for the vampire hunt together to begin. The one that blew up in my face.

"Anyhow, I'm so glad you called."

"Don't trust him, Parker," I heard in the background.

"Shut up you *piss ant*!"

I swallowed hard. The horrific scenario on the other end of the phone played out clearly through the wireless line. "Is Phil there?"

"Well, now that spoils my surprise," Nicholas said sarcastically.

"Yes, for now."

"For now?" I asked, my palms growing slick under the phone.

"Did you know that my traitor brother is a follower of God these days? Seems a little ironic considering . . . anyway, he's about to meet his maker for the first time."

"What do you mean?"

"Dead, caput, adios, gone . . . need I go on?"

My breath quickened, leaving me light headed. "You can't. He's invincible to you."

"To me, yes. To the sun, I'm afraid not."

"Don't you dare come here, Parker," Phil barked out, a tad muffled in his delivery.

Nicholas cackled. "Yeah, *don't you dare come here.*"

The sickening swagger in Nicholas' voice left me sick to my stomach.

"So what do you want?" I asked, trying to sound commanding, hearing my voice fall flat.

"You, of course."

"Just me?"

"Well . . . among other things. Bring me my mother's necklace and we'll negotiate his release, preferably before sunrise . . . or else." A hideous gurgling noise came from the back of his throat.

"And if I can't make it, won't Alora have an issue if you kill Phil?"

"Hmmm—"

"Yes!" Phil interjected.

"Cain did kill his brother," Nicholas mused.

"You have higher favor than me, Nick, and you know it," Phil argued. "Parker, don't come—it's a trap."

"*It's a trap,*" Nicholas said in a mocking falsetto.

"Where are you?" I interrupted. The constant bickering between the two put my nerves on edge, unable to use my powers to feel out the situation over the phone.

"At the same place you eluded me last time," Nicholas said with a deep throaty voice.

My stomach pitched. "The storage place?"

"Bingo."

"Can't we just meet at Mr. Pickles?" I asked apprehensively.

"We could, but Phil's unable to attend. He hasn't paid his bail yet."

I heard Phil cuss intermixed with metal clanging against metal in the background. "Let me out of here you coward."

"See you later, *Babe*. Come alone."

The phone went dead.

Without thinking, I revved the engine and sped out of the parking lot towards home. Scarlett would have to help me if we were going to get Phil out of this mess. Trap or not, I wouldn't let him fry to his death.

Luke's Blazer was parked out front meaning he and, quite possibly, Dad were home, complicating matters a little. I'd already figured I'd need to sneak out later and get to the storage facility somehow, all without driving my car. How that would happen, I wasn't sure. But the thought to *borrow* Luke's keys came to mind.

Without checking in, I dashed through the door and tore upstairs, blowing past Dad in the process.

"Hi," I called half-way up the stairs.

"You have a friend. . ." Just as Dad spoke, I halted. Someone else was in the house. Someone filled with angst.

I turned, hoping to see the face of the stranger whose anxiety was billowing up the stairway. "Who?"

"Tyler? I think. Says you two have a project due tomorrow?" Dad's face buffeted with confusion. "He's been waiting."

"Oh, right," I forced my face to light up even though we didn't have any classes together. "Let me change. Tell him I'll be right down."

I ran to my room and slammed the door, leaning my back against it like I'd just run into the end zone. Dismay filled me as the note I'd written to Phil wafted from the window's ledge onto the floor, unread.

"Scarlett," I whispered, hoping I could send her ahead of me to free Phil. No one answered.

I pressed my hand against my forehead, unsure why Tyler would stop by, not to mention shocked he knew where I lived. His mysterious ill-timed arrival made making plans to save Phil difficult and, in my distracted state, I couldn't begin to think about helping him with homework. I needed to get him out quickly and figure out a plan to hightail it to the beach.

I changed, brushed my teeth and darted back downstairs.

"Hey," I said as I walked into the living room.

Tyler bounced off the couch, still wearing his practice jersey. His hair was matted down from excessive sweat, but his calm exterior came off as being confident. On the inside, he unraveled like a loose yarn on a cable knit sweater.

"Hey. Sorry I'm late, but I wanted to go over the *outline* we're supposed to turn in *tomorrow* for *History*." His pleading eyes begged me to go along with his story.

"Sure," I said, my curiosity peaked. He had a doozy of a story to tell me and Katie was written all over it. "Let's go to my room."

"You can study in here," my dad called from the kitchen, obviously eavesdropping.

"I'd rather go somewhere quiet, if you don't mind," I quipped back, feeling Tyler's agitation double at Dad's suggestion. "Come on." I motioned to Tyler.

Tyler in tow, I took the stairs by twos, hastening our ascent to keep Dad from demanding we stay downstairs.

"Just keep your door open," he called out.

"Geez," I mumbled under my breath, feeling like I was ten again. "Oh-kay," I sing-songed back.

Tyler followed me in, but moved to the back of my room, just within eyesight of the window. He nervously shifted his weigh from foot to foot and kept glancing outside.

"What's really up?" I asked, sensing first to see if Dad was close by, then closed my door to a crack.

"I—I saw her again," he said quickly, his attention on the window.

"When?"

"Just now. After practice. I left and she was there, by my car, looking really *good* . . . and she started flirting with me and kinda put the vibe out there. And then she—"

He fidgeted some more and pressed his hand against his left forearm. He winced, radiating a twinge of discomfort.

I cocked my head, then walked over and pushed back his sleeve. Two semi-circular punctures lined the inside of his arm. I looked into Tyler's eyes with concern. He only shrugged.

"I don't know what happened, but I *really* liked it," he said, feeling ashamed. "I think she bit me."

"Geez," I said, suddenly feeling the need to sit down, my butt finding the edge of my mattress.

I ran my hand through my bangs and contemplated how much to tell him.

"How come you're not freaking out about this?" he asked, brimming with suspicion.

"Because I know stuff you don't want to know," I whispered, feeling just as ashamed. "That's why I had to talk to you earlier. When I heard you'd seen her, I was worried she'd do something like this. You've been her obsession for quite some time now and I seriously think she's behind breaking you and Mandy up."

Tyler jerked his head back. "What?"

"I think she sent those texts. And she also rearranged her schedule and took college courses to graduate early with you. She's even going to the same college." I pressed my eyebrows together at his blank stare. "Dude, she's been stalking you all year. You didn't know?"

"Whoa, really?"

I rolled my eyes. *Stupid boys.*

"But now that she's all vampy. . ." I paused and looked into his eyes as they started to glaze over with information overload.

"Wow, this is weird."

"Sorry," I said, kind of glad he took the news better than I did when I found out vampires weren't mythical beings. The last thing I needed was for him to go berserk with my dad downstairs. He looked at me, then the floor, then back again, slowly processing his new reality.

"How did she become a—what is she actually?" he finally asked.

"Vampire," I stated frankly. "Luckily she didn't infect you 'cause she's a different type of—" I avoided saying the V word again, hoping it would help him assimilate the details. "She's sterile, I guess. Normally, a bite would be enough to change you into one. So, you're cool."

"Whoa," he said and slumped to the floor. Katie must have drained a lot of blood earlier.

"You okay?"

"Yeah, just . . . a little light headed."

I'll say. I sat on the floor and put my arm on his shoulder. Tyler turned out to be a genuinely likeable person, unlike a lot of the jocks I knew. "It'll be okay. I've got friends working on the problem."

"More vampires?"

I gulped, wishing for once Scarlett could be here to interpret and help—maybe even mind swipe him. "Kind of. Remember Phil?"

"The guy that died in that fire?"

"Yeah, but it wasn't a fire."

"He's not a—"

"Yes, he's like Katie, but good."

Tyler scrubbed his hand down the front of his face. "Man."

Suddenly curiosity bounded into the room, stopping our counseling session. "Crap," I said, scrambling to my book bag and ripping out my binder and a pen. "Quick, pretend we're doing homework."

Tyler pawed into his own bag, taking out his book.

I cleared my throat. "So, I think Mr. Marshall would like something more like this for the outline . . . Oh, hey, Dad."

With a fake smile to cover his concern, Dad pushed open the door and brought with him a tray of cookies. "Thought you'd like something to snack on."

Tyler's eyes lit up as his hunger hit the scene. "Yeah, thanks, Mr. Parker."

He scarfed five before I even got to eat one.

"How are things coming along?" Dad asked, emitting thankfulness, I'm sure because he didn't find us making out or something.

"Pretty good, almost finished," I smiled. "Tyler's just about to go since it's late." I let out a quick yawn though the time was only nine o'clock.

Tyler took the hint, shoved his book into his bag and slung it over his shoulder. "Thanks, Julia and awesome cookies, Mr. Parker."

I caught his arm as he was about to leave. On a piece of scrap paper, I scrawled out my phone number and placed the slip into Tyler's hand. He looked at it and smiled before putting the number in his pocket. Together, we trudged out my bedroom door towards the stairs. Dad followed transmitting curious disquiet.

"We'll talk *soon*?"

"Yeah," Tyler said. With a wave he was gone.

"Nice kid," Dad said and put his arm over my shoulder at the front door.

"Yeah," I said, thinking now might be an opportune time to throw him off track. "I like him a lot."

"Do you?" He turned his head and studied me quizzically, closing the front door. "What about that *other* fella?"

"Huh?" I artificially displayed my confusion.

"Your brother said you were hanging with the fellow who helped you home when you had your accident."

"Oh, yeah, him." I snorted. "We were, but not anymore."

"Did something happen?"

"Naw. We're just friends."

"Ah-h," he said in relief.

Just then, Luke walked past us and buzzed up the stairs, giving off some serious skepticism. Just out of sight of Dad, he turned and glared at me, obviously listening in on our conversation. I wanted to make a face back at him but couldn't without Dad noticing.

Dad gave a few pats to my back before he made his way to his office. "Need to get some work done. We'll talk later?"

"Sure," I said, heading up the stairs. I needed to make a stop before I snuck out.

Through Luke's half-opened door, I spotted a *Vans* covered foot hanging off the bed, twitching to an unheard beat. Mustering up my courage, I stormed down the hall into his room.

"What's your problem," I said with one hand on my hip.

He put down the music magazine and removed his iPod earbuds. "Excuse me?"

"You and your attitude. Acting all pissy."

"Am I?" He rolled his eyes then resumed reading.

I walked over and forced the magazine down with a little too much force, ripping the page from the seam.

"Hey!"

"I'm talking to you," I barked.

"Geez," He got up and pushed me aside on his way to his desk. He carefully reaffixed the page with some tape. "What's your deal, Julia?"

"If anyone should be mad, it should be me. You big fink."

"Don't blame me," he said, instantly feeling guilty. "Dad was worried. I just told him the truth for your own good."

"Well, because of you, I'm on a GPS leash now."

"So."

"So? Dad knows everywhere I go now."

Luke snickered.

I contemplated forcing him to give me his keys, threatening to tell Dad about Amber if he didn't. But then he'd know I was sneaking out tonight and might tell Dad anyway. Besides, his big secret really wasn't much to blackmail him with.

"What?" he finally asked.

"Nothing." I stomped out of his room.

Lying on my bed, I stared at the ceiling, internally cursing at Scarlett. Where the heck was she anyway? Without her, trying to rescue Phil would be darn near impossible. I looked at the stupid new phone, tempted to smash it into smithereens against the wall. The anxiety of waiting was killing me.

The thought to ask Tyler crossed my mind a few times, but my better judgment warned me not to get him further involved. Scarlett would need to work her amnesia magic if Katie kept her regular little visits.

The soft melody of my cell phone interrupted my solo problem-solving moment. I looked at the phone's caller ID. No one I knew. My heart sped up with thoughts of who it could be.

"Hello?"

"She's here," a male voice whispered on the other end, his breathing a little rushed.

I sat up in bed. "Who is this?"

"Tyler," he said sounding fearful. "Katie's outside my house right now. I parked down the street, not wanting to go home when I saw her."

"Did she see you?"

"No, I don't think so."

"Then come back here."

"To your place? Are you sure?"

"Yeah," I said quietly. "I need your help anyway."

"Oh, okay," he said apprehensively.

"Park down the street. I'm sneaking out."

"Okay, be there in a bit."

Chapter Thirty-One

"Scarlett, now's the time to show up if you plan to help me," I said out loud in hopes she'd jump through the window and save the day.

Nothing happened.

"Crap," I mumbled. "Time for plan B."

Begrudgingly, I put on my jammies and went downstairs to say goodnight to Dad. To leave this early in the evening majorly risked getting caught, but I knew Tyler wouldn't wait in his car forever.

Again, I drug the wig out from under my bed and made the makeshift body. I also put on my all black spandex outfit like before, prepared for whatever situation was going to happen.

Outside on the ledge, I closed my window and sucked in a deep breath, and prayed for a little luck. The crisp night air chilled my skin and I shivered as I released the emergency second-story ladder. Somehow I had to convince Nicholas to stop being an agent for the dark side, release Phil and get back home before morning. With nimble steps, I climbed down and landed on the back patio with a thud. No one inside noticed, so I snuck out of the backyard and ran down the street to find Tyler's car.

"Thanks," I said when I sat in front seat, out of breath.

"Wow," he said, visibly admiring my snuggly fitting outfit.

"Yeah, whatever," I rolled my eyes, realizing I was wrong earlier. He was *exactly* like the rest of the boys at school. "Let's go. We don't have a lot of time."

"Yeah, sure," he said and took one last ogling peek. "Where to?"

"Behind the Boardwalk. I need to meet someone."

I folded my arms, wishing I'd worn a jacket, while Tyler zoomed away. I hoped dragging him into the mess wasn't a mistake.

"So, what should I do about my stalker?" he asked with a snicker after a few minutes of silent driving.

"I'm going to deal with that right now. But my advice is to avoid her, like you're doing. But whatever you do—do *not* invite her into your house, car, or into anyone else's house. She's trouble and her friends are even worse," I said frankly.

"Why do I get the feeling you know more than you're telling me?"

"'Cause I do, but don't want to drag you into this mess. Believe me: it's ugly. I'm just thankful for the ride."

He pulled into the vacant lot and parked. Apprehension filtered outward. "You're meeting someone here?" The worry that flared from him added to the pit already formed in my stomach.

"Yeah," I said while I looked anxiously out the windows for any signs of the others. Of Nicholas.

"Wearing that?"

My head whipped around to meet his eyes. Though what I wore seemed a little low cut and didn't leave much breathing room, I didn't think it was *that* bad. "Since when are you my father?"

"I'm just saying." He shrugged innocently.

"I've got it under control."

"Okay."

"Stay here," I implored. "Whatever happens, whatever you see, if you value your life, do *not* leave your car. You'll be protected in here, just don't invite *anyone* inside under any circumstances. Please."

Tyler looked back with terrified eyes. My speech had been more than compelling and my own fear radiated across his face. He nodded.

"Good," I said and tore out of the seat. "Wait for me."

I slammed the door and tried to run towards the structure, my feet struggling to gain traction in the mushy sand. The necklace flopped on my chest and for a brief second, I decided not to advertise its whereabouts freely on my neck and shoved the darn thing in my pocket. Though the talisman didn't work, I'd never give it up willingly. I'd guard the fickle object with my life if I had to.

As I neared the structure, Nicholas and Phil's aura's hit me in unison—good vs. evil. I leaned up against the building and listened.

"If Julia comes," Phil barked. "I swear I'll rip your throat out if you hurt her."

"She'll come. You just watch," Nicholas replied, bored as ever as he inspected his nails. "But I'd be more worried about escaping if I were you."

"She'll see through you, *Nick*. Don't underestimate her."

"Like she sees through your façade?" Nicholas snickered. "I think not. Teenage girls are all the same. Give them a little attention and they're putty in your hands. Which apparently you've been doing a lot of because she's coming right now to defend your honor." Nicholas roared with laughter, while his insults turned my legs to batter. "Traitors like you are nothing but a lying heap of—"

I grimaced at the string of insults as I snuck around the corner of the building, unprepared to deal with Phil's peril. Across the sand, Phil yanked against the bars of a cage similar to the one I'd been placed in before, cursing back at Nicholas who leaned arrogantly against the building several yards away. Venom must have been infused in the metal to prevent Phil from prying them apart. Come sunrise, he'd have nowhere to hide; his body would be burned to a crisp in the direct sunlight.

They both stopped and locked their eyes onto mine. I pushed back my shoulders and held up my chin, trying desperately to show strength, though my dashed dreams sucked my heart like a vacuum down into the soles of my grimy shoes.

A sly grin formed on Nicholas' mouth. "Good," he said, raising his right eyebrow in satisfaction, pushing off the wall. "You're alone."

Phil mouthed Scarlett's name and I shrugged ever so slightly to tell him that she wasn't with me. His mouth hung open, arms falling limply to his sides as shameless shock covered his face. I wanted to tell him I was limited on time, abandoned and forced to come alone to plead for his life—just like Nicholas predicted I would. Like a gullible idiot.

"Let him go," I commanded, glowering at Nicholas' smug smile. "You don't need to blackmail me to get what you want."

"Nice to see you too," He cocked his head to the side. "Where is it?" He fanned his hand over his chest, raising his eyebrow. "I see you took *it* off."

I mimicked his bravado, puckering my lips. "No, if I remember correctly *you* took it off. I'm not sure what happened to it after that." I threw my hair back with a flick of my chin.

He gave me a once-over and seductively eyed every inch of my body. "I bet you're just hiding it."

I folded my arms over my chest, feeling naked under his gaze. "Let Phil go, and maybe I'll tell you."

"You drive a hard bargain, my little ninja. I like that." He licked his lips and sauntered forward, giving my body a slow lecherous gaze.

I tried to remember his evil side was the one harassing me and counteracted his swagger with a little guile of my own, still glowering back with my head held high. Even though he radiated malevolence of colossal magnitude, deep down I knew he'd never hurt me.

"Wait," I said, pointing at Phil's cage. "You promised. He needs to be released first."

Nicholas laughed, glowing with more confidence. "Give me what I want, and I'll think about it."

"No deal."

"My *sweet* dear, Julia. You're out of deals." He glared, his vibrant green eyes zinging holes like an Uzi into my body. "I don't take kindly to traitors."

I bit my lip, suddenly feeling like the queen in a life-sized game of chess and Nicholas had just said "check mate."

"Phil's done nothing but good deeds since he's been back. Or are you just jealous?" I let out a *psscht* at the end to add to my delivery.

"I'm not talking about *him*."

In shock, I pulled the precious air into my lungs, feeling like there still wasn't enough. "You don't mean *me*, do you?"

His stare leveled me to the social standing of an earthworm, obliterating any warmth or kindness I'd felt for him before I arrived.

"You've become such a huge disappointment to me." He shook his head. "Such a waste of time."

I hardened my lower lip to hold back the tears, but my shoulders sunk down anyway. His words crushed me and, like a trampled flower left for dead, I wilted in his hot sun of depravity. "You made a deal on the phone."

"I did?" Nicholas rolled his eyes. "That was before I knew the truth."

"What truth?"

"That Phil's been spending the night with you in your *room*."

"Hardly," I chirped back. "He's only there during the day by order of your mother, as a spy."

"And what have the two of you been doing *all day* while you *pretend* to be sick and skip school?"

My cheeks double-crossed me, glowing bright pink as if we had done something wrong. "Nothing like what you're thinking."

"Are you suggesting you spent the whole day *alone* with a vampire and nothing happened? Really?"

"Why is that so hard to believe? We did it all the time."

"Yes. *Did.* That is the operative word here," he quipped. "I'm done playing."

Before I knew it, with lightening speed Nicholas grabbed me and took me face down to the ground. With a painful yank, he wrenched my arm back and pushed my head into the sand. I let out a moan. Any bit of struggle on my part would easily break my elbow at the joint. His lack of concern terrified me further.

"I will ask one more time. Where is the necklace, Julia?" he growled in my ear, his voice seething impatience.

Tears from the pain and a broken heart betrayed me and fell down my cheeks, pooling into the sand. I never imagined Nicholas would never physically harm me. How wrong I had been. I hated myself for believing my love for him would bring back the Nicholas I knew and loved.

"I'm not telling you," I spat with malice, fearful for whatever else he intended to inflict on me next.

Somewhere in the background, Phil yelled for Nicholas to stop, suggesting that he knew where the *thing* was. His blunder though was revealed in his inability to name the talisman appropriately.

Nicholas kept the pressure firm, distracted briefly for the moment. He knew I'd never give that type of information to anyone anyway; implicitly loyal to the secret of its powers.

"You have a choice, Julia. Live and give me the talisman or watch everyone in your family die a slow and painful death," he said, in shocking truth. "Now where *is it*?"

"I'll never tell you," I whimpered, feeling the weight of the decision, knowing whatever decision I made someone was in jeopardy, quite possibly everyone. "I'd rather die."

"That can be arranged," he said in sickening pleasure.

"You don't keep your promises anyway. My death will seal its hiding place forever," I hissed out, feeling nauseous from the pain and his unloving threats, the urge to vomit in the back of my throat. "So go ahead."

My stubbornness irked him and he puffed hot air from his nostrils onto my neck, withholding his temper and what he really wanted to do to me. I wished for Scarlett to come and telepathically infuse him with the vision of Hell so he'd let me go and fall into a screaming fit of madness, begging for forgiveness. His vamp side needed a dire fright badly.

I started to despise Nicholas' alter-ego for mistreating me without any remorse. But, more so, I felt cheated that his good side gave up, allowing the addiction to let the evil one take over and crush everything we once held dear, including my arm. The strong noble man I thought I knew ended up being a weak and spineless coward.

"I hate you," I screeched, feeling completely overtaken and unable to do anything against the horrid creature that used to be my boyfriend, now poised to haunt me forever.

"Awww," he said, grinding his teeth and my arm a little harder. "That's a pity."

I cried out, feeling the bone in my shoulder start to come out of its socket.

"Mom," I sobbed out involuntarily, looking out into the blurry horizon. Someone had to come to my aid. Instead, I only found fuzzy blobs of color illuminated from the high wires at the

Boardwalk. I was officially at the end of my life. Sooner or later, he'd discover the talisman was in my pocket the whole time and kill me. There wasn't a prediction after all.

Nicholas laughed hysterically as if feeding off my pain. "That's right, call out for dead mommy. *Mommy. Mommy,*" he wailed, mocking me.

I waited for a rescuer in vain.

"Love will set him free," I heard a woman's gossamer voice reverberate in my mind. The one that had always been my mother's in my dreams at night.

"Mom?" I thought, figuring maybe I'd already started to die and crossed over into the next world. *"Is that you? Help me, Mom."*

"Love will set him free, Julia," she said again, the voice fainter this time.

"No, please don't leave me. I can't. He hates me," I said in a whimper, stubbornly unwilling to open myself up to his cruelty, wanting her to take me away instead.

"Love . . . will set. . . him free."

The voice echoed away like a mist, leaving me there to die. In a helpless heap, I lay drowning in Nicholas' laughter as grimy sand pressed into my mouth. The knowledge that the secret in my pocket was all that prevented him from taking my life and his mother from taking over the world, stole the breath from my lungs. How could I possibly give him love?

With the little strength I had left, and in utter desperation, I opened my mouth, spit out the sand and breathed the words anyway. "I love you."

At first nothing happened, but Nicholas' sickening cackle caused me to angrily delve into my imagination and try harder. I imagined our first kiss, his lips soft on mine, our arms intertwined with one another, his hands gently caressing my cheek and mine nestled within the back of his soft hair. I pushed these memories onto him like others always pressed their feelings upon me.

Suddenly, Nicholas stopped laughing and his voice actually hitched. I took a deep breath once the weight left my chest, and felt my arm tingle from the lessening of his hold.

He fought back, radiating out hate, greed, selfishness, and destruction. I ignored the attack and with greater courage, I imagined a beam of feathery light flashing into the dark cave of his being, focusing all my love towards him, illuminating the humanity inside.

I remembered back to the night when he'd plucked me out of the night sky, saving me from the vampire that stalked me in the woods when we first met. And followed with the time he'd defeated the three in the alley. Then the dates at our beach and the weekend in the suite. I played them all like a movie, everything we'd experienced together—the kindness, goodness, and selflessness he'd given freely to me—and poured it upon his clouded soul.

The words "I love you" began to escape from my lips, over and over growing with intensity. And with each reiteration his grasp on my body weakened.

Nicholas began to bellow, still calling me ugly names mixed with foul words. I ignored my natural reaction to reciprocate the insults and kept the conduit of goodness flowing. I began to sense the real Nicholas clawing to the surface, silently calling out to me, begging me to continue.

The last flash-back I radiated was the happiness my family felt when Emma was born just a few days ago, the memory the clearest of them all. I shined out the tropical oasis of love we'd all shared, flowing outward from every cell of my body onto his. He finally let go, crumpling down next to me, kneeling into a ball.

My heart burst into elation as his sweetness trickled forth, followed by incredible thankfulness. I sprung up and crushed his neck with my arms, crying madly, nuzzling my face into his sweaty mop of hair. I just wanted him to lift his head once so our lips could touch and I could know he was back for real. He groaned, breathing shallowly.

"I'm here," I repeated over and over, still continuing to bathe him with goodness and love.

I wasn't cognizant of what or who surrounded us, or even the time, but I didn't care. Nicholas was back. We could be together again. And once he recovered a little more, we'd release Phil and escape back to his place. Then together the three of us would make plans with Scarlett to bring down Alora and all would be right with the world again.

But like a wayward gunshot, I heard someone snap their fingers. I looked up. And as if a rift opened in the ground between us, we were swiftly separated with the help of Tony and Aden.

I clawed my arms forward, just aware Nicholas—weak and debilitated—had been drug away, handcuffed next to Phil's cage. His abused body slumped to the ground in exhaustion. Tony had corralled me and forced me towards his queen.

Trying to keep a constant stream of goodness flowing towards Nicholas with my new secret gift, I buried my own fearful feelings underneath Phil's aura, who gave off plenty to share. My rapt concentration made speaking difficult though.

"Why hello, Julia," Alora said with a syrupy smile, tracing a line across my cheek with her finger. "Still in the thick of my business, I see."

I wanted to say horrible things, but couldn't without losing my triangular freeway of extrasensory protection. Forced to listen, I kept my lips shut.

Tony stretched my hand outward towards Alora who grasped it gleefully. Within my mind, I felt her tentacles clawing at the edges of my subconscious, trying to gain entry. Ever so slightly, her eye twitched as she futilely attempted to read my mind.

After a minute, she cursed and dropped my hand.

"Figures," she mumbled. "I've underestimated you." She looked over my shoulder to the cage behind me. "Phil? What's going on here?"

"Mother, my queen," he said with a bow. "Could you please get me out of this cage? My brother seems to think I'm a threat."

"How ever did he get you in there?" she asked with a chuckle.

"Long story," he said with a blush. He simulated jocularity but anxiously awaited freedom.

To my surprise, Alora didn't move, or send anyone to fetch the keys. I removed myself from Phil for a moment to feel out the scene.

Fiery mad, Alora kept composed while she surveyed the setting. She'd probably assumed, though she couldn't see the necklace, that I was still its rightful owner since she couldn't read my mind. My heart leapt at my perceived invincibility, understanding that she'd avoid hurting me because she was still afraid of the repercussions. This gave me a tremendous advantage. Once I freed myself from Tony's Herculean grip of course.

Aden obediently stood by Nicholas, bored and tired. I'm sure being a henchman didn't leave much free time. Nicholas was still out for the count, slowly recharging his battery as I flooded him with continual goodness the best I could.

"What happened to Nicholas?" she asked in bewilderment.

Phil looked towards Nicholas, then back to his mother and shrugged. "Heck if I know. He attacked Julia but ended up falling beside her. I thought she might have staked him, but . . . " He held out his hand in disappointment as if to say "here he is unscathed."

I glared at his despondency.

"I see." Alora approached the cage. "Your hand?"

Phil smiled back playfully. "The keys?"

"Of course," she said in a lie, waving towards Aden. "Go get them, Aden." Phil fully believed she intended to free him and willingly reached out his hand, until Aden floundered.

"Where, my queen?"

"You know where." She shot Aden an evil glare, flicking her nails towards the building.

He cowered and indecisively walked around the corner and stopped right out of Phil's view but still within mine. He shrugged at Tony.

"She's lying," I called out. "Aden's right over—"

"Shut up!" Tony put his rank hand over my mouth.

My warning was too late to stop her anyway. Alora already had Phil's hand and mind within her grasp. I felt his intent to try the experiment on his own, his face tense and fear evident. But Alora sent out something soothingly peaceful that fluidly washed over him and made him feel drunk. The fear stopped.

"Scarlett, now would be a great time to show up," I screamed inside.

The give and take between Phil and Alora was like before. As Alora discovered what had transpired the past few days, the mixture between surprise and betrayal bounced back and forth like a ball at a tennis tournament. Helplessly and wordlessly, I assumed she finally read all the little secrets about us.

A smug smile crossed her face when she turned and glared at me. "Interesting," she said, her teeth gleaming. "Phil?"

His half-lidded eyes moved to focus on her face. "Yes?"

"So, you took Julia to L.A., did you?"

"Yeah," he said with a snort. "And ran into those bad guys again."

"And they almost killed you?"

"No, not me. Julia, yes, but not me. I flew away from them."

Her smile hit me like a freezing ice ray and locked my body into a statue. She knew I wasn't keeper of the necklace anymore. I was a goner.

I braced myself for what would happen next, when Alora and Phil both fell to their knees and wailed. Tony dropped me and ran to his Queen, unsure what to do, wringing his hands.

I let go of everyone's aura in the nick of time before the cesspool of Hades spun around and enveloped me into its toilet bowl. Off to the side, Scarlett stood in the shadows, body ridged and eyes locked on Alora.

"Get her good," I told Scarlett with a laugh, until I heard Phil cry out in pain.

I ran over to the bars and focused on staying within my own emotions while I changed my beam of light to include him and Nicholas, enveloping them at the same time. Somehow I hoped it would help.

"It's okay, Phil," I cried, wanting to touch him, but afraid of what would happen if I did. "It's not real. I'm here. I am with you. Hang in there."

Unable to open up and gauge if my words were helping at all, I trembled as the cacophonic symphony of distress played its hateful tune. With a quick glance, I noticed Nicholas staring back at me, a hurt expression covering his face. I went to him and interlaced my hand with his.

"What's happening?" he asked, his voice hoarse, concern engraved into his face.

"It'll be over soon." I put one hand over my ear and my other nuzzled into Nicholas' chest as the chorus of groans repeated the horrid chorus. "Scarlett's doing a mind meld with Alora. She's using Phil's memories to give her a dose of her future."

"We should go while we can," he said while petting my hair, urging me to get up and finding his arm cuffed to the cage. "Who?" Nicholas let out a low growl. "Aden," he barked weakly, "Give me the keys now."

Aden backed away with his hands up, terror covering his face. His eyes darted between Nicholas and Alora, his loyalty waffling. He shook his head, evidently speechless. Tony stood with him. They looked prepared to bolt at any moment.

"Look in her pockets," Nicholas said, visibly trembling. I knew whatever we did, he needed to be free of the negative environment and fast.

Alora pawed the ground, shredding anything that got close to her fingernails. Careful to avoid her tentacle-like arm, I patted her left hip pocket, scared stiff while searching in it. Nothing inside resembled keys.

"Check the other side," he whispered.

I waited for her to shift and strained over her body to feel the right hip, finding the treasured keys. Against my better judgment, I fished inside and formed my hands around a silver ring. When I pulled them out, she shifted back and pushed me over with her body. Her hand snatched a handful of my hair.

I shrieked and held onto my head while she tossed me back and forth. Nicholas somehow forced her to let go before slumping against the cage. Alora continued to thrash about as if she was trapped in a violent dream, unaware of her actions.

I sat out of her reach, panting violently. The raw sections of hairless skin on my scalp burned, distracting my concentration. Quickly the tension in the air caught up in my throat, feeling like I was choking on bile. The distraction burst my bubble and I could no longer sustain the good-waves channel towards the guys, which was also a buffer for myself.

Nicholas, no longer receiving the benefit of my help, hunched over and the evil quickly gained a foothold, receiving tons of nourishment from the environment.

I closed my eyes, recentered myself and chose the only one I knew who could help. Scooping up the keys off the ground, I burst into Phil's cage.

"Phil, hang on," I shrieked, hugging onto his neck anyway, smoothing back his wet hair. He shook violently, his poor body tensed and his back arched.

"Stop," I screamed to Scarlett, who still stood poised a few yards away, her blue eyes fiercely focused in a trance.

"I knew it," I heard Nicholas spit. "I knew you cared more for him than me."

"No," I turned and met Nicholas' hateful eyes again. All the progress we'd made dissolved to nothing. Luckily, he was still handcuffed. "Stop messing with him, you freaking—" I stopped myself, forgetting the evil instigated and fed on negative energy.

"You what?"

"Forget it." My body swayed. Any second, I knew I was going to collapse trying to fight the torture Scarlett was putting us all through.

Then, the insanity stopped.

I inhaled like I'd finally broken the surface after being held underwater and looked to see why. Over by the building, Katie stood in horror as something similar to a Tasmanian devil screamed and ferociously clawed its way out of what looked like a suede jacket on the ground. The worst part was Tyler stood, dumbfounded and zoned-out behind her.

Chapter Thirty-Two

"Freaking cat," I heard Katie screech, followed by a sickening sound of bones crunching as she punted Scarlett, who was still in cat form, into the woods nearby.

I cringed with the realization she'd somehow covered Scarlett up with her jacket, stopping the trance. And Scarlett, probably jolted from her deep concentration, destroyed the leather coat in order to get out, angering Katie.

"Scarlett? Scarlett!" I mentally yelled, with no response.

"Stupid cat," she bellowed, holding up the shredded pile of leather threads. "This was my favorite coat!"

The need to get up and try to find Scarlett added a surge of adrenaline my body already surfed upon, and I panicked when I noticed Alora begin to stir.

"Come on, Phil," I begged as I pulled at his shirt and avoided his injured arm.

Blood oozed out from where Alora had hooked her nails into his skin during the meld. My voice had no effect and Phil continued to lay limp on the ground, taking in shallow breaths. My heart pounded harder as Alora groaned and rolled over, recovering much faster. I got to my feet and pulled his good arm towards the cage door.

"Now, Phil," I urged. "We have to go *now*."

Cold fingers wrapped around my foot and twisted. I yelped as fiery pain shot up from my ankle, forcing my body to the ground. I landed on my side with a thump.

"Where is it?" Alora seethed, slowly crawling towards my torso, dragging her paralyzed legs behind her. "I know you have it."

"Check her pockets," Nicholas said from behind me.

"No." I scooted away from her on my hands and feet, but was forced to stop once I bumped into Phil's still body.

Alora greedily closed the space between us, vanity piercing behind her eyes. I watched the future unfold in slow motion. If I didn't do something quickly, this would be it.

My head turned to study Nicholas' evil grin. His good side was my only ally right now, but no good to me trapped under the vile obsession that now had hold of him. My secret talent—the ability to impart emotion on others—would have to free him now. I held out my arm and with all my strength willed goodness in his direction. He exhaled loudly and arched his chest outward, like the very breath was being stolen from his body, and groaned.

"Tell her the talisman belongs to me," I demanded. "If there's any shred of decency left within you, make *me* the owner. I *know* you still love me. Look deep into your soul; you'll feel it. Please?" I begged, feeling almost as if electricity was shooting from my hand towards his body, infused with healing warmth.

Nicholas' evil writhed, the fight inside him evident. The slap across my face, though, stopped the beautiful connection. I turned away from Alora's hand and spit out the blood that poured from a dislodged tooth in my mouth.

Alora inhaled the scent. "Ah," she said and her hunger grew immensely. "This may work out after all."

Before I could stop her, she snatched the necklace out of my pocket. For a second, she looked perplexed at the black stone; I'm sure because it lay dormant in her hand. Then she whooped in glee.

"I finally have it!" she exclaimed, bringing the necklace to her heart.

She rose to her feet, her hands shaking as she studied her freedom, the reflection of the talisman glittering in her eyes. Tears of joy trickled down her cheeks.

"No," I instinctively said and grasped the side of her pant leg.

Annoyed, she kicked my body away, landing her heel right into my side. I wailed, doubling over from the excruciating pain. All that mattered suddenly was the strained need to breathe, only able to swallow tiny sips of air.

"You didn't have to do that," Nicholas said in the background.

"This little wench has been a thorn in my flesh this entire time. She deserves it," Alora said, using the heel of her boot to crush my hand as she exited the cage.

I yelped in agony again, my head swimming in pain, unsure which way was up.

"Stop," Nicholas said emphatically "And get me out of these cuffs."

I heard keys jingle and then Nicholas exhaled in satisfaction, finally free.

"Are you telling me you want this . . . *thing*?" Alora asked, obviously referring to me.

"You don't need to torture her. You got what you wanted," he said matter-of-factly, though pity wasn't the emotion I wanted to feel radiating from his being.

In the darkness beneath my eyelids, I wallowed in pain and confusion. How was Nicholas able to be good to me now? The moment Alora injured my bad ankle and left me with a few broken ribs, and a fractured hand, my positive feelings tank emptied. Yet he cared enough to stop his mother from hurting me further, but that was all.

"Give it to me," Alora begged. "Come on. Just say 'I give you the talisman.'"

Frozen on the ground in agony, I waited for Nicholas to repeat the dreadful words, wishing death would follow shortly thereafter. I couldn't live in a world where this woman would reign over all. How would I warn my family?

"I give the talisman to . . ."

The ringing in my ears made the silent pause seem deafening. Maybe because I knew the shriek of delight would be coming next.

I opened my eyes a crack to see Nicholas pensively staring at the necklace Alora held in the palm of her outstretched hand. Delight and anticipation flashed across her aura as she waited. But Nicholas was all over the place on the inside. He apparently hadn't totally committed to whom he wanted the necklace to go to. I held my breath and prayed for a miracle.

For a brief second, his eyes fell upon me and a stream of warmth briefly flooded out.

"Julia."

The piercing scream of pain and acrid smell of burning flesh hit me before the truth registered through my pain. I opened my eyes to see Alora on her knees, holding her smoldering hand with the other, the chain barely peeking out of the sand where she'd dropped it. In the center of her palm was a hole the size of the stone, burned cleanly through.

"How could you," she hissed and swiped at his leg.

Nicholas got out of the way, his motions too quick for me to follow. The next thing I knew, he was clasping the chain around my neck. The warm glow against my skin gave me some sort of hope all would be well as I fought to stay lucid.

"I'm sorry," he said, petting my hair, his body up against mine. Grief flowed around us like a gentle breeze.

I tried to talk, or at least thank him, but Alora's anger started to bowl over us and her body was suddenly behind his. I wanted to warn him, but she was so fast. I couldn't react quickly enough. Utterly helpless, I watched her grab Nicholas by the shoulders and chuck him across the sand into the storage building. He hit the metal wall and his body pierced the siding, disappearing inside. I cringed, listening to him moan in pain.

"*No,*" I whispered inside and flinched, thinking about what she'd planned to do to me next until I realized she couldn't hurt me.

She knelt beside me and whispered in my ear anyway. "I'm going to kill him if you don't give me the necklace," she breathed.

I lay broken and battered, unable to fight. If I knew the madness would stop if I gave her the necklace, I would have. But I'd been around her long enough to know her loyalty was only there if you did her bidding. No one was safe from her wrath, not even her own flesh and blood. Suddenly, I realized this was the clandestine moment when he'd die and I'd want revenge—just like I imagined would happen to fulfill the prophecy. My destiny.

"I know," I mouthed, trying my hardest to stay strong for the greater good.

"Fine."

In a flash she was gone. Nicholas groaned as his mother dragged him out of the building and threw him onto the sand. Bleeding cuts covered his body. I moaned softly, hoping she wouldn't kill him in front of me, but I couldn't tear my eyes away. Her fingers formed around his neck and squeezed. Katie and Tyler stood by and watched in horror, frozen like a picture in time.

"You've become nothing but a disappointment to me," she said nostalgically. "I dreamed of us ruling together someday but you chose a human girl over me, your mother. And for that, I can't forgive you."

He made a gurgling noise and his hands wrapped up around her wrists, trying to make her stop.

"Okay," I yelped. "You win."

Her head spun to meet my terrified eyes. She smiled malevolently and let him go. Nicholas rolled over and gasped for air, damaged far beyond his physical injuries. I closed my eyes and felt her coming for me, wishing for a miracle when someone new entered the scene.

"Enough," the man bellowed with a hint of a Southern drawl, leveling the tension with his voice. Alora stopped in her tracks.

"Preston," she seethed in surprise. "What are you doing here?"

"You disgust me, Alora. You would kill your own son for invincibility? Isn't immortality enough? The necklace was only intended for human protection from *us*."

I opened my eyes just enough to see Alora cower in Preston's presence, ashamed before her husband. The man she apparently *still* loved.

"If it weren't for other consequences, I'd remove you from this earth at once."

"As if you could," she said, hurt and filled with defiance.

"I absolutely could and though I still love you, don't doubt that I wouldn't." He let his threat float in the air, allowing Alora to grasp the depth of his anger and disappointment.

Unable to keep my eyes open, I closed them then heard the click of something metal. "What?" she bellowed, suddenly closer and rattling the bars next to me. "No. You can't do this to me, Preston."

She growled in frustration, obviously trapped. "And who's *this* blind human freak?"

"That's Mr. Freak to you, you leach. And if it weren't for Preston's wishes, you'd be a pile of ash right now. I guarantee it," a raspy voice spoke.

"*Harry*," I sang in my mind. "*Oh, Harry. You're alive.*"

"As if, old man," Alora spat. "Come closer." I heard the sound of teeth snapping shut.

No longer in control, all Alora's false sweet pretenses went by the wayside. Her true character revealed in full light.

I opened my eyes again to catch a glimpse of the scene. Harry flipped a stake in the air just a few feet from Alora, catching it with the precision of a sighted person. She watched him like a tiger, ready to dart out of the way, only casting out a little bit of fear. Preston was kneeling over his son, placing his hands on his body. Nicholas' pain began to vanish.

"That's enough, Alora. Harry, please attend to Nicholas for a moment. I need to assist Julia."

"Yes, sir," Harry said, turning towards Nicholas. "Hold still there, Cowboy, you ain't goin' anywhere."

Filled with weakness, my eyes rolled back into my head. Sweetness and slight guilt wafted in my direction as Preston approached. I wanted to open my eyes and greet him, but the pain was too great.

"Dear thing, what did she do?" Preston clucked his tongue and put his hands on my hand and ribs. He mumbled under his breath. With a crack and a jolt of warm electricity from his hands, the pain in my body stopped. My lung expanded from my involuntary deep breath.

"Praise, Jesus," Preston said, helping me rise to my feet.

I wrapped my arms around his neck and the tears burst forth. "Oh, Mr. Kendrick. Thank you."

"No, thank you needed, darling. I'm sorry my wife did this to you. It's my fault." He bathed me with sympathy. "I'm just glad you don't have to suffer anymore."

"But how did you get here? How did you know?" The words tumbled from my mouth before I had a chance to think. My breath caught in my throat as I looked into Preston's face—it was like looking at Nicholas' twin.

"My dear girl, Nicholas is my son," he said unabashedly. "I normally don't interfere with his decisions, but with this—" he swept his hand towards his son. "—I couldn't sit idly by."

I pushed past Preston and stumbled forward towards Nicholas. He lay on the sand, handcuffed and hissing.

"Don't touch me," Nicholas spat to Harry, somewhat struggling to get to his feet. "I'm fine. Leave me alone."

"Quiet," Harry quipped, pulling Nicholas by his arm to a standing position. "You're far from fine, Son."

"Wait," Preston said, catching my arm. "You need to stay back, Sweetheart."

"Why?" I asked. "He needs me."

"Yes, but not now." He spun me so I looked into his dark mesmerizing eyes. "The boy needs time, lots of it. You're going to have to keep your distance, I'm afraid." His eyes portrayed the pity that I felt pouring from his soul.

"Time?" I squeaked out.

Preston nodded his head. "He's unstable right now."

"But he was good just a few minutes ago," I spluttered. "He even saved my life just now."

Preston pressed his lips together. "Maybe, but he's a time bomb waiting to go off. We need to do a serious intervention."

"I want to help though," I begged.

"No darling, you can't." He patted my arm with his other hand.

In desperation, I looked around for someone else to help plead my case. Alora stood handcuffed to the cage where Nicholas was earlier, anger registering off the Richter scale. Phil sat in the open cage next to her, awake and frightened something fierce. Katie clung to Tyler on the fringes of the scene by the building. Tyler, obviously still under her vampire spell from a recent bite, seemed spaced-out. Katie on the other hand, was completely petrified, though a little smug, eyeing Alora locked up in chains. Tony and Aden were nowhere to be seen. Scarlett limped in from the bushes and collapsed on the sand.

My heart screamed for me to ignore Preston and attend to Nicholas, but he prevented me from moving. Then the unspoken needs from the others began to torment me in unison. Nicholas looked at me again and screeched. "What are you looking at?"

I turned away, the pain of his struggle too much to bear.

Shrugging off Preston's hand, I turned around and walked to Phil and knelt down. "Come on, let's go."

"You may think you've won, Julia. But I'll be back. I'll remember," Alora whispered behind me.

I threw her a wicked glance. *And so shall I. Bring it.*

Preston materialized next to her, unlocking the cuff attached to the cage with only the wave of his hand. "I said enough. Now let's go."

She glowered at Preston, but there was love between the two of them. And when Preston looked at her with compassion, she softened.

"Okay," Phil said with a shaky voice, feebly trying to stand. "Did it work?"

I looked at Phil and shrugged. "I don't think so," I said with a wave of my hand in Alora's direction. "She's the same as she was."

Alora spat.

"Don't worry about her," Preston piped in, obviously keen on what we'd attempted to perform. "We'll do an intervention with her too."

"Like hell you will," she screeched.

"And that's exactly where you'll end up if you don't knock it off, ma'am." He ushered Alora away, like a cop arresting the perpetrator.

Harry walked next to Nicholas, unassisted, towards the parking lot.

"Is that necessary?" I begged, wondering why Nicholas was being cuffed too. Was he so dangerous he'd misbehave in the presence of his father and mentor?

"Yes," Preston dropped his head. He didn't like to take such drastic measures but obviously felt it was needed.

Harry and Preston led their captives towards an idling black sedan in the parking lot.

"You're leaving?" I asked Preston in an instant panic.

"Yes, child. We need to return to Los Angeles. We'll be in touch," Preston said over his shoulder.

I dropped Phil's hand and ran towards Harry. Come what may, I wouldn't be left behind.

"No, Harry. Please," I cried out. "I love you, Nicholas. Please take me."

Nicholas only glared back at me over his shoulder, sending a heaping dose of disdain my way. I stopped my pursuit, jaw partly open. My voice became trapped in my throat, swollen with hurt and embarrassment. I wanted to hide. How could he switch back and forth so easily, mangling my trust with each flip? I turned towards Phil, who also looked betrayed.

"Sorry." I bit my lip, not wanting Phil to think he wasn't just as important—but as a friend.

In a fragile state, Phil surveyed his surroundings with mistrust in his eye, like this dreamy world would evaporate at any moment. Being teleported to Hades and back shook his confidence beyond measure.

"It's over now, Phil. You're safe," I came towards him and made him look at me while I snatched up his hand, flowing nothing but peace towards him.

He sighed, worry still creased across his beautiful features. I gave his hand a quick squeeze and led him towards Katie and Tyler. With utter sadness, out of the corner of my eye, I silently watched Harry, Nicholas, Preston, and Alora file into the car. When it drove away, I wanted to run after and scream for them to take me, throwing my dignity to the wind, until the flash of Nicholas' angry face echoed in my mind.

Chapter Thirty-Three

I felt numb, unsure what to do next, staring at the blood stained sand.

"We should get back too." Phil tugged at my hand, breaking my trance. "I think I can fly."

All I could do was look at him and blink. Nicholas left without me.

"Julia?" Phil asked. "You okay? We can't just stand out here."

He snapped two times in front of my eyes.

"Yeah," I said, finally able to speak. "Why don't you take Katie and Scarlett back to Nicholas' place and hang out there. We'll figure out a plan tomorrow. I'll ride back with Tyler."

I glanced over at Tyler who serenely smiled with glassy eyes, completely unaware what had just happened around him. I pursed my lips as Katie wiped her mouth.

"I'm not going with that *cat*," Katie whined and hugged tighter onto Tyler's arm. "I'll stay with Tyler."

"I don't think so." I grabbed Katie by the collar and put my face an inch away from her nose. "You will go with Phil willingly, or I'll have him lock you up in that cage over there and come morning, you won't ever complain again. Half this mess is your fault so you'll shut up and do as I say. You got it?"

"What?" Katie pushed my hands off her shirt and forced out her fangs to be intimidating.

I glowered back for posterity. Phil stood firmly in defense behind me. "I'm the new leader of this coven and Scarlett is a member, so listen up and listen good. Rule number one: no more drinking from Tyler or anyone else. You're going to sober up like Phil did."

"Whatever," she said with a roll of her eyes. "With Alora gone, I'm going to do what I want. And how could you be the leader? You're nothing but a *human*. I could break you easily."

"Go ahead and try." I puffed out my chest.

Tempted, Katie looked at my tiny frame, her eyes reflecting all the evil ways she wanted to flatten me into submission. Then the image of the talisman reflected back and reverence crossed her face.

Phil stood like a statue next to me, ready to pummel her if she tried anything. He might not have been cognizant enough earlier to know why Katie backed down, but Katie saw the whole incident with Alora, completely unhampered.

"You need us, Katie," I said, taking her hand and befriending her again. "Believe me, there's a whole set of future consequences you haven't considered."

Katie reluctantly submitted. "Fine," she quipped. "But if I find another coven, I'm leaving."

"Be my guest," I said and gave Phil a sideways look. We'd already experienced how friendly other vampires could be.

Then, I noticed Scarlett hadn't joined us. She still lay unmoving, like a lump on the sand.

"Oh, no." I ran to her side and put my hand on her velvety fur. Her ribs rose up and down slightly. "Scarlett?"

Worry reverberated between me and Phil.

"Is she okay?" I asked.

"I don't know." Phil gingerly scooped her into his arms. "Let's get her home."

I swirled around, instantly filled with anger. "If you ever touch her again, I'll stake you myself, Katie."

"I didn't know she was *your* cat," Katie said, her hands were raised. "She destroyed my favorite coat."

I shook off my anger. With a motherly tone, I pointed towards the parking lot. "Get in the car. It's time to go home."

"Shot gun," Katie called out and linked arms with doped-up Tyler and skipped towards his jeep.

I sighed and followed closely behind with Phil. We piled in. Phil and I got in the back. Phil kneaded Scarlett's fur, his distress lessening. Katie played with Tyler's hair as he drove. I continually had to remind him to keep his eyes and car on the road, and for Katie to keep her lips (and teeth) to herself. If Scarlett didn't survive somehow, we'd have a huge problem keeping the two lovebirds in the front seat apart.

"Oh crap, Phil. That reminds me. We need to release the blood slaves, or give them amnesia," I whispered. "And Tyler too."

Katie turned towards me and growled, her arm swung protectively across Tyler's chest. "No you won't."

I huffed, too spent to argue about Tyler's well-being.

"Tomorrow night," Phil mumbled. "We'll do it then."

"So Scarlett's okay?" I asked, trying to keep my voice quiet, but realizing two vampires were in my midst with eagle hearing. Without her power, there would be no mind erasing.

"I think so," he said, resting his head onto my shoulder.

They obviously spoke internally to one another, Scarlett apparently giving me the silent treatment. Phil started to radiate more his natural aura—emotionally spent, but cocky and confident again. The sensations were refreshing and a good thing because I had nothing left to push his way.

I leaned into Phil and put my cheek on his hair. Somehow, we'd all survived, though the outcome was far from what I'd wished. My fingers touched the talisman and the reality that Nicholas was gone sent me reeling again. He'd been lucid enough to save my life and give me the talisman, but too susceptible to the environment to stay on the good side. Would he recover? Would I ever see him again? The grief and emptiness made my eyelids heavy.

Once we arrived at Tyler's, I crawled under my bubble, not wanting to feel their unbridled lust. I tried not to interfere with Katie and Tyler's last moment together—not that they knew this was their last. My desire wasn't to ruin their budding relationship, experiencing how quickly their fondness grew. But ultimately Tyler deserved to be unhampered and live a normal life apart from Katie's seductive powers. Selfish desires weren't enough to allow his innocence to be taken if I had a say. The vampire life was a curse first and foremost. They weren't kidding when they said "ignorance is bliss."

I coughed, signaling to Katie *enough was enough*. She finished up with one more passionate kiss and patted him on his butt, sending him on his merry way. He staggered to the door and hollered "Goodbye." I cringed, hoping he hadn't awaken his mother.

"Let's go," I whispered to Phil, hoping to leave before Tyler did something dumb like invite Katie inside. Phil handed Scarlett to me and looped his arms around our waists, bursting into the air.

Katie let out an exhilarating whoop. Apparently her first ride.

"Should I take you home first?" Phil asked somberly in my ear.

"Yes." I secretly wished he could stay the night with me and keep me company. More than anything, I didn't want to be alone in my grief. "Take them back and keep an eye on Katie. I'll check on you in the morning."

Phil sent out a twinge of sadness.

"I don't need a babysitter," Katie said in defiance. "I'll be good."

For once she actually told the truth. Maybe she was actually scared we would stake her if she didn't.

"You better," I said to solidify her fear.

"I'm sorry," I mentally whispered to Scarlett. *"Please get better."*

She opened her eyes, focused on me, then closed them again, apparently too exhausted to talk.

I kept myself together for the trip, glad to finally see my house come into view. The occupants inside were asleep, unaware I'd snuck out and saved the world, again.

Saving the world was getting old.

Phil landed on the roof and gently set me and Katie down.

"So, I guess this is goodbye," he said despondently.

We looked into each other's eyes in silence as Katie huffed impatiently. Phil's face burgeoned with questions and utter exhaustion. He looked like he'd lost his best friend.

I wanted to beg him to stay with me but worried he'd misunderstand the intention. "We'll talk tomorrow," I said, dusting off some remnant sand that clung to his shirt. "Rest."

He wrapped me into his arms and kissed the top of my head. "Sleep tight and don't worry," he said into my hair.

His "sleep tight" made my heart ache harder, reminding me of Nicholas' secret text language to meet for a good night kiss on the same ledge Phil and I stood. The avalanche started and I wasn't sure if I could stop it.

"Yeah," I whimpered out, handing back Scarlett.

You have to leave now. My lip quivered. He took a hold of Katie and in a small gust of wind, they disappeared.

It took every last bit of energy to hoist up the ladder and crawl into my window. My body crumpled to the floor in a heap and I sobbed hysterically. I wanted to die. Though Nicholas was in good hands, I had a sick feeling in my stomach I'd never see him again.

Actually no one got what they wanted tonight, except Katie. Alora wanted the necklace. Phil wanted me. Scarlett wanted me to kick vampire booty and finish them all off. And Nicholas wanted to please his mom. But in the grand scheme of things, the outcome seemed best. Alora didn't need the necklace, Phil didn't need me, Katie didn't need to ruin Tyler's life and Nicholas needed family to help him recover. Did I need Nicholas? Did I deserve to have things return to normal after I'd lied for so long? All of this actually didn't seem like a fitting punishment.

I got up and used the bathroom, really needing to pee.

Done, I dismantled my dummy, returning the wig under my bed, I found a note on the ground, just outside my door.

> *Julia,*
> *I'm flying out early in the morning for a conference in Vegas. I'll be home Sunday. I know you've been worried about me, but my tests came back fine. Doc gave me a clean bill of health and I'll be out of your hair for a few days. I love you.*
> *Dad*

I wanted to run into his room, throw my arms around his neck and tell him not to leave. For some reason, I worried if he wasn't close by, I couldn't protect him. But I also wanted him to know he'd be proud of me. I'd saved his life and many others tonight by holding out, almost to the end. I also wanted to 'fess up about sneaking out, but let him know what I did was the right thing and he could trust me. And even though I wanted to run off to Los Angeles after my boyfriend, I wouldn't. No, tomorrow, I'd put on my happy face and go to school like a responsible student and daughter, still holding the secret of my mother's death and others close to my heart.

I laid on my bed, hollow inside, wanting someone to come pet my head and take away the pain. And then, he was there—Phil that is—caressing my hair, deeply wishing to remove my pain.

"I'm so sorry," he whispered, though secretly relieved. His competition, Nicholas, had been eliminated, leaving me—broken and desperate—in the wake.

"I'm not," I lied. "He'll be back. I know it."

"Maybe," he hummed, caressing the side of my cheek and neck, grazing over the talisman.

The stone semi-zapped him and he pulled his hand away. "What the?" He blew air against his burning fingers.

"Oh, sorry," I said, sitting up. "This is what all the crap tonight was over. It wards off vampires. Alora's been after this necklace the whole time. She'd be invincible with it on, but needed Nicholas to give it to her in order for it to work properly."

"Ouch." Phil shook out his hand and wrinkled up his forehead. "So, *that's* what Scar was talking about."

"Huh?" I asked. "She was talking about the talisman?"

"Yeah, she said something about helping Nicholas choose to give the talisman to you instead of Alora, right before Scar passed out. Because with it, Alora would attempt world domination or something."

An earthquake from my stomach sent shockwaves through my chest.

"What?" I sunk down into my pillows as all energy floated out of my body. "Scarlett helped Nicholas choose?"

"Yeah, why?"

I pulled the covers up to my chin and curled into a ball.

"What does that mean?" Phil got up and kneeled down on the

other side of the bed to face me. "What's wrong?"

I felt too nauseous to talk. He brushed the hair from my forehead and wiped away my tear. "Please, Julia. Don't cry. I'm sorry. I shouldn't have told you."

"I needed to know," I whimpered. "I have to stop getting my hopes up. Just in case."

"That's a good idea," he said, but not for his benefit. He seemed to know something I didn't—something bad. Something that would break my heart forever if I knew.

I cringed and continued to cry.

He continued to smooth my hair, emitting worry, obviously unsure what to say to fix my aching heart. "I'll just stay until you fall asleep, okay?"

I nodded my head, unable to speak. I didn't want to be alone.

Chapter Thirty-Four

"So? Has Nicholas called yet?" Sam asked, looking up at me through her bangs, obviously afraid to ask.

I let out a huge sigh while dissecting the uneaten Jell-O on my lunch tray. "No."

A month had passed since the incident at the storage place without a word from anyone. Sam thought Nicholas had undertaken some reconnaissance mission and couldn't contact me, which allowed me some leeway to grieve publicly to her.

"Are you allowed to call him?" she whispered, as if an undercover spy might overhear us and figure out his location.

"His phone's disconnected." *And so is my cute little keychain one.* I bit my lip. My guess was he didn't pay the bill.

To avoid Sam's sorrowful eyes, I looked away. The truth burned on my tongue.

"Why can't I tell her?" I spoke partially to myself and partially to Scarlett, if she'd listen.

"The more people know, the more danger you put them in," Scarlett whispered back from somewhere in the cafeteria.

She'd made school visits a regular habit, not just to keep track of me, but to have something to do. High school drama apparently scored high on the entertainment scale.

My shoulders sunk down anyway. Scarlett was right. The only reason I wanted to tell Sam was for my own selfish pity party and I already had friends to share my pain with. I just hated that Sam wasn't in the *know* like the rest of us and was tired of holding up the lame façade.

"Sorry," Sam said again.

"Yeah, me too." I curled up the corners of my lips. "Thanks."

Off to the side, Morgan and Dena lovingly fed each other their lunch. As of late, their decadent display of affection sickened me, which they must have sensed because they'd taken a more permanent residence at the end of our table. Cameron sat with his new redheaded girlfriend, Savannah, and her friends—their new devotion less obnoxious.

My glance happened to casually land on Tyler who watched me back. These days I hid in my own feelings, unable to cope with much. The slightest bit of loneliness sent me spinning.

He responded by wrinkling his brow. I shrugged in return.

Sam watched the interaction. "You two—?"

"Just friends," I interrupted.

But unbeknownst to Sam, Tyler and I spent quite a lot of time together back at Nicholas' house with the Fab Five Coven—two humans, two vampires, and a half-vamp shape-shifter. We'd collectively decided to give Tyler a choice. Red pill he gets his mind wiped, returning to a normal life or the blue pill where he keeps his memories. And without the beguiling temptation of the secret vampire kiss looming over his head ('cause we'd forbidden Katie), he began to think clearly. Well, as clearly as a hormone driven high school boy could think. Surprising to all of us though, he chose Katie and the dangers of hanging with those of the surreptitious vampire lifestyle. He became our fifth member.

So every day, Tyler and I faked we didn't know one another at school . . . until today. Suddenly, Tyler and Todd were on their feet, walking in our direction with their lunch trays.

"Did you do this," Sam whispered between unmoving lips, her face appalled.

"No," I said, just as surprised as Sam was.

"Can we join you?" Tyler asked, sitting down next to me. Todd took his place next to Sam and put his arm over her shoulder. She swooned.

"Sure." I smiled with a thankful look into Tyler's eyes. He knew exactly what was wrong. Our whole Fab Five knew. Daily I begged Phil to fly me to Harry's in L.A. to which he refused and I sulked.

"Cool," he said, giving my shoulder a quick hug.

At least my new coven knew why I was so melancholy. Joy for me was fast and far between. Mostly, Phil's antics would get a laugh and visiting my new cousin, Emma always was a highlight. Her sweet little feelings were so very contagious. But things trudged on as usual leaving me boyfriendless, hopeless . . . endless.

To top it off, there was another vampire reprieve over the city. And since Katie, Scarlett, and Phil didn't really have anywhere to go, they took up residence at Nicholas' place. I figured once he got back, he could kick them out.

We also cleaned up what little mess Alora left, which was minimal. The blood slaves had escaped and skipped town, possibly with Aden and Tony. Scarlett wiped Mandy's memory too, which made her seem a little day-dreamy and forgetful. But at least she was happier.

So, like before, we all had nothing to do except hang out and wait. But for what, we weren't sure. I knew eventually Scarlett would preach about my prediction and try to start an uprising. There was no other reason for her to hang out with us youngins. But without Nicholas, I wasn't doing anything of the sort.

"You holding up?" Tyler asked under his breath as the bell rang.

"I don't know," I said, holding back my tears, feeling extra weepy for some reason. "I don't know how much longer I can stand this. I have to know something. It's killing me."

"Let's talk to everyone later," he said quietly. "Maybe someone can go and get word."

"Yeah." I looked into his concerned eyes but knew the truth.

I didn't trust Scarlett to go alone. Phil couldn't go because he was *wanted*. Katie would get lost, feeding on some cute, frat boy or captured by the bad vampire gang. My only option was to drive myself, or write Preston another letter and beg for information.

Something had to change.

After school, I walked into the house and slammed my book bag on the counter.

"Rough day?" Luke asked apprehensively, sitting at the kitchen table.

I turned and scowled, betting the next question would revolve around my period or something. "Why do you care?"

"I don't. I just thought I'd say something since you haven't talked to me or been around in weeks."

"Humph." I went to the fridge and found it barren as usual. I finally settled on an orange.

Luke felt bad and so did I. After Alora and Nicholas threatened his life, I felt extra close to my family but couldn't verbalize it. Luke finked and I couldn't make myself apologize since I felt he needed to first.

"Nicholas hasn't called, has he?" Luke said with a sympathetic look on his face.

I swirled around, ready to spit fire balls at him but Luke wasn't trying to start a fight. He'd known something was up for a while and just guessed correctly, emanating genuine concern.

I gulped, holding back the tears. No one had mentioned Nicholas by name since *that* day. "How'd you know?"

Luke looked away and took another bite of his cereal. "I could just tell something was bothering you. I guessed. It's too bad. I'm sorry."

I sat across from him and peeled my orange. "Yeah, I'm sorry too."

We exchanged a glance and Luke smiled. We'd finally managed to make up. Then, unable to withstand the sappy silence any longer, Luke jumped up and washed out his bowl.

"Hey," he said, just before leaving. "You've got a letter."

He pointed towards the counter.

I rose and spotted a manila envelope on the counter. My heart flip-flopped as I picked it up and studied the front. My name and address was typed and the stamp had a Los Angeles imprint on it. My heart raced as I opened the flap on the back.

Three pieces of paper fluttered out into my hand: the lyrics to the song Nicholas was working on—the one I'd found in his house the night we'd broken in, along with a letter.

Down by the ocean tide
the still of the moonlight
Its come at the right time
The moment we caught eyes

The sun hits your eyelids
an hour too early
and your heart starts racing
too quick for the morning

Ill equipped
for pretty sights
we're just ships
passing in the night

Just say the words
and I'll be right over
I'll meet you
at your bedroom roof top

The porcelain doves
chime above the highway hum
serenade the setting sun
I'm caught in your balcony breeze

Turn around
the winter jasmine crowns are born
they're waiting for a head to adorn
a pretty little head like yours
a pretty little little head like yours.

Ill equipped
for pretty sights
we're just ships
passing in the night

Julia,
I'll be home soon.
Missing and thinking of you often.
Keep the faith. ‹ N.K.

I stood, mouth agape, and reread the beautiful words. Then, I spun around in the kitchen and let out a whoop, holding the papers to my chest.

He was coming home.

Finally.

… to be continued.

Read on for an excerpt of The Onyx Talisman.

The Onyx Talisman
Chapter One

"I need some ore," Phil said with a scrupulous grin behind his fanned out cards as his sexy dark eyes flirted directly with mine. "Anyone got any?" I marveled momentarily at his perpetually perfect shock of sandy blonde hair.

Three ore cards mocked me within my undisclosed hand, along with a few others. If I traded my ore—which I really didn't need—he might win again. His smug aura told me he pretty much had this game in the bag; it was a matter of time.

"I'll trade for a brick?" he asked, his sharp canines revealed in his smile. No one budged, though I sensed a few were tempted. "Two bricks?"

Katie caved first. "Okay. Here."

Within moments of the trade, Phil switched out his city for a settlement, pleasure beaming from him like a strobe light.

"Nice," Tyler said with a twisted grin.

"Pschtt!" I nudged Katie in the arm, pretending to be upset. "Why did you do that?"

"I need a brick and Phil's sitting on a brick factory over there." She pointed at the game board and blew aside her black bangs tinged with florescent pink highlights.

True.

Tyler's turn was next. As I watched him palm the dice, my competitive side itched for Lady Luck to grace me this turn. Normally the rolls I needed came up all the time, but not in this particular board game of *Settlers of Catan*.

Scarlett sat off to the side, dark hair falling over her shoulders in glossy waves, and read her worn *Tales* by Edgar Allen Poe. The fact that she enjoyed the stories as much as she did gave me the creeps.

Her mind-reading abilities had ousted her from playing any games with us—not that she'd play anyway.

Tyler blew into his partially closed fist. "Come on, karma! Papa needs a new set of shoes." He shot us a coy smile then winked at Katie.

I withheld my comment as Katie giggled and wove her fingers through his brown locks at the nape of his neck. If she got the karma she deserved, she'd lose every game. Quick as a flash, Katie grabbed his hand and kissed his fingers before he could fling the white cubes. The interruption discombobulated his throw, causing them to skitter across the table, and onto the floor. I peeked over Tyler's knee and watched a die move of its own accord from a four to a five.

Scarlett coughed. Her icy-blue eyes peered at us momentarily over the binding of her book.

"You so cheat," I accused Phil, who appeared bewildered.

"I didn't do it." Phil held up his hands—truth rolling off him in huge waves. "This is crap anyway."

"That was *so* a four." I pursed my lips and raised a brow as guilt billowed out of Katie like a hole in a balloon.

She snickered and waggled her eyebrows. "What?"

"Fine, it's a four. No arguing." Tyler pulled a face and finished his turn.

Katie's turn was next. I crossed my fingers for something I could use.

"Eight," she called out. While she traded out her cards and moved her pieces on the board, I playfully mad-dogged Phil. Our competitive sides quietly bantered with one another through our eyes. My turn was next. I only had one chance to finish him off. While feeling for the dice, I kept an eye on Phil when Katie's shock and sudden elation sliced through my psyche.

Her squeal, followed by her inhumanly fast flit around the table, upset the board onto the floor. Annoyed, I pushed away from the table and moved over to the couch opposite Scarlett, away from Katie's blatant display. Though she rarely won, I wouldn't indulge her poor sportsmanship with any type of congratulations.

Phil came over and sat next to me—a little too close, actually. His wonderful natural scent filled my lungs and tempted me to bury my nose in his neck.

"Awww, don't pout," he whispered in his golden honey voice.

A huge part of me wanted to lean over and kiss him right then and there, but I knew his powers of persuasion were running at a high level. I fought the temptation and pulled out my *iPhone* instead, searching for a text from my missing boyfriend Nicholas—an obsession I couldn't kick.

"I'm not," I said defiantly. "If I would have gotten one more turn, I would have won. Katie was *lucky*."

"I see." He touched the tip of my nose then pointed to my touch-screen. "Anything exciting happening at Drama High?"

With a smirk, I put the phone away in my pocket. "No. Not today. But that reminds me. My Dad's out of town this weekend and—"

"No," Phil said quickly, flipping from sexy to cold in an instant. "Out of the question. We've already discussed the dangers as a group, not to mention I will not escort you to L.A. without your father's knowledge. Not after what happened."

His words sent tiny pinpricks of pain radiating across my chest. Every day I'd conspired a way to get Phil to take me to L.A to see Nicholas and every time he'd tell me no. All to his benefit, of course. Without Nicholas around, Phil got all my attention. I couldn't complain. Alora had resurrected him from the pits of Hell and he'd practically become a saint.

But what I did hate her for was the fact she'd awakened

Nicholas' vampire side by feeding him blood. She'd hoped, by turning him to the dark side, he'd retrieve her talisman from me so she could become invincible. The plan almost worked until Phil defected from her rule and saved me in the nick of time.

The horrific family reunion came to an end once Preston, Nicholas' father and avenger of evil, came to the rescue and took his wayward wife and son back to L.A. with a promise to rehabilitate them. The only thing I'd received to even suggest he was on the mend was a letter stating he missed me and a reassurance he'd come home soon. That was a month ago.

Lyrics to a song he wrote about me were sent as well. They lay hidden safely in my pocket, practically falling apart from all the times I've read them.

I'd continually looked for clues to what he was thinking when he wrote them. But all I could decipher was that separated ships never docked at the same time. Was that how he saw our relationship? Something that could never really be?

I curled my arms across my chest and huffed. His words promised he'd meet me on my bedroom rooftop. But when? Where was he?

"I can't keep doing this day after day. I have to find out something," I finally said with clenched teeth.

"I know." Phil looked at me tenderly while he massaged my shoulder, infusing me with his stress-releasing charm. "Patience, my dear sweet Parker. Patience."

I slid up against his chest. Whether I liked it or not, Phil did make me feel better. My spirit mended in his presence and I was beginning to need him—like a drug. I shut down my empathy and closed my eyes so I didn't have to watch Katie and Tyler snuggled up together on the opposite couch as they started a movie. She of all people didn't deserve the happiness wafting around us and lately my jealousy was getting the better of me. I didn't want to be a love buzz-kill, but their blatant displays often rubbed raw the longing in my heart.

But, for some reason, I always returned to hang with the Fab Five. Sam, my supposed BFF, had all her free time sucked up with her boyfriend Todd. So, I had no choice but to melt into the coven's regular routine where my melancholy mood was understood, for the most part. Phil and Katie were our sober vampires, Tyler and I were the inducted humans, and Scarlett was the token shape-shifting half-vampire den mother—a very motley group. After school, Tyler and I would hang out at Nicholas' abandoned house where Phil and Katie hid during the daylight hours.

"Do you have homework?" Phil asked while petting my hair.

"Mostly studying for finals," I murmured. "I also need to finish my history report."

Phil scoffed. "So glad I never have to finish high school."

I nudged him in the side. "Brat."

After a few minutes and with much reluctance, I slid down onto the floor and opened my backpack. My report wasn't going to write itself. Phil continued to try to distract me by playing with my hair, but he eventually succumbed to the movie.

I started to read about Betsy Ross, the subject of my report, but my mind drifted. The group didn't know, but I'd devised a new plan to see Nicholas. Sam and I were going to Disneyland for a few days as soon as school was out for summer. She'd scored tickets from her aunt and during the trip, somehow, someway, I'd get to Preston's house and see Nicholas in person. I had to.

I refocused my attention back to Betsy Ross when I felt it. A storm of rage sped towards Nicholas' house and whomever the feelings belonged to, they weren't about to let a door stand in their way from getting inside. I stood up, eyes glued to the sunlight-blocking barrier as I held my breath, hoping that someone was Nicholas.

"Parker, what's wrong?" Phil asked before Scarlett's warning screamed in our minds.

"Hide!"

The sudden movement of vampires escaping the scene launched my notes into the air like confetti, leaving Tyler and me alone to deal with whoever was about to come through the door.

AVAILABLE NOW!

Acknowledgements

I've found that it takes a village to birth a book. With the birthing of a second book in a year's time, my village has grown. I'm surrounded by the most amazing people who continually nurture me and give generously of their talents and time. This book is a part of all of them.

First and foremost, I give thanks to God for giving me the talent to express my imagination on paper and people like you to share it with. Secondly, to my husband, Mike: thank you for your endless love and patience. You are my biggest source of encouragement and strength—from dealing with all my emotional ups and down, to taking care of our children and our home. Without you, I wouldn't have been able to even attempt this. Thirdly, to my family: for believing in me, listening to my rave reviews and promoting my books.

Pookie: I still <3 hot vampires too. Your friendship is such a treasure. Lisa: you're the best beta reader ever and all the horn tooting you do for Indie writers is priceless. (I'm afraid to put this in here 'cause I don't want to share you!) The book is on time because of your dedication and awesome feedback. Dori: my editor and friend, for your insight and helping me find my voice and see its worth. Laura: my friend/editor/hand holder, for all your hard work you do to further our pursuits. Donna: you've got eagle eyes and I'm so glad you painstakingly read each line many times with a smile. Lori, AnneMarie, Jennifer, Shannon, DeeDee: for being amazing proofers, cheerleaders, extra eyes and plot hole finders. A special thanks to Mikey Leibovich of Sherwood for writing Nicholas' love song to Julia. It's perfect! I love you all.

To Jennifer: for my sweet care package that helped keep me going. To Eleni: for hosting and putting together my book tour for TET, hosting the remake cover contests, Twitter party and being a pseudo-publicist. I'm going to snatch you up someday. To Kari and Kelsey: for organizing the awesome pre-launch book tour with TST. To all the book bloggers: who have reviewed my work, promoted it and continue to voice the value of reading—thank you. To Kim: for designing such lovely jewelry to go with the book. To Rhonda: for being my #1 fan. To the winners of the remake contest: Caitlin George, Amelia Robinson and Miriam Robinson—thanks for entering and making choosing a winner very hard! To the girls in MOPS: for supporting me and cheering me across the finish line. To Savannah: for being an amazing babysitter to my kids.

To everyone else who gave me words of praise along the way, became a Facebook fan and/or purchased a book: without you all, I'd not be here today! I wrote this sequel for you.

Follow me: brendapandos.com & facebook.com/brendapandos